"A Southern charm all its own . . . Remmes's story will have readers intrigued in part because much of her tale surrounds the Quaker beliefs in a modern-day world. She presents her characters in life's funniest yet vulnerable situations, and allows them to work through their challenges page by colorful page."
—Michele Howe, *Bookreporter.com*, New York, NY

"For those who love a terrific Southern story with fascinating characters and a genuine sense of place, this book is a must."
—Beth Hoffman, *New York Times* bestselling author of *Looking for Me* and *Saving CeeCee Honeycutt*

"Be prepared to laugh, cry, and gasp as you read Brenda Bevan Remmes' *The Quaker Café*, an intriguing story whose unique cast of characters with long-held secrets is fractured, then put back together again, piece by healing piece."
—Julie Kibler, bestselling author of *Calling Me Home*

"While Remmes explores the South of this time and place with affection, tolerance and a sense of humor, she also shows us the kind of courage it takes to make a difference in our little slices of the world."
—Kathryn E. Lovatt, South Carolina Arts Commission 2013 Prose Fellow, 2012 and 2013 winner of Press 53's Open Award for short story

"*The Quaker Café* tells an engrossing story with humor and sympathy for the people on both sides of a difficult situation."
—Katherine Mccaughan, award-winning author of *Natasha Lands Down Under*

THE
QUAKER
CAFÉ

A Novel

BRENDA BEVAN REMMES

PUBLISHING

Published by Lake Union Publishing, Seattle

www.apub.com

Amazon, the Amazon logo, and Lake Union Publishing are trademarks of Amazon.com, Inc., or its affiliates.

ISBN-10: 1477822119
ISBN-13: 9781477822111

Cover design by Charlie Olsen

Library of Congress Control Number: 2014950442

Printed in the United States of America

For Nicholas and Evan
You are my song.

Chapter One
1992

Where you decided to bury a body in the South is not a matter to take lightly, and certainly not a decision to make without adequate sleep or caffeine. The long-term ramifications could turn into a disaster.

Unlike any other place Liz Hoole had ever been, Cedar Branch folks liked to keep mom and dad close to home, usually in the front or back yard. She'd tried to discuss this oddity with her husband once. "Why does your family put graves in the backyard?"

"What?" he'd looked at her blankly.

"I don't understand why your family put a cemetery in the yard."

He seemed confused. "To bury people . . . why else?"

She trudged on. "Why not behind the Quaker Meeting House?"

"Because it's a family cemetery. If we buried family behind the Quaker Meeting House, they wouldn't be in a family cemetery."

Liz didn't feel like she was making much progress. "But what if someone should decide to sell the family home?"

Her husband, Chase Hoole, a birthright Quaker who'd left his home town only long enough to get a degree, seemed resigned. "It's just not something we want to think about."

Liz let it drop.

Twelve years earlier when Chase's sister Sophie lost a child only days after birth, a decision had to be made about where the grave should be. Since the unfortunate death came out of sequence with normal expected deaths, an endless procession ensued back and forth to the family plot to decide exactly where each person would be buried so that the generational lines were clear. Remembering that emotional task, Liz did not want to embark on anything similar with her best friend, Maggie Kendall. Maggie had to bury her father, the prominent Judge Corbett Kendall. She was not prepared and obviously shaken.

A hundred yards behind the Kendall plantation home known as Cottonwoods, the family plot sat inside a perimeter of a dozen or more pecan trees. Instead of a wrought iron fence, a brick wall had been carefully built, making it more upscale than most cemeteries around the county. Enhanced brick columns with a large decorative *K* stood at each corner.

The location had proven to be a mistake, despite the abundance of manna from heaven that the trees produced. Not only had roots become a problem as the trees aged, but in the early 1980s, due to changes in migration patterns, millions of blackbirds descended on Cedar Branch for several days every November as they headed south. They would swarm over the town like a great dust bowl, squawking and screeching before finally roosting in the trees for the night, the pecan grove being one of many favorite spots. In the morning at sunrise they'd reverse the pattern and head for the recently harvested corn and peanut fields.

The town council had called in agricultural experts to discuss the problem, but no agreeable solution could be reached. It would pass, they assured everyone. One year the birds would find another town to roost in and simply stop showing up. In fact, that's exactly what happened. One morning several years earlier, however, when Maggie was recovering from a late night election party that had not turned out well, the birds awoke her with a roar. Having taken as much as she felt obligated to, she'd yanked her father's Smith and Wesson out of his desk drawer and headed out to rid herself of the noisy pests. She fired wildly into the trees for several minutes, scattering the hordes and inadvertently killing a neighbor's dog. In addition, she had a sizeable amount of bird-do dumped on her as the flock fled.

The dog turned out to be named Spud, a beloved pet owned by the Mohatts, black neighbors living on a small piece of land they leased from her father. The Judge was horrified. This was exactly the type of incident that could fuel racial tension. *Judge's daughter kills pet of local black family.* This was not something that played well for any politician, much less a good neighbor. Maggie immediately worked out a compensation agreement with the family and bought them another dog of their choice.

The following Sunday both Maggie and the Judge accompanied the Mohatts to Jerusalem Baptist Church outside of town and expressed their remorse during the service. The following week the Judge proposed to the Town Board that Cedar Branch be declared a Bird Sanctuary so that an incident like this would never happen again. The next time someone started blasting slugs into the air, who knew what or who might be hit?

A motion was promptly made and passed that you couldn't shoot birds inside the town limits. A sign that read "Bird Sanctuary" was posted on each of the entrances to Cedar Branch. Ironically, one sat right in front of Cottonwoods.

Maggie accepted her public humiliation with grace. Gradually the jokes at The Quaker Café ceased, and the signs fused into the landscape like background music in an elevator. Now she stood in the middle of the cemetery under an umbrella of trees, pacing from one side to the other, like the two roads that ran through her town: north-south, then east-west.

"What's the problem?" Liz said, as she caught up with her.

"This is so silly," Maggie moaned. "I never expected to get so upset over this."

"Over what?" Liz looked around the small plot.

"Look, just look," Maggie demanded, as if it were too obvious to put into words.

Liz opened the gate and walked through the three rows of eleven stones, each decorated by a lyrical Biblical verse. At the stone of Maggie's mother she stopped. "So your dad's grave would be here, next to your mom . . . right?"

"And?" Maggie stared at her expectantly.

Liz continued to stare at the stones. "And . . . the cemetery is full," she finally admitted.

"Yes," Maggie exhaled. "There is no place left for me."

After a pause, Liz finally broke the silence. "Surely you and your father discussed this."

"He expected I would begin another long line of Kendalls and we'd build a second plot, out from under these damn trees. After I turned forty-five, I think he finally accepted the fact that I wasn't going to give him any grandchildren. That's when he started talking about being cremated."

"So," Liz said, "that simplifies things. He wanted to be cremated."

"No, he didn't. He just didn't want me to worry, that's all." Maggie started pacing again. "You know this really hurts. I can't cremate his body."

"Why not?"

"He seemed so big in life, such a powerful man. The idea of him at the front of the church in a bottle would be an insult."

"What if you bury your dad and then you're cremated?" Liz said.

"I'm not ready to make a decision like that."

"You don't have to. The only person you need a grave for now is your dad."

"But then, I'm stuck. I have no other option," Maggie said.

"There are always other options. Take out a wall, extend the plot."

"The bricks wouldn't match. It would look bad . . . too many roots."

"Tell you what, why don't you give it twenty-four hours." Liz softened her tone. A lot had happened in the past twelve hours. Maggie needed to give herself permission not to make a decision if she wasn't ready. "Give it time and a way will open."

"Oh, you sound just like a Quaker," Maggie said rather harshly. "Quakers take forever to get anything done."

"But when it's done, everyone is in agreement," Liz said.

4

"That's only because you wait for all the dissenters to die."

"It's not a perfect system," Liz admitted.

*****

While Maggie continued to pace and fret as she needed, Liz sat patiently, as the Quakers had taught her, and reflected on the past evening. *Had everything happened only twelve hours ago?*

She now regretted she hadn't said something immediately when Maggie and her father first walked into The Quaker Café the night before. The Judge looked pale. His breathing appeared irregular and he shuffled while Maggie helped him to the back of the room and braced the chair for him to sit at the head of the large oak VIP table. He dropped into the same seat where he ate each meal day after day. His jowls hung heavily, pulling the edges of his mouth into a perpetual pout. His head of thick white hair looked tussled and unkempt . . . not like him. Every-one noticed.

"How ya doing tonight, Judge?" asked Frank Busby, the wiry phar-macist who ate most of his meals at the café after he sold his pharmacy to Liz and Chase.

"Dubious," the Judge mumbled and motioned slightly with his left hand. Not so much as a *hello*, but more to indicate the conversation was over.

If Doc had been there he wouldn't have let that pass. He'd have been all over the Judge at that point, probably had him on the way to the hos-pital before he got through the door. Liz knew she should have done the same. Doc didn't stand on protocol, but Liz hesitated. Liz didn't have the nerve to publicly tell her best friend what she and her father should do. Better to wait for Maggie to bring up the subject. Perhaps she would ask whether Liz thought her father needed to see a doctor. Liz had learned in her twenty-five years living in the South to hold her tongue. Being *polite* always trumped being honest.

"A good meal will perk him up," Maggie said as she placed a napkin in her father's lap and got him a glass of water. "Here, Daddy. Remember what Doc said . . . hydrate, hydrate, hydrate."

Miss Ellie, the café's seventy-five-year-old owner, set a glass of sweet tea in front of the Judge, patted him on the shoulder, and leaned down to whisper in his ear. He made an effort at a smile, nodded, and she walked back to the kitchen. Then his head slumped forward. Liz nudged Maggie and cut her eyes in his direction.

"Daddy naps all the time," Maggie shrugged. "He'll rally once he gets some food in him and the conversation gets going."

Decades before, another man had died unnecessarily in this small northeastern town in North Carolina because people didn't speak up. His death had long-lasting ramifications. Ironically, Judge Corbett Kendall stood center stage in both dramas, dead or alive. That's the kind of life he led.

*****

Liz remembered that the evening had started out much the same. The café hummed with the regulars, but a smaller group than the more active breakfast and lunch crowd. Joining the Judge at the VIP table were Frank, who controlled the conversation whenever he could, and Henry Bennett, owner of some of the best farmland in the county. Both widowers like the Judge, Frank and Henry took most of their meals out. The remaining chairs rotated from day to day, usually filled by the local lawyers and business owners at lunch, seeking insight or entertainment from the Judge and his cohorts.

Timmy Bates sat with a wide grin across his face and a slick of ketchup on the side of his mouth. Wearing a tucked-in checkered flannel shirt and oversize jeans that were cinched in as tight as he could pull the belt, Timmy never had the know-how to do more than a five-year-old. He wasn't usually at the VIP table, but either Frank or Henry had footed his bill for dinner and invited him to sit down. He was as pleased as a kid who'd just been asked into the dugout at a baseball game.

For the past fifty years Judge Kendall had eaten three meals a day at the café, unless court was in session at the county seat fifteen miles away. Miss Ellie and her husband, Walter, bought the café from a Quaker couple thirty years earlier and kept the name in reflection of the Quakers who settled the community. The Judge helped Miss Ellie and Walter with the mortgage because he didn't know where he'd eat if the café closed. His monthly tab alone could have supported the place. Since Walter's death, Miss Ellie had managed the front of the restaurant pretty much on her own, while part-time help in the kitchen came and went.

The Judge had become as much a part of the fixtures as the string of Christmas lights that decorated the front year round. The lights stayed plugged in from November through January, and around then the windowsills got dusted. White sheers stretched across the large storefront window and hid what accumulated between seasons.

Reproductions of historical buildings in the community hung in frames Frank had ordered from his pharmacy catalog. Numerous colorful hand paintings by grandchildren were taped on the wall behind the register up front. A scratched oak sideboard sat against one wall, and a matching china cabinet with similar nicks sat on the other. Miss Ellie had bought the two pieces together at an estate auction.

Eight square oak tables were scattered throughout the remainder of the room, each surrounded by four captain's chairs. After Walter had died ten years earlier, Miss Ellie installed white and pastel blue checkered linoleum on the floor, which brightened the room considerably, although ten years of scuff marks had taken a toll.

After Maggie had settled her father into his chair, she joined her two best friends, Liz and Billie McFarland, at an adjacent table. Liz was not nearly so beautiful as Maggie, nor as diminutive and colorful as Billie, but she had her own set of credentials.

She'd be the one with a *great personality* on a blind date. Cute by most standards in younger days, she now approached her fiftieth birthday and could still brag about her own natural hair color. Honey curls dominated her looks and complimented her frenzied life. Ringlets cascaded to her shoulders, each with a mind of its own. When she was younger and had more time to spend on hair, she attempted to straighten those unruly twists, but inevitably nature took its course. Forever fighting extra pounds, she envied both Maggie and Billie's ability to eat French fries and desserts without suffering the consequences.

Chase sat by her side, as he did every Thursday evening. A man more prone to let Liz chatter away than speak himself, he remained a silent observer. Billie's husband, Gill, hadn't joined them. A retired psychiatrist, he spent his days painting in an upstairs studio of their home. He accompanied Billie only when moved by hunger he could not satisfy with her gourmet leftovers. These two couples, in addition to Maggie and her father, were the only diehard liberals in town, the fact that cemented their relationship and brought them together each Thursday evening to share a meal.

Frank reached over and turned up the volume on a small TV that sat on a side table. The television had been added in the mid-1980s when UNC played in almost every final ACC basketball tournament. In small towns like Cedar Branch that sat like scattered prairie dog hills between I-95 and the Outer Banks, sports were the primary entertainment. Following the basketball season the set remained silent except for weather alerts or breaking news.

Now there was some.

"Oh, boy, listen to this! This is gonna do him in for sure," Frank said loud enough to get the attention of everyone in the room as on-screen Gennifer Flowers walked through a throng of reporters accompanied by her lawyer. A sex scandal appeared to threaten the candidacy of a young political newcomer.

The door to The Quaker Café swung open. Sheriff Howard removed his hat as he walked in. Although he looked like a stereotypical Southern lawman, the Sheriff was known throughout the county as much for his gentle disposition and fairness as for his law enforcement.

"Sheriff," Henry waved him over to the table. "Come over here and watch this."

Broad shouldered and burly, gun holstered to his hip, the Sheriff nodded his way across the room.

"Whoa," Frank let out a laugh. "Twelve years? I wouldn't want to be in that man's shoes when he goes home to Hillary tonight."

"He'll deny it. You know he'll deny it," Henry chimed in immediately before the young candidate came to the microphone.

"I categorically deny the statements made by this young woman," Bill Clinton said. "I did not have an affair with her."

The VIP table burst into boisterous guffaws. Timmy Bates joined in, not sure what it all meant, but wanting to be a part of the party.

Maggie followed the hoop-de-do with some annoyance. Elbows on the table, she pulled her long black hair behind her ears with both hands. A shock of gray ran down the left side, a genetic snafu like her one brown and one blue eye. She inhaled. She and her father had supported the young governor from Arkansas as an early favorite. She could hear the taunts before they even started. "Men . . ." she muttered shaking her head. "Please Lord, help me survive this election."

"What do you think, Judge?" Frank said.

"How much more time would you give him?" Henry asked.

"Maybe a face-lift will do the Democrats good; something different from Carter, hey?" Frank egged him on. "Can't accuse him of lusting only in his heart."

Sheriff Howard pulled out a chair at the opposite end of the table as all heads turned to look at the Judge. "Think he's still your first choice, Judge?"

Maggie shot a glance at her father, and waited for a retort that didn't come. He hadn't taken the bait. This was unlike him; even when tired, the Judge would always rally to defend Democrats, and rarely missed the chance to insert a sexual pun when the opportunity arose. He excelled at verbal banter and innuendos.

Maggie turned to look over her shoulder. She sat close enough to reach out and touch him. "Daddy, say something." What she meant was *say something witty. Knock them out of their seats with one of your fast comebacks.* She paused . . . stared back at him and held her breath. Still nothing. Maggie rose from the table and turned cautiously to her father's chair, leaning in towards him. "Daddy," she said, and placed her hand on his shoulder. "Daddy, are you okay?"

Frank reached over and turned off the TV.

"Daddy, do you want to go back home to Cottonwoods?" Maggie's hand slipped from her father's shoulder to his wrist. "He's cold," she whispered.

A murmur rippled through the room. "Oh my God!" someone said.

Liz was on her feet immediately. "Get him on the floor." She didn't hesitate now as her nursing background kicked into action.

Miss Ellie appeared within seconds. She looked around frantically, "Someone get Doc Withers." So many other nights Doc was there. Why not tonight, too?

Chase and Sheriff Howard moved to either side of the Judge to lift him while a jumble of hands and arms struggled with his legs. Well over two hundred pounds, his body hit the floor with a thud, but he was feeling no pain.

"Judge," Liz said loudly, and shook a shoulder as she'd been trained. She hadn't practiced nursing for years. She spent her days organizing and operating blood drives throughout the eastern region of the state, but still completed CPR training every year.

Feeling no pulse, she tilted the Judge's head back, grateful that his eyes were closed. His lips, tinged blue, were cold and pasty. When she pressed her mouth over his, it felt like kissing a cold piece of ham, not at all like Annie, the manikin she had practiced with. Her heart skipped a beat. She knew the odds.

"His chest moved," Maggie gasped. "He's still alive. Where's Doc?"

"He's on his way," someone in the room reassured her.

Liz knew that what Maggie had seen was merely her air filling his lungs, but she didn't stop to speak. Thirty times; pump, pump, pump; pinch the nose. Cover the mouth. Blow twice. Again and again and again. *Where was Doc?* She prayed he was sober and picking up the phone.

"Oh, thank God," Maggie murmured in relief as Doc Withers burst through the door still in a rumpled coat and crooked tie, probably directly from a long day in his office. These two men had been friends since Doc set up his shingle in town forty years ago. Together Doc and the Judge had enormous influence within the community. Ten years younger, Doc was a heavy smoker and sundown drinker, but his willingness to show up anywhere, anytime, outweighed his personal frailties.

"Everyone get out of the way, and let Doc through," Billie ordered as she pushed people aside. The third musketeer in Maggie and Liz's trio of friends, Billie could be surprisingly forceful for someone so petite.

Chase moved next to Doc and steadied him on one side as he braced himself with a chair on the other and sank to his knees with visible effort.

"It's okay, Liz," Doc told her. "You can stop." A stethoscope in hand, he listened for a heartbeat, and felt for a pulse. He checked a second time. With unexpected immediacy he clasped his two hands in a fist over his head and struck the Judge on the left side of his chest with all the force he could muster. Several people winced. Again he checked with his stethoscope. A second time his fists came down hard on his friend's lifeless body. For one last time he moved his stethoscope over his heart and searched.

Doc's shoulders sagged. He bowed his head and wiped his nose with a sleeve. "Maggie," he said, "I'm sorry . . ."

11

No one moved.

Maggie appeared confused. "Daddy," she whispered, and leaned down closer to his ear. "Doc?" She looked at him and her eyes pleaded. Doc shook his head.

She leaned back towards her father. "Daddy, can you hear me? I know you can hear me. Open your eyes . . . please."

Doc put his arm around her. "He's gone, Maggie darling. He's gone."

Maggie didn't seem to hear. "Daddy," she said. "This is no joke. Please." Her voice trailed off.

Miss Ellie stepped up and rested her hands on Maggie's shoulders. If she could have been on the floor next to Maggie she would have, but her knees wouldn't bend down as easily as they used to. Someone moved a chair up behind her and she sat. "Could we give Maggie a little space, please, a little time to absorb what's just happened?" She added more softly, "Maggie and *me*."

Heads nodded. People pulled napkins out of the dispensers to wipe their eyes. Billie immediately slipped back into the kitchen and started to clean up. It wasn't her kitchen, but the two women followed her lead. Billie McFarland, a known commodity in both the white and black communities, could organize anything at the drop of a hat, and proved so once again.

She returned to the dining room with Styrofoam containers. First in pairs and then in groups, people scraped their meals into the boxes and left money on the table. Chase and Billie removed the dishes. Maggie, Doc, and Liz remained on the floor with the body, while Miss Ellie sat, her thick layers of make-up now streaked with tears.

"Shall I call the funeral home?" Doc asked so quietly that only Maggie, Liz, and Miss Ellie heard.

Maggie looked at him bewildered. "Not yet."

No one moved.

"Could you get him a blanket?" Maggie asked. "It's cold here on the floor."

Liz looked at Doc, and then up at Miss Ellie.

"Of course, dear," Miss Ellie rose. "I have a couple in the back." She returned with three blankets. Two she spread over the Judge and the third she draped over Maggie's shoulders.

"Could I just have a few minutes alone with him?" Maggie asked.

"All the time you want, honey," Doc said as he strained to pull himself up. "We'll just go in the back room."

Miss Ellie retreated to the kitchen to finish cleaning and usher the staff out the back door. Chase and Liz huddled for a moment and then Chase headed home to relieve the babysitter watching their two youngest of four. Their older boys were now young men living away from home, no longer available to babysit as they once did.

Doc, Billie, and Liz retreated to the meeting room off the dining area that provided a little privacy for groups of no more than fifteen. "We'll stay with Maggie," Liz insisted. "We'll call when she's ready."

"Thanks," Doc said. Suddenly he looked tired, and much older. Undoubtedly he needed a drink. "I'll alert the funeral home to expect a call."

Sitting on the floor alone with the Judge, her legs curled beneath her, Maggie brushed back her father's thick hair. She had reminded him to get a haircut, but he'd procrastinated. With long strands hanging across his forehead he looked oddly disheveled and stale, not at all like the Judge who had held court for over three decades, and demanded proper attire for anyone who entered.

A knot as big as a persimmon jammed in Maggie's throat. She felt a stinging sensation race up the inside of her nose. She took a deep breath. "Daddy," she whispered. ". . . we had more to do."

Judge Corbett Kendall was the last male descendent of five generations of the Kendalls who had built the old plantation home, Cottonwoods, on the edge of Cedar Branch. The whole town knew that he had dreamed of the day his only child, Maggie, would marry and produce heirs to carry on the family name; but now unmarried and fifty-five, with a law degree that shouted, I AM WOMAN, she made it clear the only house she ever intended to clean out was either the one at the North Carolina State Capitol or in Washington, DC. When she moved back to be closer to her father and take over his law office, *politics* had become her only child.

A sob, like an echo rattling restlessly through a cavern came from nowhere. A chill ran up Maggie's back. Had that been her? She found herself in the grip of a spasm unable to completely catch her breath. A sensation of drowning seized her and she gasped several more times before she could steady her breathing.

She laid her head on her father's frozen chest and ran her hand down his arm until she clasped his hand; but there was no warmth, no reassuring squeeze as she laced her fingers in his. Her cheek wet his shirt and she unconsciously wiped her nose on his coat. "Maggie, dear," she could hear his gentle reprimand. "A young lady needs a handkerchief at all times." She waited. Wouldn't he have something to reassure her that he had not left her yet? But the night remained as cold and sequestered as his corpse.

Maggie let out a moan that seeped into the floorboards and traveled the length of the room into the next. Liz and Billie waited and wrapped their arms around one another in a hug.

"What am I to do?" Maggie sputtered.

There had been issues he had promised her he'd resolve before he died. She felt betrayed—orphaned—vulnerable.

Rage suddenly seized her and she kicked a chair hard, sending it over backwards as she yelled loud enough for Liz and Billie to both jump: "Damn it, Daddy! DAMN, DAMN, DAMN!"

CHAPTER TWO

When Liz drove Maggie home it had been past midnight. The headlights from the Judge's Cadillac illuminated the asphalt avenue that stretched for a quarter mile to the formidable six columns rising out of the ground, up past the piazza on the second floor to the third-floor pitched roof. The front steps vaulted to a main entrance off the piazza. The old Federal-style plantation on the edge of town was dark. Reflections from the headlights on the crystal glass suggested the possibility of ghosts. Liz had no doubt that ancestors of the hallowed halls had gathered already to welcome their new arrival. She might not have felt the same if she still lived in St. Paul, but after living in the South for decades Liz understood that ghosts and old homes were as much a part of the culture as chopped barbecue and vinegar.

She drove around to the side entrance of the ground floor where a pair of French doors opened into the downstairs living area. Maggie got out of the passenger's side and walked in ahead of Liz. Billie promised to be at the house by 7:00 the next morning so that Liz could get to work for a few hours. All three knew that come daylight, the phones would not stop ringing.

"I'm going to fix a cup of tea," Liz offered. "Would you like one?"

"That might help," Maggie replied as she started up the stairs to her apartment. "There's a sofa bed in Daddy's office."

An eating counter divided the den from the kitchen on the ground floor. Years ago Maggie and her father had their own bedrooms at the other end of the large room, keeping the entire living section of the house on the bottom floor. This was after a major renovation in the wake of her mother's and grandparents' deaths. The house had suddenly become too big for just two people. But as Maggie grew older and wanted more privacy, her father acknowledged that she needed a bathroom and study space of her own. An apartment had been added behind the living room/dining room area on the second floor. Three bedrooms were on a third floor. The Judge converted Maggie's old bedroom on the ground floor into an office for himself, thus eliminating the need for him to climb stairs.

Liz put water on to boil and walked back to the Judge's bedroom. A crumpled shirt lay across the bed, several pairs of shoes were pushed to one side, and a dresser drawer sat open. This was out of character with the rest of the house, which remained neat and picked up; but Liz knew Maggie and her father didn't do the cleaning themselves. She closed the bedroom door and walked into the office. A light on the roll-top desk emitted a soft glow. The sofa had a pillow and a blanket at one end, as if it had been used recently. Liz didn't check for sheets. It didn't matter. The bedrooms were larger on the third floor, but she didn't intend to go up there. She knew the rooms would be dusty, and that sleep would be hopeless.

The whistle on the kettle sang and Liz fixed two mugs of hot tea and walked up the open kitchen stairs to the main floor and Maggie's apartment.

"Maggie, you okay?"

No answer. She heard the shower turn off and walked into the formal dining room and placed one mug on the marble top of the credenza. *How ironic*, Liz thought as she surveyed the array of Kendall portraits hanging from the walls. *Of all the people in town, Billie and I are the ones with her now. The outsiders. The Yankees.*

It had never really crossed Liz's mind that Cedar Branch would become her permanent home. She knew that Chase would want to practice in North Carolina, but she had wrongfully assumed that he would choose somewhere in the Triangle Area between Raleigh, Durham, and Chapel Hill. When Frank Busby called to tell Chase he wanted to retire and hoped that Chase might consider buying the pharmacy, Liz was stunned. Had she not been so crazy-in-love, she probably would have objected more; but the excitement in Chase's eyes, and the fact that she was pregnant and hormonally imbalanced, convinced her otherwise.

After they moved to his home town they got a loan and poured their money and hearts into making the pharmacy a viable business. With a one-year-old baby and a second on the way, they initially moved in with Chase's mom and dad, both devout Quakers. Liz, a Presbyterian, knew very little about her husband's faith.

When she'd asked Chase, he simply shrugged his shoulders and said, "It's not so different. There's just no minister and no music." He might as well have said that a banana split wasn't so different from vanilla ice cream without the banana, chocolate sauce, whipped cream, and two other flavors.

When Cedar Branch had been settled two hundred years earlier, 80 percent of the members of the community belonged to the Society of Friends, otherwise known as Quakers. Up until fifty years ago the Quaker meeting disowned anyone who married outside of the faith. This shrunk their membership significantly. Quakers married Baptists and became Baptists or married Methodists and became Methodists. Rarely did the reverse happen. Just about everyone in town could talk about a Quaker grandmother or grandfather who had been *read out of meeting*.

In general Quakers were quiet, deliberate people with a focus on the testimonies of peace, simplicity, integrity, community, and equality. Liz felt as if she was constantly under the scrutinizing eyes of Chase's mother, Euphrasia Hoole, who encouraged Liz to simplify her ever-complicated world. Euphrasia had an uncanny ability to keep Liz on the defensive without saying anything derogatory. Chase insisted Liz misinterpreted his mother's words. Liz believed that what Grandma, as she called her, said, and what Grandma meant, were two different animals.

When Liz and Chase finally built their own home on the Potecasi Swamp, she felt a surge of freedom. She had grown to respect the Quaker testimonies, and would be forever grateful that their four boys had been raised in a small community with a strong religious base and grandparents close by. But Liz could never quite shed the omnipotent expectations of her mother-in-law, Euphrasia.

The Quakers lived at one end of the town and the more prominent families of this small community inhabited the other. Blacks lived outside the town limits. This arrangement guaranteed that all elected town officials would be white, although the competition for county commissioners was dicey. The election always hinged on which race could get the most voters to turn out.

Downtown consisted of two blocks of stores. From one end of the town limits to the other was less than a mile in both directions, with the white Methodist Church, Baptist Church, and Quaker Meeting spaced two blocks apart. After integration, the black school outside of town had been merged into the white school building on the Quaker side of town. No one lived far apart. The next little burg of a town was less than ten miles away, and small clapboard houses and trailers dotted the road between one town and the next.

But distance is never measured by miles, and just as blacks and whites moved in different social circles, so did Quakers and non-Quakers. Grandpa and Grandma Hoole ate only infrequently at The Quaker Café, *an unnecessary extravagance.* Initially Liz's knowledge of Maggie and the Judge rested only on what Chase told her. The Hooles frowned on idle chatter about other people, and Chase rarely indulged in gossip, although Liz was sure he heard plenty on a daily basis between the pharmacy and the café.

As a newcomer, Liz missed the municipal parks in her Midwestern home town that provided opportunities to meet other young parents at playgrounds and in the recreation centers. Impulsively, after living in Cedar Branch only four years, she decided to challenge the current county commissioner from their district. Grandma and Grandpa raised their eyebrows and told her to follow wherever her inner light leadeth.

Chase chuckled and said, "Go for it."

Liz had been in Cedar Branch long enough to realize the black vote rested within the black churches, and that the white vote surfaced somewhere between the country club and the back room poker games. She jumped at every opportunity to visit a civic club or church, and talked passionately about the public swimming pools and tennis courts in St. Paul and how much they provided for the community. She was good on her feet. She received polite applause and got trounced in the election.

While licking her wounds, she was surprised one evening when she and Chase stopped by The Quaker Café, and the Judge and Maggie pulled up chairs to their table. They had followed the election with interest and liked her spunk. Long after the regulars had left, they'd talked into the evening. They warned her that she needed to leave St. Paul out of the mix since few Southerners cared what they did in St. Paul, or anywhere else as a matter of fact. And she'd hit a sensitive nerve by running on a platform as racially charged as recreational facilities.

"It isn't a black-white issue," Liz protested.

"Everything is a black-white issue," Maggie warned her.

*****

Although Maggie and the Judge had rarely used the formal living room at Cottonwoods anymore, Liz had been to many gatherings here since that first meeting. Besides election night celebrations, there'd been a legendary New Year's Eve party where the Judge greeted each guest he didn't recognize with the query, "Who's your daddy?"

Liz knew the names of each of the figureheads in the portraits, all Kendalls, a formidable lot dating back before the Civil War. When she mentioned being impressed by their wealth, Grandpa Hoole had gently reminded her that originally the wealth came from slave labor.

Now Liz sank into one of the antique wing chairs and gazed across at the picture of Maggie's mother, Sarah Richmond Kendall, with Maggie's odd eyes, one brown and one blue. She looked so frail, not at all like Maggie. Liz rested her head on the back of the chair and dozed off. When she awoke with a start, her heart jumped and her pulse raced.

Maggie sat motionless in the chair next to her, staring at her mother's portrait.

"I'm sorry I never knew her," Maggie said.

Liz took a deep breath.

"Daddy met her in New Orleans, at Mardi Gras, of all places. She was several years younger. He and a bunch of his law school buddies had just graduated, and Daddy was headed for an internship in Raleigh."

Chase had told Liz parts of the story after she met Maggie. It remained one of the great tragedies of the town's history, a love affair that went badly awry.

"You would think he had more sense than to marry on impulse. If he'd brought her to Cedar Branch first, I'm sure she would have refused to live here." Everything Maggie knew about her mother she'd been told. Sarah's death after Maggie's birth had left Maggie motherless.

"Do you think I look like her?" Maggie asked.

Liz looked across at the portrait in the dim light. "The eyes are a dead giveaway. You can't deny the eyes."

"They are, aren't they?"

"But you're your father in and out—your personality, your gorgeous black hair. You're tall like your daddy. Your mom wasn't all that tall, was she?"

"They tell me only about five foot two. Like Billie, I guess, shorter than you."

"You have your mama's straight, narrow nose," Liz said.

"Daddy had a narrow nose, too, before he got kicked by that horse. Look at the picture of him downstairs on his desk, when he was about eighteen."

They sat together, staring at the portrait, waiting for Sarah's voice to break the years of silence and answer the many questions that surrounded her past.

"Well," Maggie said as she stood up suddenly, "I might as well decide where they're going to dig the grave. Let's get it over with."

A dull headache hovered at the base of Liz's neck. She had hoped to get some sleep before taking on what the new day would bring. "What time is it?" she asked.

"Almost 6:00. The sun's starting to come up. I need your advice."

When Maggie headed down the stairs, Liz followed. Once on the ground floor Maggie detoured into the kitchen and banged around, pulling out filters for coffee.

"I need to call Chase," Liz said across the room. When he picked up the phone instantly, Liz could hear Nicholas and Evan in the background, and an occasional bark from their two collies, Jasper and Lady. Evan was undoubtedly teasing them with dog bones in his partial efforts to teach them to sit. Actually, they sat pretty well. They were old dogs, not inclined to learn tricks or, for that matter, to perform any of the old ones. Generally they could be found lying on one of the two dog carpets in the family room or in the sunny part of the front yard.

"How's Maggie? Chase asked.

"Okay, I guess."

"And you?"

"Exhausted. We're headed out to the cemetery to decide where to dig."

"You going into work today?"

"I have to, at least for a few hours. Billie promised to be here by 7:00."

"I'll get the boys to school."

"Chase, do you think you need to call your folks? I thought about them last night."

"I know," he said. "I'll try to catch Dad at the café before he goes in, so I'm with him when he gets the news."

"That would be good."

Since Liz and Chase had moved into their own home, Chase's dad joined him every morning with coffee in hand. At first Euphrasia had made the coffee for Grandpa to take with him, but in more recent years, Grandpa let Grandma sleep in. He stopped at The Quaker Café, picked up two cups to go, and two ham biscuits, and carried them across the street to the pharmacy. This bonding time between father and son had become somewhat of a ritual, and if Grandpa didn't show up, Liz or Chase would always call to check.

"Good luck with the grave thing," Chase said.

As it had turned out, she needed more than luck. Maggie got more distraught by the minute.

Chapter Three

In a Southern town, where good manners take precedence above honesty, Maggie was one of few who would give it to you straight. Her father's prominence made it possible; but there were times that her blunt remarks made even the Judge shake his head and lower his eyes in a quiet gesture of disapproval.

She was her daddy's darling, but some things were not said in public. In Cedar Branch you never knew if unintentional remarks might reawaken racial tensions that hovered beneath the surface like thousands of fire ants.

Over the years Liz had figured out that the town had wounds that had never been healed. She imagined that some were related directly to the Kendalls, given their position in local society; but she never could find out exactly why. Specifics were distasteful. When she hinted for more information, mouths snapped shut and eyes twitched. The past was better left buried beneath the layers of civility and politeness. It kept neighbors from having to build too many fences, or worse yet, buy more guns.

In contrast, the Quakers chose to remain silent unless clearness led them to be a witness to their faith. They had witnessed against slavery. They had witnessed against segregation. Their witnessing now focused on education, prison reform, and adequate housing for the poor. Their social interactions were much like their meetings for worship; full of quiet waiting and gentle but persistent nudging.

At Cottonwoods, Billie arrived on time as promised and climbed down from Tank-Tank, her burgundy Land Rover, as Maggie marched into the house. Billie lifted her black Scottie, Webster, out of the seat. This morning Webster was adorned with a lavender rose collar that matched

Billie's blouse. Billie had a large silk flower pinned to her bodice and a loose-fitting magenta skirt. A thimble of a woman to go with a thimble of a man, Billie dressed in an array of pink outfits she'd brought with her when she moved ten years earlier from New York City with her husband.

No one in town wore something like this for anything other than a party, much less on a Friday morning. Billie wore such outfits every day of the week and set the standard for fashion in this small corner of the state. But first impressions could be deceiving. She was a hard hitter. She had survived New York City, and could damn well make it in Cedar Branch, too.

Some thought her most impressive accomplishment was surviving Gill. Gill was a moody man, not prone to a lot of social interaction, possibly because his career in psychiatry had taught him that when you knew too much about people, you didn't usually like them all that well. He had thought that if he and Billie retired to a small rural town as complete strangers, he'd be left to pursue his painting uninterrupted by the constant demands of the city. Quite the opposite, small towns make individuals even more conspicuous, and those who are the most secretive attract the most attention. In contrast, as evidenced by her dress, Billie loved attention, and for the most part provided enough gossip to alleviate Gill from having to furnish any more. A stranger to no one, she quickly ingratiated herself with everyone in town and loved the way she could stand in a grocery line and gab her way into anyone's life. She asked questions. People answered. When she'd hired a black maid and invited her to sit with her on the side porch every day for lunch, Maggie and Liz fell in love with her. Her naiveté about Southern norms was irresistible.

Billie joined Liz at the back door of Cottonwoods and listened to Maggie banging around in the kitchen. "How are things going?" she asked.

"Not too smoothly."

They entered together and cast their eyes across the room as Maggie slammed a cupboard door.

"She's badmouthing Quakers and swearing at the burial options," Liz said.

"There are options?"

"She can't figure out whether she wants to be cremated or not."

"Whether *she* wants to be cremated?" Billie's eyes opened wide, "I thought she needed to bury her father."

"Well, it's evidently a package deal."

"Can either of you fix this?" Maggie shouted into the den. "This damn coffee pot isn't working."

"I'll get it, Maggie," Billie said and moved towards the kitchen. "Go sit down."

In that way Billie began to do what she did best—manage. Just as she managed her home, the finances, and Gill's eccentric lifestyle, she was competent in any social setting. The Judge was well-known throughout the state. There would be dozens of inquiries from people who would expect to be recognized and treated with some deference. Billie would acknowledge them with courtesy and respect. Maggie was apt to ignore everyone and head off in God-knows-what direction. Billie could provide balance.

"What would you like for breakfast?" Billie asked.

"Just coffee, lots and lots of it," Maggie said.

Liz walked over to Maggie, who had started pacing again. "I need to get home and change and then head into the office for the morning."

Liz had a thirty-five minute commute to her job in Westtown. "Billie will be here to help with the calls."

"Oh," Maggie said. She seemed surprised.

"Just for a few hours, hon. I have to clear a couple things off my desk and make sure someone else handles them. I'll be back by lunch time, promise."

"I understand," Maggie said. "Hey, listen." Her voice softened and she walked over and put her arms around Liz. "I appreciate what you tried to do for my dad at the café last night."

Liz felt her throat tighten: this was Maggie, fussing at you one minute, and hugging you the next. "I'll be back soon, promise."

"After lunch would be good," Maggie said.

The French doors opened and in walked LuAnne Perry, surprising Liz and Billie. LuAnne had been coming in at 7:30 each morning to help the Judge with whatever he needed before he went to the café for breakfast. In recent months, as the Judge's needs had become more demanding, Maggie had talked about finding extra help. LuAnne was getting older. She'd often be sitting on the couch reading scripture to the Judge as they waited together for Maggie to come down. Maggie would joke that the Judge was bathed, shaved, and saved before she was even out of bed.

LuAnne had fed Maggie breakfast and gotten her off to school when she was a child. LuAnne had been there for Maggie when she got home. She was as much a fixture at Cottonwoods as the Judge and Maggie. But now almost seventy, she only did light cleaning: straightened up the rooms and washed the few cups and saucers in the sink. Once a week she changed the sheets. Most of the clothes went to the cleaners. Given that the Judge and Maggie ate all their meals at The Quaker Café, LuAnne never cooked.

Silence enveloped the room. Maggie immediately crossed the distance between herself and LuAnne. Now Maggie must provide comfort.

"It was so peaceful," she reassured LuAnne as they folded into each other's arms. "He had friends around him. He just slipped away, almost as if he'd stepped out of the room for a minute." Tears brimmed in both their eyes. "I kept thinking he'd come back to us . . . open his eyes and sit up and start talking again, but he didn't."

Then LuAnne was once again the caretaker. "Oh my baby, my poor little baby." She reached up and took Maggie's face in her hands and brushed back Maggie's hair. "What's my baby going to do without her daddy?"

CHAPTER FOUR

Liz drove back to the home she and Chase had built and did her Houdini shower and change. Their house was a mere half mile away from Cottonwoods, but sat on the edge of the Potecasi Swamp outside of town. In some ways Liz found this appropriate, since even after twenty-five years she was still considered an outsider.

The size of their house was deceptive. At first glance it appeared to be a one-floor ranch with a wrap-around porch, two bedrooms and two baths, and a large family room and open kitchen. When Chase and she had it built, they insisted on large windows to incorporate the hardwood growth and the vines and plants of the wetlands. In contrast to the dark, sluggish feel that most people associate with swamps, she found them mystical and calming.

They had picked this particular location because the land dropped dramatically behind them as it plunged into the soggy black waterway. This allowed for no flooding, to date anyway, and a half basement that couldn't be seen from the front of the house, plus an additional view of the swamp from the lower level. The extra eight hundred square feet of space downstairs allowed for two more bedrooms, a bath, and a playroom large enough for a ping-pong table. When their two oldest boys, Nat and Adam, were in high school, the basement had become the *man cave*, which they kept as dirty or neat as they pleased. Since it was out of sight, Liz never fussed and rarely went down. For the time being, Nicholas and Evan were sharing the second bedroom on the main floor, but Liz knew a time would come when they'd move downstairs, too.

Liz pulled up to the curb in front of The Quaker Café and ran in for an order to go. The family's pharmacy sat directly across the street, with the hardware store, the bank, and the Judge's law office on the same side. The post office, a small grocery, a barber shop, and a gas station shared the side with the café. All the buildings dated back to late 1800s, when a fire had swept through the one block of business and devastated all the wood structures. From that point on North Carolina red brick was the only thing anyone used to build.

The morning crowd had begun to form; the talk on everyone's lips was of the Judge. At a corner table Timmy Bates sat with a grocery sack of roasted peanuts that he methodically shelled and sorted into a row of miniature bags. He sold each bag for fifty cents. Liz stopped by his table, picked up one of the five bags, and dropped two quarters. Timmy gave her a snaggletooth grin.

Timmy's older brother, Marshall, who'd owned the Bates Peanut Processing Plant on the edge of town, had taken care of his brother all his life. Timmy slept in a small apartment attached to the plant. When he left the stove in the efficiency kitchen on overnight one time, Marshall took out all the appliances and made arrangements with Miss Ellie for Timmy to get his meals at The Quaker Café.

Timmy helped out with odd jobs from time to time; sweeping the town sidewalks, washing store fronts. When business was slow, Marshall gave him a big grocery bag full of roasted peanuts to sell. When Marshall died without warning from a heart attack, his wife sold the business and moved Timmy into a trailer they still owned on a small piece of land. She reached an agreement with the new plant owner that Timmy could continue to get a large sack of roasted peanuts every weekday. Timmy used the money he made from shelling the peanuts to pay Miss Ellie for his meals, although Marshall's wife still sent Ellie a check monthly. Sometimes Miss Ellie took Timmy's money, more often she didn't. Just as often someone else at the café would pick up Timmy's tab.

"How's Maggie?" Miss Ellie asked as soon as Liz approached the register.

"She's doing okay. I don't think any of us slept much last night."

"I didn't, either," Miss Ellie nodded.

"You should have closed the café for the day," Liz said.

"And do what? Sit at home and cry? This is the very day I need to be open, so people can gather together to grieve and reminisce."

"Has Grandpa Hoole been in already?" Liz asked.

"He has. Chase was here to meet him."

"Good," Liz said. "I'm going to run across the street. Would you fix me an egg sandwich and a cup of coffee to go and I'll pick them up in a few minutes."

"Sure honey, they'll be ready."

*****

Liz walked across the street to the pharmacy that had lured her husband back to Cedar Branch twenty-five years ago. Ceiling to floor windows stretched across the front with a raised shelf on the inside large enough for placard billboards propped up in one side and two patio chairs and a circular patio table decorated with a red checked table cloth in the other. Billie had helped touch up the display with gala accessories implying that ice cream floats and a juke box awaited you once you entered. Nothing was further from the truth, though years ago such a scene had indeed existed.

An elegant black and white checkered marble floor stretched the breadth of the room with the pharmacy in the back. At one time a soda fountain had provided coffee, sodas, and ice cream at a long counter near the front entrance. When Chase was a teenager the pharmacy was the meeting place after school, and he spent happy days as the soda jerk behind the counter. Liz and Chase had kept the old juke box and toyed with the idea of cranking it up, but in the late '60s they were eager to get their business started without any wrinkles.

Frank had closed down the soda fountain in the midst of the civil rights demonstrations and unplugged the juke box. The possibility of black and white teenagers socializing together seemed to unhinge many in the community. It occurred to Liz that whites in the South worried too much about who might sit next to them, and as a result denied themselves more than they gained in return. *What a waste*. But that was the Yankee in her talking.

While Chase filled a prescription for a customer in the back, Grandpa Hoole sat at one of the six circular tables that remained after a half century. Liz slipped into the chair across from him. She looked into the eyes of the man her husband would become twenty-five years down the road. He was almost completely bald and the bit of hair around the ears was gray. Heavier than Chase, he carried the extra weight well.

"Grandpa, I'm so sorry." Liz pulled out the chair across from him.

As Grandpa looked up at her, his thin lips curved down. The two furrows that ran from each side of the bridge of his nose etched prominently up the middle of his forehead. "It's a loss," he said, "a loss to the whole town."

"The two of you made quite a team," Liz said. She knew how hard it must be to watch the people you'd grown up with your entire life die one by one. Grandpa and the Judge had similar hopes for the community. They'd worked on many of the same committees over the years despite the difference in their personal lives.

"A team?" Grandpa looked bewildered. "He understood the politics. He was good."

"And you are the most patient and persistent man I know," Liz added. "It was a great combination."

"Well, it worked on a few things," he said.

"Cedar Branch is a better community because of both of you." Liz wanted Grandpa to accept that he was as responsible for the positive changes as the Judge. They had served together on numerous boards, including education and health, but the accomplishment they could both be the proudest of was the zoning and funding resources for numerous low-income housing projects that eliminated the majority of the shacks that littered the county less than two decades ago. 96 percent of the population in the county now had indoor plumbing and electricity.

Speak truth to power. If ever there was a Quaker phrase that exemplified Grandpa, this was the one that fit him best, Liz thought.

Grandpa didn't respond. He shook his head just short of disagreeing. Liz wondered why Grandpa was so reluctant to accept a compliment. She was convinced he was the finest man in town, just short of Chase. Even Euphrasia would admonish him at times to step forward and receive the recognition he deserved, but he refused.

Grandpa braced his arms on the table to stand up. "I need to get back to the house and tell Euphrasia."

"You want me to go with you?" Liz asked.

"No, no, she'll be fine but she'll want to do something for Maggie. Anything she needs?"

"She seems to be focused on arrangements for the funeral," Liz said. "She'll be okay."

"She's a strong woman."

Liz accompanied her father-in-law to his car. He walked slower, bent lower, and hesitated longer than usual at the curb. It bothered her to think of his getting old.

Once Grandpa was gone, Liz ducked back into the pharmacy, behind the counter in back of Chase and slipped her arms around him with a hug.

Liz had met Chase at The University of North Carolina, Chapel Hill, where Chase received a full scholarship. At that time, a 6'3" basketball guard was considered tall. Chase Hoole loved the game and gave it everything he had.

They were in a chemistry class together. Chase wanted to be a pharmacist and Liz wanted to be a nurse, someplace where flowers bloomed in March. She remembered vividly her first spring in Chapel Hill when she walked across the campus and was spellbound by the beauty of the azaleas, dogwood, and camellias. *Good Lord*, she thought. *Where have I been all my life?* Then she remembered: *St. Paul.*

For the entire first semester Chase sat in the back of the classroom, unnoticed, as she fluttered up front asking the professor one question after another. One day she ended up at the tutorial center, and as part of his work-study scholarship Chase Hoole stepped forward to help her. No one was more surprised than she.

The real stunner came in January when basketball season heated up. As Liz followed the team, she realized for the first time that Chase excelled, not only in chemistry, but also as a star player for the Tar Heels. Liz was in love, and to her delight he appeared to be equally infatuated. After a whirlwind courtship, they married at her home town Presbyterian Church in St. Paul and moved back to Chapel Hill. Chase worked to complete his Doctor of Pharmacy degree and she took a job as a nurse, but soon found herself pregnant. Fifteen months later, back in Cedar Grove living with his parents, she was pregnant again. *No one ever told her you could get pregnant if you were nursing,* she confessed.

Gone were the days when Chase's basketball cronies used to call him Icabod. A nice cushion of flesh softened his middle. She barely came up to his shoulder, making them the butt of multiple Mutt and Jeff jokes. She slipped her arms around his waist.

"Watch that, little lady," he said in his best John Wayne accent. "If my wife catches you here again, there will be hell to pay."

"I need a hug," she said.

He turned and wrapped his arms around her and kissed the top of her head.

"Just want to feel alive, that's all. Let's do something crazy," she said as she felt the comfort of his embrace.

"Well, we've got about thirty seconds. Here comes your favorite customer."

"Maybe later," Liz said as he let her go.

When the bell dinged on the front door, Liz could see Helen Truitt enter in the mirror from the back counter. Even before eight Helen was in a suit with stockings and low pumps. When her husband had died, out of respect for his thirty years as a county commissioner, the board had appointed her to serve out the remainder of his term. She had assumed his responsibilities with a zeal that far exceeded his, and then she filed to run in the next election.

She would be a time-consuming customer, Liz knew, and she didn't want to get trapped into a conversation about the Judge. More importantly, however, Liz had filed to run against Helen in November for the position of county commissioner. Twenty years had elapsed since she had first dipped her toes into the political arena; Maggie had convinced her that the timing was right for a Democrat. Maggie's backing would be crucial. The local elections wouldn't heat up until September or October, but Liz already knew that Helen was miffed.

Liz and Chase joked about the convenient layout of the mirrors around the walls of the store. While they were originally installed to discourage shoplifters, Liz found them more helpful to avoid certain people.

"I'm slipping out the backdoor," she whispered.

"Go on," he said, and kissed her curls again. "By the way, the boys want to spend the night with the Browns tonight and watch the Carolina game there. I told them they could."

Chapter Five

When Liz returned to Cottonwoods later that day LuAnne was arranging a platter of sandwich meats on the kitchen counter. Liz frequently imagined that she could easily age like LuAnne and become rounder above and below the waist.

"Are you okay, LuAnne?" Liz asked.

LuAnne took a tissue and wiped her nose. "Yes ma'am, I'll make it." LuAnne was twenty years older than Liz, but always called her "ma'am" despite Liz's constant objections. It was part of Cedar Branch for a black maid to speak this way in a white home; but on Liz's part, it was also Quaker tradition never to use any prefixes to a name that would imply that one person deserved more respect than any other.

This had been an adjustment even for Liz. Several years passed before she got used to her children addressing the elders in their meeting by first names. To have a black person, particularly an older black person, always address her as ma'am continued to make her uncomfortable.

"You've been a saint," Liz ran her hand across LuAnne's shoulder. "Maggie's going to need you now more than ever."

"Miss Maggie will always be my little girl."

Billie came halfway down the stairs leading to the formal living room and called to Liz. "Reverend Morgan should be here in a few minutes. Maggie wants to meet upstairs. Bring him on up, will you?"

Liz picked up a piece of roast beef and put it on a roll. She looked at LuAnne. "Why is she meeting upstairs? That's a long climb for the Reverend."

"I'm not sure," LuAnne said. "Maggie's been in her office all morning. Dozens of calls, but Billie's been taking them."

Liz walked to the door as a car pulled into the drive. Reverend Morgan heaved himself out of his '88 Buick LeSabre looking like a man who had already put in a full day's work in one of the nearby fields. To the contrary, he was nursing his flock, many of them elderly widows who tempted him with generous offerings of pastries and pies. A sinner of gastric proportions, he found temptation too great. His waistline and arteries proved that this bake-off competition was a deadly business.

Liz welcomed him and directed him to the stairs. "Maggie's waiting for us in the living room," she said.

Reverend Morgan sighed, paused momentarily, and then began the climb. He was breathing heavily when he reached the top step and stopped to catch his breath. Maggie appeared from her office and walked over to greet him.

"Oh, Reverend, I wasn't thinking. It's been a long night. Oh my goodness. I am so sorry." She bent slightly to accommodate his shorter frame and gave him a kiss on the cheek. Then she took his hand in hers and gingerly walked him across the dining room and into the formal living room. "I didn't realize it would be such a hard climb for you. I just wanted some privacy."

Although late March was still cool, the Reverend took out a handkerchief to wipe his forehead before he sank into one of the vintage chairs. Billie quickly poured him a glass of sweet tea and set it down next to him. Liz started to offer to get him a diet drink, but the Reverend grabbed the glass immediately and drank the tea with relief.

Once he had regained his composure there were some pleasantries exchanged, and Reverend Morgan began to reminisce about the Judge and the numerous stories that surrounded him. There were dozens to be told, but the Reverend picked the one most closely related to church attendance. "Remember that young man they picked up for drinking and driving one Sunday morning?"

Everyone knew the story throughout the county, but Liz, Billie, and Maggie listened politely as Reverend Morgan told it one more time.

"When he appeared in court, your father frowned and said, 'Is it true you were drinking and driving on a Sunday morning?' and the young man admitted with shame, 'Yes, Your Honor, it is.' To which the Judge bellowed, 'Thirty dollars court fine and fifty dollars for not being in church on Sunday.' They say that young man went to church every Sunday after that, although he never stopped drinking."

Everyone chuckled politely and Reverend Morgan fumbled in his coat pocket for a sheet of paper. "Now about the service, Maggie . . ."

"Actually," Maggie said, preempting him, "my father and I discussed his funeral before he died."

Billie and Liz exchanged glances as Maggie continued. "Liz, would you jot a few things down here. Billie, I'm going to need you to help out also."

Billie immediately obliged by handing Liz a piece of paper and a pen she'd placed on the sideboard after taking one for herself.

The Reverend returned his list to his pocket and sat back. "I'm delighted to know that your father had already given this some thought. More people should do that."

Maggie began. "I'd like for his body to be at Cottonwoods for a wake on Saturday evening."

"That's between you and the funeral home. I see no problem," said Reverend Morgan.

"Billie," Maggie said, "if you would arrange the food for the wake and whatever else you think we might need for people dropping by tonight, it would be a big help. I guess we'll also need something at the house following the funeral. That's a big task."

"I can do that," Billie nodded.

"Get a caterer, whatever. Make sure there's plenty of food."

"Okay."

Returning to the Reverend, she continued. "I want the funeral to be this Sunday, early afternoon after church."

Reverend Morgan bit his lower lip and took a deep breath. "Well, of course, we can probably do that. We don't usually do funerals on Sunday, since it's a church day, but if that's what you want. It's awfully quick, though, Maggie . . . to get notices out, line up the organist and choir—prepare the burial site."

"That's where I'm hoping Liz will help me out. As soon as you leave, she and I will work on the obituary to get to the funeral home and newspapers. Word spreads fast. Besides, more people could come on a Sunday than a weekday."

"I understand," he said. Liz jotted down *obit* on her sheet of paper.

"On Sunday, I'd like for the church bells to continue to chime from the noon hour until the funeral at one. I plan to have the casket placed on one of our farm wagons and pulled from Cottonwoods to the church. I will walk with the casket the half mile to the church and then back from the church to our family cemetery."

"You'll need to check with Sheriff Howard," the Reverend said.

"I'll take care of that, Maggie," Liz offered and added it to her list. This was the sort of thing she was good at. Liz loved to make a list and check off one item after another to the point that her youngest boys, Nicholas and Evan, begged her *not* to put anything else down in writing. No more charts with their chores pinned to the wall.

"Reverend Morgan," Maggie leaned forward a bit in her chair. "You know my father always worked hard to bring this community together."

"He did, indeed, Maggie. He was a pillar among us."

"He had hoped within his lifetime there would be some resolution to the conflicts in our racial past and more economic stability for everyone."

"And there has been. Why, when I think of where we were thirty years ago and where we are today, there have been tremendous strides."

"Strides—yes. Resolution—no." She paused. "He felt our family had a particular obligation since we benefited from the hard labor of so many people."

"Goodness, Maggie," Reverend Morgan straightened in his chair, "the Kendall Family has managed their resources well. The town has benefited. Our church and community are indebted to your generosity."

"Reverend," Maggie paused for emphasis. "I feel this is an appropriate time for us to break the racial barriers that exist among our churches and have a truly integrated service that includes the black community. My father would want that."

Reverend Morgan appeared confused. "Why, Maggie, if members of the black community wish to attend the funeral service, we would not keep them out."

"I would hope not," Maggie said, "but I would like to take it further than that. I would like to have Reverend Melvin Broadnax co-officiate the service and the Jerusalem Baptist Church Choir sing. I would also like to have fully half of the pews set aside for the black community to join us. I don't want them standing outside the church."

There was silence. Reverend Morgan removed his glasses, took out his handkerchief and wiped his forehead again. He picked up his glass of tea and took a long swallow. Maggie Kendall had just put him in a very awkward position. Cedar Branch remained a small segregated town in many ways. Liz remembered the loud arguments over court-ordered school integration shortly after she first arrived. There had been many visits to the Hooles' home asking Nathan and Euphrasia to support the building of a private academy. The Quakers stood by the public schools throughout, but twenty years later segregation still prevailed within private schools, swimming pools, clubs, and the greatest bastion of separation, the churches.

"Maggie, dear," Reverend Morgan began after a long period of silence. "This is a very difficult period for you."

"Of course it is," she responded. She leaned forward even more in her chair and her eyes were locked on the minister. Liz knew she had anticipated his reservations; she was obviously prepared. "It is also an opportunity," she said softly.

"This creates quite a number of problems." Reverend Morgan shook his head.

"For example?"

"We have never had a black minister or choir at our church before. There needs to be more preparation before we do something as dramatic as this. The parishioners just aren't ready for it. These things take time."

"We don't have that much time, Reverend," Maggie said. "We just have until Sunday."

"That is the problem. I would really need to discuss this with my church council."

"Maybe some thoughtful prayer would do," Maggie coaxed gently. "There would be nothing that would have pleased my father more than to believe that in his death he was instrumental in bringing about the first truly integrated religious service in our town, where black and white sat side by side, worshipping together. It would be a first, Reverend, and you would make history."

"No doubt about that," Reverend Morgan said nervously. He shifted, trying unsuccessfully to cross his legs. Instead he raised his glass for more tea. Billie immediately grabbed the pitcher and gave him a refill.

"Why now, Maggie?" the Reverend finally asked. "Help me explain this to my congregation. Why does this have to happen right now?"

"Because my father is dead now, and I have to bury him."

"I understand that. But could we not plan this for a future date? Does it have to be done this Sunday? Perhaps we could discuss a community service at Thanksgiving?"

"With all due respect, I just don't think it would have the same impact then. Think of it, Reverend, we will have people coming from all around the state . . . judges, lawyers, politicians. It will make a statement about the kind of town my father hoped we could become. It will be a statement of what we believe. It will set the standard for new initiatives in race relations."

The Reverend looked helplessly at Maggie.

"I could always ask Reverend Broadnax if we could have the service at his church," Maggie said.

Liz knew immediately this was a benign threat, but it was what the Maggie she knew would say—more confrontational.

Reverend Morgan struggled to find his voice. His chin jutted forward and his mouth dropped open. "Maggie, you don't mean that. You'd have the service in the black Baptist Church instead of your father's home church?"

"Well, of course I'd rather have it at the Methodist Church, but if you feel that my request is simply not something you can do, I don't want to force you. Who knows, perhaps Reverend Broadnax won't be able to accommodate me, either, but I could ask."

"No, no, Maggie. I don't want you to do that." Reverend Morgan was shaken. "Do you truly believe these were your father's wishes?"

"I believe," Maggie said. Liz watched her measure her words carefully, because Liz knew that above all else, Maggie Kendall was a political animal like her father. ". . . my father would feel honored and pleased that a tribute such as this would come about as the result of his death."

"Ask Reverend Broadnax to call me," Reverend Morgan said with a woeful tone of resignation. "I assume you'll also ask him about the choir?"

"I will, thank you," Maggie said with a genuine tone of appreciation, "and one more thing . . ."

"Yes?"

"Daddy didn't want any long eulogies, and he didn't want a lot of politicians and lawyers grandstanding."

"That surprises me some," the Reverend said as he rose to again tackle the stairs, "but surprises appear to be the order of the day."

Maggie followed him to the steps and Billie slipped in front of him. "I'll walk you to your car, Reverend," Billie said. Billie sashayed a bit more than necessary in her magenta skirt as she led the way in front of the minister, but perhaps she lifted his spirits.

"I don't think you'll regret this," Maggie called down the stairs as an afterthought.

Reverend Morgan nodded his head and emitted a long sigh. "We'll see, won't we?"

When the Reverend was out of hearing distance Liz turned to look at Maggie. "Do you know what you're doing?"

"I do," she said confidently.

"Do you really think it'll help?"

"I think if people would come together regularly they might find out they like each other. With friendship comes forgiveness."

CHAPTER SIX

The air was still cool, but the promise of spring and March Madness invigorated the conversation, despite the occasion. A group of Chase's friends gathered on the patio outside the side entrance to Cottonwoods. Liz and Billie had predicted that Friday evening would fill the house with Maggie's friends from Chapel Hill and Raleigh. With the Judge lying in the living room, Saturday evening would undoubtedly be more somber.

Chase stopped, exchanged handshakes and grabbed a beer from the cooler. When Liz went inside to help Billie she was surprised to see only a few people from the black community, all women, who stood in a small circle around LuAnne. Liz stopped to speak, embarrassed, that she didn't know each by name. LuAnne introduced everyone and extended Reverend Broadnax's regrets that he was unable to attend due to a wedding. They left shortly afterwards.

Most of Maggie's professional friends were upstairs in the main living room, or circling around a dining room table laden with cold cuts and finger foods. Meanwhile Helen Truitt held court in the middle of the downstairs den.

"I understand that Maggie has invited the Reverend Broadnax to participate in the funeral on Sunday," she said with a look of disdain. Her mouth puckered, adding wrinkles to her already withered lips highlighted with bright red lipstick. She stood straight as a board in her uniform dark blue polyester suit and pumps. Her bifocals caused her to tilt her head forward or backwards depending on her need. "And . . ." she added, "the Jerusalem Choir will be seated in *our* choir loft."

"Oh my," Mary Law, the church organist, gasped. "Am I to accompany them?"

"Why don't you ask Liz," Helen said. "She and Billie seem to be running the show."

Heads turned. Liz stood awkwardly on the fringes, not wanting to speak out of turn. "Maggie's made the arrangements with Reverend Broadnax and Reverend Morgan. You'll have to talk to her."

"Where is she?" Helen asked, surveying the room.

"Upstairs with a number of her Chapel Hill friends," Liz said.

"Chapel Hill," Helen huffed, "not surprised. That's where she gets all of her liberal politics. We all know what they teach at Chapel Hill." Helen eyed her companions with a knowing nod and appeared to dismiss the unspoken invitation to go upstairs. Instead she said, "Poor Reverend Morgan is just beside himself over the whole thing. Maggie should have realized what stress this puts him under."

Liz moved across the room in an attempt to distance herself: she didn't want to enter into a debate with Helen over social or racial norms.

Liz and Billie knew that most people would leave before nine. The Tar Heels took center stage from then on. A North Carolina basketball game preempted any competing event. In this case, the only people expected to abstain from watching were perhaps Helen and the body lying in the coffin. Even then, it could be a toss-up. It always made for good politics to be able to quote scores and reference certain players' assets and more than one fan had asked to be propped up in front of a television prior to internment. If observers witnessed that the deceased did not rally when Carolina scored, then it was permissible to proceed with burial plans.

As 9:00 approached, Chase eyed Liz and motioned her towards the door. "Game," he mouthed, tapping his watch.

The crowd began to thin rapidly as people climbed the steps to pay their respects to Maggie before leaving.

"Basketball, Billie," Liz carried an empty platter into the kitchen where she found her wrapping up leftovers.

"I know. You go on home. You were up most of last night. I'll straighten up some and then I'm leaving, too."

"Thought you were going to stay with Maggie?"

"Some of her Chapel Hill friends are staying to watch the game. She told me to go home. Think I will."

"Okay, then. You know how Chase is about basketball."

"Yes, I do," she said, and waved Liz out of the room.

*****

Liz knew when she married Chase that basketball would remain an obsession. The fact that their children were all boys just heightened the intensity of each game. Four boys, all different in their own unique ways, and all wonderful. She never failed to appreciate the fact that even though you loved one more than you could stand, when another came along, your love expanded exponentially. Nat, their oldest, was given Grandpa's name. Born within the year after they married, he'd graduated from Wake Forest four years ago and was engaged to be married in October. The wedding plans already had Liz in a spin. She had tried to stop talking about it all the time as Maggie had obviously grown weary of the topic. Billie, however, was her main confidant. She was ready to coordinate the whole shebang despite the fact that the role fell to the bride's family.

Adam, their second son and the one who most resembled Liz, married Heather, his childhood sweetheart, after their sophomore year at Guilford College. Their desire to tie the knot prior to graduation had given Liz a severe case of gastritis, but they had both graduated on time and joined Teach for America in New Mexico. Happy on a limited budget, they were expecting their first child in November.

Liz's two youngest, Nicholas and Evan, were a midlife surprise that she'd never regret. While having children in your forties with the prospects of sending them to college on Social Security had never been in their long-term plans, both children were a joy. There was a wisdom that came with parenting as you got older. The small stuff didn't matter so much anymore. Liz tended to be kinder to herself—to give herself a break when things went wrong. Alas, if her mother-in-law would only do the same.

With the one exception of Grandma, all the Hooles were avid basketball fanatics who shouted and screamed and jumped up and down with each score. Grandpa would sometimes join them, since he and Grandma still hadn't taken the leap into the purchase of their own television set. Grandma preferred a good book.

Liz made a big deal of having chips and dip and sodas and other junk foods around for the games. College rivalries of their two sons added to the hype, but the Darth Vader on the bracket sheet was always Duke. ABD: *Anybody But Duke.* Liz knew Chase would miss the boys that evening, but he most certainly would not miss the game.

"I'm going to go soak," Liz said as Chase turned on the TV.

"Right," he said while he flipped through the channels.

"Then I want to make mad passionate love to you," she added with a wink.

"Uh-huh," he responded, as he adjusted the volume.

Liz ran the water and poured an ample amount of bubble bath under the faucet. She glanced through the tapes that sat on the shelf to the left of the sink and debated between Andrew Lloyd Webber and André Gagnon. The Gagnon tape was from a second honeymoon she and Chase had taken to Québec. She flipped André into the recorder, loosened her hair clip from her hair, and slid into the tub.

Though she could hear the background noise of the television, once the tape started, the noise was gone. She submerged in the water and let her mass of copper curls become wet and heavy. They always made her feel as if she had a giant rubber tube around her head fighting to stay afloat as the rest of her body sank under the water. She had bleached her hair blond her first year away at college. Her mom had a fit, as she knew she would. In reality, she remembered being quite satisfied with the outcome, not on her hair, but on her mother. Now, the curls simply did their own thing. She tried to keep them corralled with scarves, cloth headbands, or an extra-large clip at the base of her neck.

The tension began to drain from the muscles in her back and legs as the warm water enveloped her, but her mind wouldn't let go of the events of the past twenty-four hours. If she wanted to get any sleep she'd have to find some way to wind down completely. Her body liked routine, and didn't react well to all-nighters or skipped meals. Sex would do it. *Sex*, she thought. She must be crazy. Sex . . . Basketball. Sex . . . Basketball. She weighed the two in her head. No, she didn't think she was up to the challenge.

André Gagnon began to play *Vue sur la mer* and a wave of remembrance washed over her. How could she forget? It was a row boat in the middle of an isolated lake north of Québec City. They had let it drift and despite Chase's initial objections, she had seduced him into making love in the middle of the day. They were lucky the dinghy hadn't capsized. It was great sex, even Chase admitted, although he'd resisted her initial advances.

"We're not in public, Chase. Just the two of us here," she teased.

"It's a public place."

"We're in the middle of a lake, no one else around."

"They could be, any moment."

"We'll make their day," she persisted as she slipped off her blouse and brassiere.

She loved how she could fluster Chase with the least bit of public affection. If she pinched his butt or ran her hand up under the front of his shirt, he'd immediately blush and grab her wrist. While Quakers certainly weren't opposed to sex, they were restrained. He admitted that he'd never seen his parents do more than give one another a gentle peck on the cheek. Liz liked to rattle that cage for him.

She believed her spontaneity was one of the things that attracted him. It was so different from how he had been raised. Chase was so practical, always the one to balance her exuberant, over-committed lifestyle. He was the head and the soul of their family. Liz was the heart and spirit.

Liz began to fantasize. Tonight might be a good test of her talents. It would be quite a conquest to score against the Tar Heels. She let her imagination set the trap.

She climbed out of the tub and began the laborious task of drying her hair. That accomplished, she put on make-up and sprayed herself with a sample blend of L'Eau de perfume from her Clinique bonus package. She slipped in a tape of *The Entertainer* and after maximizing the volume she wrapped a large fluffy pink towel around her and sidestepped out of the doorway into the den.

Liz knew Chase would be ensconced on the sofa. With her back towards him she took four long sideways strides so that she stood immediately in front of the television set, still facing backwards and effectively blocking the screen. Liz spread her arms wide, holding either end of her pink towel, and then let it drop. While she knew that her derriere was a bit more ample than ideal, she also knew what turned him on. She had great boobs.

Running her fingers up through her hair, she slowly lifted her arms over her head and did an abrupt turn, bending her right knee and turning it in a bit for a Kewpie-doll look. Her next step was to bite the tip end of her index finger and coyly flutter her eyes.

Liz didn't get that far. She stopped cold. There in front of her, wide-eyed and slack-jawed, sat Chase. Next to him with a frozen stare so alarming that she thought perhaps he had stopped breathing, was Grandpa Hoole.

If lightning had struck her dead at that moment, she would have welcomed it. Liz catapulted to the bathroom as fast as humanly possible and locked the door.

She slammed the off button on the tape recorder and collapsed in a heap on the bathroom floor. The television in the next room clicked off. A car started and pulled out of the driveway. One of the dogs barked. The house was quiet. Eventually there was a knock.

"Liz. Are you going to come out?"

"No."

"You're going to have to come out, honey, sooner or later."

"Later, maybe."

"Okay, I'll wait." Another thirty minutes passed before there was a second knock.

"Liz, please come out."

"I don't think I can."

"I wish you had stuck around to see the look on Dad's face. I don't think I've ever seen that look before in my entire life." There was a chuckle.

"Chase, this isn't funny."

"Actually," he responded through muffled cracks in his voice, "it's perhaps the funniest thing I've ever seen."

"Oh, this is just great. You're laughing." She threw a UNC plastic cup that sat on the tub at the door.

The guffaws increased a level and now he couldn't catch his breath. Liz snapped the door open and stood buck-naked shaking her finger in his face. Tears in his eyes, Chase doubled over. She couldn't remember the last time she'd seen him laughing so hard.

"You stop that right this minute," she demanded, leaning down and retrieving the pink towel that was still on the floor. "This is NOT funny!"

Chase collapsed on the sofa holding his sides and rocked from side to side. "If you could have seen him, Liz! Dad stood up straight, cleared his throat as if to say something, and then just turned and went for the door. He'll never EVER watch Carolina or Ohio State again with the same expectations. He'll keep waiting for you to make your bump and grind entrance from the sidelines."

Liz let escape a long sorrowful moan. "How can I ever look him in the eye again? What must he think?"

"He must think Mom has really been holding out on him all of these years." Chase gasped and went into another contortion of laughter.

"OH," Liz wailed. "Euphrasia!" The thought that her mother-in-law would hear of this almost paralyzed her. "What if he tells your mom?"

"Are you kidding? He won't ever tell Mom. What would he say? He just saw a great pair of boobs?"

Liz stood mortified.

"I will say," Chase said through tears, "it was a bit extreme, but I do think you've probably cured Dad of walking in unannounced."

"Chase, listen. Stop it and listen!"

He wasn't listening. "I'm sure it took his mind off the Judge, too," he said.

"Chase," Liz took a more controlled tone. "You have got to promise me you won't ever tell anyone about this. No one! Hear? Not your sister, not a soul at the pharmacy. No one! Understand?"

He wasn't quite ready to let up. "Whatever possessed you?" he blurted out.

"We were alone. The kids were gone. I thought it would help us break the tension so I could sleep."

"It did. It most certainly did." Chase pulled Liz down on the sofa next to him and started to play with the top of the towel. Then with eyes that sparkled brighter than she had seen in months he rolled over on top of her. "I do love you, you know, very, very much."

"Chase, listen to me now. You must promise me or I won't ever leave the house again. Promise me you will never tell anyone else about this. Promise me!"

"I promise," he said softly.

It wasn't exactly the evening she had planned, but it was the one time in her life that Liz scored more points than Chapel Hill. The Tar Heels lost by seven.

CHAPTER SEVEN

The following evening the crowd was much smaller as Liz weaved her way across the den. Billie refilled glasses from a bottle of Chardonnay in one hand and Pinot Noir in the other, and made small talk about the election with two of the county commissioners. A silk cerise ribbon that matched Billie's slacks was pinned to her tea rose blouse and hung loosely in four strands down the left side of her bodice. Nestled into a pillow on the sofa, Webster would come alert momentarily for anyone who stopped to scratch his head. He wore a cerise collar with several sparkling glass jewels embedded.

Liz greeted several of the guests; a more reserved group, no cooler of beer on the outdoor patio. Leland Slade, one of the Quaker elders, nodded at her wordlessly as he turned to leave. A giant of a man with a bushfire beard that concealed the bottom of his face, he saw little use for idle chatter. Liz was never sure how to approach him.

Kate Pearson, recently retired, also a Quaker, came up and slipped her hand into Liz's. "I know you and Maggie are good friends. If there's anything I can do . . ." she left the words suspended in air.

"Thank you," Liz said. "I think things are under control for right now, but I'll let you know."

"I've heard what she's requested for the service," Kate continued. "There are some in town who are critical, but you know I've been through that. Different ideas are not always appreciated. I hope she knows many support what she's doing."

"Thank you," Liz said, "I'll tell her."

Kate's offer was genuine. Twenty years earlier when her daughter had married a young black man, her own Quaker meeting had failed to reach a consensus to approve the marriage. Ralph Edgewater felt that it was an unwise decision; he refused to step aside, making it impossible to grant approval. He was set in his ways and could not be moved. The wedding was held in the Philadelphia Meeting instead of Cedar Branch.

Liz knew Kate was deeply hurt by the lack of support, even if it did rest on the shoulders of one individual. That has been one of the challenges of being a Quaker: consensus has to be found. One person has the ability to block a decision from moving forward.

A big pot of coffee and tray of cookies sat on the counter. Liz sidled up to Billie. "Where's Maggie?" she asked.

"She's upstairs with the casket," Billie said.

"Alone?"

"There are a few others up there with her; ladies from the church. Helen is one. Your mother-in-law and father-in-law went up a bit ago. I think they're still there. Want a glass of wine?"

"I'll take it," Liz said, needing something to fortify herself before an encounter with Grandpa Hoole, given the previous evening's surprise.

Liz took a swallow and then put the glass back in front of Billie, who obliged her with a refill. As she put the glass to her lips Billie nodded to the stairs as Euphrasia and Nathan cautiously descended. Liz considered chucking the wine in the sink and ducking out of sight, but they had already seen her.

They both looked weary, their skin taut, their eyes dark with circles. Grandma Hoole wore a loose-fitting gray dress. Grandpa wore a traditional collarless white shirt and black trousers with suspenders. Liz had seen him only once in a suit, at her wedding in St. Paul. She had wondered why he'd made that one exception. Like most Quakers, he never wore a tie; and although he still had one of the wide brim hats, he wore it only in cold weather to protect his bald head. Liz hadn't seen Grandma in her bonnet in years.

Wearing hats was becoming a thing of the past, except for Leland, who stuck to the old ways. He could always be seen working on his farm, in town, or around his house, wearing either his black or brown wide brim hat. The custom dated back to the beginnings of Quakerism when George Fox refused to take off his hat to anyone. Fox insisted that to be required to remove one's hat in respect to another implied that the two men were not on equal footing. Since all men were equal in the sight of God, they were likewise equal in the sight of other men. He was thrown in jail on numerous occasions for what the English saw as a failure to respect the many tiers of social stratification within that society.

Liz embraced Grandma. They were about the same height, although Grandma had shrunk a bit in recent years. She kept her hair pulled back in a severe bun. Liz always felt that if she could convince Grandma to loosen her hair, maybe even go to a hair dresser, a different style would soften the features in her angular face; but Liz didn't have the nerve to make such a suggestion. Grandma never wore make-up or jewelry and discouraged vanity in any fashion.

Chase's sister, Sophie, looked like her mother, and was a beautiful woman in her simplicity and style. She started to wear a small bit of make-up when she followed Chase to UNC. After she married Jack Reardon, a dentist, and moved to Charleston, she paid more attention to style with her hair and clothes, but always in modest good taste.

"Where's Chase?" Grandma asked.

"At home with the boys. He came last night," Liz said.

"You call him to come pick you up. You don't want to be driving after drinking."

Liz looked as obedient as she could: "Yes, Grandma."

"I'm glad he's staying with the boys, though. They shouldn't be left with babysitters too often."

"They're not, Grandma," Liz kept her voice steady.

"Nathan?" Grandma turned, expecting he might add something.

Grandpa Hoole murmured. He took out a handkerchief and wiped his nose. He had not yet made eye contact with Liz.

"Can I get you a cup of coffee or a cookie?" Liz asked.

"No, thank you, dear," Grandma said. "You go on up and sit with Maggie. She needs her friends around her tonight. We'll see you at meeting for worship before the funeral tomorrow."

Liz walked with them to the driveway, opened the car door, kissed them both on the cheek, and went back into the house. Billie met her with her glass of Chardonnay.

"Thanks," Liz said. "Remind me not to drink and drive."

"Helen is still upstairs. Probably should take the whole bottle if you're going up."

"I'm not enthusiastic," Liz said.

"Better you than me. You're a political rival. She won't want to say anything you can use against her in a campaign. That could help."

Liz climbed the back stairs and heard the low mumbling of several voices. Through the dining area she saw the casket on the opposite side of the living room under the portrait of Maggie's mother. A yellow cascade of roses, orchids, snapdragons, and lilies placed at the head filled the room with the perfumes of spring flowers. A spray of confederate roses interspersed with cotton bolls rested on top of the lower half of the casket.

Liz stopped at the partition between the dining room and living room. Maggie sat in a winged Queen Anne chair half facing her father's body. Helen and two other women had their backs towards Liz.

"Maggie, dear," Helen was talking. "Your father would not want to be remembered in this way."

"In what way, exactly?" Maggie asked. Liz knew by the tone in her voice that Maggie had already grown weary of Helen.

"Well, he would not want his death to be the cause of a split within the church. Surely you can see that."

"Who's planning to split, Helen? You?"

The other women shifted uncomfortably in their chairs. This was never a good way to approach Maggie. Unlike her father, who would spend days, even years cajoling and negotiating a mutual agreement, Maggie had neither the patience nor the inclination to play games.

"Maggie, we have a small congregation," Helen said. "You know that. There are only thirty or forty regular members. If anyone should leave," she hesitated, "well, a loss of five or more would make a big difference." Helen paused a moment and looked at Maggie. Maggie was not receptive.

Helen continued. "I hear talk. Quite a number of people are upset that this situation has been thrust upon the church with no warning. This is so unlike your father."

"No warning, Helen? You know my father spent many years in an effort to improve race relations in this community. He was an invited guest at Jerusalem Baptist and other black churches in the county numerous times. Not once did our church reciprocate with an invitation."

"He never made a formal request." Helen fiddled with her pearl necklace.

"Oh, Helen! He suggested several times that he thought Martin Luther King, Jr.'s birthday would be an ideal time to invite a member from the black community to preach. It never happened."

"For good reason," Helen's lips pursed in disgust. "I never approved of that holiday anyway. That man encouraged civil disobedience."

"Helen," Maggie's voice rose. "The entire American Revolution was based on civil disobedience."

"I don't want to argue with you." Helen softened her voice in contrast to Maggie's, which had the desired effect. Helen appeared in control; Maggie appeared to be losing hers. "I think you're turning this funeral into a political statement of sorts, perhaps to help Liz out in the election. This is your agenda, Maggie, not your father's."

Maggie took a deep breath in an obvious effort to calm herself. "My father's agenda included better education and improved economic opportunities. He worked vigorously with men like Nathan Hoole," she nodded at the stairway in reference to Grandpa's recent departure, "to get subsidized housing, mental health services, improved roads, water lines, and industry into our county. He did all of that not just for the benefit of a few people in the community, but for everyone. That was my father's agenda and I stand by it."

"That's all well and good, Maggie, but your father understood politics and he knew that without the right timing you could lose everything overnight. To be honest, I don't think you've got your father's knack for timing."

"Maybe, maybe not," Maggie conceded. "I guess we'll see."

Everyone knew they had reached an impasse. Helen's face softened with sympathetic insincerity and she reached out and patted Maggie's hand. "I understand why your family feels it owes so much to the black community. On the other hand, those of us in the community who don't have the same guilt struggle to just keep things on an even keel. Be careful, my dear. Don't start something that you can't control."

Maggie stood and stretched her frame to its full 5'10". Her long dark hair, which was normally pulled back and twisted upward, had come loose throughout the day. Now fugitive strands framed her face and accentuated the streak of gray. "Perhaps it's time you left," Maggie said in a more controlled voice.

The two other women scurried to get their handbags and immediately headed past Liz for the stairs, not stopping to acknowledge her presence. Helen deliberately took more time. She reached for her bag, stood up, and pulled back her shoulders to gain some height. The lines on her face complemented her steely voice. "You're making a mistake, Maggie Kendall, a very big mistake."

"I'll pray on it," Maggie said. "Perhaps you should do the same."

Helen turned and walked to the steps. She saw Liz and shook her head in hopeless resignation.

"Those idiots!" Maggie said, and dropped back into her chair. "What gall!"

Liz walked over and sat opposite her. The Judge lay serene, no longer stale, but dressed in a tuxedo and wine plum cummerbund. He might have enjoyed the previous exchange, although Liz couldn't help but wonder why he had left Maggie to do the job instead of handling it himself. Too old, too tired . . . maybe too much water under the bridge?

CHAPTER EIGHT

Chase and Liz walked the half mile from their home to the funeral. Countless cars parked at angles along the street and up into various yards throughout town. The Sheriff had patrol cars blocks away from the church to prevent congestion. The chimes that the Judge had donated to the church in memory of his wife played "A Mighty Fortress is Our God," followed by "For the Beauty of the Earth."

As Liz approached Cottonwoods she saw a horse-drawn wagon at the bottom of the staircase that descended from the piazza and the main entrance to the house. Journalists hovered around with small groups of lawyers and various county officials in the front yard. Liz and Chase slipped in the side patio doors and walked up the back stairs. LuAnne stood awkwardly in the corner of the living room, lost in a roomful of dignitaries. Liz sidestepped the crowd to get to her.

From the other side of the living room next to the door, Billie waved at them frantically. "Come here," she mouthed, and pointed at the empty space beside her. Liz grabbed LuAnne's hand and motioned to Chase to follow her as they wedged their way through the crowd.

As they watched, the casket bearers moved the casket out of the room onto the piazza. Maggie followed like a bride awaiting the cue for her entrance. Billie discreetly held up her hand to stop the rest of the line. The choreography was in place: this was Maggie, all Maggie, the last of the Kendalls, who now stood alone at the top of the stairs to Cottonwoods watching the descent of her father's casket for his final journey. Cameras flashed from all angles. It was the most published photograph of the day and appeared in all the state papers the next morning.

Once the casket was securely in the wagon, Billie motioned for Senator Winston Gray to join Maggie. With his enviable full head of richly dyed brown hair and his closely cropped beard, he took his place to Maggie's right as the line began to move.

Miss Ellie was next in line on the arm of her son, Josh Cartwright. Josh worked with the State Department and lived somewhere around Washington, DC. It had been years since he had been in Cedar Branch. Liz remembered meeting him only a couple of times. Ellie's two girls, Susan and Cathy, were further back in the line with their husbands. Chase and Liz walked with LuAnne between them.

Billie and Gill followed. Liz had never seen Billie in black before, but today she conformed to dress etiquette. Her black chemise dress bore a large silk pink flower on the right shoulder and there was a pink belt around her waist. She also wore pink sunglasses and heels. Liz couldn't remember having ever seen Gill in a suit. A small man, he looked quite dapper. A pink tie added bit of flash. He and Billie made a handsome couple.

In contrast, Liz felt pretty uninteresting in a knee-length good-for-any-occasion black polyester dress. The only salvation was that it was draped in chiffon that gave it a bit more upscale appearance. With an attractive head scarf and a long string of pearls, this was her fallback outfit for any occasion.

The procession walked the four blocks to the Methodist Church with "How Great Thou Art" ringing through the town. Maggie stayed just a few steps behind the casket. Jackie Onassis had nothing on Maggie Kendall, other than a few million more mourners. As they approached the church Liz saw at least two hundred people standing outside. Folding chairs had been set up and a microphone system was in place. Chase nudged her and nodded to the roof line below the steeple, where a large white bird perched reviewing the parade.

"Look at that," Chase said. Hawk?

Liz looked up. "Couldn't be. Owl, I think."

The casket was rolled through the double doors of the church and up the aisle to the front as the Jerusalem Baptist Choir sang "Just a Closer Walk with Thee." Their soulful tones echoed out into the churchyard.

Behind the reserved rows, the pews were filled with members of the black community on the left, and the white congregation on the right. Liz wondered whether they had been seated that way, or if a process of self-selection had placed the two races on opposite sides of the aisle. A small three-piece band of a keyboard, the drums/cymbals, and a saxophone assembled in front of the pulpit: apparently the Jerusalem Choir had brought their own musical accompaniment.

Miss Mary Law sat at the organ with her eyes straight ahead on the sheet music in front of her. In her black suit and pill box hat, she looked every bit the Chair of the Methodist Women's Auxiliary and church organist.

When the remaining participants were seated and the choir finished their first hymn, Reverend Morgan rose to the podium. "Welcome to the Methodist Church and the celebration of the life of Judge Corbett Marshall Kendall. How pleased we are to have representation from all of our community here with us today," he began. "It is not often that we come together to worship. How fitting that the Judge helped us make that happen."

His words sounded sincere. Liz recognized what a difficult situation this was for a man who had ministered only to white, conservative congregations for forty years. She fully appreciated his efforts to make this a service of inclusiveness.

"Let us bow our heads in prayer." The congregation fell silent. "Our Father in Heaven, we are gathered here today to celebrate the life of our recently departed brother, Corbett Marshall Kendall. As we do so, we ask for your blessings on his friends and family as they struggle with their loss, even knowing that he is now with You in Heaven. Amen."

At the organ, Miss Mary Law now burst into "Joyful Joyful We Adore Thee" as the congregation searched for their hymnals. Once through the prelude with only a minor key adjustment, she paused with a long chord and was rewarded by a sea of voices that joined in as she belted out the first verse. Rarely had this church been filled with so many singing their praises to God. When she concluded all four verses, her face reflected genuine satisfaction with her performance.

Reverend Morgan rose again. Liz looked at the program and could see that he planned to dominate most of the service; after all, the service was in *his* church. The Reverend Melvin Broadnax's opportunity to speak came after the second song by the choir.

"Maggie," Reverend Morgan began, "Reverend Broadnax, distinguished guests, friends of the family, and members of our community. This week we have suffered a terrible loss. We have all lost a friend, a mentor, and a community leader of substantial proportion. And Maggie, our dear Maggie, has lost a father.

"But let not our grief overshadow our joy; the joy of having a man such as Corbett in our midst," Reverend Morgan continued with steady nerves and a more even tone to his voice. "Our beloved Judge Corbett Kendall has not left us. He has merely gone ahead to wait for us and perhaps stand before our heavenly Father in defense of us when our turn comes for the final judgment. What better representation than to have a judge waiting for us at the pearly gates?"

There were a few smiles and snickers. At this point Liz thought she heard soft music in the background. As she scanned the front of the church, she looked first at the organ: a quick turn of Miss Mary Law's head indicated that she'd heard the music, too.

It didn't take long for all eyes in the congregation to focus on the young black man seated at the keyboard. With his back towards the congregation and his face uplifted, he provided background music similar to the theme song for the soap opera *Days of Our Lives*.

Engrossed in his own words, Reverend Morgan did not yet appear to be aware of the accompaniment. Mustering up more wind power than he normally displayed, he sang out with conviction, "The Judge sits today with his Maker. Our Judge Kendall has met the Heavenly Father, the Greatest Judge of All."

A few respectful "Amens," called out from the black side of the church. Reverend Morgan seemed a little surprised. He paused before resuming.

"Corbett Kendall was the creator, preserver, and protector of so many memorable contributions to our community that it is difficult for me to know where to begin. I must mention his great love for his home town of Cedar Branch where he was in a succession of a long line of Kendalls dating back to the late 1700s. Corbett Kendall loved Cedar Branch."

When the keyboard increased in volume, Reverend Morgan finally took notice.

"Everywhere he went he would announce, 'I am Corbett Kendall from Cedar Branch . . .'"

Several voices joined in to complete the sentence with him, "*the crown jewel of North Carolina.*"

At first startled by the communal response, the Reverend then seemed pleased. "Yes sir, *the crown jewel of North Carolina.* That is indeed what he called his home town."

"Corbett Kendall loved his daughter, Maggie," Reverend Morgan went on, with force.

Pop, pop! The drummer hit the drum twice. "Amens" resounded in the church. The drummer smiled. Reverend Morgan leaped into the air with a start, causing the reading glasses at the tip of his nose to fall to the floor. Simultaneously the majority of the white membership jumped several inches above their seats.

Reverend Morgan disappeared momentarily behind the pulpit to recover his glasses and then paused before speaking directly to the drummer. "Judge Corbett Kendall is sitting with Jesus today."

The drummer nodded.

Reverend Morgan continued. "I cannot speak for Jesus. I can only imagine that Jesus spoke to Corbett as Matthew records when God said, *This is my son with whom I am well pleased.*

"For surely, most surely, God is pleased," the Reverend added in a solemn tone.

Though a few "Amens" rang out, the drummer appeared to be under control.

Liz was both surprised and proud of how well Reverend Morgan handled this new approach to worship. This was unlike the stoic Methodist congregations who regularly sat in front of him on any given Sunday morning—*the frozen chosen*.

Reverend Morgan now juggled several things at once. His eyes shifted between his notes and the drummer as he resorted to a safe passage in the scriptures. "Let us not forget the words of John 14, 1–6 in this time of our grief: Jesus said to his disciples, *Do not let your hearts be troubled. Believe in God, believe also in me.*"

The Reverend continued through the verses without interruption. The drummer was silent. The extended delay appeared to the choir to be their cue to begin the next song. Confused and obviously not expecting to be cut off quite so prematurely, Reverend Morgan moved to his chair while the Jerusalem Choir sang an *a cappella* rendition of "Down to the River to Pray" that floated through the church as if angels themselves had cast a spell over the entire sanctuary.

At the end of the five verses Reverend Morgan was not about to try to top their performance. After a pause, Reverend Melvin Broadnax took the podium. This powerfully built man in his fifties with bushy eyebrows that dominated a smooth, shiny head played to the percussion instruments, and they played right back. Liz couldn't help but be fascinated by the fact that the black congregation appeared to relax. Faith was not a burden for them, but a celebration.

"Maggie, Maggie," Reverend Broadnax said with his eyes on her. "While we cannot begin to understand the loss that you must feel, we are here today, ALL gathered here today to share your pain and be a witness to the life of a great man."

Several "Amens" were softly heard from the black side of the church.

"But I bring you good news. We are confident."

Pop went the drummer.

"Confident," *blam* went the cymbals, "second Corinthians tells us CONFIDENT," *pop, blam, "that while we are at home in the body we are absent from the Lord,* but today, yes, TODAY, Maggie . . ."

A drum roll began in the background, softly at first, but gaining momentum. "We are CONFIDENT that while your father is absent from the body, HE . . . IS . . . PRESENT . . . WITH . . . THE . . . LORD. Amen."

Pop, pop, blam, blam, blam.

"Amen" was raised in unison from the black congregation.

"Let the people say, AMEN," Reverend Broadnax repeated.

"AMEN."

Liz joined in with a few respectful "Amens" from the white gallery.

"Let the church praise the Lord and echo to the ceiling our belief that Corbett Kendall now sits with the Lord. Are you CONFIDENT, brethren? Say AMEN." *Blam.*

"Amen" poured out from the black side of the aisle and with less enthusiasm from the white parishioners, who obviously weren't quite so confident. Liz noticed Reverend Morgan mouthing the words, but without much fervor. Miss Mary Law didn't look confident one bit.

The Reverend Broadnax and the drummer were now involved in a duet they practiced Sunday after Sunday. The drummer knew when to come in, and the Reverend knew when to let him.

"It has not always been a good time for us here in Cedar Branch." The Reverend lowered his voice to a softer pitch. "We have suffered some bad days here in our little town."

Scattered "yeses" arose.

"There were days when a man was judged by the color of his skin, instead of the content of his character."

As a tense hush blanketed both sides of the aisle, Liz could sense a new level of discomfort.

"We all remember days of struggle, days of hardship—days when we failed. Yes, we FAILED. We have failed to demonstrate the compassion and love due our brothers and sisters of both races."

No one said a word. Even the music had stopped.

"But brothers and sisters, I stand here today to tell you the Judge was a fair man. He recognized injustice. He stood up to criticism. He stood up to controversy. And he stood before God and man to do what was right."

Now the drummer was back in the game: *pop, pop.*

In the front row Liz could see Miss LuAnne and Miss Ellie dabbing their eyes with handkerchiefs. Maggie sat in front of Liz with her shoulders squared and her emotions intact.

"And I have more good news, Maggie. Your father, the Judge, did not walk up the golden steps to meet his Savior with any regrets. He was not bent over with his face to the ground. He stood straight and tall. Your father knew when he met his maker that he had served his Lord, his God with all his heart, with all his mind, and all his soul."

Blam, blam, blam.

The percussion instruments were again a part of the game plan as the Reverend launched into a series of "Hallelujahs" and "Amens."

"Cedar Branch is a better place, and we as individuals are better people because of Judge Corbett Marshall Kendall."

"Hallelujah" echoed through the black side of the church.

"Yes, Praise Jesus, he is with his Maker."

The drummer was now alternating the cymbals by lightly feathering them with wire brushes until the minister reached a crescendo.

"Let not your heart be troubled, Maggie."

Blam.

"Let not your heart be troubled, friends."

Blam.

"Let not your heart be troubled, citizens of Cedar Branch. Let not your heart be troubled, North Carolina."

The keyboard joined in with the cymbals and shouts of "No, No."

Liz noted that Reverend Morgan did look somewhat troubled, however, and Miss Mary Law was most definitely troubled.

"For I go and prepare a place for you in my Father's mansion, and I will come again and receive you to Myself, that where I am, there you may be also."

"Hallelujah" poured out from the black congregation.

After a loud chorus of "Amen," he stopped abruptly.

Knowing that he had both the capability and reputation for preaching for an hour non-stop, Liz was surprised. The saxophone player rose and three members of the choir stepped to the front of the church and joined the keyboard in a chorus of the gospel song "On My Way to Heaven."

Some of the foot tapping and hand clapping appeared to be coming from the white side of the aisle. Liz was very sure that no one in the Methodist Church had ever tapped a foot inside the sanctuary up until that day. At the end of the song there was generous applause from one half of the church and polite applause from the other; Liz felt that the wheels of community had been greased a bit. It was a beginning.

When the song reached its finale, Reverend Morgan rose and almost tripped in an effort to regain control of the podium. Reverend Broadnax acquiesced and respectfully withdrew to his seat.

Without another word Reverend Morgan seemed intent on reminding everyone that this was his church: "First Corinthians, 15:51," he thundered out as loudly as his voice allowed. *"Behold, I tell you a mystery; We shall not all sleep, but we shall all be changed."*

And that, Liz thought, might have been the most profound statement of the service.

Reverend Morgan then nodded firmly to the funeral home director who approached the front of the church to begin the task of removing the casket. A member of the Jerusalem Baptist Choir rose and in quiet velvet voice began a slow *a cappella* rendition of "I'll Fly Away."

At first it was very soft as the casket was rolled down the aisle. Maggie stood and turned to wait for the usher, then leaned across the pew and gave Liz a hug. "Thank you," she whispered in her ear.

She gave a similar hug to Billie; Liz's eyes began to water. Maggie and the first rows were escorted out, and more of the choir joined in the chorus as the tempo picked up.

Once outside, Billie and Liz put their arms around each other's waists. Through the speakers they could hear that the keyboard, drums, and saxophone were all now involved in a zippy rendition of the song. People stood in silence to hear the final three verses as the casket was loaded onto the wagon.

"Boy," Billie leaned into Liz. "I want that choir at my funeral."

Still a bit choked up, Liz couldn't speak. The church emptied and the entourage followed the horse-drawn carriage back up the street to the family cemetery behind Cottonwoods.

At the cemetery Reverend Morgan provided a few brief words as Maggie placed the first of several single confederate roses on the top of the casket. Liz was close enough to hear her whisper, "Good-bye, Daddy. I hope I got it right."

Then she turned and walked back to Cottonwoods with the legal power and political junkies following her. The mantle had been passed.

CHAPTER NINE

When Liz walked into the Red Cross building the next morning, her secretary, Debbie Bradshaw, was busy with her brightly painted finger-nails dancing around the keyboard.

"New dress?" Liz asked as she sat down beside Debbie to review the weekly schedule.

"Yeah, my ex's new wife gave it to me." Debbie gave her a big toothy grin. "Like it?" With a thumb on each shoulder of the dress, she showed it off and fluttered her fingers.

"Very nice," Liz knew before she asked the next question that the answer would be good. "You mean to tell me you get clothes from your ex-husband's new wife?"

"Sure, we're good friends. I gave her my husband as a hand-me-down and she hands me down her clothes." Then without missing a beat she added, "I got the best end of the deal."

This woman made Liz laugh at the beginning of every day. Tall, with long shapely legs that got a second look in most restaurants, Debbie was upbeat despite the ongoing soap opera in her life. She was at her desk at eight on the dot every morning, took each of her breaks to the minute in order to get her cigarette fix, and walked out the door at exactly five to begin her afternoon routine with her two teenage children.

"So tell all," Debbie ordered. "I'm dying to hear the details about the funeral."

"There's not so much to tell," Liz said.

"Are you kidding? It's the headlines. Lookie here." She whipped out the *Raleigh News and Observer*, or "The Disturber," as she chose to call it, with the picture of Maggie on the front page as the casket was carried down the front steps. "I looked for you. Figured you were there in the background someplace, but didn't see your picture."

"I wasn't the main attraction by a long shot," Liz said.

"Lots of bigwigs, I bet, from all over the state?"

"Lots of them," Liz said.

The phone rang and Debbie picked it up in a smooth transition. "Red Cross Donor Recruitment Office, Debbie speaking. Oh, *Hiiii* there Mr. Baughman," her voice squealed as if she had been waiting breathlessly for his call. "Ms. Hoole will be *soooo* pleased to hear that. I'll get her that message right away. September second would be great. And I look forward to seeing you there also. Thank you so much."

"Ted Baughman." She gave Liz a thumbs-up as she put down the receiver. "Confirmed the September drive at Dexter's Small Engine Company. They've got four hundred employees—lots of blood."

"Great," Liz said, and marked it in her day planner.

Liz often commented to Chase that the best part of her job as Director of Donor Recruitment was her secretary. Debbie wore clothes that were too tight and too short, and exposed an excess of cleavage. She also upped donation statistics more than 10 percent at every drive she worked. Redneck to the core and proud of it, Debbie could figure out anything from cost reports to computer repairs while filing her nails at the same time. Had her high school guidance counselor done a better job she would have gotten Debbie into college, but instead she simply asked her what she liked to do.

"Fix hair," Debbie said, and ended up with a one-chair beauty salon in her basement. After a nasty divorce that left her with two kids and no benefits, she decided to refresh her typing skills. Computers had just entered the work place and businesses were scrambling to find employees who could adapt to the new technology. Debbie found it as natural as eating grits and cheese. She tutored Liz. In turn Liz worked with Chase and Maggie on the inevitable transformation into the computer age. Debbie was a diamond in the rough. Her only flaws were her indiscriminate taste in men and a weakness for two-bit bars.

"I've got a new boyfriend," Debbie said as they began to review the work ahead. Boyfriend reports were part of her ongoing repertoire. "You're gonna like this one."

Having seen too many of Debbie's boyfriends come and go, Liz was skeptical. "What's to like?"

"For starters," Debbie almost blushed as she shot Liz a coy glance that promised a revelation into his personal assets, "he's got all his own teeth."

Liz laughed out loud. "Already an improvement! You're definitely aiming higher."

"Second, he's not married." She went into her first tier of requirements that Liz knew by heart.

"Most important, he's got a job—a real one. One that pays money and has benefits."

"This one is definitely a keeper." Liz felt Debbie deserved so much better than she'd had, but she had learned long ago not to give boyfriend advice. "He's a lucky guy."

"So back to the funeral," Debbie said. Although Liz thought that topic was closed. "Is it true?"

"What?"

"That Maggie had the body at the house all night before the funeral?"

"She did."

"Oooooow," Debbie scrunched up her nose. "That gives me the willies. You know that for sure?"

"I do, I was there," Liz said.

"Really? You stayed with her the whole night?"

"I did."

"Did you see the Judge's ghost?"

"Nope."

"You sure? I heard people saw a light out in the cotton field. They say if you see the ghost the night of their funeral it means they're coming back to get someone else."

"That's nonsense," Liz said as she stood up and handed Debbie her disk with updates that needed confirmation letters. "Where in heaven's name do you hear all of this stuff?"

"I'm well connected," Debbie said with a devilish smile.

"Then how about start connecting with that keyboard? We've got work to do." Though Debbie could get easily sidetracked, Liz had learned how to stop her. The rest didn't matter. Debbie added a bit of glitz to an otherwise sterile medical atmosphere.

As Liz sat down at her desk she shook her head in resignation. At some point she knew someone would claim to see an apparition of the Judge. He himself had spoken of ghosts at Cottonwoods, and older homes were fodder for such stories. The fact that there were family graveyards throughout the area and that the Quakers had provided sanctuary for runaway slaves during the days of the Underground Railroad added to the folklore.

Liz's personal favorite was the story of the lady on the big brown mare who rode across the old Quaker farm at daybreak when the mist was heavy. Her own son, Adam, had said that he saw her once when he was out early scouting cotton. And then, of course, there was the rhyme that all her boys sang at sleepovers with their friends. At night they'd sit on the back porch staring out into the swamp looking for the telltale lights that Chase and Liz tried to explain to them was swamp gas. Once in a while one of them would claim to see a light: they'd scream "corpse candles," and run inside.

Liz would try to hush them up. If it was the middle of the night, Chase would get up and get them off the porch and back into their bedrooms.

"Isn't anything out there but the swamp," he'd try to convince them, but then Liz and Chase would hear the chant again as squealing from the basement bedrooms. Kids can't let things go.

> *Listen my children and you shall hear,*
> *The screams of a man who runs in fear.*
> *They hung him high in a cypress tree.*
> *Deep in the swamp of Potecasi.*
> *He mourns his wife and weeps for his son*
> *And swears he'll come back for revenge with a gun.*
> *So, if there's a man with a lantern, be wary,*
> *It may be the ghost of Isaac Perry.*

CHAPTER TEN

Though Chase had promised to talk to his mother about the upcoming Easter Parade as well as her grandson Nat's wedding, he hadn't gotten around to it. He and his father had discussed both over coffee at the pharmacy, but apparently neither of them bothered to give Euphrasia any of the details. "Let's not worry her," Grandpa had said. "She's pretty flexible."

Liz fretted over both. *Flexible* did not describe Euphrasia in her thinking. Grandma might appear flexible to Chase and his father, but Liz knew she would run into objections from Euphrasia on both issues. Grandma never confronted Chase with her concerns; she'd always come straight to Liz. She'd assume that Liz either had a lapse in understanding or a complete disregard for Quaker values.

Not true, Liz wanted to jump up and down saying. She may not have been raised Quaker as Chase had been, but she'd attended Quaker meeting for worship for twenty-five years now, and together they'd raised all four boys within the Society of Friends.

Both the Easter Parade and the wedding required some concessions, concessions she'd discussed with Chase. Liz had fond memories of Christmas trees decked out with presents underneath, and Easter egg hunts. She wanted to embellish the concept of Santa Claus and the Easter Bunny and would not give up the festive, albeit commercial, aspects of the religious holidays.

Chase knew that when Liz insisted on all the wedding trappings for her own wedding, that she would never deny her children the same luxury, should any of them ask for something similar.

Their second son Adam had married his childhood sweetheart from another Quaker family in town. The wedding was traditional; a meeting for worship that was held in silence. Afterwards a potluck was held on the grounds of the Meeting House. Grandma Hoole had made the wedding cake herself.

Nat, the oldest and Grandpa's namesake, fell in love with Alexandra Louise Lloyd at Wake Forest University. Given that she was from a prominent Episcopalian family in Charleston, South Carolina, their wedding would be elaborate in contrast.

Grandpa had always been so grateful that Liz and Chase raised their four boys in Cedar Branch where they were a part of his everyday life, that he never objected to Liz's desire to re-create special memories for her own children. *Let each person seek clearness and find their own path in the light* was his firm belief. He had allowed Chase and Sophie to do so. He had no intensions of denying his grandchildren the same choices.

Grandma, on the other hand, feared that a lackadaisical approach into the more universal religious traditions of uniform prayer, ministered worship, hymns, and the sacraments, instead of simple silent worship, would lead her grandchildren to become Baptists or Methodists. She was only now trying to grasp the fact that a great-grandchild might be an Episcopalian.

With the Easter Parade less than two weeks away and Mrs. Lloyd having already called to discuss wedding plans, Liz became insistent. Chase agreed that an evening at The Quaker Café over an informal dinner might be best. They'd just mention things to Grandma in passing. The two boys would come along; Liz knew they'd create a buffer. Grandma would cushion any remarks she made in their presence.

Evan, their seven-year-old, dressed in his sky blue Tar Heel T-shirt and a pair of jeans, played with Matchbox cars, which he ran along the side of the table. He had just gotten two new ones in his collection that he wanted to show Grandpa. His long thin fingers held a blue Ford T-Bird Turbo and a yellow Lamborghini Diablo. He made small revving noises as he slid them down the table. Dark silky bangs partially covered his eyes. Liz made a mental note to get him a haircut over the weekend.

"My golly, look at those," Grandpa said as he and Grandma joined them. He picked up one and examined it. "Bet you're the only one in town with those two beauties. I'll give you a dollar for them."

"Nooooo." Evan grabbed them both and hid them behind his back.

"Two dollars?" Grandpa asked.

"Nooooo." Evan smiled. This was a game he and Grandpa played over and over with his cars, although Grandpa never went higher than two dollars, and Evan never agreed to sell.

"I could have fixed something at home," Grandma said as she pulled up a chair to the table. "No point in spending money to eat out."

"The boys like The Quaker Café. We thought we all deserved a treat," Chase said. "It's been a hard week."

"Whatcha got there, son?" Grandpa turned his attention to Nicholas, who was focused on a hand calculator.

"Calculator," he said. "Ask me something. Ask me anything."

"What's fourteen times fourteen?" Grandpa asked.

Nicholas punched in the numbers and quickly came up with 196. "Something harder," he insisted.

"The circumference of the world divided by pi," Grandpa teased.

"GrandPAAAAAAA," Nicholas groaned. A mathematician at heart, Grandpa had predicted Nicholas would be the math teacher or the scientist in the family—always fascinated with anything he could take apart or calculate. In fourth grade he was already running circles around Liz on the computer and helping her figure things out whenever she got stuck. With curly hair the color and texture of Liz's, he was more intense, more focused than any of the other boys.

"How's Maggie doing?" Grandpa asked.

"She needs some time," Liz said. "She was on her way to Raleigh the last I heard, but I plan to stop by her house tomorrow after work."

The café's door opened. In walked Timmy with a basket of small brown bags each containing roasted peanuts he'd shelled. He stopped next to Nicholas and gave each of the boys a high five. "Peas?" he asked.

Nicholas and Evan giggled and slapped his hand. He was a big kid to them, old in years only. Timmy walked in and out of the local businesses in Cedar Branch throughout the day selling his peanuts. Liz found his total acceptance by the community to be heartwarming, a statement to the adaptability of small towns and how they took care of their own.

Grandpa pulled three dollars out of his pocket and handed them to Timmy. "Put a bag in front of everyone," he said. Timmy proudly placed a bag in front of each person, took the three dollars, tipped his Atlanta Braves cap, and moved on to the next table. Before long he'd have enough to pay for dinner—six dollars and fifty cents.

"Euphrasia, Nathan, good to see you," Miss Ellie said as she placed a tray with six glasses of water and a basket of biscuits on the table.

"Ellie," Grandma Hoole reached out and took her hand, "come sit with us tonight. It's not that busy."

Miss Ellie squeezed Grandma's hand. "No rest for the weary."

"I'm so sorry about the Judge," Grandma said. Involuntarily everyone glanced over at the VIP table where the Judge normally sat. No one had returned to their usual places. Memories were still too raw.

"It's a hard pill to swallow, but life goes on, doesn't it?" Miss Ellie said. "We wake up every morning and put one foot in front of the other to start the day."

"That we do," Grandma said.

"What can I get you folks tonight?" Miss Ellie said as she took orders. Nicholas and Evan beamed at the opportunity to have a soda and peanuts as an appetizer. The rest of the family began to reduce the basket of biscuits to crumbs.

"How are wedding plans coming?" Grandma casually asked.

"I think everything's under control," Liz said. "I don't have much say, anyhow. It's the bride's wedding."

"Well, I hope you're not letting this get out of hand. After all, Nathan is a Quaker. Her family needs to respect that," Grandma said.

Liz gave Chase a nudge under the table. He ignored her. Wedding chatter continued. Miss Ellie sat a plate of fried chicken in front of Chase and two hamburgers with fries next to the boys.

Nicholas jumped into the talk. "Mama says Evan and I get to wear tuxedos?"

There was a pause as Grandma Hoole looked from Liz to Chase.

"Tuxedos? People are going to be wearing tuxedos?"

"It's going to be a formal wedding, Grandma," Liz said as she gave Chase something more akin to a kick instead of a nudge. *Jump in any time now,* she thought.

"Quakers have simple weddings," Grandma said.

"Episcopalians don't," Liz said.

"Nat is not Episcopalian."

"Lexa is," Liz said, and there was a poignant pause.

"Who is Lexa?"

"Euphrasia," Grandpa raised his eyebrow. "Alexandra."

"Alexandra is such a pretty name. Don't know why she shortens it. Lexa sounds like a car."

"Look," Chase interjected, "Liz and I have discussed this. We'd like to cover all of your expenses for this wedding. Dad, we'll rent a tuxedo for you. Mom, if you'd like to go buy a new dress . . ."

"Nonsense," Grandma snapped. "We're not going to be renting tuxedos or buying new clothes. We are who we are. We'll not dress up to pretend to be someone else."

"Fine," Chase said. "That's fine, Mom. You and Dad can wear anything you want. Nobody's insisting you do otherwise. We just want you to be there. It's very important to us that you and Dad are a part of the wedding."

"And we will be, son," Grandpa Hoole broke the tension. "There's nothing that could keep me away from the wedding. But we will attend as Quakers, not Episcopalians."

"What will I attend as?" Evan asked.

"You're going to be a penguin," Nicholas teased.

"I don't want to be a penguin," Evan complained loudly.

"You're not going to be a penguin," Liz tried to reassure him and shot a warning glance at Nicholas.

"Will there be a bubble machine like in the Easter Parade?" Evan asked.

"Bubble machine?" Grandma said with such surprise that Liz realized that neither Grandpa nor Chase had mentioned that possibility.

"No need to go into that now," Grandpa said, snatching control of the conversation. "Do you know your grandmother and I will be married fifty years in just two months? That's a long time, isn't it boys?"

"Wow," Evan's eyes opened wide. That's before there were cars."

Grandpa laughed. "A little after that. But I did ride my horse all the way from Cedar Branch to Holly Hills to see her one summer." He looked over at Euphrasia with obvious love. "That was twenty-five miles. Twenty-five miles there and twenty-five miles back."

"Why?" Nicholas asked. "What did you do when you got there?"

"Slept," Grandma said. "I gave him a glass of lemonade and then he lay down on the sofa and went to sleep. When he woke up he got on his horse and rode home."

"I loved that horse," Grandpa winked. "She was one fine animal."

Smiles circled the table. Grandma didn't say anything, but she relaxed and fell into lighter conversation. An unspoken truce had been called, one of those truces that only married couples who've been together for many years understood.

"Hey," Grandpa said as he pulled two baseball cards out of his pocket. I found a Cal Ripken, Jr. and a Barry Bonds card. Either of you boys interested?"

"Me, Grandpa, me," said both boys as they held out their hands in anticipation.

For the first time since Liz had so brazenly interrupted his basketball game by surprising him in the buff, she looked straight at Grandpa. Her eyes thanked him. Grandpa nodded.

Chapter Eleven

The morning of the Easter Parade nothing went as planned. Chase had been up throughout the night. At about five in the morning, he shook Liz awake. His voice was strained.

"What's wrong?" she said, struggling to unravel the fog in her head.

"We've got a problem."

More alert to his level of anxiety, she sat up. "What?"

"I threw Jitters into the washer and dryer." Chase choked and Liz thought she saw his eyes water. "He's never gotten into the laundry basket before, I didn't think to check."

Jitters was Evan's pet hamster. Despite his girth he had developed a magical ability to escape from his cage on a regular basis. He had done it so many times that it was normal to see Jitters scamper across the floor behind the television set, or pop out of the sofa from under a cushion. The family had turned his disappearance act into a family game of "Where in the World is Jitters Now?" Nicholas even suggested they change Jitters's name to Waldo to coincide with the real game, but that never happened.

This mischievousness entertained the family endlessly. Even Liz, who had not been overly excited about a hamster to start with, had become attached to the slippery little bloke. Their two aging collies would lie listlessly on the floor as Jitters dashed in front of their noses or across their tails.

"Is he dead?" Liz asked—as if there were a possibility that a hamster could survive a wash and rinse cycle, be tumbled dry, and come out refreshed and invigorated.

"Very."

"Do we have to tell the kids?"

"I think we do." Chase looked ghastly. "We can't lie to them about it."

"I could," she volunteered. "I would have no trouble at all lying about this."

"No, we'll talk to them at breakfast and then I'll take them with me down to the school. There'll be some other kids and their dads there; maybe that will distract them."

And so it was agreed. The boys were up by seven and hurried into their clothes with great expectations for the day ahead. Evan had one pair of Levi jeans and a blue Tar Heel T-shirt that he wore year round. His commitment to this particular outfit required that at least one load of wash be done nightly. Liz had tried duplicating the outfit, given that there was an endless array of the same exact jeans and shirts, but to no avail. Somehow Evan always knew. The others were *too scratchy, the neck was too tight* or *it just didn't feel right.* Liz and Chase conceded they had become soft with age, and they reconciled that one of them start the washer every night.

Chase fried bacon and scrambled up eggs while Liz packed the car with decorations for the float. The boys put on their clothes and taunted one another over who could find the most eggs. When they sat down to eat, Chase finally spoke up. "I've got some sad news boys. Jitters had an accident."

Evan and Nicholas turned their wide dark eyes on their father in nervous expectation. "Accident?" Nicholas said. "What kind of accident?"

"Jitters was hiding in the laundry basket and I threw him into the washing machine by mistake." Chase struggled with the words.

Liz could see Evan's lower lips start to quiver. "Is he okay?"

"Actually, he's not. I'm afraid he's dead."

Big wet tears began to roll down Evan's cheeks and he wiped his nose on his shirt. "He was my pet," he said, trying to contain a sob. "I was going to take him on the float with me today. He was my favorite."

"You have the two dogs, honey," Liz said, as if dogs and hamsters had anything in common. "Jasper and Lady will be on the float."

"But I wanted to take Jitters."

"Well, you can still take Jitters if you want." Chase spoke up. "We could make a little box for him to lie in and it could be his farewell to everyone before we bury him."

"Would it be like his funeral?" Evan stopped the sniffling and took interest in this new proposal.

"It will be a celebration of his life and the fun he had. He's still your pet and he will always be your pet even after he's no longer with us in the house." Liz let Chase take the lead. He seemed to have gained some ground. "You finish your breakfast and then we'll all go down to the pharmacy and pick out the right box to put Jitters in. How does that sound?"

The idea of picking out a box for Jitters seemed to put a new light on the death of the hamster. Evan and Nicholas got up from the table. "Where is he, Daddy?"

As they looked at the dead hamster laid out on a towel in the laundry room, Liz had to admit he had puffed up rather nicely all things considered. One side of his head was a bit flatter than the other from the spin/dry cycle, but Chase had arranged him in a way that didn't show too much. Liz cleared the table and they all headed out the door and in two separate cars. After they left the pharmacy, Liz would head over to the float, while Chase took the boys to the egg hunt.

As the two cars pulled up in front of the pharmacy Liz saw that Frank had already opened the store. He substituted for Chase when needed, a tremendous help. He stuck his head around from the back room when they walked in and waved. "Thought you'd be at the school by now."

"We will be shortly," Chase said, "got to pick up a couple of things first."

Frank walked around in front of the counter and shook hands with each boy. "Do you look like your dad," Frank smiled down at Evan and then over to Nicholas. "And you, young man, you're the spitting image of your mom."

"He's got my looks, but more of my mother's traits," Liz said. "Now Adam, I think he's got my personality."

"Oh yes, he's a honey. Still out in where is it? Arizona?"

"New Mexico," Liz corrected. "Baby due in November."

"And Nat's wedding. That's soon, too, isn't it?"

"October."

"Isn't that grand?" Frank patted Evan on the top of his head, which Liz knew Evan hated. "I remember when your dad was a soda jerk here every day after school. He ever tell you that?"

"Yes, sir," both boys said simultaneously, obviously wanting to join their father.

"Yep, your dad was one of the best soda jerks I ever had. Always on time. Didn't give away free sodas to his friends. Used to have a soda counter, right over there." He pointed up towards the front underneath one of the large mirrors. "Good boy, your dad was. Good boy."

The boys knew this story by heart. Chase had told them many times how he loved working here; the memories were the reason Chase became a pharmacist. In the mornings in the front part of the pharmacy, men would gather for a Coke with Bromo-Seltzer to settle their nerves, or a Coke with a shot of ammonia for a morning boost. Up front there was a checker table. In the backroom behind the pharmacy counter a few regulars met daily for several hands of poker. Chase's job was to have the poker table cleared of the drug orders no later than 3:00 when the game started. If Grandma and Grandpa Hoole ever knew what went on in the back room, they never said. *If you don't want to know the answer, don't ask the question* was a pretty standard motto, although not a Quaker one.

"Come here, boys," Chase called out from the back. "See if one of these boxes will work." The spell was broken and the boys ran to join their father. Chase gathered cotton to stuff in the appointed box. Upon hearing of Jitters's demise, Frank rose to the occasion and offered his condolences and approval for an appropriate send-off. Things seemed to be back on track.

"I expect Dad will be in before long," Chase said to Frank as they started out the front door.

"Hope he brings coffee." Frank held the front door open and patted each boy's head one more time as they walked by him. Nicholas grimaced; Evan ducked. Liz hopped in her Toyota and called out a parting reminder to come to the float directly after the egg hunt.

*****

The activities began at 10:30 a.m. with the Easter egg hunt, then the parade a half an hour later. Meanwhile downwind, the pork barbecue was being prepared on the opposite end of the school yard, where a team had been up most of the night with the smokers. At 2:00 that afternoon, the baseball play-off of the various small town men's clubs started as middle-aged men pretended to be in their prime and pulled their colored T-shirts over their sweatshirts. By the end of the game most realized that they were older than they thought, and still out of shape. There would be a lot of pulled muscles, hamstrings, and backaches the next day.

The pharmacy was prepared. Each year when Liz and Chase collapsed into bed at the end of the festivities, Liz would rub Chase's shoulders and say, "Do you think all that work was worth it?"

"Absolutely," he'd say as he adjusted his ice pack.

*****

Historically, the Easter Parade had been initiated by the churches and decorated with appropriate religious themes. There had been a traditional parade where people dressed in their Easter bonnets and walked down Main Street. The Quakers, in contrast, dressed in their regular browns and grays and sat on benches on the back of a flatbed.

Over the years the parade had become more eclectic. The high school band joined in playing "Peter Cottontail," and the volunteer fire department added their fire engine and sirens. The barbecue sales were initiated as a fund-raiser for the fire department. The men's club offered to do the egg hunt. The town began to solicit more entries for the parade and invited the homecoming queen, cotton queen, tobacco queen, and peanut queen, all to join, riding in a variety of vintage cars shined and buffed for the event.

Liz had the Quaker float assigned to her by default. This year she had arranged for the float to be the grand finale with the bubble machine streaming throughout the town. Liz had seen such a float the past summer when she'd been with the boys at a July Fourth parade in St. Paul, and they had begged her to do the same thing for the Cedar Branch parade. Why not? This was for the kids. They could bring their pets. They'd have bubbles. It would be fun.

When she got to the staging site Henry Bennett had already parked one of his flatbed trucks at the end of the parade line in the space marked *Quakers*. Billie and Webster were waiting. Of the few young Quaker women left in town, all were working the country store and craft booths. Liz had recruited outside help *just to keep the rabbits at one end and the dogs at the other*, she'd said. Billie had been her usual good sport.

Bedecked in a gigantic deep carmine pink silk bow that took up the front of her cherry blossom sweater, and a pink floral Easter bonnet the size of an umbrella, she looked anything but Quaker. Webster had on a Persian pink tutu and ribbon. *Not really a Quaker image, either*, but Liz wasn't about to look a gift horse in the mouth. This wasn't exactly a Quaker-looking float, anyway.

"Everything on schedule?" Billie asked.

"It's been a tough morning," Liz sighed as she opened the trunk and began to pull out streamers and crepe paper. "We started out the day with a death in the laundry room. Jitters got washed and dried overnight."

"Oh my God," Billie said. "Are the kids okay?"

"Evan's pretty upset. Chase took him down to find a burial box at the pharmacy. He'll probably be carting the corpse when he comes."

"Who else is coming?"

"Well, I know the twins plan to be here with their two beagles. Their mom is working on a crafts booth behind the school, though, so she can't ride with us. Chase's sister, Sophie, is here from Charleston, and her two children will ride the float. They're bringing their old Basset Hound, Hubert. The Joneses' three girls will be here with their cats and two rabbits and then my two boys and their dogs. That's nine kids, nine animals, one dead hamster, and you and me."

"Where's Maggie?"

"Lord knows. I tried to get in touch with her last week. She's been in Raleigh dealing with legal stuff. Don't know if she's got a case going over there or what. You know Maggie. She's shut down temporarily."

As they worked to arrange the bales of hay Henry had put on the float, Billie made idle chatter. "I'm free next weekend to do some shopping with you. You really need to take this mother-of-the-groom dress seriously. Time is running out."

"Can't possibly do it next week, Billie," Liz said. "I've got to get my guest list together with addresses for Lexa's mom, and figure out the rehearsal dinner. Let's wait a few months."

"Months?" Billie gasped. "Mark my words; you're going to regret that."

Within an hour the float looked reasonable, not spectacular; but after all, it was a Quaker float. No need to get too carried away.

"My God, Billie," Liz said in self-admiration when the electrical cords for the boom box and bubble machine were all plugged in and tested. "Look at what we've done. We're technological giants. All we need is the banner that Sophie promised to bring—and of course the children."

As if on cue, Chase pulled up. The boys and the two collies climbed out of the back seat. Evan clutched a small silver box filled with cotton and Jitters.

"Oh, honey," Billie said, "What a lovely box. Jitters looks *so* peaceful."

"He's dead. Daddy drowned him in the washing machine."

A painful look crossed Chase's face, but he said nothing.

Liz changed the topic. "How was the Easter egg hunt?"

"There were a lot of kids from out of town," Nicholas said with obvious disdain for the intruders. Evan held up a basket with eight plastic eggs and a giant bunny lollipop.

Chase lifted Evan up onto the flatbed with his small box in tow and the seven-year-old surveyed his options before taking a seat on the hay bale closest to the bubble machine. Other cars of kids fresh from the festivities turned quickly into the Armory driveway as children scrambled onto their designated floats.

Chase's sister, Sophie, arrived with seven-year-old Estelle dressed appropriately in a traditional Quaker ensemble: a black dress and bonnet. Five-year-old Stin had on black pants, a white collarless shirt, and a black wide brim Quaker hat.

"Oh my golly, they're cute. Where did you ever find those outfits?" Liz cooed, and tried to avoid the thought of her boys' jeans and sweatshirts.

"Made them," Sophie beamed. "I thought they turned out well."

Chase gave his sister a peck on the cheek and lifted his nephew and niece onto the float. "How's the house coming?" he asked.

"A disaster, as one would expect," she said. She and her husband had taken on the restoration of an old house in the historic district of Charleston following Hurricane Hugo three years earlier in 1989. "It'll take us years."

Chase helped his sister to dislodge their Basset Hound from the car. "I promised Mom I'd get her baked goods down to the school," Sophie said.

"Sophie, the banner—did you bring it?" Liz called out before Sophie could start her engine.

"Oh yes, silly me, almost forgot." She went around the car and pulled out a tube that contained two beautiful banners: *Cedar Branch Quaker*

Meeting. They were masterpieces. Sophie had done it again. There was a reason she taught art. Somehow she could manage a family and a job and still cook, sew, and do crafts. Liz was no match.

Billie and Liz whipped out the two staple guns and began to affix the signs to each side of the flatbed. At the same time Chase was trying to lift eighty-five pounds of Hubert into the air.

"Come on, ole boy. Help me out here," he grunted with each effort to get the hound off the ground. Hubert's large droopy eyes gazed upward with a total lack of interest. There appeared to be no bone mass. When hoisted around the middle, Hubert simply collapsed like an army duffle bag of wet clothes. His ears brushed the ground and Chase moved to the rear in a second effort to gain altitude.

Liz finally put down her staple gun and went to help Chase heave the dog onto the flatbed, where Hubert collapsed with a thud next to Evan and the bubble machine. The children let out a triumphant cheer.

The three Jones girls and the twins arrived with two cats and two rabbits in a cage. The twins had their beagles. Their parents dropped them off, waved, and were gone.

The floats at the front began to move. Henry came wheeling into the lot and greeted everyone with hellos. "Not too late, am I?" He surveyed the mélange of animals and children and gave one of his famous broad grins that stretched across his weathered face. "Whoa," he said as he started to climb into the cab and saw Billie's hat. "Some Quaker bonnet you got here."

"Henry, don't turn on the boom box until we get onto Main Street," Billie said as she retrieved her hat from the cab of the truck. She added, "But then crank it up, as high as it will go."

"You got it," he beamed. "This is a Quaker float to beat all." With that the float began to inch forward.

From the get-go the rabbits were none too pleased with the presence of the dogs. "Estelle, honey," Liz said. "Why don't you go sit up with the other girls and talk to the rabbits to calm them down." Estelle inched her way across the flatbed, took a tumble as the truck jerked a bit, and came up with her dress covered in straw.

"Auntie Liz," she sniffled, "my dress."

"There, there," Liz caught her balance and put her arm around Estelle. "Nothing to worry about, we'll just pick it off. Little Quaker girls used to roll in the hay all the time," she tried to assure her.

When Billie chuckled, Liz silenced her with a look.

"There's a place on the end. Sit there, so you can show off that pretty Quaker outfit," Liz suggested to Estelle.

Everyone rearranged themselves to accommodate Estelle. The twins looked a bit annoyed that they were now stuck with a bunch of girls. One of them shifted to the middle bench, which started another round of musical chairs as the animals rearranged themselves according to positions of their owners.

Without warning the cats arched their backs and began to hiss at Webster. Webster responded with a round of barks. Billie, who needed ample room to accommodate her hat, tried to hush him. Webster looked nervous and fidgeted in his little skirt. Evan cradled Jitters, describing to him all that was happening as if he were listening intently.

As the float approached Main Street, Stin inched his way over to where Liz sat and whispered, "Auntie Liz, I have to pee."

"Oh, darling," Liz grimaced, "just hold it. This isn't a long parade. It'll be over in ten minutes. Can you hold it for ten minutes?"

"I don't know, Auntie Liz. I don't think so."

"Let's you and I think light thoughts together," she cajoled him. "I'll switch on the bubble machine." The effect was electrifying. "Look at all of those bubbles, Stin. See how light they feel, floating up into the air. It makes you want to float away with them, too, doesn't it?"

The kids' total attention was now focused on the massive amount of bubbles flowing out across the street and into the yards behind the float. It was even better than Liz had imagined. The wind was just right; there wasn't any humidity to force the bubbles to the ground. They took off and danced through the air, reflecting the sunshine with a waterfall of colors.

Squeals and giggles erupted along the parade route as children pointed at the bubbles and jumped up and down in an effort to pop them. Liz looked back at Billie and gave a thumbs-up.

As the float approached the turn onto Main Street, Henry turned on the boom box and switched the speakers up as high as they would go. *Great*, Liz thought. Despite the sound of the band in front of them, the music was audible above the rest of the street noise. Everyone could clearly hear the "Critters" song.

The flatbed stopped and then jerked forward as Henry made a sharp right-hand turn. Liz's eyes focused on the bubble machine to make sure it didn't slip, and then glanced over at Evan to see that he still had a firm grasp on Jitters's box. He did. From that point on chaos ensued.

The rabbit cage shifted and tumbled off the hay bale. Estelle let out a shriek. Lady and Jasper and the two beagles immediately rose and rushed to get to the other side of the float.

"Grab the dogs, Nicholas," Liz shouted.

Nicholas seemed confused. Something else had caught his attention and he stared at the back of the float. Liz feared they might have lost the bubble machine.

She tried to get to the other end of the flatbed near the cab in order to help with the rabbits. With one swoop she grabbed the rabbit's cage and lifted it up above the dogs. Billie soothed Webster, who whimpered and shivered.

Liz gave the cage to the girls and grabbed the leashes of the two beagles to pull them back to the other end of the truck. She noticed Hubert get up and shift his weight so that he was practically on top of the bubble machine.

Out of the corner of her eye, Liz saw Evan near one of the hay bales next to the cab trying to help Stin get his pants down so he could pee. He had left Jitters in the box sitting precariously on the bench. When one of the cats spied the unprotected hamster, in one long leap she knocked the box into the straw, grabbed the rodent, and shook it two or three times by the neck.

Liz's heart jumped into her throat. She looked over at Evan. He had been momentarily distracted by his cousin's predicament.

One of the girls squealed and jumped to the other side of the hay bale. Liz grabbed the cat by the nape of the neck to make her release the gnawed body of Jitters, and as fast as possible stuffed the pet into the pocket of her fleece. She gave a silent prayer that Evan had not witnessed any of her antics.

"Mom," Nick called over all the commotion. "Mom, look," he said, pointing behind the float.

Fearing that perhaps the bubble machine had taken a plunge, Liz looked up and gasped. It had not been there in the lineup. It had not even been on the list of floats; but there it was. On another float directly behind them with a twenty-foot cross, with a live man positioned on a thin ledge midway up, replicating an image of the crucifixion. Above the cross a large banner read, *The Holy Church of Everlasting Redemption knows the TRUE meaning of Easter. DO YOU?*

The bubbles poured out and danced around the Christ figure. Meanwhile the boom box blared: "*All God's critters got a place in the choir . . .*"

Liz turned to Billie, who was wide-eyed. "Turn off the bubble machine. Turn it off," she motioned. Liz moved over to where Hubert had planted himself, with his backside up against the switch on the machine.

"Hubert, MOVE," Liz ordered. She tried to push down between his rear end and the machine, but he only pressed harder against her hand.

"Tell Henry to turn off the generator," Liz yelled at Billie.

"What?" She yelled back.

"The GENERATOR! Tell Henry to cut it off." Liz motioned by slicing her index finger across her throat several times. "The generator," she yelled.

Billie eased herself up to the cab and braced herself as she tried to make herself heard. "Henry," she yelled. "TURN OFF THE GENERA-TOR!"

"WHAT?" Henry called.

"TURN OFF THE GENERATOR!" she tried again.

"IT'S AS LOUD AS IT WILL GO!" he hollered back.

They were now halfway and bubbles floated throughout Main Street. The children's joyous outbursts were mixed with nervous giggles and finger pointing.

"Wow, look at that," Evan said. "The bubbles are taking Jesus up to heaven."

"Help me, kids," Liz pleaded. "Help me push Hubert off the bubble machine."

Estelle placed her little hand on her hips and in a manner that reflected her grandmother, pointed a finger at Hubert, and said in the familiar plain English she'd heard by some of the elders. "Hubert, thee must move thy weighty bottom now."

The rest of the children started rocking Hubert trying to get him to budge. It became a game. Hubert appeared quite content.

Mercifully, the high school band stopped. They had reached the end of the parade route. The float turned off Main Street and headed back on a side road to the Amory.

Henry flipped off the boom box and hollered back. "How was that?"

"Great," Billie called back without much enthusiasm. She looked over at Liz, who sat holding her head in her hands.

The float of the Holy Church of Everlasting Redemption continued straight up the highway to the next town carrying the Easter message.

The bubbles continued to trail behind the float down the street and into the side yards. Evan suddenly dug frantically around in the straw. "Mom," he wailed, "Where in the world is Jitters? I can't find him."

Liz feigned a brief moment of searching and then took him in her arms. "He was taken up during the parade, honey. Raptured, I think."

Billie's jaw dropped. Nicholas gave his mother an incredulous look.

"What's raptured?" Evan asked.

"It means when God's ready he just comes and takes you."

"But we were going to bury him, Mom," Evan said.

"I know, but God was in a bit of a hurry today. Jitters' time had come."

Evan tried to comprehend. Liz stared straight at Nicholas and begged him with her eyes to keep quiet.

"I hope Jitters liked the parade," Evan finally said.

"I know he did, honey. That's probably why he was ready to leave us so quickly." Liz put her arms around her youngest child and squeezed. "It was a great send-off."

"Do you think God will come down and take me up like that one day?" Evan asked, obviously taking her explanation deeper than Liz intended.

"No, honey, not for years and years and years—not until you want to go."

"Promise?"

"That's a promise, sweetie," she said, knowing that her little white lie conflicted with the Quaker beliefs in honesty, heaven, the rapture, and probably a dozen other things. Surely they could understand. There was no need to break a child's heart unnecessarily.

Chapter Twelve

The children and pets were parceled out and Henry took care of the flatbed clean up. When Chase asked about Jitters, Evan and Liz said with serious looks on their faces, "Raptured."

Chase raised his eyebrows, but one look told him not to take it further. When in doubt, he always chose silence.

After they took the pets home, he and the kids headed back to the school where the festivities for the afternoon were getting started. Billie and Webster left for the craft show. The last thing Liz wanted to do was face the crowds. She imagined the ribbing she would get over the float. She didn't feel up to it, not yet.

As she expected, The Quaker Café was deserted. Liz poured herself a cup of coffee from the coffee pot, took a seat, put her head in her hands and closed her eyes.

"Liz," Miss Ellie said as she walked out of the kitchen carrying a tray of silverware rolled into cloth napkins. "Parade over?"

"Most definitely," she sighed.

"You look like someone forgot to put the frosting on your cake."

"The Quaker float was a disaster."

"Oh, now, how bad could that be?" Miss Ellie placed the tray on the side table, poured herself a cup of coffee and sat down.

"The pets fought, the children screamed, my nephew pulled down his pants and peed, a cat chewed on Jitters, and a float depicting Jesus on a cross pulled in behind us. Jesus was crucified in bubble land. To top it off I lied to my son. If the Quakers still disowned members, I'd be on the street."

Miss Ellie stopped her. "What did you say happened to Jitters?"

"He drowned in our washing machine, and then the Joneses' cat tried to eat him."

"Oh, dear." She stifled a smile. "Does Evan know?"

"I told him he had been taken up."

"You told him what?" Miss Ellie said in surprise.

"I told him Jitters had been *taken up*, like in the rapture. That's why he was gone." She pulled out the gnawed creature from her fleece pocket and gave Miss Ellie a quick peak. "I couldn't let him see his pet looking like this."

"Ohhhhh," Miss Ellie winced and then burst into laughter. "I do believe, Liz Hoole, you are the most entertaining mother in town. Let me get you a piece of pie or something."

"I'd really rather have a sandwich. I'm hungry, and barbecue is not the ticket."

"How about a tomato sandwich and a bowl of chicken noodle soup?"

"That would be great."

Miss Ellie poked her head into the kitchen to give the order and then rejoined Liz. "Now tell me everything from beginning to end. When the crowds come in this evening I want to be sure I've heard the original version."

"Don't tell anyone the rapture part, would you? It's bad enough already."

"My lips are sealed," she said with a warm smile.

To Liz's ears the story didn't sound any funnier the second time. But a trip to the bathroom to wash up followed by hot soup and a sandwich provided a definite improvement.

"Did you see Maggie?" Miss Ellie asked.

"No, has she been in the café this week?"

"Not at all. Do you reckon anything's wrong?" Miss Ellie looked concerned.

"I don't know," Liz said. "She does tend to go into hiding when she's brooding. Tomorrow I'll find LuAnne. She'll know where she is."

Liz finished her soup and sandwich but didn't want to leave. It was quiet and Miss Ellie was a good listener. "Miss Ellie," she ventured.

"What, hon?"

"That funeral for the Judge . . ."

"Uh-huh?"

"What do you think that was all about?"

Miss Ellie raised her eyebrows and cleared her throat. "I don't know." She started to ignore the question but then added, "It's hard to say about these things, but of course, her father never got over that lynching. Maggie probably wanted to find closure for that blemish on his reputation."

"She never talks about it. Chase warned me not to bring it up."

"It's all in the past," Ellie said.

"Evidently not. It seems to be the elephant in the room everyone knows about, but no one wants to discuss."

"Sometimes ignorance is bliss," Ellie said.

"I still want to know."

Ellie shifted in her chair and looked around the restaurant. "Oh, Liz." She started and stopped. The barbecue was in full swing down at the school, and crowds wouldn't start coming in for supper until after the baseball games.

"Sarah Kendall was a sassy little thing when she arrived in Cedar Branch," Miss Ellie began. "I have no idea what Corbett was thinking when he married her. She sashayed into town expecting a plantation home and a big social life to go with it and, well . . . you live here. And it was worse back then—mostly Quakers. No offense." Her eyes offered an apology.

"No offense taken," Liz said.

"Sarah was in shock."

"I can imagine," Liz said, remembering her own first impressions.

"Old Man Kendall and his wife tried to find something she enjoyed doing in order to fill her days. Corbett was finishing up his clerkship in Raleigh at the time and gone most of the week—home on weekends."

Miss Ellie got up from the table and refilled her coffee cup. When she sat back down she motioned with her head to the Quaker side of town. "She started riding horses out at Hansen's barn." She paused for a long time and then glanced back towards the kitchen, lowering her voice. "That's where Corbett found her with Isaac Perry."

"Found them doing what?" Liz asked in disbelief. She was sure what she imagined was worse than what could have actually happened.

"Fighting."

"Fighting?"

"Struggling. Depends on who tells the story."

"Over what?"

"Well, some say he tried to force himself on her, but to a lot of folks that didn't make sense. Course, no one in the black community believes for a minute that Isaac ever touched her. He had a good job with the Kendalls and he loved his wife; a church-going man, pillar of the community. But he did hit the Judge, and he couldn't get away with that."

"The Judge and he fought?"

"Oh yes. The Judge ended up with a broken nose."

"Maggie told me he got kicked by a horse."

"That's what he started telling folks. Just didn't want to go into it all anymore." Miss Ellie took a deep sigh. "It's best forgotten. Just brings up bad feelings all over again. Of course the black community's never forgotten. It's like a bad tooth the doctor can't pull."

"What happened to Isaac?" Liz asked.

Miss Ellie looked at her and shook her head. "Lynched, honey; they strung him up. The Judge took Sarah to Raleigh with him the next week, and well, you know the rest. Nine months later Maggie was born, and Sarah died in childbirth."

"So Isaac was lynched for a fistfight?"

"Honey, you and I grew up in different times. The way the law saw it, Isaac had physically threatened a white woman and brutally attacked her husband when he came to her defense."

"There should have been a trial at least," Liz said.

"Sometimes you've just got to let things go." Miss Ellie rose from her chair and pushed it under the table. "Old Man Kendall was a hard man. There was no way he'd let his son be shamed like that. Someone had to die, and that someone was Isaac Perry."

CHAPTER THIRTEEN

Quaker meeting was almost too much for Liz to bear. She wanted to stay home, but Chase insisted her absence would only cause concern and result in a stream of visitors after meeting was over. Given the options, she chose to attend.

"We appreciate your effort," Anna Reed said in a hushed voice with a loving pat on her hand at the break of meeting.

Dana Everett moved her jaw to the left and then back to the right to readjust her false teeth. They clicked into place. "The children are all talking about the bubbles. The float made quite an impression." She ground her teeth a second time.

Plain spoken and direct, Leland said what Liz believed everyone was really thinking. "Didn't like your float. Too much confusion. Keep it simple next year."

Next year? Please, dear God, let there not be a next year, Liz thought.

Of course it was inevitable that Grandma Hoole would have her say. Liz dreaded her criticism the most. "Liz," she said, "I know sometimes our ways seem old fashioned, but there's a reason we persist in doing things the same year after year. It speaks to simplicity and modesty in the way we live. I can't see where that float really represented what Quakers stand for."

"I see that now," Liz said humbly, and slipped away.

The only saving grace was Chase's father and sister. Grandpa Hoole took both of Liz's hands in his and gave them a squeeze. He stooped down and kissed her cheek. "Thank you, my dear," he said. "You add so much life to our meeting."

He could never know how much that meant to her. He was the one man whose forgiveness she needed. If Grandpa Hoole could see past her weaknesses, she'd survive.

Sophie slipped her arm around Liz's waist as they walked out to their cars and said, "You're great, you know. My kids had a terrific time. It's probably the one parade they'll remember for the rest of their lives. Don't let the others get you down."

"Oh, Sophie," Liz returned the embrace. "I can't even handle a simple float in a ten minute parade. How am I ever going to make it through a formal wedding in Charleston?"

"Don't worry," Sophie said. "I'll be there to help."

*****

Late afternoon Liz headed over to Cottonwoods to try to dislodge Maggie from whatever hole she'd climbed into. There was no answer at the door. As usual everything was unlocked. Liz opened the door and called Maggie's name, but got no response. When she returned to her car she saw LuAnne back in the cemetery. She had on a loose-fitting plaid flannel shirt, workpants, and gardening gloves. A wheelbarrow filled with the dried wreaths from the Judge's grave sat just outside the brick wall.

Liz called out so as not to frighten her. "Hey, LuAnne. Don't you know for every stitch you sew on Sunday you'll have a thousand to take out with your teeth when you get to heaven?"

LuAnne looked up. "Don't think that message ever got to poor folks."

"Whatcha doing?"

"Just cleaning up a bit."

"I'm looking for Maggie. Is she around?" Liz asked.

"No, ma'am, she's in Raleigh—been there most every day since the funeral."

"We've missed her. I've talked to her on the phone a couple of times, but she didn't mention she'd be in Raleigh so long." The fresh dirt on the grave reminded her that it had been less than a month since the Judge died. "She promised she'd be at the Easter Parade."

"She must have forgot." LuAnne leaned down and picked up a bouquet of dead roses. Liz took them from her and threw them into the wheelbarrow outside the wall and then bent down to help with the remaining assortment of dried-up arrangements held together with ribbons and metal ties.

"Court's on Wednesdays. She's always back for court days."

"What are you going to do with all this?" Liz asked, motioning to the dried sprays of flowers.

"Put it in the burn pile back yonder," LuAnne said, nodding in the direction of the cotton field. Though it was still too early for planting, with warmer days they'd soon start turning the fields.

Liz moved in next to LuAnne and worked by her side. She knew that LuAnne didn't drive. "How did you get here?" Liz asked, knowing it was pretty easy for LuAnne to get a ride, although she wasn't afraid to walk the mile between her house and Cottonwoods.

"My nephew's daughter was in town for church. She dropped me off on her way back to Norfolk."

Liz realized with some embarrassment that she knew very little about LuAnne's family while LuAnne knew a great deal about hers. "She got children?" Liz asked.

"Thank goodness, no . . . only seventeen. I'm hoping she might go to a community college for a couple of years before she starts having kids. Lord knows, these young 'uns are in such a hurry to get on with life."

"So, LuAnne, do you have brothers and sisters?" Liz was trying to connect the families.

LuAnne stopped what she was doing, straightened up, and applied pressure to the small of her back with her left hand. "Just one brother . . . he's dead, Miss Liz."

"Oh," Liz paused. "I'm so sorry, LuAnne, I didn't know."

"Yes ma'am," she said and looked Liz in the eye. "You knowd . . . Isaac Perry. He was my brother."

At a complete loss for words, Liz's mouth went dry. She knew LuAnne was a Perry, but there were so many. It seemed everyone in the black community was Perry, Wilson, McFadden, or Jones.

LuAnne picked up a rake against the brick wall and started to run it across the grave. "You heard of Isaac Perry?" she asked.

"Yes," Liz said. "I've heard of him. I'm sorry about all the hurt it had to cause your family. The memories must be very painful."

"We're all sorry," LuAnne said as she continued to rake the trash into a pile. "Sorry don't do a lot of good."

"People won't talk much about what happened," Liz said. "I don't know what to say."

"People want to forget what happened." LuAnne shook her head and made a *humph* noise as she picked up more trash. "I think about it every single day."

Liz was desperately trying to think of anything that might sound consoling. "Chase told me a lot of folks don't believe he did anything wrong."

"He didn't," LuAnne spit back. "He was the kindest, most gentle man you'd ever want to know. Lived his life only doing good for others. Could have been a preacher. Loved his wife, Molly, and adored that baby boy of his, Johnson." She grit her teeth. "They hurt lots of people. They killed Isaac, but that was only the half of what all happened afterwards."

"Was there a trial?" Liz asked.

"Trial?" LuAnne turned and stared at her. "Trial?" she repeated the word in disbelief.

"I meant for the men who lynched him." Liz already knew that Isaac hadn't gotten a trial.

"Pshaw, they said they had no proof who done it. But they was parading around town like they was heroes—people shaking their hands, laughing, having a grand time. It tore me up inside. Filled me with so much hate."

"So nobody ever knew for sure who did it?" Liz said, a bit surprised.

LuAnne bent over and scratched the rake in the dirt with disgust. "I know. I know who done it. Their faces are burned in the side of my brain."

"Are they still in town?" Liz said, suddenly terrified that LuAnne might actually give her names. She didn't want to know. They might be people she saw at The Quaker Café, people she liked.

"All dead. I trust they've each had their reckoning with God and Isaac was waiting for them when they tried to pass through those pearly gates." LuAnne raked up the last of the rubbish. "I could have taken a gun and shot every one of them myself, but I was scared back then. Scared of what they might do to my mama or me. That was then, and this is now, and I stopped being scared a long time ago. I seen being scared don't help. And I seen what it's done to Isaac's wife and his son."

"What happened to them?" Liz said with genuine concern.

"Molly, she died a broken woman. A broken heart, really . . . what they done to Isaac just killed her, too. And Johnson, he's been an angry man all of his life, in and out of jail. Blames white folks for everything that ever gone wrong. I'm praying for his kids, though. Praying somehow they can get by this."

"I'm sorry, LuAnne," Liz said. "I'm so sorry your family has had to suffer like that."

"Me, too, child. But God gives us all our burdens to bear." She straightened up and bent her head back to the sky to stretch the muscles in her neck. "You just hadn't had to shoulder yours yet."

Chapter Fourteen

Maggie Kendall made her way across the café on Thursday evening as if nothing unusual had happened during the past month. She stopped to talk at each table as locals rose to greet her. Based on the premise that you can never be too thin, Maggie looked good, in a striking tan suit with a peach-colored blouse that matched her heels. She was actually wearing make-up at the end of a workday.

Liz and Chase sat with Billie and Gill watching her entrance. Billie was in a carnation pink jumper with a long-sleeve cherry blossom pink blouse. Gill looked like he'd just gotten a white wash in the local drive-through.

"Listen, about last weekend," Maggie said when she reached their table.

Liz didn't say a word. She was irritated that Maggie had pulled one of her disappearing acts without as much as a phone call. "Maggie, we were worried about you. You went to Raleigh and didn't tell anyone."

"I told you," Maggie insisted.

"You said a couple of days. It's been over two weeks."

"Well, I'm a grown-up. I don't have to check in."

"You don't," Liz conceded, but still felt slighted that Maggie didn't acknowledge the importance of their friendship.

"You missed quite a show at the Easter Parade," Billie piped up.

"I heard things didn't go well," Maggie said. She looked at Liz, but couldn't even get eye contact. Liz screwed her mouth into a pout.

"What's happening in Raleigh, Maggie?" Chase made an honest effort to break the tension.

"I'm looking at a job possibility, and *I'll be back in Raleigh* next week," she said with emphasis directed towards Liz.

"What kind of job?" Billie asked.

"Everything's only tentative. It's a political appointment, so I don't know what my chances are with a Republican governor right now."

"But a Democratic legislature," Chase said.

"Which brings us to your campaign." Maggie focused the conversation back to Liz. "Have you started thinking about what you'll do?"

Liz looked a bit surprised. "It's only April, Maggie. You were the one who told me not to worry about doing anything before October. We're talking basically hitting churches and putting up a few billboards."

"October's a big month," Billie said. "Wedding, campaigning, new baby due in November, and then the holidays; it never hurts to plan ahead."

"Nat and Lexa are driving up this weekend," Liz said rather defensively. "Possibly we can get things finalized for the rehearsal dinner. I can give some thought to the campaign after that."

*****

Nat and Lexa announced that Frogbelly would join them when they came for the weekend. The thought of seeing Nat and his fraternity brother Frogbelly had Nicholas and Evan bouncing off the walls. Frogbelly had been considered part of their family since Nat and he were both in Kappa Alpha at Wake Forest University.

"It *is* his real name," Evan insisted as he sat on the floor next to Lady stroking the dog's blond hair, which seemed to be a magnet for every piece of material in the house. Liz had opted for This End Up Furniture so that the dark plaid cushion covers could be removed and washed frequently, although frequently was less often than she intended, and the blond hair on the dark colors was hard to miss. But the furniture itself proved to be durable, so much so that they were long overdue something new.

Nicholas paced in front of the window hoping to see the lights of his brother's car turn in the drive. "Is not," Nicholas said.

"Is too," he and Evan ricocheted back and forth.

"Mom, Frogbelly is his real name, isn't it?" whined Evan.

"No, honey, it's a nickname."

"What's his name then?"

"Arthur McBride Tiller."

"So why does Nat call him Frogbelly?"

"I don't know. Why don't you ask him?"

Nat and Frogbelly both majored in business and now worked with competitive banks. For three years they had rented a house together with four other Wake Forest grads at the corner of Providence and Wendover in Charlotte, but a year ago Nat had moved into an apartment with Lexa. This Chase and Liz did not mention to Grandpa and Grandma Hoole, but they considered it a sign of another passage into adulthood, surpassed only by the day he started to pay all of his own bills. Step-by-step he was breaking the ties. The wedding would be the grand finale.

Their second son, Adam, just thirteen months younger than his older brother, was gregarious and outgoing like Liz. Adam was the story teller in the family. He had worked the farms during his summer months and turned everyday occurrences among the farmers and laborers into evening entertainment around the dinner table. Liz and Chase planned to pay for him to fly to the wedding in October. Heather would be too pregnant to make the trip safely.

Shrieks of "Frogbelly" and "Nat" escaped as Nicholas and Evan bolted out the front door at the sound of a car engine. As Nat stepped out of the driver's seat and Frogbelly opened the rear car door, they hurled themselves like miniature football tackles into waiting arms. Nat stood tall and lanky, the spitting image of his father at that age, same eyes and dark hair a little too long over his ears and forehead. He scooped up Evan and gave him a hug.

Frogbelly crouched in a defensive position while Nicholas and he bumped shoulders and did a little shadow boxing. This ritual was a "must do" any time Nat or his friends came home. Frogbelly was much shorter than Nat, with wide muscular shoulders and thighs that kept him solidly pinned to the ground. A slight paunch suggested the beginnings of a beer belly. His sandy hair was cut short with a little twist of bangs to one side of his face.

While Nicholas and Evan tugged at them both, Nat shook his father's hand and slapped shoulders before giving Liz a hug and a kiss. Frogbelly followed suit and after several more minutes of male bonding antics, everyone finally noticed Lexa.

Lexa stood quietly at the passenger side of the car taking in the homecoming. A lovely young lady, raised South of Broad in Charleston, South Carolina, she came from a family of old money. Willowy, with long blond hair that fell across her shoulders, she spoke more frequently with her azure eyes than with words. Her thoughts transferred directly through body language and Nat read her slightest gesture with precision. They moved with a rhythm that set them apart. They belonged together.

Once inside the house, Liz got everyone something to drink. It was late, but the level of excitement was too high to go to bed right away. Instead they talked through the usual check list: jobs, Lexa's parents, and Frogbelly's folks back in Georgia. Nat got an update on his brother, Adam, and the baby-watch and then turned to the latest Cedar Branch happenings. Liz reluctantly recounted the great tragedy of the Quaker float, which everyone else thought hilarious. She was able to find some humor for the first time. Evan somberly described Jitters's rapture as they listened wide-eyed while Liz gave hand signals behind Evan's back not to ask any questions.

"Saw that Maggie may get an appointment to the Board of Transportation," Nat volunteered after the description of the Judge's funeral at the Methodist Church.

"Really?" Both Chase and Liz looked at him in surprise. "Where did you see that?"

"*Charlotte News and Observer.*"

Chase raised his eyebrows. "That's big. That's really big."

"Guess the Kendall name still has some clout," Liz said.

"A lot of political hopefuls wanted that position," Nat said.

"Would she have to move?" Liz asked.

"Sure," Chase said. "It would be a full-time job in Raleigh."

*****

Over breakfast the next morning Frogbelly was the first to bring up the wedding plans. "Miz Hoole," he said with great emphasis on the *Miz*. "We are about to save you a ton of money."

Liz put another stack of whole wheat pancakes in the middle of the table. "Uh-huh?" She waited for the next line.

"We all know that Nat has a lot of friends because he's such a great guy, raised by such a great mom and dad." Frogbelly paused and favored Chase and Liz with a display of all of his pearly whites. "We, his KA brothers, would like to do something really spectacular to celebrate the fact that Alexandra Louise Lloyd has finally agreed to marry him." A big deferential grin was focused on Lexa this time.

You couldn't help but love this young man, Liz thought, but he was indeed *full-of-it.*

"And because your son, our friend, Nat here, is from the eastern part of North Carolina where folks are not quite so sophisticated as in other parts of the world, like Georgia, no offense intended, Miz Hoole, we feel like he needs our advice and guidance on his rehearsal dinner so that he might duly impress his future in-laws—the Lloyds of Charleston."

Frogbelly said this with great exaggeration and let the *L* sound roll off his tongue with an inflection of an enhanced Southern drawl over and above the one he already had.

"Therefore," he continued, his eyes darting back and forth from Chase to Liz to Lexa, and then to Nat, "we, the men of KA, the financial investment giants of the Southeast, and I must add, experienced connoisseurs of true Southern cuisine, propose that the rehearsal dinner take place at a beach house, one that has already been secured, mind you, where his closest friends will barbecue a pig in his honor."

There was silence. Liz wasn't sure she liked the vision that formed in her head reminiscent of some of the fraternity parties she'd heard about: beer kegs, nudity, drunken brawls. This sounded like a dangerous undertaking.

"Whoa," she said, raising both of her hands to stop the bull hockey. "Back up."

"Is there a problem?" Frogbelly looked at her, apparently surprised that there might be any reason to question him.

"Well, there certainly could be. I need to ask you a few things."

"Shoot, Miz Hoole. There's nothin' I can't handle." Frogbelly was gushing with sincerity. Nat sat by quietly and watched attentively, a replica of his father, always in the background reserving his comments until all the information had been vetted. It was Liz who sensed the worst-case scenarios.

"Well, first and foremost, what do you and your parents think of this idea?" she deferred to Lexa. The idea that the Lloyds of Charleston would buy into this with equal enthusiasm was highly questionable. "I mean, after I last spoke with your mom, she suggested we take advantage of their membership to reserve a room at the Carolina Yacht Club for the rehearsal dinner. I agreed and she's done that."

"They're fine with it, Mom, really," Nat quickly interjected. This was his standard response. Over the years Liz had come to respect his attempt to reassure her he would handle things and she should not get involved; but a rehearsal dinner was not something she felt at liberty to turn over to his past fraternity brothers, investment bankers or not.

"Lexa?" Liz turned her attention on the bride-to-be.

"They're comfortable with whatever you want to do," she said.

"But what do *you* want? That's what I'm most concerned about. Don't let these boys talk you into a party that isn't to your liking. After all, it is *your* wedding.

"It's Nat's, too," she said quietly and followed with an unspoken exchange with Nat as their eyes met.

"Have you talked to your parents?" Liz asked.

"We ran it by them. They said it sounded like fun," Lexa said.

"Are you absolutely sure?"

"Yeah, they said they were fine with it," Nat said. *There was that word 'fine' again.*

"They can just cancel the other reservations," Lexa added.

Liz wasn't convinced. "Nat, I feel like I need to touch base with Lexa's mom to be sure they're on board, but if you honestly think it's okay with Lexa and her folks, we'll consider it."

Liz turned back to Frogbelly. "Where is this house at the beach?" she asked.

"Folly Beach. The KAs rented it one year. We've already checked and it's available." Frogbelly's cheeks were a rosy pink. Liz had to admit that his enthusiasm was contagious. Her scowl broke into a skeptical smile.

"You mean they'll rent to you again? Did you tell them you were KA?"

Frogbelly lowered his eyes in a mock look of disappointment. "We left it spotless. They love us."

"I'll bet. I've been in a house or two after the KAs had it for a weekend," Liz said with skepticism. "Who's going to cook this pig?"

"Me."

"Arthur, have you ever in your life cooked a pig; a whole pig?"

"Miz Hoole, you are looking at the master—the pit master, par excellence, no less. And my assistants . . . did I mention I will have two assistants, the Big-Pig Team? They have even more experience than me."

"The Big-Pig Team? Arthur how many pigs, I mean real whole pigs, have you and *the Big-Pig Team* cooked from beginning to end?"

"Two. Buck did one and Spanky did one . . . and we always cook both ends." He laughed at his own joke and then stopped. "They were good, real good, Miz Hoole."

"Buck and Spanky? You mean to tell me my caterers for my son's rehearsal dinner to Miss Alexandra Lloyd of Charleston would be Buck, Spanky, and Frogbelly?"

"Yes, ma'am, the famed Big-Pig Team of BS Frogbelly. You couldn't be in better hands." His eyes danced and his grin was so loose and broad Liz figured at any moment he could pull his lower lip over his eyes and play a game of peek-a-boo. She suddenly had new insight into where the "frog" came from in his nickname.

Liz smiled at him, but in truth she was nervous as hell. This did not add up to what she considered an airtight plan. Already, she saw sleepless nights loom into her near future: frantic calls to buy barbecue when the pig wasn't cooked, warm beer, side dishes in the sun, not enough chairs, and canopies. Would they need canopies? Plumbing? When was there ever adequate plumbing for a crowd on the beach, particularly a beer-drinking crowd?

Chase, who had said nothing to this point, finally leaned forward and asked Nat the most basic question of all. "Son, is this what you want?"

Nat, who thus far had been letting Frogbelly spin his pitch, nodded. "Yeah, Dad, I'd really rather have a barbecue than a dinner at the Yacht Club."

"Okay," Chase said firmly. "A barbecue it will be."

Frogbelly rubbed his hands together. "Yahoo! Nat, your mom's not as unreasonable as you told me." He gave Liz a quick wink.

"Enough with the sweet talk," Liz looked at Chase and nodded. "Okay."

Frogbelly stood and turned to Nat with a high five. "Now, I'm going to take these little rug rat brothers of yours outside and teach them how to play real football while you and your mom make a list." He tilted his head towards Liz coyly and raised one eyebrow. "I know how fond you are of lists, Miz Hoole. Every KA knows about your lists. Don't forget, the pig's on me."

Chase, Nat, and Liz sat and looked at one another for a long minute. Lexa slipped her hand into Nat's and waited quietly.

"There are at least a hundred things that can go wrong here," Liz said. "It's a far cry from the Yacht Club. Are you absolutely sure?"

"I'm sure," Nat said.

"Then, let's get to work."

CHAPTER FIFTEEN

Nat, Lexa, and Frogbelly spent most of Saturday afternoon touching base with a few of Nat's childhood friends who were still in the area, and then drove out to Bates Peanut Plant to get a case of roasted nuts to take back to the guys at Wendover and Providence. Liz had planned to have Grandpa and Grandma over for dinner that evening, but Nat insisted on The Quaker Café.

"I didn't drive all this way to miss out on Miss Ellie's fried chicken and biscuits," said Nat. "My treat."

"You need to call Grandpa and Grandma about the change of plans," Liz said. "I'm not calling. They'll be more apt not to argue with you, but Grandma's got some pretty strong opinions about the wedding, so brace yourselves."

That evening as the Hoole family all gathered at The Quaker Café, Nathan and Lexa were the center of attention. Everyone stopped by the table to say "hello."

"Banker now, so I hear," said Henry as he slapped Nat on the back.

Nat stood and shook hands. "Yes sir, investment banking."

"Got any stock tips?"

"No sir, I avoid giving friends stock tips. I wanna keep them as friends."

Henry chuckled, nodded to everyone else and moved on to the VIP table.

Miss Ellie walked over as soon as she saw Nat and gave him a hug. "My, my, don't you look good, honey," she said. "Everything going okay?"

"Yes ma'am, they're treating me fine. Miss Ellie, you remember my fiancée, Lexa Lloyd?" Lexa stood and embraced Miss Ellie.

"Of course I do. We're all so pleased to hear about the wedding. Just wish it was going to be up here in Cedar Branch."

"You're invited to Charleston, you know," Nat said. "We wish you would come."

"I wish I could, too, but I doubt if I'll be able to make it," Miss Ellie said. "But you'll have plenty of people there to help you celebrate. Now what can I get you folks besides biscuits?"

"Fried chicken all around, country style with whatever vegetables you're serving tonight," Nat said, "and give the bill to Frogbelly over there. He's paying for everything."

Frogbelly eyes opened wide and there was laughter.

Grandma had seated herself directly across from Nat and Lexa. She wasted no time in cornering the conversation. "Have you ever been to a Quaker wedding, Alexandra?" she asked.

"No ma'am, I haven't," Lexa said. "Nat has told me about them, though."

"They're really quite lovely. Simple, nothing extraordinary. It's actually part of the regular meeting for worship."

"So he said."

"No bridesmaids. The bride might wear a new dress, but nothing fancy. Have you picked out your dress already?"

"Yes, ma'am, I have." Lexa knew she was about to get the third degree, and proceeded cautiously.

"Bridesmaids? Will there be bridesmaids?"

"Yes, ma'am, my sister and a few special friends I've invited to stand with me."

"A few?" Frogbelly let out a guffaw at his end of the table. "Miz Hoole, that church is going to be so weighted down with groomsmen and bridesmaids at the front end, the sanctuary may collapse. If I were you, I'd get there early to make sure they don't prop you up in the stairwell. It's going to be a spectacle to behold."

If looks could kill, Frogbelly would have been on life support, but he was too busy cracking open hot biscuits and slapping butter in them to notice. When the conversation ceased altogether he looked up in surprise, swallowed the food in his mouth, and beamed at everyone.

Grandpa Hoole made an effort to soften Frogbelly's remark. "That sounds like something I want to see," he said with a warm smile.

"Let me tell you about our wedding," Grandma glanced over at Grandpa and then looked again at Lexa. "We had it at New Garden Friends Meeting across the street from Guilford College. I had a short white dress that my mother made for me. About halfway through the silent service, Nathan and I rose and stood in front of our friends and God to say our vows to one another."

"No party afterwards?" Nicholas asked somewhat disappointed.

"Oh yes, there was very nice gathering afterwards. Everyone brought something to eat for a pot-luck. Some of the girls in my dorm had made us a cake. That was it. We were married . . . one of the most memorable days of my life."

"Nobody else spoke or sang during the service?" Lexa asked.

"Well, I think one or two people rose and spoke. To be honest, I don't remember a word, I was so nervous. Do you remember anything that was said, Nathan?" She looked across at Grandpa.

"Only you, my dear. Only what you said."

"Is that legal?" Lexa asked.

"It is. There is a wedding certificate that everyone who is present signs to verify that the vows were exchanged. It's recognized as a legal document. It's framed on our wall if you'd like to take a look."

"I'd love to," Lexa said. "Could we do something like that? Would the Quakers allow us to have a wedding certificate signed by everyone present?"

"Well, I'm quite sure," Grandma said, pleased that Lexa seemed interested.

A high-pitched voice interrupted the conversation and heads turned to see Helen Truitt holding court with her regulars. Across from Helen sat Irene Lambert, a lamppost of a woman, and the Barker sisters on each side. Billie referred to them in code as the OHIO Squad, with Helen on one side, skinny Irene across from her and the sisters who measured identical in circumferences. They were all in their seventies, and seemed to be always gunning for someone.

Liz wanted to avoid Helen, but knew it was impossible. Helen wouldn't pass up the opportunity to speak to Nat and meet Lexa. Liz saw her push out her chair and then make her way to their table.

"Nat," Helen said, "it's always good to have you come home. We see you so seldom now that you've got that important job. And is this the lovely bride-to-be?"

"Yes, ma'am," Nat said as he rose to greet her and give her a peck on the cheek.

"I've heard it's going to be quite the wedding. Something different from the Quakers, huh?" she said as she looked between Grandpa and Grandma. Neither made a comment.

This is good, Liz thought, sensing a potential advantage. *Nothing better to get Grandma on Nat's side than Helen making some wisecrack.*

"I've heard the guest list is top heavy with all of those Charleston bigwigs, but I wouldn't be able to make it, anyway," Helen elaborated. "So don't worry about my invitation. Travel costs, hotel, and all. It would be much too expensive."

"It is a long drive," Grandma said, practicing honesty to the letter.

Receiving no further response on the wedding Helen deftly changed the subject. "We haven't seen Maggie here for a while. I can't help but wonder what she's been doing lately?"

"She's been in Raleigh," Liz said. "She's involved in a case there and working on the Judge's estate. You know it's considerable." Liz knew it was entirely inappropriate for her to say anything, but she just couldn't resist the temptation to tweak Helen a bit given her attitude about the Judge's funeral.

Eyes opened a bit wider. Liz went further. "Maggie told me she intends to give the Methodist Church a very generous gift. She was very appreciative of the way the membership responded to her father's funeral. It meant a lot to her."

"Oh, really?" Helen said coolly. "We haven't seen her in church at all since then."

"It's just over a month since her daddy died. She's been busy," Liz said.

"Well, I did read in today's paper that she withdrew her name from consideration to head the Department of Transportation," Helen said. "That surprised me."

Ears perked up. Helen paused and her eyes lit up as she realized that she had information the others hadn't heard. "I didn't even know she was being considered, but I guess if you have the right name and the right contacts, you can pull the right strings."

"Where did you see that, Helen?" Chase asked.

"It was in today's paper, under Capitol News. There's probably a copy still around." Helen scanned the room.

Several issues of the papers were folded and tucked on top of the corner cupboard. Chase got up and walked over to retrieve one. They had all been too involved with wedding plans that morning to even look at the paper. He turned to the second page and read under the heading *Dobbs to get Transportation Board* several lines down . . .

There had been considerable speculation that the appointment would go to Marjorie C. Kendall, the daughter of the recently deceased Judge Corbett Kendall from Cedar Branch, however, citing personal reasons, Ms. Kendall withdrew her name from consideration.

Everyone sat stunned. "What's going on with Maggie?" Nat said. "I can't imagine her passing up such an opportunity."

Liz raised her eyebrows. "I don't know, but I plan to find out."

Chapter Sixteen

Liz pushed open the patio door to Cottonwoods with a tub of chicken salad in one hand and a basket of chocolate chip cookies in the other. The smell of homemade soup wafted across the room. Having arrived before Liz, Billie puttered in the kitchen in a hot pink apron with ruffles. Webster nestled into his usual corner of the sofa.

"When did she get home?" Liz asked.

"She told me on the phone it would be late. I didn't ask *how late*, but I told her we'd be here with lunch. Let myself in. I don't think the door's been locked the whole time she was gone."

Within minutes the sweet smell of whole wheat and Parmesan cheese filled the room. A few minutes later Maggie came halfway down the stairs and stared at Liz and Billie with a blank expression.

Both Liz and Billie did a double take. It had been two weeks since Liz had seen her at the café, but this was not the Maggie she remembered. Her black hair lay wet and limp across her shoulders. She wore a long, blue terry cloth robe with a sash tied at the waist. Her face appeared more angular than ever before. Without a hint of powder or blush she looked gaunt and colorless. Webster jumped to the floor and ran to the bottom of the stairs barking.

"Hush that, Webster," Billie scolded. The Scottie stopped and then retreated.

"Something smells wonderful." Maggie took a deep breath, and came down the remaining stairs in her bare feet.

"Oh, you can thank Liz for this," said Billie. "Come on over here and get something to eat and tell us all, Maggie. We've missed you."

Liz sat speechless. The first thing to cross her mind was depression. Billie made a circle of plates and ushered everyone to the table. "Everyone, come sit and eat."

With uncharacteristic obedience, Maggie walked over to the table and joined them. "It's good to be home," she said. Things didn't go as well as I'd hoped in Raleigh." Maggie picked up a strawberry off the salad.

"Tell us what happened," Liz said.

Maggie let out a small grunt and rolled her eyes. "I suppose everyone saw my name in the paper?"

"Of course," Billie said. "What else do we have to talk about?"

"And rumors are flying."

"Not so many, but we could start a few," Liz said.

"The timing's bad. I'm not up to the challenge right now."

"Really?" Liz said, surprised. Never before had Maggie shied away from a challenge: it was the sort of thing she usually relished.

Things got quiet. Maggie only picked at food she normally loved. Liz went to the kitchen counter to retrieve the chocolate chip cookies, and then put them in the middle of the table.

"Wow, homemade chocolate chip cookies," Maggie said as she took a small bite, and put it down on her plate next to the uneaten salad and roll.

"Maggie," Liz said. "You're not eating. Do you feel all right?"

"I just haven't had much of an appetite lately. A virus or something . . . it seems to come and go. I'm tired, that's all."

"Have you seen a doctor?" Liz asked. She wasn't going to make the same mistake she did with the Judge, and shy away from asking questions.

"A psychiatrist? Nope, I thought I could sit down and talk to Gill free of charge. He could tell me I'm experiencing post-traumatic stress or some such thing."

It was a weak joke. No one laughed.

"A regular doctor? A family physician or internal medicine doctor?" Liz pressed.

"I have," she said, "since you're so concerned. They're running tests. I should know something next week, but I think what I really need is just a lot of rest. My stamina's gone." She rose from the table with the cookie in hand and turned to go back upstairs. "Thanks for everything. That was really good."

Billie and Liz watched her climb the stairs and looked at one another dumbfounded. "That's it. That's all the time she has to spend with us after three weeks?"

Billie said, "Something's not right."

*****

When Maggie didn't show up at The Quaker Café for dinner on Thursday night, Billie and Liz were insistent that they drop by Cottonwoods after their meal. "Something's going on," they tried to convince Gill. "Maybe you can figure it out."

Maggie sat with her legs tucked under her on the couch, dressed in baggy shorts and a tank top. Summer was closing in, but an evening breeze kept the humidity down and the temperatures moderate. Maggie appeared better than their previous visit, a little flushed, but closer to normal.

As they walked in, they realized Maggie had other guests already. Opposite Maggie sat Reverend Morgan with a much younger man. They both rose to shake hands.

"This is Liz and Chase Hoole and Gill and Billie McFarland," Reverend Morgan said as he greeted everyone. "I'd like for you all to meet Reverend Richard Shannon."

A stocky man in a pair of tan slacks and a blue Polo shirt, the young minister seemed poured into everything he wore. Liz guessed that he had probably put off buying that one-size-larger in hopes of a successful diet plan. A mass of brown curls crowned a round head and a wide smile stretched across his face. When Liz saw him she had a flashback to the Big Boy Restaurants of her childhood and the enormous mannequin that stood in front of each store as he held a giant hamburger up to the heavens. She liked him immediately.

"Richard, please call me Richard. And Billie is short for?" He paused, waiting for Billie to fill in the blank.

"William," she said without flinching. "My dad wanted a boy. I was his only shot, so I have his name, William McConnell McCoy. Imagine my delight at marrying a McFarland and adding that to the list?"

"Imagine *my* delight," Gill added unexpectedly. "All of our legal documents are signed as Gilliam and William. Everyone thinks I'm gay."

Reverend Morgan flinched, but Richard laughed out loud.

"Maggie, you may have heard that I will retire at the end of this month," Reverend Morgan said.

Maggie looked surprised and a bit alarmed. "I hadn't heard that, Reverend. I truly hope that I didn't cause that."

"Oh no, my dear, it's long overdue—time for younger blood." Reverend Morgan put his hand on Richard's shoulder and patted his back. "This young man is going to be the new pastor at the First Methodist Church beginning July. I think we are all very fortunate. He's a recent graduate of Duke Divinity School and comes with high references. I'm taking him around and introducing him to a few folks in town. He'll be moving with his family in another week or so."

A general round of "ohs" and "ahs" were exchanged.

"You have children, Richard?" Liz asked.

"Yes, twin daughters, two years old."

"That's great," she said. "We have a seven- and a nine-year-old, both boys."

Liz knew he was doing the math to decide if he would look as old as she did in five years when his girls turned seven. Liz, likewise, had done the math and figured he was about the same age as her son Nat.

"We started a second family late in life," she added to help him out. "One of those little surprises to remind folks to read the small print on their birth control products."

Richard appeared amused. "How old are your other boys?" he asked.

"Both already out of college. We'll be working until we're eighty to get the other two through."

His smile broadened.

"The McFarlands are members of our church, although we don't see Gill as often as we'd like," Reverend Morgan said and he cast a reproachful eye in Gill's direction. In reality, Billie told Liz, Gill never went, but Reverend Morgan gave him the benefit of the doubt.

"The Hooles here are Quakers. They don't come to our church," Reverend Morgan added.

"Oh, that's too bad." Richard looked genuinely disappointed.

"Not as bad as you might think," Maggie smirked. "Liz won't be in charge of your Easter float."

"Maggie Kendall, don't go there." Liz clutched a throw pillow in the corner of the sofa and eyed her as if she intended to throw it in her direction.

"Ah, yes," Gill took up the tease. "Did the Reverend tell you that you're required to do an Easter float?"

"An Easter float?" Richard appeared confused.

"Well, not really. Not everyone has to do it; it's up to the congregation." Reverend Morgan stumbled over his words as he tried to decide how to explain it.

"I'd suggest you forget animals," Billie said.

"Animals?" Richard asked.

"The bubbles were a good idea to start with," Chase said.

"Bubbles?" Richard looked more confused than ever.

"Ignore them, Richard," Liz said. "It's an inside joke."

"I liked the music, too. The music was good," Gill added.

"But not a good idea as far as Jesus was concerned." Maggie raised her eyebrows.

Richard started to laugh nervously. Reverend Morgan bit his lower lip, but remained silent.

"Of course, Hubert really created the problem by not moving his butt since he was sitting on the bubble machine," Billie said.

"Personally," said Gill, "I think it boiled down to Jesus. After all, nobody knew he was coming. He wasn't invited."

"But, it was HIS parade. He shouldn't have to have an invitation," Maggie said.

"Well, just out of common courtesy, He should have let people know He planned to attend," Gill continued. "He deserved a better spot in the lineup."

"The Lord doesn't always give us advanced notice on His plans," Richard jumped in and immediately had the approval of all present.

Liz tried not to smile, but for the first time she found the whole mess funny. The look on Richard Shannon's face was priceless.

"Did you want to get in one more punch line?" Liz asked, "Or shall we let the new Reverend have the last word?"

"I think the topic's been adequately covered," said Maggie.

"Okay, DONE," Liz announced. "I think I've been sufficiently roasted, and I think we all owe Richard an apology for making him believe he's moved onto a ship of fools."

"A toast," Billie said, raising a mock glass.

"A toast," everyone agreed.

"Here's to Richard Shannon. May he learn to love the finer things in Cedar Branch, and live long enough to forget everything else."

CHAPTER SEVENTEEN

Two weeks later, Billie called Liz at five in the morning. Dr. Withers had sent Maggie in an ambulance to the hospital in Murphy twenty miles away. Her fever had spiked to 104 degrees; she was delirious. They were contacting the doctor she'd seen in Raleigh and waiting for reports. Liz left immediately to pick up Billie and drive to Murphy.

The doctor was a young internist apparently inundated with other patients who had mystery diseases that required referrals. Already slightly bent from overwork and fatigue he carried the weight of his responsibilities on his shoulders like Atlas. He delivered the report from the hematologist as if he was reading a teleprompter. Maggie was weak and confused. Billie became alarmed. Liz got angry.

"I want to refer you to an oncologist at Duke," the doctor said.

Maggie hesitated and looked at Liz. "Oncologist?" she questioned. "Is this cancer?"

"Yes, ma'am, there's a strong possibility that it is," he said.

"Serious?"

"No cancer should be taken lightly."

"What kind of cancer?"

"Well, it looks like cancer of the blood, but that can be better explained by an oncologist."

"Leukemia?" Liz asked.

"Very possibly," the doctor said.

"Is it curable?" Maggie asked.

The young doctor rubbed his forehead first and then his eyes and paused.

Read the damn teleprompter, Liz thought to herself. *Didn't they teach you the right answer for that question in medical school?*

"It's hard to say, Miss Kendall. An oncologist could give you better odds than I can."

Odds? He's talking odds? Where did this kid do his residency? Liz was furious.

"I want to go to Chapel Hill," Maggie said, trying to focus.

The doctor nodded, "I understand," he said. "I only suggested Duke because they have a specialist who is nationally recognized for his work in this field."

"What field?" Liz pressed him.

"This particular leukemia," he said.

"And that is . . . ?" she questioned.

"Nothing is certain yet," the doctor sidestepped the question. "I'd rather an oncologist review it before we reach any conclusions. Your fever is coming down. We'll keep you overnight and then send you home, but wherever you choose to go, I recommend that you not delay."

*****

As soon as Liz got back to her office she was on the phone to contacts at Duke, Chapel Hill, and Wake Forest.

When Richard Shannon dropped by Cottonwoods the next evening, she had four recommendations she was reviewing with Maggie.

"I just saw Billie and Gill at The Quaker Café and they told me you haven't been feeling well," Richard said. Maggie sat in a pair of cut-offs at the kitchen table picking at a BLT sandwich. The tomatoes from the local gardens were in their prime, but Maggie didn't seem to care.

"Thanks, Richard," Liz said. "We've just been considering specialists for Maggie to see."

"In oncology?" Richard asked. "That's what Billie told me."

"Honest to God," Maggie said under her breath. "Can't we keep anything in this town under wraps for twenty-four hours?"

Richard appeared unsure whether to continue. "I just stopped by because I wanted to tell you that I have a good friend who has a double MD in hematology and oncology. He's just completed a fellowship at Johns Hopkins. If you like, I'll call him."

"Where's his office?" Maggie asked.

"I got to know him at Duke. He's at the Medical University over there."

"Duke?" Maggie's left eyebrow shot up. "I think not."

"Duke's a problem?" Richard looked confused.

"I'm not going to Duke," Maggie said.

"Why not?" Richard asked as Liz looked across at him and rolled her eyes.

"I don't like Mike Krzyzewski, that's why."

"He's the basketball coach," Richard said.

"That's right," Maggie said.

"Did he reject you as a walk-on for the team or something?" Richard chuckled.

"What's his name?" Liz interrupted. "The doctor, what's his name?"

"Sreenivas Rao," Richard said.

"Maggie, he was recommended by three other people. Maybe he's our man," Liz said.

"He's tops in his field, Maggie," Richard added. "Hates basketball. Never watches basketball. He just does medicine. Loves Chapel Hill, wanted to go to Chapel Hill more than ever, but they didn't have a vacancy at the time."

"I think I'd rather die than go to Duke."

"Well, that's a choice, too," Liz said and regretted the words as they left her mouth.

Maggie hesitated and groaned.

*****

Two days later Liz and Billie were on the road to Duke with Maggie grumbling the entire way. The mention of Dr. Rao's name received accolades from everyone Liz spoke with. She was convinced this was their best option, but Maggie didn't like the idea of a Dukie with celebrity status. "It's bad enough I'll have to look at little blue devils everywhere, but if he's a pompous ass on top of that, I'm out of there."

They concurred this would be a trial visit. Richard had helped to get an appointment in two days, which was unheard of. It would be foolish to not at least check the man out.

When Dr. Rao walked into the exam room he had on a UNC cap with a Tar Heel T-shirt under his lab coat. The heaviness in the air lifted immediately.

"Ms. Kendall, what a pleasure," he said as he extended his right hand. His full head of jet black hair and dark eyebrows accentuated his flawless brown skin. Whereas Liz had always thought of most Indian men as being of slight build, Dr. Rao was solid and squared off in both face and figure. Liz acclimated quickly to his clip, enunciated English.

"I hear from Richard you are a big Tar Heel fan?" Dr. Rao said.

"Yes, I am," Maggie said.

"Ah yes. To tell you the truth, I'm a closet Carolina fan myself, but I have to keep a low profile here. You understand?"

Maggie smiled. "I'm sure you do."

Billie and Liz introduced themselves and there was a polite exchange about Cedar Branch, Richard, and their mutual friendship before Dr. Rao referred to the papers in his hand. "I have just received the lab reports from your doctors in Raleigh and Murphy. They were faxed this morning. Tell me, what do you already know?"

"It's a cancer, probably leukemia. That's all I know. That's not good news," Maggie said.

"That's correct," Dr. Rao said. "It is, indeed, a cancer. Of that I am certain from your lab work. I'd like to run a couple more tests a second time to confirm that it is AML."

"AML?"

"Acute Myeloid Leukemia. It frequently helps to double-check lab results. I always do that before recommending a treatment plan."

"It's serious?" Maggie said.

"Serious, yes, but untreatable? No. We can treat this cancer, Ms. Kendall. It's not an easy treatment protocol, but you are relatively young and appear to be in good health otherwise. You're strong. I hope you're determined to fight."

"You think I could beat this?"

"What makes you think that you can't?" Dr. Rao asked.

"Nothing," Maggie said after a pause. "I can do this. I just never thought I'd have to do it at Duke with doctors and nurses who have little blue *D*s on their pockets."

"They're good people, Miss Kendall," Dr. Rao said. "I'm sure they'd be at Chapel Hill if they could, but heaven can't accommodate everyone."

*****

Liz walked into her office at the Red Cross and stopped at her secretary's desk. Debbie's face was lit up like a Christmas tree and she announced with an accent as country as Texas, "Guess what? I'm a-gonna be a grandma."

"A grandma?" Liz sat down next to her with a thud. "Was there a high school graduation or a wedding I missed?"

"There you go, always looking at the glass half-empty." Debbie never knew a cliché she hadn't worn to a frazzle. That was one of her favorites. "You know where I'd be if I always thought of everything that could go wrong? Living in the toilet, that's where. When life gives you a lemon, it's time for a Cowgirl's Prayer." This was one of her favorite alcoholic concoctions of tequila, lime juice, and lemonade.

"Congratulations," Liz said and regretted her lack of enthusiasm. "When's the baby due?"

"March."

"Listen, I wanna hear all about this, but I need you to do something for me first."

"Shoot."

"We got some bad news. Maggie has been diagnosed with leukemia."

Debbie's face froze in mid-sentence. "Oh, I'm so sorry. That's not good."

"Not good at all." Liz didn't say anything for a minute and then took a deep breath. Up until this moment she had kept her emotions pretty tightly under wrap, but she knew too much. This was one of the disadvantages of working in the medical field. When friends tell you about their health, a nurse always thinks of the worst-case scenarios.

Debbie picked up on Liz's momentary lapse and went to the water fountain in the hall. Her skirt was again too short and her blouse too tight.

"I'm so sorry," she said as she handed Liz a paper cup of water. "What can I do?"

"Thank you," Liz swallowed the water. "Maggie's going to be in and out of the hospital a lot."

"Bless her heart."

"It's going to be tough and she will need some blood because her red cell count will get very low. I want you to put in a request for a list of donors with her blood type in our region so I can make some calls. I want to be sure we've got plenty on hand and I know who to call if we need more."

"I'm on it," Debbie said. "You know her blood type?"

"I need to confirm it. It's in our main record bank out of the Atlanta office. Just ask them to fax the names and blood types of donors in our regions—and let me know as soon as the fax comes in."

*****

"Got your list for you," Debbie said as she walked into Liz's office later that day. "Marjorie C. Kendall, right?"

"Yep, that's her."

Donated last two years ago in 1990; Marjorie C. Kendall, O positive. And her husband donated last in 1982."

"No husband."

"Oh, that's right. He died, didn't he?"

"Debbie, she's never been married. Who've you got there?" Liz got up from her chair and walked around to the other side of the desk to look at the paper.

"Oh shit," Debbie said, and then paused. "That's her dad." Debbie flushed. Skewing her mouth and wrinkling her nose, she shook her head slowly from side to side and said softly, "Don't know if you want to see this or not."

Liz looked at her for a long moment and then took the papers out of her hand. *Marjorie C. Kendall, blood type O positive; Corbett M. Kendall, blood type AB.*

"Crap," she said. "Holy crap."

Debbie quietly slipped out of the room and closed the door behind her.

Liz sat by herself in her office for the next hour staring out the window. Judge Corbett could not be Maggie's biological father. She would have to have an A or B as part of her blood type to be his daughter. Did it matter? *If ignorance is bliss what fool wants to know?*

Once Liz had gathered her wits she walked out of her office and sat down at Debbie's desk. "I need to remind you of something. This information is all confidential."

"I know that," Debbie said, slightly insulted that Liz seemed to imply she didn't.

"Well, I'm just reminding you so that you will continue to remind me. If we let this slip to anyone; my husband, one of your boyfriends . . ."

"I got it."

"Not your kids, best friends . . . no one, Debbie."

"I know that," she said. "I like my job. I don't plan to lose it."

"Okay, that's understood. We can't make a mistake on this. Someone could get hurt."

"I hear you, boss lady," Debbie used a term she frequently called Liz, but one look at the expression on Liz's face told her this was not a time for jokes. "My lips are sealed."

"Good," Liz said, "Let's try to get ourselves back on task for the rest of the day. Tomorrow we'll talk about your new grandbaby."

*****

Later that evening as Liz packed up to leave she poked her head into Debbie's office.

"I've got a question. Do you still have your clippers from your beauty salon?"

"Yeah, I still do hair for a few folks out of my house."

"How do you feel about shaving heads?"

"Oh, boy," Debbie beamed. "You gonna have a party? Should I bring my Dolly Parton wigs?"

CHAPTER EIGHTEEN

The hair thing was a big deal. When Dr. Rao told Maggie that the chemotherapy would virtually guarantee she'd lose her hair, it became her major obsession; not the fatigue, not the nausea, not the diarrhea or possible skin rashes, but the hair. The idea of having no hair broke her composure and brought her to tears.

Billie, Maggie, and Liz sat in the den at Cottonwoods, each with a glass of wine. Billie was in a collarless oversize blouse and puce shorts. Liz wore her usual jeans and T-shirt, and Maggie seemed to have settled into a loose-fitting sleeveless "garden dress," as Billie called it. Liz called it a "moo moo" but was corrected at once with instructions that fashion was only as good as its name. A "moo moo" brought up images of a barn. A garden dress, on the other hand, implied a more upscale label.

"Bald can be beautiful," Billie said.

"I don't see many women shaving their heads in hopes of looking better," Maggie said. "And I'm not beautiful to start with."

"Maggie, you're so knock-out beautiful I'll bet no one even notices," Billie said.

"That's a load of bullroar and you know it," Maggie said.

"You know you don't have to shave it," Liz said, "just wait until you go into the hospital and see how it goes. Maybe it won't fall out."

"I know." Maggie took a tissue and wiped her nose. "It's just I can't stand the thought of waking up with hair all over my sheets—of running a comb through my head and having clumps come out. I'd rather just get it over with all at once."

"Whatever," Liz said. "It's your call."

Maggie cut a piece of cheese and picked up a cracker from a tray Billie had put in front of her. Big meals had become a thing of the past, but Maggie would nibble throughout the day. "So tell me again about this friend of yours who would come here to cut my hair," Maggie said. "Is she any good?"

"The best," Liz said.

"Does she cut hair for a living?"

"Well, she's not in business anymore. She still cuts hair some, but only after hours. I told you, she's my secretary."

"But you've never let her cut your hair."

"I've just never thought about it. She's *my secretary*," Liz said. "It just didn't seem to be appropriate for me to ask her to cut my hair."

"Why did she stop cutting hair?" Maggie leaned back in her chair and raised one eyebrow.

"Got divorced. Wasn't making enough money to support her kids. Needed benefits."

"And you like her?"

"I love her. She's great. Makes me laugh on a daily basis and is darn good at what she does."

"But you wouldn't let her cut your hair."

"Look, Maggie, I've just never asked her to cut my hair. I'd have no problems letting her cut it, though." Liz got up and poured herself another glass of wine. "But hey, you don't have to do this if it bothers you. I just made an offer because I knew someone who would come to the house."

No one said anything for a long time. Each sat there with their glass of wine in hand and their eyes focused on the ceiling. Finally Maggie broke the silence, "You know, I always wanted a wedding cake."

"What?" both Billie and Liz shrieked in unison. "You want a wedding?"

"Hell, no, I'm not interested in a wedding. I just want the cake."

"Cake we can do. Do you want it tonight?" Liz asked.

"No, not tonight. When I get through this let's throw a party with a gigantic wedding cake."

"I love it," Liz screamed. "A cake without the trouble of the wedding. I wonder if I can talk Lexa and Nat into that?"

"Lord," Maggie groaned, "now I've tripped the switch."

"I won't talk about it, promise," Liz said. "It's just that Euphrasia is going to flip when she gets to Charleston and sees how *not* simple this wedding is. Plus, and this is a big plus, there's the alcohol, the live band with the music and the dancing and the alcohol."

"You already said alcohol," Maggie moaned.

"That's because she will very much disapprove of the alcohol."

"But you and Chase both drink."

"I know. She knows," Liz said. "I give them credit. Grandpa and Grandma try to let their children live their own lives."

"So live it," Maggie said, "and stop worrying about all of the 'what ifs.'"

"Then, there's the rehearsal dinner with the BS Frogbelly gang at the helm," Liz continued.

"Are you having alcohol at that?" Billie asked.

"Of course! You think a house of KA brothers would show up for lemonade? And then, there's *my* mom and dad. Do you realize how close I am to a nervous breakdown?"

"Speaking of alcohol . . ." Billie refilled her glass and popped the cork on another bottle. "I've always found that a little more wine makes the world a bit rosier."

Billie poured another round and Maggie took a swallow, raised her glass, and said, "Call your friend. If she can come over tonight, ask her to bring her clippers and we'll go down to one inch. Leave a little something up there for me to run my fingers through."

*****

Liz made the call.

"Great, this is going to be fun," Debbie said with what Liz feared might be a bit too much enthusiasm from the other end of the line. "I'll bring the tequila and be there in an hour."

"Okay, ladies," Liz said, "to the kitchen. We're going to put together a party."

Kitchen cabinets were emptied, the liquor cabinet sacked. They grabbed anything and everything that Maggie expressed the least bit of interest in eating. Two frozen pizza went in the oven. There were chips. Billie whipped up a dip from sour cream and dried onion soup. Liz found some pimentos and made some pimento cheese for crackers. There was an unopened jar of olives in the back cabinet. Nuts were in the liquor cabinet, and glory be, there was Cointreau that had never been opened, probably a bottle someone had given the Judge.

As promised, Debbie arrived an hour later loaded down. In addition to tequila she brought limes, music tapes, wigs, mirrors, capes, and a clipper with several guards that could cut to a specified length. Liz met her at the door as she burst in overloaded with bags. It looked as if she had just arrived home for the holidays. Squeezed into a pair of skin-tight plaid shorts and a white T-shirt that hid nothing, she wore a Dolly Parton wig the size of a ten gallon hat on her head. She hollered out, "Howdee, y'all ready to partee?"

"*This* is Debbie Bradshaw," Liz said with a majestic wave. Billie's mouth dropped open and Maggie shot a look of total disbelief at Liz. The thought occurred to Liz that she hadn't done anything to prepare them.

"Let me help you with all of that." Billie jumped to assist.

"Thank you, hon," Debbie said to Billie. "Love that outfit. Can you get those blousy things at K-Mart?"

Billie appeared taken aback. The idea that anyone would suggest she shopped at K-Mart startled her, but it didn't matter. Debbie had already moved on to the next topic. "Where's the tape deck?" Billie pointed to the corner cabinet.

"Liz, I need a little help for just a minute," Maggie said and motioned her to the downstairs bedroom. Liz followed. "*That* is the woman who is going to cut my hair?" Her face had turned pink. "I think *not*. Where on earth did you find her?"

"Look, Maggie. If you don't want her to cut your hair, she won't. Just tell her you changed your mind. But I promise you, if you decide you want her to, she'll do a great job."

"Yeah, you, who have never let her touch your own."

Dolly Parton's "9 to 5" burst forth from the adjoining room and there was a tap on the door. "Don't want to bother you girls, but I thought I'd get started on the margaritas. You said you had some Cointreau stuff?"

"I'll get it for you, Debbie. Come on." Liz motioned her towards the kitchen.

"I brought my own music, honey. Hope y'all don't mind."

"Whatever," Maggie said rather rudely.

Liz ushered Debbie back into the den. She figured it would be best to leave Maggie alone to pull herself together.

Debbie strutted a bit and shook her head so the curls swung around her neck. "This one's my favorite. I brought three others, though. You can take your pick."

"Do you actually wear those things out in public?" Billie asked, a bit subdued as she was momentarily out-bedazzled by Debbie's fashion statement.

"Lord yes, honey, every Friday and Saturday night at Billy Bob's Dance Barn. Them cowboys love big hair."

"They love big lots of things," Liz said.

"Yeah, I got a couple of them, too." Debbie gave a wink and wiggle. "Now, let's get down to the drinkin' part."

Everything was laid out on the counter and Debbie started mixing things up. She paused long enough to look at the bottle of Cointreau and pursed up her lips. "The fancy stuff," she said. "This is gonna be good."

"Well, damn," Maggie emerged from the bedroom and plunked her glass down on the counter. "I think I deserve a good party. This may be my last chance to drink for quite a while."

"Atta girl," Debbie dipped the mouth of the first glass in lime juice and then salt, filled it, raised it in a toast, and handed it to Maggie. "This here your place?"

"It's mine," Maggie said as she took a sip and then another.

"Niiice," Debbie said.

By the time Dolly Parton made it to the end of her first album everyone had emptied two margaritas and Billie went to the kitchen to mix another batch. Debbie put Tammy Wynette into the player and she started up with "Your Good Girl's Gonna Go Bad."

"So, Debbie," Maggie ate a couple of crackers and started to warm up a bit, "Liz tells me you used to be a beautician?"

"Sure did. Cut lots and lots of hair. Did perms and dye jobs, the whole bit."

"But you no longer do that?"

"Nope, got a pro-fession-al job. I work in an office now with the boss lady here."

"Why?" Maggie asked.

"Why?" Debbie seemed a bit confused. "Because she pays me money."

"No," Maggie said. "I mean, why did you stop cutting hair?"

"Well," Debbie finished up what was left of her drink and tucked her legs up under her hips, "you know everything eventually boils down to a man. My husband ran into his high school sweetheart after twelve years of marriage and suddenly remembered those good-ole days in the backseat of his Pontiac Grand Prix when everyone's hormones were revving like a hot rod motor and their girlfriend's belly was flat. He was a sorry bastard anyway. Left me with the kids. Him and his flat belly girlfriend took off for Vegas."

She motioned to Billie as she came in the room and waved her empty glass in front of her. "I was kind of glad to see him go. Biggest problem was when we got the big D, he had a better lawyer than I did and minus his health insurance I wasn't helping myself by being self-employed. That's when I interviewed with the boss lady, here." She referenced Liz with a nod.

Billie refilled the other glasses while Tammy launched into "Womanhood."

Debbie stood up and pulled down at her shorts to get them away from cutting into her crotch. "Actually, his new wife and I get along fine. We exchange clothes. These shorts, here . . . they're hers. I just keep cramming my big butt into them to prove I can."

"You know," Billie said in an obvious effort to give some fashion advice, "with your body, you would look really well wearing Ralph Lauren."

"When you see Ralph, you send him my way," Debbie said with a twinkle. "I'm at my best wearing nothing at all, and you can tell him that, too."

"I'll let him know," Billie said, and raised her glass.

"So what do you do for Liz?" Maggie asked.

"Whatever she wants. Follow up with all of her arrangements for blood drives. Make sure the locations and rooms are locked in. Send out confirmation letters. Secure the vehicle and equipment. Confirm arrangements with whatever volunteer groups plan to help out with refreshments or donate thank you gifts such as mugs or T-shirts. Whatever."

"And just what does Liz do?" Maggie said.

Debbie launched into one of her glowing appraisals of Liz. The good part was that it wasn't just good office politics on her part, she actually meant it.

"Oh, Liz is the up-front lady. She's the one who visits all of the muckety-mucks in their businesses and at the college campus and talks them into invitin' us to come. She's the one who writes the reports and goes to all those meetings in Raleigh. She's the boss lady who makes sure everyone's doing what they're supposed to. Whenever there's a problem, they come lookin' for her."

Liz was suddenly aware of her shabby cut-offs as she sat listening to the accolades being bestowed on her, and she didn't wonder that her friends would have a hard time believing Debbie's description. Around town she looked like a worn-out mom who didn't own an iron, but Debbie made her sound like a business tycoon.

"And what do all of you fine lady people do?" Debbie was relaxed and seemed comfortable with the group. That was one of her qualities that never failed her. She enjoyed just about anybody and could readily make conversation with whomever she was entertaining. "You all got husbands as good as Mr. Chase?"

Maggie let out a humph. "Not me," she volunteered. "Haven't yet met the man who's my equal."

Debbie laughed. "That's tellin' it like it is. Me and you. We're just hard for those men to handle, ain't we?"

Maggie didn't respond, but she didn't object, either. Liz thought she might be adjusting to the idea that she and Debbie had something in common after all.

"I'm married," Billie spoke up, "to a fine man, a bit moody sometimes, but he's a fine man."

"A *bit* moody," Maggie echoed. "Billie, he's always moody."

"He is not," Billie insisted.

Liz sensed that Billie was offended. "You just don't understand him, Maggie. He's a very deep man. Introspective, you know. Most of the time his mind is just elsewhere."

"Most of the time he'd prefer to *be* elsewhere."

Billie got defensive. "That's not so. He loves Cedar Branch and he loves you, too. Can't you see that?"

"Well, he's got a heck of a way of showing it." Maggie realized that perhaps she had gone too far and hurt Billie's feelings. Her look softened.

"Come on, Maggie," Liz jumped in. "You and Gill are two of a kind. You just see too much of yourself in him; headstrong, independent, self-confident, expect privacy."

"Maybe," Maggie conceded, "but Billie you pamper him way too much. He expects you to wait on him hand and foot."

"You know what," Liz argued, "if Billie keeps Gill happy and Gill keeps Billie happy, and they've got a system that works for them, who are we to question it? Right, Debbie?"

"You got it," Debbie agreed. "Shall I tell you about my motorcycle honey with the pony tail and how I keep him happy?"

"NO," everyone chimed in.

As Tammy Wynette launched into "Stand by Your Man," Billie took the bait and started to sing along. Debbie jumped up, threw out her arms and wailed, *bad times* to which Maggie and Debbie both raised their glasses and chimed in *good times*. Billie sashayed to the middle of the room pumping her hips left and right. She picked up a candle off the side board, flipped it upside down and put it to her mouth like a microphone.

That did it. Liz grabbed a green candle off the desk. Debbie veered over to the bookcase, jacked up the volume, and grabbed two white candles. She handed one to Maggie. Everyone lined up in formation behind Billie, who was singing her heart out as the lead.

Once they hit the chorus the room was rockin'. At the tops of their voices they belted out *STAND . . . BY . . . YOUR . . . MAN* and even made an effort at leg kicks, putting their arms around each other's waists and trying to get into uniform step. Billie latched on to the end next to Liz and counted out loud to try to get everyone in sync. It was hopeless. Having had more to drink than advisable, Maggie started to lose her balance, and all four collapsed in a pile on the floor laughing.

Maggie slammed down the candle and said, "I'm ready for a haircut."

"I figured you were gettin' close," Debbie said. "It usually takes about three. If you want to whip up one more batch, we can all strip naked and dance before I get started."

"Good Lord, no, Debbie," Liz blurted out. "Nobody's dancing naked."

"Can you cut straight, honey?" Maggie asked. "I just wanna be sure you're sober enough to cut straight."

"Ain't nothin' to it," Debbie said. "I just stick this old guard on the clipper and it'll hold even on us. It ain't the clippers that are the roller coaster. It's the bumps in the head."

"Well, that's reassuring," Maggie was tipsy and she exaggerated her words while she eyeballed Debbie.

Liz pulled out the kitchen bar stool and Debbie whipped out the cape and swung it around the front of Maggie. "One more for the road," Maggie said and raised her glass. Billie headed into the kitchen to make up another batch.

As Debbie went to her bag of clippers she motioned to Liz and pulled out a large plastic bag. "When I cut," she said, "I'm gonna hand the hair to you to put in the bag. It's better than lettin' it all fall on the floor in front of her."

While Liz took the bag, Billie went over to the tape player and slipped in Ray Charles singing "Bye Bye Love."

Maggie sat on the stool and closed her eyes. The giggles stopped. Only Debbie's chatter broke the new level of tension. "You know, I did this for another woman once and she told me she got more pick-up offers bald than when she had hair. Then she went out and got a tattoo on one side of her head. I always wondered whether the ink soaked into your brain if you did that, the tattoo thing, I mean, but she seemed to be okay, 'cept she went from havin' blue eyes to black eyes."

"Debbie," Liz said. "Stop, you don't mean that."

"I do," she said. "I saw it."

As the clippers hummed Liz and Billie couldn't take their eyes off the swatches of long thick hair that Debbie handed over strip by strip. Liz wanted Maggie to keep her eyes closed and never open them again until everything was back to normal. By the time Ray Charles had gotten into "Hey, Good Lookin'," Debbie was done.

"Lord, that's a beautiful head," Debbie exclaimed. "Honey, you are gorgeous. I'm tellin' you, I know some bikers who would fight over gettin' you on their Harley."

Maggie ran her fingers through the fine bristle on her head and appeared to struggle for her next breath. Billie shot Liz a glance. Liz stood behind Maggie holding the bag and suddenly felt an overwhelming sense of doom. She turned her back to everyone and took several deep breaths.

"Debbie," she said abruptly, turning around. "Cut my hair, too."

There was a moment's pause, but Debbie picked up on it immediately. "You want a fine-looking haircut like this, too? Okay, boss lady. You sit your pretty ass right up here on this stool and I'll make you beautiful."

A horrified expression crossed over Billie's face and then she downed another margarita in one swallow. "Me, too," she called out, "me, too."

"Liz, Billie, don't be silly. You don't have to do that for me," Maggie said.

"Why not? I want to do it *with* you, not for you." She was determined now. "Debbie, cut my hair."

"Here, Billie. You hold this bag for us, darlin," Debbie said. "I'll hand you the hair."

Billie hesitated, but then took the bag. Liz could tell that Billie's resolve was breaking. She watched the first tangle of curls handed to Billie and closed her eyes. Maggie's way was best. Listening to Ray Charles sing "Just a Little Lovin' Will Go a Long Way," and the hum of the clippers, her stomach twisted into a knot.

"All done," Debbie said. Liz opened her eyes and the expression on Billie's face said it all. Whatever impulse Billie had a few minutes earlier was gone. She looked at Liz and gulped. "Gill would kill me."

"Forget it, Billie. Don't do it," Liz said, wondering if the reason she'd changed her mind was related to how bad she now looked.

141

Debbie didn't waste a minute. Ignoring Billie's gaping mouth she grabbed the Dolly Parton wigs and said, "It's Dolly time." She helped Maggie and Liz adjust the wigs onto their heads while Billie struggled with hers. As a foursome they stood in front of the mirror in the den. "Not bad, not bad at all."

"I think we could use another round," Maggie said, and Billie dutifully returned to the blender. From there on they sang "It's a Little Too Late" and "Walking Shoes" with Tanya Tucker. By the time Deanna Carter finished up with "Strawberry Wine," they were all snockered.

With heads thrown back staring at the ceiling and legs stretched out across the coffee table, Dolly Parton curls cascaded down the back of the sofa. Maggie spoke. "You know what?"

"What, babe," Liz said.

"I hate country music."

"Well, now you tell me," Debbie said. "I've got every song that Elvis ever sung in the car. I could hav' got that."

"Don't worry about it," Maggie said. "Liz?"

"What, hon?"

"I feel like I'm ridin' naked into the wind." Maggie closed her eyes.

"Hot dog, we gonna get naked?" Debbie giggled.

"Forget it," Liz eyed Debbie. "Grab a sofa and sleep it off."

Chapter Nineteen

When Chase came to pick up Liz, a silly little grin appeared on his face at the sight of the Dolly Parton wig. "You gals been having a good time?"

"You bet," Liz said.

"You up for some more fun?" Chase asked.

"I've got a surprise. I gotta tell you something," Liz said.

"Okay?" he said, his grin got bigger. "I'm game."

"I shaved my head."

"No, you didn't." Chase gave a bit of a snort.

"Yes, I did."

"I don't believe it." The silly grin was completely gone.

"You wanna see?"

"Yeah, prove it."

"Wait until we're in the house."

When they were in their bedroom Liz took off the wig. Chase's eyes widened and he stammered. "You really shaved your head."

"Yep."

"You look sort of like Ben Kingsley."

"I was hoping you'd say Demi Moore."

"Well, I'll try to think Demi Moore and not Ben Kingsley in bed tonight."

Liz threw a pillow at him, grabbed her nightgown, dropped into bed and pulled the covers up over her head.

When she opened her eyes in the morning she considered the possibility it was all a nightmare, but the headache was real. Chase was in the shower. Her head felt cold and weightless. She ran her fingers through the bristles on top and slowly approached the mirror. It was then that the realization hit her. *The wedding! Oh my God, this is what I'll look like for the wedding.*

*****

Maggie and Liz made their bald debut at The Quaker Café the next Thursday evening. Liz wore a UNC baseball cap, but Maggie was out there; no scarf, no cap, nothing. She had decided to tackle it cold turkey, get it over with in one fell swoop. She'd go to the café one last time before she left for her four-week stay at Duke and answer all of the questions and hopefully put to rest whatever outrageous rumors had started to circulate.

Chase admitted he had grown accustomed to Liz's curls, but they had married through "thick and thin" and he'd honor the wedding vows. Besides, he admitted his own pate was getting a bit bare these days, so he couldn't point fingers.

Liz became her own worst enemy. She hated her bald head but didn't want to say anything for fear Maggie would feel responsible. As Liz knew all too well, she was the victim of her own poor judgment and too much alcohol. In her younger days the same kind of decision making could have gotten her pregnant. She had been lucky. Now all she could do was wait; her hair could grow back. Besides, given all that Maggie was up against, how could she be so selfish as to fuss over her hair?

"Like it, Maggie, like it," streamed forth from various tables around the The Quaker Café as Maggie and Liz made their entrance. Liz noticed nobody was giving her any hi-signs.

"When do you leave for Duke?" Miss Ellie sat down at their table.

"Monday morning," Maggie said.

"I could help . . . come sit with you, if you like."

"No, thank you," Maggie patted her hand. "We've got it all worked out. Billie and Liz have volunteered to alternate days. Richard is coming at least once a week to give them a break. The doctor tells me I won't feel like company anyway."

"You change your mind, you let me know," Miss Ellie said. "I'd close this place down in a heartbeat to be by your side."

"I know you would," Maggie said, "and I appreciate it."

"Liz," Miss Ellie turned to her. "You'll keep us updated?"

"I promise," Liz said.

"Where are Billie and Gill tonight?" Miss Ellie asked.

"Norfolk," Liz said, "went to catch a show."

Clayton Collier, a lawyer from Murphy who had worked closely with the Judge throughout their careers, walked into the café and immediately headed for Maggie. His reputation as one of the good-ole boys reached far and wide, and he played it to his advantage every time he stepped into a court room. With a toothpick always protruding from the corner of his mouth, he would roll it around with his tongue and let it pop in and out with the agility of a lizard. It was distracting. Whenever he cross-examined a witness, he mesmerized them with this toothpick trick and they'd get lost in their testimony. Although complaints had been raised by a few opposing lawyers, Clayton insisted the toothpick was a medical necessity. It stopped his ears from ringing.

Clayton spoke to several others before kissing Maggie on the cheek and pulling up a chair next to her. "Figured I might find you here. Nice head," he said. "Is there anything I can do for you, darlin'?"

"No, Clayton," she said. "Thank you, I think everything's taken care of."

"Well, if you get into anything legal you want someone to handle, you know I'm always available."

"I appreciate that," Maggie said. "Liz has healthcare power of attorney and is executor of my will if it should get to that."

"Good Lord, we hope not," Clayton looked taken aback. "I was thinking more about your month to month accounts and investments. You aren't planning on dying on us, are you?"

"Nope," Maggie said. "I plan to forgo that option."

"Well, by all means, please do. Losing one Kendall was painful enough."

Maggie returned his smile. She was being very upbeat, and Liz knew she had reserved her energy to do just that.

"You take care of her," he said looking at Chase and Liz. "If there's anything I can do, just any little thing, you don't hesitate to give me a call."

"Thank you, we'll do that," Liz said as he got up to leave.

Clayton gave Maggie's hand a pat and kissed the top of her bald head as he rose. He didn't so much as comment on Liz's UNC cap; she felt slightly offended.

Helen got up from her table in the far corner and started over. Liz groaned. She'd hoped they could get in and out without anything more than a *good evening*.

"Maggie, dear," Helen said as she stood by their table. "I just want to wish you the best during your stay at Duke. We're all praying for your quick recovery."

"Thank you, Helen."

"Liz, I just wanted to suggest that with all you two have to deal with, we need to make a gracious agreement not to spend money and time on this silly campaign. Let it run its course; not get caught up in any pre-election speaking and posters and all of that useless paraphernalia. All of your energy needs to be about getting well, Maggie. And the only thing you should spend extra time on is helping Maggie in any way you can, Liz. Wouldn't you agree?"

No one said anything for a moment. Liz didn't want to commit to anything she hadn't had time to consider. Maggie spoke up. "That's a gracious offer, Helen. I'll certainly encourage Liz to think about using her time wisely."

Helen nodded, uncertain if her offer had been accepted or not. She hesitated and then added, "Well, Maggie, the best to you. We look forward to your quick return to Cedar Branch," and she returned to her corner table.

"Interesting," Maggie mused, and then changed the subject. "Would you come by Cottonwoods in about an hour? Just want to show you a couple of things."

*****

Liz dropped Chase off at the house, ran their Thursday night babysitter home and drove over to Cottonwoods.

Maggie lay on the sofa, obviously spent after her event at the café.

"Liz, I need you to follow up on a few things until I get back. I could have asked Clayton and will, if you'd rather not."

"Of course, what?"

"For starters, there are some bills that will come in mid-month. I've gone ahead and signed the checks. If you would just fill the amount in when they arrive, and stick them in the mail for me?"

"That's no problem. Where are the checks?"

"Upstairs, in my third desk drawer on the right."

"Can do."

"I've also taken out about four thousand in cash and put it in the safe to cover the four weeks I'm gone. LuAnne and the farmhands get paid on Fridays at noon. I've made out envelopes for each one with their names on them and put the cash inside."

"There's a safe?" Liz asked.

"Of course there's a safe. You don't think I'd leave thousands of dollars in a drawer, do you?"

"So where's the safe?"

Maggie straightened and stood up. "Come on, I'll show you."

They climbed the back stairs. Liz noticed Maggie moved more slowly than usual. On the fifth step Maggie stopped briefly, closed her eyes and took a long slow breath. At the top, she paused again, held onto the railing, and again, bent forward slightly and took another breath. This was a new development in Maggie that Liz hadn't noticed before.

Then, just like in the movies, Maggie approached the portrait of her grandfather, Marshall C. Kendall, Jr., and removed it from the hook to reveal a safe flush with the wall.

"He was a Scrooge, you know?" Maggie said as she tilted her head towards the picture.

"So you've told me."

"We thought we'd let him protect the money since he thought so highly of it. I guess one day I'll need to give it away, set up a scholarship fund or something."

Maggie stepped back and let Liz move in front of the safe. Maggie recited the combination and let her open it. The safe was about two feet wide, two feet high, and a foot deep. A stack of envelopes sat on the right side with a rubber band around them. Several documents were arranged across the back and a number of small jewelry boxes were stacked in front. On top of everything was a cloth sack with oil stains on it.

"What's in the bag?" Liz asked.

"A gun," Maggie said.

"Your father's?"

"Of course." She took the bag and pulled out a Smith and Wesson with the letter K engraved into the handle. "The bullets are in this separate bag, if you ever need them."

"Not me. I don't want anything to do with a gun. Quaker. We're those conscientious objectors, remember?"

"I remember." Maggie set the gun on the credenza. "It belonged to Daddy, but I don't know when he ever used it." She shuffled through the contents. "Daddy's will is in here. I'll put mine with it."

Maggie pulled out several small jewelry boxes and handed them to Liz one at a time.

"What's in these?" Liz asked.

"Necklaces, rings, and things. Don't know what I'll do with it all. No relatives. You want any of them?"

"No, Maggie, I don't," Liz scolded her. "For God's sake. Who knows in five to ten years what you might want to do with them."

"Let me show you something," Maggie said as she opened one box. Inside was a necklace with a blue sapphire that shone from an antique silver setting attached to a delicate rope chain. She walked over to the portrait of her mother and held up the necklace next to the painting, and there rested the necklace around her mother's slender neck. "That's the only thing I have from her; that and her wedding ring. Daddy gave it to her on their wedding day. Told me it was a Kashmir Sapphire."

"That's special," Liz said.

Maggie glanced at the necklace and then back at the portrait. "I've always wondered what really happened between them." She twisted the necklace in her hands as she looked at both sides. "I sort of thought he might marry again. There were lots of women."

"I think he had too good a deal going between Miss Ellie cooking his food and LuAnne cleaning the house. Why mess it up with a marriage?"

"He did adore Miss Ellie."

"So why didn't he marry her?"

"I kidded Daddy about that after Walter died . . . her being available finally. He just waved his hand and shook his head."

Maggie walked back to the safe to replace the necklace and then stopped. "Here," she said. "You take the necklace and wear it at Nat's wedding. The necklace will be a reminder that I wish I were there."

Liz hesitated. "If you put it like that, I'd like that."

Chapter Twenty

The check-in and prep at Duke made both Maggie and Liz tense. Only when Dr. Rao walked in did Maggie brighten. He appeared confident and wore his UNC cap and a Tar Heel T-shirt visible under his lab coat. Liz wanted to kiss the man.

"Liz, Liz Hoole," she reintroduced herself when she realized that he didn't recognize her without her hair.

"Ah, yes, of course, Miss Hoole. "I see you got matching hairdos." His eyes darted from the top of Liz's head to Maggie's. His eyes were the thing, followed by the tone of his voice. They would become Liz's instant clue as to how well Maggie handled each treatment.

Dr. Rao sat down opposite Liz and pulled his chair up close to Maggie's bed. Liz loved the way he did this. In lieu of standing, he put his chart down, put one hand over the other in his lap and leaned forward. It spoke volumes about his commitment to a conversation. "May I call you Maggie?"

"Yes, please do," Maggie responded.

"And you may call me Sreenivas," he replied.

Maggie chuckled, "Dr. Rao is easier."

"Whichever you prefer." After a pause, he continued, "You've got a nicely shaped head, you know."

What a funny thing to say, Liz thought, but the remark seemed to please Maggie.

"I'm getting used to it," Maggie replied.

"I think to cut your hair was a good choice. A lot of patients do so before treatment begins and say they were glad that they did. And Miss

Hoole?" he said as he redirected his attention. "You've got your head all covered up with that hat. Have you got a lumpy head?"

Liz took off her cap. "I just don't want to look like Ben Kingsley."

"Ah, yes, our Gandhi," he said as he surveyed her head in a glance. "Beautiful head, too. Rest assured you do not look like Ben Kingsley." Unconsciously, he ran his long fingers through his own thick hair.

Dr. Rao leaned in a bit closer to Maggie and fixed his eyes directly on hers. "I want you to know that I have gone ahead and put out a request for a donor match for a bone marrow transplant."

Maggie appeared startled. "I didn't think that would be necessary."

"It's just a precaution, because sometimes it takes a while to find a match. It is better to begin the process now and have it available should we want that option."

Maggie glanced over at Liz as if she wanted advice.

"It sounds like a wise thing to do," Liz said. Liz had known all along this was a strong possibility: the main reason she wanted to be sure there was an adequate blood supply in Maggie's type. Not until now did she realize that Maggie viewed the procedure only as an outside chance.

"Maggie, am I correct, you are not married?"

"That's right."

"No children?"

"No children," Maggie replied. Liz knew exactly where Dr. Rao was headed. She assumed Maggie did, too.

"And your mother and father?"

"Both dead."

". . . any brothers or sisters, maybe half brothers or sisters?"

"Not to my knowledge," Maggie looked at Liz a second time. Liz was becoming very uncomfortable at what might be going through Maggie's mind. She should have better prepared her.

"It is rare that we get a close match with a half brother or sister anyway. The best matches are always with a direct sibling," Dr. Rao said.

"Not to worry. You'd be surprised how often we do find a donor match." He casually brushed the topic aside and brightened. "So are we ready to get started and add the good stuff to that IV?"

"Well, this isn't exactly where I had planned to spend the month of August, but given my options, I guess I'm as ready as I'll ever be."

"Remember what I told you, Maggie. This is going to get harder before it gets better." He placed his hand over hers and continued, "I have a pager. The nurses can get me any time of the day or night. Have them call me if you need me."

Liz could see the lines softened in Maggie's face. "Thank you," she said. "I appreciate that."

With that, Dr. Rao stood up and did what would become his signature exit after each visit. He tipped his UNC baseball hat, winked and said, "You can do this, Tar Heel." Then he left.

Maggie looked over at Liz. "I like him."

"Even if he's a Dukie?"

"In name only. His heart's in the right place." Maggie ran her hand over the sheet and watched as Dr. Rao spoke with a nurse in the hall. Then she said more tentatively, "Would you go talk to Miss Ellie for me?"

"About what?"

"You know. I want to know about the possibility of any half brothers or sisters."

Liz's mind shifted into reverse. Such a conversation wouldn't make any difference. The Judge was not her biological father, but Maggie didn't know that. She stammered trying to come up with an appropriate excuse. "Oh, Maggie, I'd be embarrassed to ask her."

"Listen, no one knew my father better than Miss Ellie. If there is the slightest possibility that he had an illegitimate child, she would know."

"Are you sure you want to know?"

"If it could save my life, I sure as hell do."

*****

Liz rotated between work and Duke the rest of the week agonizing constantly over how to deal with Maggie's request. At times she considered a simple lie. She'd tell her she had, even if she hadn't. But what if Maggie later found out she'd never followed through? Chase championed the home front, making sure the boys got to school and softball practice. They agreed that this would just be one of those periods in their lives when they'd have to make some sacrifices to help out a loved one. Life happens—you adjust.

Maggie seemed more fatigued on each visit and Liz knew the worst was yet to come, but she asked each time whether or not Liz had spoken to Miss Ellie. Over and over again, "Did you talk to Miss Ellie, yet?"

"Maggie, I haven't been in town this week when the café isn't busy," Liz would beg off, but finally she capitulated. "I'll go by on Sunday after the church crowd leaves."

"Promise?" Maggie said.

"I promise."

And so as they cleaned up after lunch at Grandpa and Grandma Hoole's following meeting for worship, Liz mentioned that she had promised Maggie she would speak to Miss Ellie that afternoon. The boys had deserted the table with Grandpa to play a game of Chinese checkers in the den.

"What does she need from Miss Ellie?" Grandma Hoole asked, thinking perhaps if Maggie had a special food request, she could send something.

"Maggie may need a bone marrow transplant," Liz said without softening the news.

"Oh," Grandma stopped washing the dishes and looked at her. "Tell me what that means."

"She has a type of leukemia that has caused a severe drop in her red blood cells and platelets because her bone marrow, where blood cells are made, is defective."

"How did that happen?" Grandma sat down at the kitchen table and gave Liz her complete attention. She wanted the details.

"Nobody knows."

"So what will they do?"

Liz tried to simplify a very complicated disease. "First they try to kill off the cancer cells. That's what the chemo does, but it will also kill off the normal cells in the bone marrow."

"And that's what they're doing now . . . in the hospital?"

"Yes, that's why she has to stay for four weeks, to let unaffected blood cells replace those they've killed off."

"What if it doesn't work?" Grandma asked.

"Well, they'll repeat a similar procedure in another month or so after she recovers from this and if that doesn't work they will try to do a bone marrow transplant."

"Which means?"

"They would take bone marrow from someone who is a match and put it in Maggie's bone so that the new cells can then generate more healthy blood cells."

"Oh," Grandma said. Her eyes wandered upper right and Liz could tell she was thinking through the process. She had a sharp mind and she never hesitated to ask for further explanation if she didn't understand something. "So what is it that she wants Ellie to do?"

"See," Liz said, trying to think of how to be delicate, "ideally that other person is a brother or sister, because they are more likely to be a match. Maggie doesn't have any brothers or sisters, at least none that she knows about. She seems to have gotten it in her head that Miss Ellie might know if her father had any other children. She wants me to ask her."

"Oh, my goodness, dear." Euphrasia's hand went to her mouth. "Do you really think that's an appropriate thing to ask Ellie?" Grandma exhaled audibly. "I just don't see what good that could do. Not now. Not after all of these years."

"Grandma, I agree with you. Honestly, I do. But Maggie made me promise. She's just not going to let me off until I ask."

Chase had more dishes in his hand as he walked in from the dining room. The conversation stopped and Chase glanced at his mother and then at Liz with a question on his face. "Did I interrupt something?" he asked.

"Your mother was just asking about Maggie," Liz said.

Grandpa walked in. "Anyone making coffee?"

"I'll get a pot on right now, Grandpa," Liz said.

"What's with all the long faces?" he asked.

"Nothing, Nathan," Grandma Hoole said. "I'll explain everything later."

The background conversation of a checkers game between Nicholas and Evan played out while Chase and Liz had a cup of coffee with his mom and dad and one cookie each; oatmeal raisin made with whole wheat flour and wheat germ. In truth, Liz would have eaten a half dozen of any cookies that Grandma baked. Desserts were the one thing she cooked to perfection, but she always handed them out sparingly in good Quaker fashion: *everything in moderation.*

"I still can't believe you shaved off that beautiful hair of yours," Grandma said to Liz after Chase bent to give his mother a kiss on the cheek. Liz thanked her for lunch. "And just two months before the wedding . . . whatever were you thinking?"

"I wasn't thinking at all, Grandma. It's just something I did."

She shook her head and kissed both boys as they opened the door. "You just need to slow down. Stop and think more often before you make rash decisions like that."

"You're right, I should," Liz said.

Grandma handed each of the boys an extra cookie.

CHAPTER TWENTY-ONE

Chase dropped Liz off at The Quaker Café. The Sunday noon buffet of country ham, turkey, dressing, and a wide assortment of overcooked vegetables had been cleared. A couple of small bowls of banana pudding still sat on the dessert cart. Miss Ellie picked up one and brought it over to Liz, sitting at the table in the far corner.

"Would you like some tea, Liz?" she asked graciously.

"No, thanks, we just had lunch with Chase's folks."

"How are they?"

"They're fine."

Miss Ellie looked tired. Two large floor fans rotated in opposite corners of the room and despite the rattle of the window air-conditioning unit, Liz could still feel the heat from the vacated crowd and the food warmers. Miss Ellie brushed back a stray lock that had slipped out of the rose barrette in her hair and picked up a cloth napkin and wiped her forehead. A large smear of moist powder left its mark. Annoyed, she looked down at it. "I don't know why I do that. I know they've got to be cleaned. I just don't remember to use a paper napkin."

"Big crowd?"

She nodded and wiped her forehead a second time. "I hope you've come to tell me about Maggie. I understand so little about what's happening to her. I want to see her, but they tell me she can't have visitors."

"She's not really up to visitors right now." Both looked down at the pudding that Liz hadn't touched.

"Just doesn't seem fair."

"No, it doesn't. Miss Ellie . . ." Liz started in, trying to work up the nerve to ask the question she'd promised Maggie she would. "I'm embarrassed to ask this," she finally said, "but I promised Maggie."

Miss Ellie tilted her head attentively.

"Maggie grew up eating almost every meal she had with her father and you. She adores you."

"I love her, too." Tears began to pool in Miss Ellie eyes and she wiped her nose with the smudged napkin.

"She believes you knew her father better than anyone else in town." Cautiously, Liz tried to measure her words by the expression on Miss Ellie's face. "Is there any chance that Maggie has a half brother or sister?"

Miss Ellie seemed startled, her mouth slightly open, but said nothing.

"Did the Judge have another child by someone else?" Liz rephrased the question.

"What are you asking, Liz?" Miss Ellie straightened up and sat back in her chair. Her expression had changed. Her lips firmly set. The tears disappearing.

"Maggie wants to know if she has any half brothers or sisters."

"Why?"

"I think she hopes to find a match as a donor for a bone marrow transplant." Liz repeated the explanation she'd given to Grandma about Maggie's disease. Miss Ellie seemed to wander in and out. When she finished, Liz felt her explanation had probably made things worse, not better.

"Oh, my . . ." Miss Ellie let out a long sigh. "She really should have asked her father that question, don't you think? If he'd wanted her to know, he would have told her."

"I promised her I'd ask. She made me promise to ask you," Liz said in defense.

"Sweet child," Miss Ellie's face softened. "Does she think for a minute that Corbett didn't love her more than anything else in this world? He completely changed his life around for that baby."

"There's no question that she knows that, Miss Ellie."

"He left Raleigh and moved back to Cottonwoods so that his mama and daddy could help him raise her. He opened up his law practice here in town and put aside his dreams for a senate seat. He ate just about every meal with her."

"I think everyone in town knows how much he loved her," Liz repeated.

"They do. We all watched him raise her, in front of our eyes."

"What was she like?" Liz knew this didn't answer her question; but Miss Ellie's voice seemed more relaxed as she began to reminisce.

"My goodness, she was something! Pretty as a picture, but strong willed. When she got it in her head that she wanted something, she wouldn't let go of it. He used to call her his little Magpie, until one day she decided the name was not a compliment, and she fussed at him to stop. He did, of course."

"She hasn't changed much, has she?" Liz said.

"She was spoiled. Yes, indeed, Corbett spoiled that child. She pretty much got things her way." Miss Ellie paused and then added, "But I guess things aren't exactly going her way now." She took her time and folded her napkin in her lap thoughtfully and then looked back up. "Liz, some things are worth remembering, and some things we need to put behind us. This is one of those things. The truth has consequences. People can get hurt. Tell that sweet child I can't help her, and let it go."

The heat was playing havoc on Miss Ellie's make-up. The weary look on her face aged her the ten years she'd reclaimed with cosmetics. Liz had asked the question as she'd promised Maggie. She saw no sense to take it any further, and that was exactly what Liz told Maggie when she visited the hospital the next day.

*****

Hoole family evenings at The Quaker Café became more frequent. Between work, the pharmacy, and Duke, both Liz and Chase were simply too tired to cook when they got home. With three more weeks before school started, Nicholas and Evan were enjoying the shift in their dinner routine.

"Why aren't *we* going on vacation this year?" Evan asked. Liz looked over at him and thought he'd grown another inch in the past week. He would soon be the same height as Nicholas, although two years younger. Chase saw basketball potential.

"We're saving our money for Nat and Lexa's wedding. Your vacation this year will be in Charleston in October," Liz said.

"That's just a three-day vacation," Nicholas complained. He had his calculator and appeared ready to do some math. "What will it cost?"

"Costs more than our usual ten-day vacation," Chase said, trying to see the humor.

"So what do you think we spend on our regular vacation?"

Nicholas pondered seriously. "Well, let's see, gas and restaurant stops, and one night in a motel on the way up."

"Plus whatever we spend while we're there," Liz added.

"Then the trip back," Nicholas was busy punching numbers into his calculator. "I'd say . . . five hundred dollars."

"Not a bad guess," Chase said.

"You're going to spend more than five hundred dollars on the wedding?" Evan asked.

Chase nodded. "A lot more."

"That's not fair," Evan whined.

"Lots of things aren't fair," Liz said, offering her standard reply to such complaints.

"What about Grandpa and Grandma Reynolds? We're not going to Minnesota to see them?" Evan asked.

"We'll see them at the wedding. They'll all be there."

Nicholas and Evan mulled this over for a few minutes between hamburgers and French fries.

"You know," Nicholas finally piped up. "Some of my friends go to the beach for vacation. Some of my friends go to Disney World for vacation. Some of my friends go camping in the mountains for vacation."

Chase and Liz looked at him and knew further analysis would be forthcoming. They weren't disappointed.

"Every summer we go to St. Paul for vacation. The same place every year. No one else goes to St. Paul but us. My friends haven't even heard of St. Paul. They think it's a church. And this year, we can't even do that. We're going to a wedding. For only three days."

"Not just any wedding, though," Chase said. "Your brother's wedding with Frogbelly and all of his other friends. It will be one big party."

Liz didn't think that was the best twist to put on a wedding, but given the present discussion, probably appropriate.

Nicholas chewed on that thought and dropped the subject for the time being. As they treated the boys to bowls of chocolate ice cream, the door opened and Richard Shannon entered with his wife, Sandra, and the twin girls. Sandra had gotten a part-time teaching job at the community college twenty miles away immediately after arriving in town. Jobs were not easy to find and her ability, not only to land one, but to then arrange for babysitters in such a short time period, was impressive. All in all they seemed to be settling in rather nicely.

Evan and Nicholas entertained the twins for a few minutes. When the topic of Maggie arose, Chase shifted his chair back from the table. Both Liz and Chase worked to balance their conversations so that their home discussions didn't always involve Maggie in order to try to maintain some normalcy.

"Come on, boys," Chase said. "Let's head home. We'll leave your mother here to talk to the Shannons for a bit."

Nicholas and Evan scrambled from their chairs and out the door.

"How's Maggie today?" Richard asked.

"Not good," Liz said. She didn't want to get maudlin about her visits, but at present they were weighing heavily on both her and Billie. Maggie was dreadfully sick. "She feels like she's dying . . . lots of nausea and back pain. Billie and I spend all of our time feeding her ice chips and giving her back rubs. It's exhausting."

Miss Ellie walked over to the table and sat down in the chair just vacated by Chase.

"Do they think they'll end up with a bone marrow transplant?" Richard asked.

"Don't know," Liz said. "Gotta find a donor match first."

Miss Ellie shook her head sadly. "Is there anything I can send to her that would help?"

Liz wanted to reassure herself, as well as the others. "The doctor tells us she'll begin to feel much better in a couple more days. Another week and we'll have her home, and then you can start sending over those buckets of chicken soup."

"Well, I'm looking forward to that day," Miss Ellie said as she took the Shannons' order.

"So what's the plan?" Richard asked.

"We're going to move her bedroom downstairs so she won't have to deal with steps. Billie plans to stay overnight with her for as long as necessary and sleep on the day bed in the Judge's office so someone will be there during the night if she needs anything. LuAnne is coming in the mornings. Billie or I will check in from time to time during the afternoons."

"That's good," Miss Ellie said. "Let me know as soon as you've got a date for her to come home. I'm going to fill up her refrigerator."

"Anything else I can do?" Richard asked.

"Listen, having you there once a week is a tremendous help. Billie and I are worn to a frazzle. If I didn't believe this was going to be over in another week, I don't know how much longer we could keep it up."

Chapter Twenty-two

Maggie had hoped to be home for Labor Day, but Dr. Rao delayed her release by a week. Billie went to pick up Maggie at the hospital. LuAnne and Liz were in the final stages of moving the contents of her upstairs bedroom and office to the ground floor.

Two of the farm hands were supposed to arrive shortly to move her mattress, desk, and filing cabinet downstairs. Liz knew they should have had this done sooner, but she wanted to be involved when they shifted Maggie's files. There might be documents from work, and Liz was acutely aware of the need to protect the confidentiality of any files Maggie may have at the house.

"That Mr. Gill, he's a strange animal," LuAnne said as they piled papers in a laundry basket.

"He's harmless," Liz said. "Don't let him bother you. You're a big help to Billie right now, and Maggie will want you around in the mornings when she gets home. I doubt if you'll even see Gill over here that much. He stays in his studio painting most days."

"You ever seen what he paints?"

"I have . . . mostly abstracts."

"Does he sell them, or what?"

"Yes, he actually has a bit of a following up in the Virginia Beach area. There's an art shop that carries his work."

LuAnne mulled this over while Liz pulled the next pile of papers out of the file. A loud thump shocked her as something slid to the bottom of the drawer. She jumped. There lay the Smith and Wesson with the bullets rolling across the inside drawer. "What the?" she said.

LuAnne peered down at the gun. "Lawd, Lawd," she stepped away.

"What's that gun doing here?" Liz asked.

"I don't know, but stick it someplace else, Miss Liz. The Judge kept it in his desk drawer until Maggie killed that dog. I remember he locked it in the safe."

A call from downstairs alerted them that the field hands had arrived to move the furniture. Liz shoved the gun and the bullets under the papers in the basket and LuAnne headed to the stairs to direct them. Two hours later, the last piece of Maggie's furniture had been carried downstairs and LuAnne and Liz were straightening up the room in final preparation for Maggie's arrival.

"Don't say anything about the gun," Liz said to LuAnne. "I put it in the Judge's desk drawer, but I'm not sure I want her to know that yet. Let's just see how things go."

*****

As Maggie slowly made her way into the downstairs den, LuAnne rushed to the door and embraced her. "Child, you gotten thin. We got to get more food in you."

LuAnne was right. Maggie had aged. She had lost enough weight for her clothes to look baggy. Her skin remained blotchy from the chemo, and the lack of hair added to her years. She reminded Liz of Chase when he had gotten a bad case of the flu some time ago.

Maggie dismissed the concerns with a wave of her hand. "I'll find that weight, don't you worry. I'm already feeling a lot better now that I'm home. This place sure does look good." She dropped onto the sofa and petted Webster, who had jumped out of the back of Tank-Tank and already found his cushion.

Billie scurried in behind with a small suitcase and headed for the downstairs bedroom. "They've got you all set up in here, your dad's old room," Billie called back. "I see Liz got your files down, so you can work in your dad's office, too."

"Can I get you something?" LuAnne asked.

"Not a thing. You sit right down here and tell me everything that's happened since I've been gone. Tell me about the election. How are things going?"

Liz grimaced. "To be honest, Maggie, I haven't done a thing in regards to the election. We've been too busy keeping up with you."

"That's gotta change. Now's the time you need to be out there asking people for their votes. You know people expect to be asked. They expect you to stop them on the street and say, 'I'd really like your vote.'"

Liz groaned. "You're right. I just haven't had the time."

"I suppose you've still focused on the wedding?"

"Well, it does require some attention."

"She hasn't even bought her dress yet," Billie tweaked from the sideline.

"Do you think I could steal Billie for a trip to Virginia Beach?" Liz asked.

"You two go," Maggie said. "For God's sake go buy the freakin' dress and get that chore out of the way. LuAnne will be here if I need anything, won't you, LuAnne?

"Of course I will, Miss Maggie. I'm here for as long as you want."

*****

Every day Maggie got stronger. Food, phone calls, and flowers poured in from around the county. Billie handled it all with the skill of a personal manager. Meanwhile, Liz contacted donors from the Red Cross list at work and spoke with ministers, business resource directors, and student activities coordinators on college campuses to encourage blood donations and emphasize the need for bone marrow donors. Campaigning was at the very bottom on her priority list.

By mid-month Billie and Liz agreed that the time had come to make a dress run to Virginia Beach. Liz would go with the intent to buy. She didn't want to be bothered with more than one trip. "So how do things stand?" Billie asked on the drive up.

"Invitations are ready to go out. I'm dealing with flowers now," Liz said.

"What do you need flowers for? You're having a beach party."

"Louise Lloyd called me to recommend the florist they are using for the wedding reception for the rehearsal dinner. I took that to mean I am supposed to do flowers. Do you have any idea what flowers cost?"

"You're looking at a thousand for starters, and it can skyrocket from there."

"Right! A thousand dollars for something that's going to get thrown out the next day. I can't stand it. Honest to God, Euphrasia will die."

"There you go with Euphrasia again. Give it a rest. She's not that bad." Billie let out a long sigh. "You should have known *my* mother-in-law. My God, she had all this money, and she hung it over our heads like a puppeteer."

"Why didn't you just say, *screw it* and forget the money?"

"It was a lot of money, Liz. A lot of money is hard to turn your back on."

*****

Billie pulled Tank-Tank into the parking lot of a circle of small shops. Celeste's Evening Wear was to the left with several hipless mannequins in dazzling arrays of sleek shimmering gowns that promised endless cleavage and limited waddle room for anything a half size above a four.

"Billie, I'm not going to find anything here," Liz said. "This is where skinny people come. As you can see . . ."

"Nonsense! You haven't even looked. Focus, Liz, focus."

More stunning dresses were displayed on four other mannequins placed in strategic locations around the shop. A cozy seating area with Queen Anne arm chairs in the middle featured a coffee pot brewing on a side table. Mints and a plate of cookies sat on a second coffee table between the chairs. One end of the store smelled like Evening in Paris and the other like chocolate chip cookies. Liz headed for the baked goods.

Built-in open floor-to-ceiling carpeted cabinets displayed dresses hung along the sides. The sections were divided into short cocktail dresses, long basic dresses, and finally, long designer ones with beads and ruffles. One entire wall was basic black.

Liz stood at the entrance in her jeans with a slip-over knit shirt (at least it had a collar on it) and a UNC baseball cap. A svelte lady in her early sixties approached them wearing a breezy forest green skirt with a silk scarf draped fashionably over a tea green blouse. She had a zippy haircut that went in several different directions at the same time. The blonde part had been paid for, but the color made her look younger, even at sixty. Liz wondered if she could ever carry off such a look, but before she opened her mouth she knew she'd been set up.

"Billie," the woman was buoyant, "what a delight to see you. How have you been?"

Billie beamed, and they kissed cheeks. "Celeste, I have brought a dear friend with me today. This is Liz Hoole," she said as she stepped back for a formal introduction. "I've mentioned her to you before. She's getting ready for a wedding. She's the mother-of-the-groom."

Celeste gave a gracious smile, took Liz's hand and led her over to one of the chairs. "Oh yes, I've heard so much about you already. This is a big wedding, I understand. You'll have so much fun. Let's just have a seat and talk for a bit so I can get an idea of what you hope to find. Coffee? Sherry?"

Taken a bit off guard, never having actually sat down and chatted about a dress over a glass of sherry, Liz accepted coffee and a cookie and breathed in the intoxicating aroma in the midst of evening gowns.

"So tell me, Liz. Where is this wedding?"

Billie jumped in, "St. Michael's in Charleston."

"Say no more," Celeste said with a smile. "I've already got the picture."

"Well, not really," Liz interjected. "You see, my son is Quaker."

"And that is a problem because . . . ?"

"There's no problem exactly. It's just that Quakers believe in simplicity."

"Are you thinking of basic black?"

"I don't know what I'm looking for at the moment. Not necessarily black, but yes, basic, and not too expensive. You see my mother-in-law would die if I spent too much on a dress."

"Is your mother-in-law paying for the dress?"

"No," Liz said, somewhat annoyed.

"Do you give her a report of what you spend on your clothes?"

"No, of course not."

"I don't see the problem. If she asks, just lie."

"I couldn't lie to her."

"You couldn't?"

"No, I can't lie."

"You never lie?"

"A few times, maybe, but I try not to."

"So lie this time. This isn't a heaven or hell issue, is it?"

"That's true." The twenty questions game was taking a toll. Liz got up and started browsing through the rack of short black dresses. "You know what? I think I could use that glass of sherry now."

"Splendid idea," Celeste beamed and left for the back room. Liz immediately began to dig into the inside of the sleeves to find the price tags.

She leaned over to Billie, who had obviously enjoyed the exchange. "Billie, what have you gotten me into? I can't afford this place."

"Of course you can, and you'll never regret it." The tinkling of a silver tray with three long stem Waterford glasses and two bottles of sherry interrupted her. Celeste set them on the side table next to them.

"Do you prefer a sweet Moscatel or an Oloroso?" Celeste asked.

"Moscatel," Billie answered immediately.

"I prefer something a bit dry," Liz said, as if she could even remember the last time she had sherry.

"Wonderful," Celeste said as she poured a generous glass for each and then added a dollop to her own cup of coffee. "Now, when is this wedding?"

"Five weeks."

"Good Lord! You waited until five weeks before the wedding to go shopping?" Billie shot Liz an I-told-you-so glance. "Well, not to fear," she said. "I've been in tighter binds. Now, what do you like?"

"A simple, basic, not-too-expensive, mother-of-the-groom dress."

"Ah, yes. Stand up and turn around and let me have a look at you."

Liz took a sip of the sherry, which was not bad at all, and did as she was told.

"Take the hat off, dear."

Off came the UNC cap.

"Uh-huh, uh-huh," Celeste repeated as she twirled her index finger a few more times to encourage continued rotation. "Tell me about the hair."

"The hair? Well, I cut it off."

"Uh-huh. I can see that. Is it a political statement or are you on chemicals?"

"I have a friend with cancer. It's more of an affirmation for a friend."

"How important is the hair for the wedding?"

"I don't quite understand. What do you mean?"

"I'm just wondering whether you want to coordinate a head dressing with the dress, wear a hat, or add accessories. Let's see, you'll have another half inch in a month. It'll cover your head, lie close and flat, could be rather chic. You know, what dress we pick would make a difference."

"I hadn't really thought about it. What do you recommend?"

"I'm thinking," she said, and then twirled her fingers a couple of more times and Liz did another turn and a half before picking up the sherry glass and taking a second sip.

"You have wonderful breasts," Celeste eyed her chest. Liz blushed. "We'll want to do something to bring the look up. Accentuate the positive, you know. Now the hips. Did you bring your foundations?"

"Foundations?"

"Your underpinnings."

"Underpinnings?"

"The things you wear under the dress, my dear, to hold everything firm and together."

"I'm wearing a bra and underpants. Do they count?"

"Oh, my, no. That is the first place we have to start. No point going any further." Celeste immediately rose and returned to the inner sanctum of the back room.

Liz took another swallow of sherry and gaped at Billie. "Foundations?"

"She'll fix you up, honey. If you're going to do it you want to do it right, don't you?"

"What's this going to cost me?"

"You brought a credit card, didn't you? Not to worry. You'll look like Greta Garbo by the time she gets finished. It'll be worth every penny."

"Greta Garbo's dead, isn't she?"

Celeste returned with five different brassieres; three were strapless. In addition, she had upper thigh and enhanced spandex hip panties with a midriff that fastened onto the bra, as well as three different styles of body suits that included a bra in the suit, and enclosed the entire upper body below the shoulders. Two were for strapless dresses and one slipped over the arms and shoulders. Prices were not marked on any of them.

"My God," Liz said as she spread each one out and explained which kind of dress each one was designed for. "How do you pee?"

"Don't drink anything before or during the wedding reception," she admonished.

"Can you breathe in them?"

"We highly recommend breathing," Celeste smiled. "If when you try it on you find yourself short of breath, we probably need to order a larger size."

Liz took another drink of sherry and Celeste refilled her glass. "Couldn't I just wear the bottom for the hips and forget the other pieces?" Liz asked.

"Probably not a good idea, because the objective is to hold everything in. Just wearing the bottom piece simply pushes those extra pounds up, and then you have an expanded waist and midriff. The point is to smooth out all the rough edges. No panty lines, no bra straps that show through the dress. No little unsightly bulges popping out."

"Yeah, but if you keep pushing it up, eventually you have a triple chin," Liz said.

"No really, most of it goes into the bosoms, and that's a plus. You get the full impact of smoothing out everything below the breasts and then enlarging your cup size so it all blossoms forth over the top."

"Oh," Liz said. "I hadn't thought of that."

"Now," Celeste said with a flourish, "let me get you set up in the dressing room and I'll take some measurements and then bring you some dresses so we can get a feel for what you like."

"Couldn't I just browse through the racks?" Liz asked as she stood a second time and started to make her way back to the racks.

"No, no, no. That's a mistake far too many people make. Clothes look much different on you than they do on the racks. If you don't try it on, you'll never know."

Three and a half hours later, in a dressing room equal the size of the entire front room and surrounded with mirrors and sofas, this had become a team effort. It crossed Liz's mind that only hospitals and fittings rooms required women to forsake any hope of modesty. Liz let Billie and Celeste zip and tug and push and stuff her in and out of a series of dresses. Liz really just wanted to munch on chocolate chip cookies and drink coffee or sip sherry, but the spandex reminded her that eating and drinking were both high-risk behaviors.

With each dress she'd do a twirl or two and Billie and Celeste would discuss the pros and cons. There was one dress that Liz liked, black, short, and simple, and two that she loved. One black floor-length dress had an impressive drop-dead neckline that gave her a Dolly Parton bust and a lady-of-the-night air.

"It's not for comfort," Celeste said, as she and Billie concluded that the black flattered Liz most. "It's a show-stopper for sure, the kind that lets you stand beside the bar or a mantelpiece with a glass of Chivas Regal, looking glamorous."

"What if I wanted to dance?"

"A waltz, perhaps . . . no tango, though. None of this boom-boom, shake-your-bootie stuff. I have to special order those. I don't carry them in the showroom."

"But I have to sit at some point."

"Why?"

"Well, I'd have to sit down in the church. And I'd have to get in and out of cars. You don't get transported flat to a church unless you're in a hearse."

"That's true. That actually may be the only time you could wear that dress in a church, so we should probably drop that particular one from consideration. Can't upstage the bride or the mother-of-the-bride. You're lower in the pecking order at this event, *but*, you do look fabulous in it. Perhaps you'd like to go ahead and get it for another occasion, a second honeymoon, or a lucrative divorce settlement?"

"Right! Any divorce I have wouldn't be lucrative, and I don't think Chase could sleep with me if I showed up in a dress like that," Liz said.

"Don't kid yourself," Billie chided, "a man would sleep with *anyone* who showed up in a dress like that, which might lead to that lucrative divorce."

"Okay, that dress is out, unless Billie wants to buy it. Let me try on the teal again." The second dress, a long teal with a square neckline and a short-sleeve jacket trimmed in white lace, was more appropriate for the mother-of-the-groom, but fit a little too intimate around the hips. Liz had a vision of seams that tore apart as she lowered her spandex-encased butt into her seat in the front row of the church.

"Not to worry," Celeste reassured her. "I'll get our seamstress in here and she'll have it fitted to you without any trouble. You buy better quality clothing and they don't skimp on the extra material in the seams. There's room to expand."

"Tell you what, Celeste," Liz finally said. "I need to run some numbers and see if I can afford any of this."

Celeste looked at Liz with sad green eyes. She obviously wasn't used to customers who put money ahead of fashion. "Dear," she said, sweetly, "you're not buying a condominium. You're buying a dress."

Liz smiled back. "I still need to run some numbers."

"Very well, I'll leave you two alone. Let me know when you're ready."

"Billie, we're talking four hundred dollars," Liz said after adding up the cost of the dress and foundations. "That's twice as much as I'd hoped to spend, with shoes and everything."

"It's a steal," Billie said, "but I guess we've got enough time to drive over to Richmond and look if you really think it's too expensive." Billie shook her head sadly. "And then of course, we could try Raleigh next weekend. You'll still have four weeks left."

"Stop it, Billie," Liz groaned. "I'm not going through this again. The thought of doing it all over next weekend makes me dizzy."

"So you go cheap on shoes, and we'll go through my jewelry and Maggie's and come up with something. Plus, you don't need a hat with this outfit . . . nice earrings and a necklace and you're all set. Look at it as an investment. You will have your wedding dress for every wedding for the rest of your life."

"Oh," Liz moaned. She got up and walked over to the dress on the hanger and looked at it again. "I do like it."

"You know," Billie beamed as if lightning had just struck. "I once went to a party at the beach where instead of flowers the hostess had used clear flat bowls, the cheap kind you get at Pottery World in Smithfield. She had a votive candle in the middle of each with sand and seashells scattered around the outside of the centerpiece. It was quite attractive and very appropriate for a beach barbecue rehearsal dinner. Voilá. I just saved you one thousand bucks."

"I like it, Billie. That's a great idea."

"How about the dress? You look stunning in it. It's you. Honest," Billie prodded.

Fifteen minutes later Billie went to get Celeste. "Splendid!" she exclaimed as they walked together back into the fitting room. "I already called the seamstress. She's on her way over."

Turning to Billie, Celeste slipped her arm around her waist directing her back into the showroom. "While we wait," she said, "I have an adorable hot magenta skirt with a rose pink blouse I pulled off the rack for you to try. I thought of you the minute it came in. Would you like another little sip of sherry?"

CHAPTER TWENTY-THREE

There was a knock at the side door into the den. "Afternoon," LuAnne said.

"Hi, LuAnne," Liz said, with more than a hint of surprise. The last time she remembered LuAnne coming to their house was when she babysat for Nat and Adam years ago, but then without explanation declined any further requests. Liz had replaced her with a transitory stream of teenagers. "Just getting out of church?"

"Wondered if I could talk to you about something?"

"Sure. Come in." Chase and the boys were glued to a football game between North Carolina and Mississippi State, but they all looked up. Chase rose from his chair.

"We're just going out on the porch." Liz motioned to the sliding glass door. The three males all turned their attention back to the game, grateful to be dismissed.

"Iced tea?" Liz asked.

"That would be nice," LuAnne said as they detoured through the kitchen. Liz loved the way that all the rooms on the top floor had sliding glass doors that led onto the porch. Throughout warm weather, with everything opened, there was a delightful cross-breeze.

"It's been a great help knowing that you're with Maggie during part of the day," Liz said, and motioned to the two rocking chairs on the porch. She couldn't imagine why LuAnne had come. *Maybe she wanted to quit? Maybe the work had gotten to be too much. Perhaps she needed money?*

LuAnne tugged at her skirt, and then sat down in the rocker. The edge of her knee stockings showed at the hemline. After one more effort to pull her skirt down, she ignored them, and looked at Liz over her glasses. "Miss Liz, can we straight talk?"

"Of course."

LuAnne squared off her shoulders and leaned forward. The fullness of her lips would have been a cherished feature to any model. She rolled them inwards, tightening them before she spoke. "I been taking care of Miss Maggie since she was seven years old. I know what she's got now is bad. Reverend Broadnax talked about it again in church today, and told everybody she needs a match."

"You're right," Liz wanted to be as honest as she could with LuAnne. "We spoke about it at our Quaker meeting as well."

"So a black person like me might be a match."

"As a bone marrow donor?"

"I guess. That's what they say she needs."

"The odds are best with a brother or a sister. After that they go to a national search. There's always a possibility you could be a match, LuAnne, nothing's impossible, but in all honesty it's highly unlikely. Besides, you're too old."

"I ain't that old."

"No, you're not *that* old, but you're still past the age limit to be a bone marrow donor. You can always give blood, though. She needs blood, too."

LuAnne was quiet for a minute as she looked at the floor. "Miss Liz, what if . . . just what if, Miss Maggie might have a brother or sister out there someplace?"

Liz raised her eyebrows. This was unexpected. She caught her breath and leaned in closer. "LuAnne, that would be very important. Do you know of a brother or sister?"

LuAnne remained silent and stared straight ahead. The edge of one of her lips started to twitch.

"I won't tell a soul," Liz nudged her along. "If there is someone out there who is a brother or sister to Maggie, I could talk to them about being a donor. No one would have to mention that Maggie is their sister. I would never bring up your name."

"You promise?"

"I give you my word."

LuAnne remained quiet for a while longer. She owed a lifetime of employment to the Kendalls. Not only had the Judge made sure she got her Social Security, Maggie continued to give her some additional weekly cash to work a few hours a day. LuAnne was better off than the majority of black women her age, and she knew it. This could be a double-edged sword for her. Liz needed to be careful.

"Miss Liz, I have my suspicions. I can't prove what I think, but I know what I think."

"I understand."

"Ever since they murdered Isaac . . ." Her eyes darted to the north side of the screened porch and she gazed out at the swamp. "Isaac was older than me and worked for the Kendalls before I did. My nephew, Johnson, is his son. I told you that."

"I know."

"Lawd, Johnson, he grew into a bitter man. Too many hateful memories of white men lynching his daddy, and of his mama just falling to pieces. He still fightin' against the world, intent on avenging his daddy's death. Fighting all his life, in school and outta school. He bought a gun. His mama, Molly, poor Molly, bless her soul, she got frightful scared, losing Isaac like that, and then Johnson talkin' crazy. She was scared she'd lose them both. And she did. In different ways."

Liz sat quietly not knowing where the conversation was headed.

LuAnne's eyes began to tear up, and a twitch reappeared at the corner of her mouth.

"Molly sent him up to Norfolk to live with a cousin. He'd get some better for a while, and then he'd end up back in jail for just doing crazy stuff; stealing, takin' drugs, talking trash, and threatening someone at work. Married. Divorced. Has two kids, a girl and a boy. They've got a good mama, although I'm afraid he hasn't been much of a daddy to them. I told you about my niece."

Liz nodded. "You did. She visited Cedar Branch in the spring. Took you to church."

"Johnson's back in jail, but we got hopes for his kids, Felicity and Alex." Her eyes glistened a bit. "He's never forgiven me, you know."

"Forgiven *you*? For what?" Liz asked.

"For working for the Kendalls. He hates 'em, and he accuses me of being their nigger."

Liz gasped. "LuAnne, surely not."

"You wouldn't understand, Miss Liz. You don't know what the Kendalls did to my family. My mama thought I could help set it all straight. That's what I tried to do."

LuAnne took a swallow of tea and her face hardened. She looked out across the back screen again and her voice dropped, replaced by a dry rattle. "That swamp's got no good memories for me, only bad things, horrible things."

Liz sat numb, a feeling of trepidation caught her unexpectedly.

"I was there. I seen it all."

"What?" Liz wasn't sure she'd heard her right.

"I was there when they lynched Isaac up in that tree."

"Oh my God, LuAnne. No one ever told me that."

"Ain't no one who knows, but me and my mama, and she made me promise not to tell another soul. For fifty-six years I ain't told a soul. Mama was frightful scared if those men found out, they'd kill me, too."

"My God, LuAnne, how old were you?

"Fourteen. Isaac, he was twenty-four."

"Why did you go with him?"

"I didn't at first. When he came runnin' home that afternoon, he was shakin' all over. He told Mama that there was a big mix-up between him and Mr. Corbett. He'd tried to explain, but Mr. Corbett didn't listen. Isaac said Mr. Corbett started swinging a shovel at him, so he just run.

Mama told him to go to the swamp and she'd come get him when things calmed down. Isaac, he left. Mama and Molly dressed up and went up to Cottonwoods to try to talk to Mr. Corbett and Old Man Kendall, but they said there weren't no talking goin' on. Everybody just yelling. The Sheriff and old Doc Hewitt was there, and they told Mama and Molly that Isaac could do his talking in court."

LuAnne rubbed her forehead and closed her eyes. "Like a black man ever get to see the inside of a court . . . we knowd that was a lie." LuAnne stopped and looked out into the swamp once again, and then back. "Later that night Mama fixed some food for Isaac and sent me to take it to him. She told me to tell him to keep on running. Go to the other side of the swamp and get as far away as he could. That's what I did. I knew where he'd be . . . a place we fished at."

"LuAnne, you were only fourteen. You must have been terrified." Liz could hardly imagine what she heard. The thought sent shudders through her and she wrapped her arms around herself to try to ease the chill.

"I was. I was so scared of the dark and the water moccasins, but more 'an anything I was scared of those white men, and what they'd do to my brother if they found him."

"Jesus," Liz whispered. The mental image kept her frozen in her chair.

LuAnne nodded. "The worst day of my life, I can't ever forget."

"Did you find him? Alive?"

"He was right where I knowd he'd be. He told me he'd gone to pick up Miss Sarah from her horseback riding. He went early on that day 'cause they got word Mr. Corbett would get home unexpected from Raleigh. When Miss Sarah didn't come out the door of the barn, Isaac says he went in looking, thinking she's still out riding. He says he heard something in the stall in the back and walked back to see if her horse was there. He says she comes running out of the back stall yelling at him to get out of the barn and she's all undone and all, her clothes, you know . . . and she starts shoving at him."

"And Corbett Kendall walks into the barn?" Liz said. She could see the scene in her head now, as clear as day. She understood exactly what happened.

"That's right, the Judge comes in . . . that's what he sees. The Judge picked up a shovel and started swinging at Isaac, but Isaac ducked. The Judge keeps swinging, like a mad man, but he loses his step and falls. When he falls, he lands on a board from the stall and breaks his nose. He ain't never told the story that way, but that's the way Isaac told it."

"Then what happened?"

"Isaac runs, like I told you. And when he runs, he sees a white man running in the opposite direction from the back of the barn. And he's thinking, *Which one is going to tell the truth to protect me? Miss Sarah or that man running away?*" LuAnne hissed through her teeth in disgust and let out a loud *humph*. "Neither of 'em."

When LuAnne paused and kept peering out over the swamp, Liz sat silently. She couldn't think of any words appropriate to share LuAnne's grief. She sat, as she would at Quaker meeting . . . her eyes closed in prayer . . . seeking words that might comfort.

LuAnne rocked back and forth and back and forth.

"We heard 'em," she began again. "We heard the dogs first, then the shouts. I begged Isaac to run deeper into the swamp, but he's scared for me, now. He don't want to leave me. I beg him to run for his life. I scramble into a tree. Isaac looks up at me and says, 'You stay there. You hear me? No matter what happens. Don't move. Don't cry. Don't scream. LuAnne, don't even breathe if you can help it. Don't let it be on my soul that something happens to you.'"

LuAnne got silent. Her hands twisted in her lap. "That's what I did. For six hours I didn't breathe."

"You saw them lynch your brother?" Liz said, her voice trembling.

"I did." She got up and walked over to the screen and looked out over the swamp. "I was wrapped so tight around that tree, I 'bout grew bark, but my insides done froze so cold I thought maybe I be dead, too. All night long I stayed there, 'til even the critters weren't making any noise. When it starts to get light I tried to move, but my bones won't unwind. Then bit by bit, first my fingers and then my feet and then my arms move, like I don't even know how, and I start to climb down. I think I got to try to get Isaac out of that tree, but I can't even look at him. Instead I start to run and run and run with my sobs choking me and the tears coming so fast I can hardly keep up with them."

Liz stood up and walked over to LuAnne. She put her arm around her and cradled her head on her shoulder. They began to sway together, rocking back and forth. Liz began to hum, "*Rock my soul . . . rock my soul . . . rock my soul . . . oh Lord, rock my soul.*" At first LuAnne sighed, and then her body went limp. As the sounds of the swamp penetrated the darkness, they shared their grief in the arms of Abraham.

*****

"There's someone out there that knows Isaac Perry was hanged an innocent man," LuAnne said after a long period of silence. "There's someone out there been sittin' on the truth for fifty-six years and as God is my witness, his day of reckoning must come, too."

"Do you know who that man is, LuAnne?" Liz asked.

"I suspect."

"You think that man was Maggie's real father?"

"I believe that."

"Do you think the Judge knew?"

"I believe Miss Sarah was cheatin' on him. I think the Judge figured it out, but he loved Miss Maggie so much the truth wasn't important. I think he knowd his daddy had done the Perrys wrong. That's why he came lookin' for me."

"And you went to work in their house? Why?" Liz asked.

"Weren't nobody who'd give work to any of us Perrys after that."

"Mr. Corbett came to me some years later. By then his folks were dead. I was walkin' along the road one day on my way back from Wednesday night prayer meeting and it started to rain. When a car pulled up beside me, I was scared. This white man inside says real nice, 'LuAnne Perry, I'm told you're good at keeping children and I've got a little girl who needs some looking after. I'd like to offer you a job.' I just stood there in the rain shaking my head because I knowd it was Mr. Corbett Kendall. He waited. Then he says, still nice and all, 'You think about it, hear? You come see me at Cottonwoods if you change your mind.'"

"And you took the job?"

"I wasn't gonna take it. I didn't want to be workin' for that hateful family in the big house, but my mama convinced me it would be best for us all. She sensed Mr. Corbett was tryin' to send a message to the rest of the town folks. And she was right. After I started workin' there, Molly got a job and then two of my cousins got jobs, and so did some of their family members. I think Mr. Corbett knew he had to try to right some wrongs, little as it was."

"Things did get better, though?"

"Better? I suppose. I can't say I wanted to work there, but I started to love little Maggie, and Mr. Corbett, I came to believe he respected me. I figure, God in his wisdom took Isaac from me and gave me Miss Maggie in return. Strange, ain't it, God's way of teaching us?"

"You helped the town heal," Liz said.

LuAnne looked at Liz with pity. "It never healed, Miss Liz. That's the problem with white folks. They think if everything is going along smooth like; as long as black folks doing their work and not getting uppity, they think things are okay and then, just like that, you turn around and some-body's killin' someone and everything's in a mess, and white folks open their mouths and say, 'Why, why is this happening? We was all getting along so good. Must be the black man's fault. He ain't ever satisfied.'"

In the absence of any way to respond, Liz reached over and filled LuAnne's tea glass and waited. Finally, when it seemed apparent she wouldn't continue on her own, Liz said, "Who was that man, LuAnne . . . the man who was in the back of the barn?"

"Well, I ain't saying for sure. Like I said, I can't prove a thing. And even with proof, a black person's word ain't worth much in this town."

"LuAnne, does that man have children?"

"If it's the one I'm thinking, yes, he does."

"So they would be Maggie's half brothers and sisters?"

"That's right."

Liz took a deep breath. "LuAnne, will you give me a name?"

"Open your eyes, Miss Liz. Look at Miss Maggie and look around town at who she looks like, and if you get your eyes and your mind working together, you'll know it weren't Judge Corbett who was her daddy."

Chapter Twenty-four

The next week Liz took a half day off work and went to the county museum with a magnifying glass and notebook in hand. Hattie Winslow could not have been more helpful. Shoulders wider than her hips, peering through big round glasses, she padded around the room and took pictures off the wall. She laid them out on an oversize table and began to pile books alongside of everything else.

"What . . . are . . . you . . . looking . . . for?" she asked.

"I'm not sure yet," Liz said.

"I . . . could . . . help . . . more . . . if . . . you . . . could . . . give . . . me . . . a . . . name."

"If I had the name, I wouldn't be looking," Liz smiled.

Hattie's claim to fame in the county was that she was a slow talker. Her deliberate use of the spoken word pertained neither to her lack of intellect nor capabilities. She simply enunciated each word that she spoke and paused before the next. Her mother had spoken the same way in order to control a stuttering problem, so Hattie's speech pattern shouldn't have been a surprise to those who knew her family history. Only those who didn't know Hattie sometimes mistook her speech as a sign of being somewhat slow.

After Hattie retired as a special education teacher, she volunteered at the new county historical museum. The museum reclaimed a corner grocery store across from the court house in the county seat of Maywood. It was filled with keepsakes that were deemed too valuable to discard by those cleaning out the attics of deceased relatives. The hours that Hattie volunteered to be available quickly became the hours the museum remained open. This arrangement worked out well. Other than an occasional class field trip, the museum's visitors numbered only one or two a day. Hattie viewed Liz's visit to get help with research as golden.

"Hattie, you've lost weight since I last saw you," Liz said as they sat down side by side at one of the larger tables. Having struggled with her own weight, Liz never passed up an opportunity to compliment anyone who could adhere to a successful diet.

"Yes . . . I . . . thought . . . I . . . was . . . getting . . . *a* . . . *little* . . . heavy.

"What did you do?" Liz asked.

"Well . . . I . . . bought . . . a . . . book . . . and . . . did . . . what . . . the . . . book . . . said."

"What did it say?"

"Not . . . to . . . eat . . . so . . . much."

Liz smiled. *Just read the book and do . . . what . . . the . . . book . . . says.* At times answers could be quite simple. Why couldn't she master that one task?

Liz figured the person she was looking for would be between twenty and twenty-five years old in 1937. He would look somewhat like Maggie; tall, dark hair, slender. She knew all the characteristics might not be the same, but she had to start someplace.

"Who is this, Hattie?" Liz asked over and over again as they scanned one picture after another. Eventually, she and Hattie started to resemble two owls *who*-ing back and forth, although as time ran short Liz hoped the *forth* part of the conversation would go faster.

All in all, Hattie entertained her with lots of trivia about various individuals in the county. But when Liz left she was no further along in identifying the mystery man. *Buy a book and do . . . what . . . the . . . book . . . says* remained her best insight of the day.

*****

A week later Liz decided to take a different tack. Instead of looking for older men in their fifties who looked like Maggie, she decided to look for young children who looked like Maggie at about the same age.

"Where are your school annuals, Chase?" she asked.

"I think Mom put them in boxes in the attic."

"Would you mind if I collected them and brought them over here?"

"I don't care. It's a storage problem. I'd rather the boxes stayed in their attic instead of ours, but I guess eventually we'll need to either move them or toss them."

Euphrasia seemed less enthusiastic. "I had just assumed they would stay here until your boys and their children wanted them as part of their collection of memories."

"Do you want me to bring them back when I'm finished, Grandma?"

"No, that's not necessary, if you think you can find an appropriate spot to keep them. Mildew's a terrible thing, you know, and you built that house in the swamp where everything stays so damp."

"I'll bring them back," Liz promised.

The first evening that Liz sat on the floor in the den, Nicholas and Evan scanned the book in fascination. They thumbed through the old annuals and found pictures of their dad and Aunt Sophie, plus the dads and moms of several of their friends. They laughed at the bowl haircuts. Chase identified the Quaker children.

"There were lots of Quaker kids," Nicholas said, his first realization of how few Quakers now lived in Cedar Branch compared to fifty years ago. "Why's that?"

"People moved. Some married Baptists and Methodists and joined those churches. A few were read out of meeting for not following the testimonies."

"Read out?" Evan asked. "What's that mean?"

"Asked to leave. Not allowed to attend anymore," Liz said. This tradition had remained a curiosity to Liz, even now, although she'd never heard of Quakers practicing such a thing in recent years.

"They would kick them out for good?" Nicholas asked.

"Well, never for good. They always hoped that the individual would change their ways and return and ask for forgiveness or bring their new family into the fold of the Quaker faith."

"Doesn't look like their plan worked too well," Nicholas noted dryly looking at the picture. "There were a lot more Quaker kids back then."

"You're right. It didn't," Liz agreed.

"I wouldn't wear those plain clothes," Evan announced.

"You'd have to if you lived back then," Nicholas said.

"No, I wouldn't. I wouldn't do it."

"Then you'd be read out or eldered," Nicholas said, referring to the traditional custom in some meetings when the elders called a member forward in order to reprimand unacceptable behavior.

"They wouldn't," Evan reasoned sensibly, for he was aware of how many times he'd worn his jeans and Tar Heel T-shirts to meeting.

"You're correct, they won't now," Chase agreed. "It's been a very long time since I recall anyone being eldered."

Eventually Chase and the boys lost interest. Liz sat with a pile of books in the middle of the floor. Not until three nights later did a thought occur to her. She called Maggie.

"Maggie, how old were you when you got that streak of gray in your hair?"

There was a laugh at the other end of the phone. "What on earth brought that up?"

"We're sitting here looking at some of Chase's old school albums and I noticed you didn't have that streak when you were little."

"I would hope not. You noticed I had hair then, too," she said. "I think it first started to change my senior year in high school. In college it became really prominent. I was afraid all my hair would turn gray, but only ever that one streak. I dyed it for a few years and then just let it go."

Liz hung up and started looking at pictures of all the senior girls in every annual. It took her a while, but she found what she was looking for; a pretty girl in a loose-fitting brown dress with a touch of white on one side of her bangs. She didn't look particularly like Maggie, but her older brother in seventh grade compared to Maggie in seventh grade could have been brother and sister. Liz denied the similarities at first. She continued to compare other pictures, but kept coming back to those two. The eye simply refuses to see what the mind won't believe.

"Chase," she said when she climbed into bed that night. "When did Sophie start dying her hair?"

He wrapped his arms around her and snickered, "She wouldn't appreciate you knowing that. She's very proud of her long dark hair."

"I'll bet when she got to Chapel Hill. Grandma wouldn't have approved."

"You're quite the detective," Chase said as he nuzzled her neck. "What else did you figure out?"

"That I married the best looking guy in the class of '61."

CHAPTER TWENTY-FIVE

Debbie stood at the door to Liz's office. "Your father-in-law is here."

Normally Liz's first thought would have been that he made the thirty-mile drive to Westtown to see someone in the hospital, and had stopped by to have lunch. This day was different. Liz knew in the pit of her stomach that this visit was not about lunch.

"Grandpa Hoole," she took both of his hands in hers and stood on her tip toes to kiss his cheek. "It's always good to see you over here in my neck of the woods. Someone you know in the hospital?"

"Thought I'd stop by," he said. His face was strained, and a deep crevice of lines on his forehead met in the tip of a V at the ridge of his nose. He'd been pulling at his eyebrows again, a fidgeting habit when he worried that Liz saw repeated in Chase and two of her boys. It made him look as if he'd gotten a bad eyebrow wax at a two-bit salon.

"Debbie, hold my calls." Liz closed the door to her office and pulled two chairs away from the desk so that they could sit at an angle to each other. "Would you like something to drink, Grandpa? Water or coffee?"

"No, honey, not now."

"Are you feeling okay?

"Well . . ."

If Liz had learned anything at all from Quakers, it was to sit patiently and give people time to reach clearness. The fact that he'd come at all spoke volumes. As Liz sat, she also realized why Grandpa had chosen to speak to her in her office. Not only was it away from Cedar Branch, but her work environment required confidentiality.

"I'm very concerned about Maggie," he finally said.

"We all are."

"I have reason to believe that I might be able to help her." He shifted slightly in his seat, took a deep breath and looked directly at Liz. "There's a possibility that I might be a match for her bone marrow."

Liz felt an overwhelming desire to flee. Whether more for him or for herself, she did not want her image of this gentle Quaker giant who devoted his life to his family and community to be altered in any way. There was still a possibility she had guessed wrong about Chase and Maggie. Deep down she didn't want Grandpa to confirm her suspicions. She hastily interjected, "Grandpa, that is extremely generous of you, but they wouldn't allow you to be a bone marrow donor because of your age."

"That's why I'm here, Liz. If I'm right, I want you to find a way for them to let me be the donor."

"Grandpa, it's probably pointless. They would just never do it. It's a difficult procedure to endure. At your age it might endanger your own life."

"So be it."

There was a pause. "I just don't know what to say, Grandpa."

"Don't say anything." He lowered his head and closed his eyes.

She folded her hands in her lap in silence. Grandpa broke the silence sooner than she expected.

"I was so impulsive, so in love. I am ashamed of the truth." He paused and reflected. "The truth," he repeated. "What a complicated requirement of faith."

He looked down at his folded hands in his lap. "Do you think the need for truth outweighs silence, Liz?"

"I don't know. I'm like a pebble in the Grand Canyon when it comes to religious philosophy," Liz confessed. "You know so much more than I do."

His lips curled ever so slightly. As always, he weighed his words before he spoke. "Maggie's mother, Sarah, came from New Orleans, a city of entertainment and lights. She didn't fully understand what to expect when she got to Cedar Branch. Corbett went to Raleigh each week. She was homesick. She didn't have anything to do. Corbett's father arranged for her to take horseback riding lessons from my Uncle Charles."

"At the Hansens' farm?" The vision of the ghost lady on the horse came to mind.

He nodded. "She turned out to be a good rider, and after a few lessons she wanted to ride every day. Uncle Charles didn't have the time. He asked me to meet her at the stables until she could get her horse saddled and unsaddled properly by herself. *Keep an eye on her*, he advised me. *Make sure she grooms her horse the right way.*"

Grandpa Hoole stopped and looked at Liz. The implications were all there. Liz hoped he might let it go at that. Nothing else needed to be said.

Grandpa's brow wrinkled into a tighter knot as he rubbed his forehead in an unconscious effort to erase this memory. After a couple of minutes he continued. "I was a shy lad of twenty. She was a year older, from a big city. She believed Corbett Kendall and Cottonwoods would give her social status and financial security."

"Maggie has told me her mother was unhappy here," Liz said.

"You know," Grandpa looked up at Liz, "I worried about you when Chase first brought you here. Worried that you'd be as miserable as she was, but you have been amazing. Have I ever told you that, how impressed I've been at your willingness to adopt Cedar Branch as your home?"

Liz started to say something, but he didn't seem to need an answer.

"Sarah thought Corbett was fun," Grandpa looked off in the distance and started to ramble a bit. "That's what she called him, *fun* . . . when he was home. On the weekends everything revolved around him. People poured into Cottonwoods and he entertained them. The rest of the week she tried to amuse herself. Once a day she went riding. I met her at the barn. She talked. I listened. And then, to my own surprise, I began to talk and she listened. I couldn't believe that I had anything to say of interest, but she convinced me that I did."

"So you met her at the stables before her rides?"

"I not only met her at the stables, I began to ride with her every day. The crops were in. I worked on the bookkeeping for the farm in the morning. We rode in the afternoons. She told me about New Orleans. I told her about Quakers, and farming and horses. She was so delicate and beautiful. I was captivated. I hadn't ever talked to a girl like that. I fell in love."

Grandpa stopped for a long moment and took out a handkerchief from his back pocket to blow his nose. When Liz offered him a glass of water again, this time he nodded. She walked past Debbie's desk and shook her head as Debbie rose to assist. Once back in her office, she set the water beside Grandpa.

"Of course, I knew she was married. I knew that we could only be friends, but the world had suddenly opened a door to a delicious sliver of happiness that no one told me existed."

"That's not bad, Grandpa. Friendship is a good thing." Liz wanted him to stop.

"Friendship is one thing. But then I began to feel guilty that I had stolen a moment of joy from Corbett that she'd never shared with him. I know now that guilt was an indicator that I had overstepped an invisible boundary, but I refused to listen to my inner voice. She wanted to ride horses. I was there if she needed help. It was that simple. Of course, if it had, indeed, been that simple, I wouldn't have kept our relationship a secret from my parents and Uncle Charles."

There was a quiet tap at the door. Grandpa stopped and Liz got up to speak to Debbie.

"I'm off to lunch," Debbie whispered. "You want me to bring you anything?"

"Nope," Liz said.

"Shall I put the answering machine on for the phone?"

"Please," Liz shut the door and sat back down across from Grandpa. "Grandpa, there's no reason you have to tell me any of this."

Their eyes met. "But there is," he said, not to be dissuaded. "One afternoon, as I helped to unsaddle her horse, she kissed me on the cheek. You can't imagine how many times I've thought about that first kiss. I turned my head to look at her face and then with an intensity I never knew that I had, I kissed her back."

He stopped again and stared out the window. A ray of sunlight shined through onto his eyes. Liz wanted to get up and flip the blinds, but she felt a strong need to remain still until he spoke again.

"I don't know what else to say. I should have stopped at that first kiss, but I didn't. The fact that I believed with all my soul that my fixation on her night and day must be love seemed to justify whatever we did. I believed that somehow things would work out so that we could be together. Now I look back on that fantasy and marvel that I could be so naïve. But when you're young, reason often plays second chair to desire."

"That was so long ago, Grandpa," Liz said. "What difference does it make now?"

He ignored the question. "Corbett came home without warning a day ahead of time for Christmas vacation. Isaac came early to get Sarah and tell her. He had never come into the barn before. He always waited for Sarah by the car, and I would clean up and water the horses after they left so that he wouldn't know I was there.

"But this day he walked into the barn and surprised us. Sarah begged me to go out the back barn door." Color rose in Grandpa's face. Liz suddenly realized how embarrassing this must be for him. In more ways than one she regretted being the recipient of the story he told.

"We scrambled to get back into our clothes. Before I could slip out, Isaac walked back to where we were, probably thinking Sarah might need help with the saddle. She went rushing out half clothed, yelling at him to leave, when I heard a car pull up. Then Corbett came into the barn, and suddenly everything happened at once. We had slipped from a world with just the two of us into chaos: the sound of a car, the shouts, horses neighing, loud voices and screaming. I heard Corbett yelling at Isaac, and Isaac and Sarah shouting back. During the confusion I was able to get out the door without anyone seeing me."

Grandpa rose for the first time. He walked over to the picture window in the office and looked out across at the hospital. Slowly he shook his head from side to side and then continued in a monotone that Liz could barely hear. "Shaken, I went back an hour later to water the horses and check if anything might be out of place. There was blood in some of the straw up front and a broken board on one of the stalls. A shovel lay in the middle of the floor. My mind began to race as to what might have happened after I left. I imagined a fight between Sarah and Corbett. I wanted to believe that she confessed to him that she loved me. I worried that perhaps he had hit her. I cleaned up the straw and replaced the board so that my Uncle Charles wouldn't ask questions. Then I ran home to borrow my father's car. I drove to Cottonwoods and saw old Doc Hewitt's car there and the Sheriff going into the house. When I knocked on the door, Mason Jones answered."

"Mason Jones?" Liz had never heard that name before.

"He worked at Cottonwoods back then and was one of the inside servants. He was a bent, elderly man with hardly any weight on him. I told him that I had come to see if Miss Sarah was all right. He seemed disturbed by my visit and anxious to have me leave."

"Did anyone speak with you?"

"No. I could hear loud voices. I told Mason I wanted to see if there had been trouble with the horses since things were not as they should be when I returned to the barn to clean up. Mason said no one could talk to me then. I asked him to please tell the family that I had come by, and he said he would."

Grandpa turned and sat back down into the chair. "It wasn't until the next morning that I heard that Isaac had been lynched overnight in the swamp." He closed his eyes. "Oh my God, Liz, what had I done? I heard the arguing. I knew there had to be a misunderstanding and I ran.

That event has haunted me every day of my life." Grandpa lowered his head into his hands.

"You never told anyone?" Liz asked.

"I knew I had to. The only thing to do was to go to the Sheriff. But while the mind was steadfast, the body became weak. I began to vomit. My legs would not hold me upright. I went into violent shakes and my mother found me curled up on my bed. After Uncle Charles arrived at the house, he and my father stood in the back yard talking. I could hear them. My mother insisted I was too sick to see them."

Grandpa picked up the water cup and took another swallow. He leaned his head back and closed his eyes and continued. "A small child showed up at the back door with a letter. Mother recognized the boy as a grandchild of Mason Jones. At least an hour or more passed before I had the nerve to open the letter and read it."

Grandpa Hoole stopped. He reached inside his shirt pocket and pulled out an envelope brown with age and tattered around the edges. "The letter," he said, as he handed it across to Liz. "She called it *friendship*."

"You still have it?" Liz breathed out the words with no attempt to cover the surprise in her voice. Then she read.

December 23, 1937

My Dearest Nathan,

My heart is breaking. Mason told the family that you came by Cottonwoods last night out of concern for me. My heart nearly stopped fearing what you had planned to say. Please, please, dear Nathan, don't do that again. How could it possibly help things now?

Corbett says we will go to Raleigh immediately after Christmas. He has found a house for us. That was the surprise he came to tell me. He feels guilty for leaving me alone in Cedar Branch these past few months and has accepted part of the responsibility for what happened. I cannot tell him the truth, not now. Isaac should never have come into the barn and after he hit Corbett there was no turning back. The truth will only make things worse for the Kendalls and your family. Imagine the scandal it would become. Think of your dear mother and father.

I will leave this town, but this is your home. Hopefully, I will find more happiness in Raleigh, although I will never find the friendship that I found with you. Please promise me that you will not reveal our secret to anyone. Our fate is that we must be apart, haunted by God for the rest of our lives. Is that not punishment enough?

I know not what you must do to regain that inner peace that you told me all good Quakers have. You are such a sensitive soul. I know you will suffer. Please forgive me. You will forever be in my heart.

Love, Sarah

Liz could avoid the question no longer. There was only one reason Grandpa was here to tell her this story. "Grandpa, you think Maggie is your child?"

Over closed eyelids, Grandpa arched his eyebrows. He raised his left hand to his temple and then opened his eyes and looked directly at her. "Yes, I do," he said. "I feel certain she is my child."

"Certain?" Liz said.

"I remember the first day I saw her. She was almost six years old." A slight smile crossed his lips. "Corbett held her hand as they walked to The Quaker Café. I had only been back in town a couple of months. I stepped out of the hardware store and Corbett stopped to talk to a friend on the street. I don't even remember who, I was so captivated by Maggie. He hadn't seen me. He stood there with his back to me holding Maggie's hand. She turned. The instant she stared up at me with those same mix-matched eyes of her mother I knew she was mine."

"It was that sudden?"

"It was that sudden. I knew, and then of course as Chase got older, I could see the resemblance; same build, same hair, same facial structure. I thought everyone in town would see it instantly, but I've never heard anyone say a word."

"I never saw it, Grandpa."

"Really?"

"Honestly, I never thought about it until recently."

"That's amazing," he said, shaking his head.

"Would you like to be tested as a possible bone marrow match?"

"I would."

"I will try to arrange it. I'll add that we do these tests with complete confidentiality, but I should also tell you that I don't think there's any way they will consider you as a donor, regardless of the results."

"I just ask that you try."

"I will do what I can. We'll need to go to the office in Durham. I'll take you."

"You just tell me when."

When Liz looked at him, for the first time she saw a wounded man. A quote from a play by Thornton Wilder, which she'd read in college, came to mind: *Without your wound, where would your power be?* It suddenly made sense. All these years he had worked to seek redemption for the wound he had inflicted upon the community fifty-six years ago.

"I will hold you in the light, Grandpa, and pray a way will open."

"What a Quaker you have become, my dear." He rose, more burdened by his years than Liz had ever seen, and he bent down to kiss the top of her head. Then he walked out the door.

Chapter Twenty-six

Every Thursday evening since Maggie's diagnosis, Richard Shannon had come by Cottonwoods to sit with her while Billie and Gill met Liz and Chase at The Quaker Café for supper. Things were better, not great, but better. Billie had become the watchdog in the afternoons and the bouncer when visiting hours were over.

"How's Maggie today?" Liz asked when Billie sat down.

"As long as she takes her Percocet every five hours, she's all right. She's tried to stretch it to six hours. The medicine makes her drowsy and when she wants to catch up on some legal work, she'll delay taking it. That's when she runs into problems."

"Lord, she should just forget everything at the office," Liz said.

"Shoot, I think that's why she gets up every day; the office and the elections. She's worried that you're not getting out enough, Liz, and she's not able to campaign for you like she planned."

"My heart's just not in it. I shouldn't have let her convince me to file."

"Word is the Democrats have a chance of reclaiming the governorship with Jim Hunt. Maybe you can just slide in on his coattails."

"I don't even know if I want to anymore?"

"For God's sake, don't let Maggie hear you say that. She's already voted, you know. She requested absentee ballots for both her and the Judge," Billie said. "Unfortunately the Judge's death was too well publicized; but give her credit, she tried."

Miss Ellie brought two plates of fried chicken with mashed potatoes and green beans, and two bowls of chicken 'n dumplings. "What's this?" Gill asked as Miss Ellie put the dumplings in front of him.

"What you ordered," Billie said. "Chicken 'n dumplings."

"There's chicken in here some place?" Gill pushed his fork around the plate.

Billie looked up at Miss Ellie and shook her head. "Ignore him. He's in one of his picky moods."

Miss Ellie refilled everyone's glass of sweet tea. "I've got a pot of chicken soup in the back for you to take to Maggie," she said.

"She'll love that," Billie said. "She always loves your soup."

"Is she eating better?"

"She's eating because she knows she has to," Billie reassured her.

"I talked to my son Josh up in Baltimore. He's promised me he'd give some blood for the donor tests." Miss Ellie looked straight at Liz. "My two girls and I went over to give blood on Tuesday. They say a lot of people have come in since Sunday when all of the preachers announced it in church."

"It's really helped out our blood reserves, and we're grateful," Liz said. "Chase and I have donated blood, and I think Sophie and her husband have also."

"Well, I hope they find a match," Miss Ellie said, and continued her loop through the restaurant with the pitcher of tea. Liz noticed Helen's lips in fast forward with the OHIO Squad. Liz knew Helen had hit the campaign trail, working her way through the white community, and prophesizing doom and gloom if a liberal outsider, such as Liz, ever became a county commissioner. Liz sighed. She'd lost the fire in her belly when Maggie got ill.

They finished their dinner and while Chase and Gill paid the bill, Liz went over to retrieve her sweater off the coat rack.

Helen spoke as she walked by, "I understand wedding invitations have all gone out."

"We're all pretty excited," Liz picked up her sweater and gave her a pleasant nod. "Getting close now, just a few weeks until the end of October." Liz really didn't want to get into a public conversation with Helen, but Helen had an agenda.

"A wedding and the election, all rolling in at the same time. I imagine you're tired, dear."

"I am, Helen," Liz conceded.

"I guess it will be a big wedding," she continued. "St. Michael's in Charleston and the reception at the Mills House—sounds elegant and expensive. Nathan's fiancée must be quite well-off?"

"They're a fine Charleston family."

"Just what do her parents do?"

"He's in real estate. She owns her own business, interior design."

"Oh, my, guess they wouldn't profit much from those skills here in Cedar Branch." Helen threw a puckish grin around the table.

"That's probably why they don't live in Cedar Branch." Liz returned the look.

"Well, it sounds like a pricey wedding. Not very Quakerly."

"They're Episcopalian, Helen—St. Michael's *Episcopal* Church."

"Of course, well, I couldn't go, even if I'd been invited, you know. It's much too expensive for me to afford. Pity about your hair."

Liz flushed, knowing that her light complexion had just turned bright pink. Biting back a sarcastic remark, she kept her mouth closed and turned to go. Helen tugged at her sweater. "By the way, how is poor Maggie?"

"A bit stronger each day."

"Well, that's good to hear. Have you had any luck?"

"Any luck with what?"

"Well, I understand you hope to find someone who is a brother or sister to Maggie for a transplant."

Liz was startled. "You must have misunderstood, Helen, we're looking for a match for Maggie. They will try to find someone through a national registry."

"Oh," Helen said with lack of conviction. "I thought I heard that you had asked around to find out if Maggie had a half brother or sister."

Speechless for a moment, Liz felt herself start to puff up like a blow fish. Others now eavesdropped on their conversation. The one thing about The Quaker Café was that nothing said there ever remained private. "Helen, that's simply not true. I don't know what you heard, but you heard wrong." Liz knew Helen had caught her in a lie, but she simply refused to confirm the rumor. She responded to her guilt with anger.

"Sorry," Helen said sheepishly, raising her eyebrows. "I certainly didn't mean to offend anyone."

"But you do, Helen, over and over again. And you, ladies." She turned to face the remainder of the OHIO Squad. "Why do you let her do this? Surely you all have better things to talk about than town gossip." She could feel herself bubbling over like a lava flow.

Chase walked over and put his hand in the small of her back. "Come on, Liz. Let's go."

Helen had stiffened, her mouth puckered up. "Liz Hoole, if Nathan and Euphrasia could hear you talk."

"Don't bring my in-laws into this, Helen. Damn it. Just give it a rest, would you?"

"Liz," Chase took her shoulders and pointed his wife in the direction of the door. "Good night, ladies," he said as he nodded and then ushered Liz out.

"Whew," he said once they were out.

"I was just getting started."

"I could tell."

Billie scampered out of the restaurant behind Liz while Gill kept his distance. As they walked to their cars, Billie was in a titter. "My God, Liz, bet that will keep the old biddy quiet for a while, especially if you're in the room."

"She just aggravates me to death. I declare, what to do with that woman?"

"It might have been better to *declare* instead of swear back there, but you made your point," Chase said softly.

"I didn't swear," Liz said. She knew full well that swearing was never considered appropriate by Quakers, nor by the Hooles. Years ago she'd learned to control colorful language.

"I believe you did," Chase said.

"What did I say?"

"*Damn it* comes to mind."

"No, I didn't. Did I really say damn it?"

"Yes, you did, yes, you did," twittered Billie. "Loud and clear."

"Well, damn it!"

CHAPTER TWENTY-SEVEN

The day after Liz deposited Maggie at Duke for her consolidation treatment she picked up Grandpa Hoole and headed back to Durham to the Donor Center. Grandpa said little on the way over. Liz made small talk about the boys and school.

Liz had called Rachel Wells, her only contact at the Donor Center, and explained the dilemma and Grandpa's unusual request. Liz knew Rachel on a professional level but Liz didn't think that Rachel would make any concessions. Her reputation throughout the Red Cross offices was one of high expectations and rigid regulations.

"Liz," she said when they talked on the phone. "They're just not going to let him be a donor. He's too old."

"I promised I'd try, Rachel," Liz pleaded. "He's dead set to find out whether or not he's a match. Can't you just give him the test?"

Rachel greeted Grandpa with a frozen smile that Liz imagined went with the job. Smartly dressed in a tailored blue suit, her look said management. She glanced at Liz's Tar Heel baseball cap and Liz expected to be the brunt of a joke before Rachel realized the hat covered a cropped head. Whatever Rachel intended to say, she stopped. Liz's name was Hoole. Grandpa's name was Hoole. Her mind weighed the possibilities. Instead, she turned and ushered them into her office.

Grandpa and Liz stepped into a well-organized room with notebooks lined up in alphabetical order by county, topic, and data on long, dust-free shelves. Rachel offered each a seat and positioned herself behind a spotless clear-top table fashionably sized to be a desk. Liz envisioned an immaculate house, void of children. The thought resulted in an uncomfortable stomach spasm similar to ones she experienced when visiting her own mother.

"I hope you had an easy trip over. How long did it take?" Rachel asked.

"Oh, a bit more than two hours . . . mostly country roads, not too bad, as long as you don't get behind a school bus."

Rachel's smile remained unchanged. "Your call last week surprised me somewhat, Liz. I've never had this particular request before and I never expected one to come from you. I had to check with a couple of people first. I had a busy day yesterday and didn't have time. I just touched base with some of our staff this morning."

"I know how busy you are," Liz said, this more as a courtesy and because she wanted something out of her, not because she felt the least bit sympathetic. Liz always got annoyed at anyone who wanted to make a point of how busy they were. Everyone's busy. She resented being told she didn't make their priority list. Rachel might as well have said, "What you want simply isn't that important to me."

Rachel continued. "Mr. Hoole . . ."

"Please call me Nathan," Grandpa corrected.

"Mr. Hoole," Rachel continued without flinching, "what you want to do is exceedingly generous. I understand your deep love and concern for the individual involved." She cast her eyes from Liz to him. "There are several reasons we have age limits on who can be a BMT donor."

"BMT?" Grandpa Hoole looked at Liz.

"Bone Marrow Transplant, Grandpa."

"Sounds like a sandwich."

Liz smiled.

Rachel appeared momentarily flummoxed. "One reason is we're concerned about you, the donor, and your health."

"I'm in good health. Only medication I take is for blood pressure and a little something for indigestion every now and then."

"Yes, I realize there are many people in their seventies who are in excellent health, but there are concerns about a general anesthesia with older citizens. Even more important is that the success rate for the patient is not as high when the donors are older. The chances for success would be greater with a match from a younger donor."

Though Grandpa didn't respond, he didn't seem satisfied with this answer. "What if there isn't a younger donor?"

Rachel ignored his question. "This is a difficult procedure. It's difficult on the donor. It's difficult on the patient. We want to be very sure that we've maximized the possibility of success before we put them through it."

"When will you know if you find another match?" Grandpa rephrased his question.

"Does this individual have any brothers or sisters?"

"Not full brothers or sisters . . . a half brother and sister." Grandpa didn't look at Liz when he said this. Liz's mind immediately jumped to Chase and Sophie. They didn't know. She couldn't tell them.

"Well, that's interesting. With full brothers and sisters, there's about a one in four possibility that one of them will be a match. We need to have seven out of ten antigens match when we test for donors."

Grandpa raised his eyebrows and she rephrased: "Antigens are sort of a coding marker that's found on your white blood cells. Half come from the mother and half come from the father. There are millions of combinations, but we focus on ten of them for a BMT. Sometimes we find what we call a half match. There are numerous studies on that possibility right now, but so far we don't have any clinical data to put it into practice."

"Is there a possibility that a half brother or sister would be a full match?" Grandpa asked.

"Anything is possible, but it would be extremely rare. There is, however, a new procedure that has been successful with cord blood from an infant. If there is a match there, the antigens don't have to be quite as many to make it work. Anyone in your family expecting a baby?"

Grandpa and Liz looked at each other. "Yes, in November in New Mexico."

"How are they related?"

"My first grandchild?" Liz bragged.

"How would that child be related to the patient?" Rachel seemed more interested.

"My husband is her half brother." As the words came out of her mouth, she couldn't believe she'd actually verbalized that Chase and Maggie were siblings. It was the first time she'd said it out loud. "So the baby would be a great-nephew or -niece of a half brother." Before Rachel spoke, Liz knew the answer.

"Not probable." Rachel shook her head and seemed to dismiss that option, although she added, "But it might be worth testing. Even if it isn't a match for the individual in mind, it could be a wonderful gift for someone else. Cord blood can be frozen."

"It would have to be collected in New Mexico," Liz added.

"That's not a problem. We ship blood around the world, as you well know." She glared at Liz over a raised eyebrow as if to say, *of all people, you should know.* Liz disliked this woman more and more.

"I presume that the doctor has already placed this patient on a national registry list for a donor. Depending on the ethnicity of the patient, if she is a white American, we have a fairly high chance of a match, usually in two to four months. You would be better off to go with an anonymous match than a half match of a relative."

"All the same, I'd like to be tested." Grandpa was not to be put off from his original purpose and appeared completely oblivious to the tension that was building between Rachel and Liz.

"Mr. Hoole, you would be responsible for the cost due to the fact that your age does not permit you to be a donor."

"Even if I were the perfect match?"

"Even if you were the perfect match, which is not likely."

"I don't see why it's less likely than finding someone in Ohio or Montana who's a full match. I'd like to be tested," he insisted.

"Very well. I will walk you to the clinic and they will handle everything from there. Count on a couple of hours with paper work and wait time. We'll just need to draw a little blood."

Grandpa was on his feet and waited for Rachel to lead the way.

"And how would you like your results reported?" Rachel asked as they followed her.

Grandpa looked over at Liz. "Would you just call Liz and let her know?"

"That would be fine," Liz said. "Call me at my office."

Two hours later and after an early lunch in the cafeteria they retraced their steps down the red-dotted corridor to the blue corridor to find Maggie.

Richard Shannon came to the waiting room, stripping off his mask. "Hey, didn't know you all planned to come by." He appeared fatigued and frustrated.

"Well, we had to come to Durham, and thought we'd stop in. How's Maggie doing?"

"Not too good right now. I'm at a loss for what to do. She's had some kind of reaction to the chemo . . . blisters in her mouth and throat. She's very uncomfortable. For the time being I'm pretty much shoveling ice chips into her to suck on, which seems to be the only thing that helps."

"Is there anything we can do?" Liz asked.

"I'd welcome any help."

After Liz showed Grandpa how to put on the PPE outfit, with masks over their faces they slipped into the room. "Maggie," Liz whispered, and brushed her hand across her damp forehead, "Grandpa is with me. We had things to do in Durham today."

Maggie's eyes flickered between Liz and Grandpa like a frightened animal. "I'm dying," she said in a hush so quiet that Liz could barely hear her.

"No, you're not, Maggie. It's the drug making you feel this bad. It's going to get better." Liz tried to control the tears. "Roll over, hon, let me rub your back."

Maggie struggled to get on her side. Richard still sat in front manning the ice chips. Liz stood on the opposite side of the bed with the hospital gown strings loose as she rubbed lotion into Maggie's back and shoulders. In a chair behind Richard, Grandpa closed his eyes and folded his hands in prayer. The room became very still.

Within fifteen minutes, Maggie began to sleep peacefully. Liz and Richard sat back in their chairs and joined Grandpa in silence. Forty-five minutes later, Liz and Grandpa got up to leave.

"That was amazing," Richard said. "What a difference. Thank you so much."

*****

"Grandpa," Liz said as they made their way back to the Interstate. "Have you ever said anything to Chase or Sophie about Sarah?"

"No."

"Does Grandma know?"

"Not yet."

They merged with the traffic onto I-85 and ran into road construction, which seemed to be never-ending. The drive back and forth should have been second nature to Liz by now, but she found that she became increasingly annoyed at minor delays.

"Are you planning to tell anyone besides me?"

"I keep thinking of all the people who will be hurt."

Liz sighed. "You know that I am bound by confidentiality?"

"I understand."

"Grandpa?"

"Yes, honey."

"Don't make me lie to my husband."

"I'd never ask you to do that . . . never."

Chapter Twenty-eight

The phone rang as Nicholas and Evan gathered their books for school the next morning. Long ago Liz had given up on forcing them to make up their beds or pick up their clothes from the floor. It was enough just to get everyone out the door on time; they didn't want to start every day with a battle. Sunday morning became "pick-up day." Every other morning was just "let's get up and out without a fight."

In her bedroom Liz wrestled with a pair of panty hose that grabbed at the thighs and threatened defeat before they hit her crotch. She wondered what marketing genius had ever convinced women to wear these things.

"Can you grab the phone, Chase?" Liz yelled.

"Got it," he called back.

As Liz walked into the den she heard him say, "Yes, this is Mr. Hoole. I don't understand. Would you say that again?" He looked over at Liz and waved his free hand with a confused look on his face and mouthed, *Duke Medical Center*? "You want me to come in today? Are you sure you have the right Hoole? Chase Hoole?"

Alarms went off in Liz's head. "Let me talk to them, Chase." She tried to grab the phone, but he had already gotten an answer.

"I'm afraid you have the wrong Hoole. There are two Nathan Hooles. One is my father and one is my son, but I still don't understand why you're calling."

"Let me talk to her, Chase," Liz insisted. Chase's eyes scrunched up as he handed his wife the phone. "This is Liz Hoole. We're in the middle of getting everyone out the door to school. May I call you right back? Yes, yes." She jotted the number down on the pad next to the phone. "In about ten minutes."

"Boys, run on out to the car." She motioned to Nicholas and Evan who had stopped what they were doing and turned their attention on their parents, sensing something amiss. "They'll be late, Chase."

"Oh, no," he said with a frown. "You're not going to dismiss me like that. Who was that?"

"A woman from the blood donor center at Duke," Liz said.

"Why is she calling me?"

"She called for your dad. She told you that," Liz answered.

"She said they needed me to come in to donate platelets today if at all possible. Why would she want my dad to donate platelets?"

"I don't know what it's about. I'll call her back." Liz tried unsuccessfully to dismiss the conversation, but Chase was having none of it.

"Oh, come on, Liz. Why should she talk to you instead of me?" Chase was getting annoyed, an emotion foreign to him. In their years of marriage, Liz could count the number of times Chase had lost his temper on one hand.

"Because I have health care power of attorney," Liz said, sounding more defiant than she had intended. "Let me return her call, would you please? Go on, take the boys to school and I'll stop by the pharmacy before I go to work."

Chase turned sharply. Evan looked at both of them meekly and said, "We got plates. How many plates do they want?"

Chase gave him a little nudge with the back of his hand and Liz heard him snap at the boys in the driveway. "In the car, both of you, *right now,* and not another word. I'm not taking questions this morning."

Liz called Rachel's office. Her secretary answered. "Is Rachel in?" she asked.

"No, I'm sorry. She's in meetings all day today. Could I give her a message?"

"This is Liz Hoole. I believe you just called my home phone number."

Silence from the other end.

"I was there yesterday with my father-in-law, Nathan Hoole, who left a blood sample to be tested for a donor match for Marjorie C. Kendall. If you check her record you will see that she has signed a release form for you to talk to me about her medical condition."

Silence.

"The instructions on the chart were to call my office phone. You called my home phone. You reached the wrong Mr. Hoole. You spoke with Chase Hoole, not Nathan Hoole. In the future, please ask for Liz Hoole or Nathan Hoole before you speak to anyone."

Silence.

Liz knew all too well the secretary was now in a panic, because there had been a breach of confidentiality. The secretary had spoken to the wrong person and revealed information concerning someone else's blood donation . . . an honest mistake, but still a mistake. Liz would confront Rachel with it later, but at the moment she wanted to know about the reason for the call.

"You asked Nathan Hoole to come to Duke today to give platelets. Can you give me any more information?"

"I'm sorry, I am unable to provide that information," the secretary said, lapsing into a defensive mode. She knew she was in trouble and was cutting her losses. Liz didn't waste time arguing with her. She knew the standard response to requests for information about other people's records. The secretary was following the letter of the law. She could not be sure Liz was who she said she was.

"Just please circle the correct phone number in Nathan Hoole's folder and I'll call the doctor," Liz said. After she'd pulled Dr. Rao's pager number out of her address book and called, an answering machine asked for a call back number. True to his word, Dr. Rao returned her call within fifteen minutes.

"Dr. Rao, this is Liz Hoole, Marjorie Kendall's friend. I have a signed release in her records that you may talk to me about her health."

"Ah yes, Miss Hoole. I am glad you called."

"Is there a problem?"

"Yes, as a matter of fact there is. Miss Kendall's body is not responding to our platelet transfer treatment."

"But she responded okay to it last time?"

"Yes, she did, but sometimes the body will, shall I say . . . change its mind the second time around and start to reject the platelets. That's what it seems to be doing now. There's a chance that we can get a better response if we can obtain platelets from someone who is related to her."

"Related in what way?"

"Any way; cousins, half brothers or sisters, nephews or nieces."

"How many people do you need?"

"At least two. Three would be perfect."

"Blood type doesn't matter, right?"

Liz knew enough about platelets to know they didn't have to be the same blood type, but this was the first time she'd heard that rejections of platelets might be overcome if they came from relatives.

"If the donors could come two days apart that would be wonderful, as we can only store platelets for about five days," Dr. Rao continued. "If we could get at least three people this week and then if they would come again next week . . . I think that would do it."

"I'll see what I can do, Dr. Rao. Thank you."

Liz got on the phone and called Grandpa Hoole. "Grandpa, have you taken any aspirin in the past forty-eight hours?"

"No, should I?"

"Don't take a thing. Could you go with me to Durham again today if I picked you up at lunch?"

"Yes, I believe I could. Why?"

"You've been called to give some platelets for Maggie. She needs them today."

"I'll be ready."

"And Grandpa?"

"What?"

"Drink lots of fluids before I get there."

Next Liz called Nat in Charlotte. "Hi, hon."

"Hey, Mom. Everything's on track at this end. Everything okay there?"

"Yes, wedding plans are all good, but Maggie could really use your help right now. She needs additional platelets."

"From me, Mom?"

"Well, actually, darling, we need them from everyone. I know this is a busy time for you, before the wedding, but do you think there is any way that you could get to Durham on Saturday and donate some platelets?"

"She needs them this week?"

"Yeah, sweetie, it's urgent. You could help her out a lot."

In true Hoole spirit, he said, "Sure. Yeah, I'll do it for Maggie. Should I bring anyone else?"

"They can always use blood from any of you boys. Bring as many people as you can get in the car. It'll take a couple of hours, though. Just nobody take any aspirin for forty-eight hours ahead of time. Can't use anyone who's sick. No colds. No alcohol between now and then. Could you do that?"

There was a pause, and then, "Sure, we can do it. What time and where?"

"I'll call the hospital and make an appointment and get back to you within the hour."

Next came the hardest part. Liz pulled in front of the pharmacy and went inside. Two customers were in line at the counter and she sat down at one of the tables up front until both had filled their prescriptions and left.

"So tell me what you found out," Chase said rather coldly as he worked on the orders in the to-fill basket.

"They do need you to come to Duke to give platelets." Liz stopped and then added, "day after tomorrow, if at all possible."

Chase extended his arms and laid both hands flat on the counter. Looking down at her he spaced his words. "Liz, what's going on?"

"All I can tell you is that Maggie needs your platelets this week."

"All you can tell me . . . all you can tell me?" He stammered in frustration. "You're asking me to take off a day of work and drive to Durham to give platelets when you and I know they've got plenty of platelets at Duke Medical Center and that's *all you can tell me?*"

Liz looked down at the floor and didn't respond.

"I'm not a fool, Liz. I'm a pharmacist, for crying out loud."

"I never meant to imply you were a fool. I know you're not; that's why this is so hard."

"Liz," Chase said with exasperation. "I'm not doing anything without an explanation."

"I would give you an explanation if I could," she said. "All I can do is to tell you that Maggie would benefit greatly if you would go to Duke to donate platelets this week. I can't make you do it. That's your choice. All I can do is to ask. The rest is confidential information."

As Liz turned her back on her husband and walked out of the pharmacy she knew that for the first time in their marriage she had stepped on a line of trust that had cemented their relationship for the past twenty-seven years. Was it worth it? She didn't know. When this all started to unravel, she wasn't sure who was going to get hurt, but someone had to start telling the truth . . . and it couldn't be her.

Chapter Twenty-nine

Nat stuck his head in Maggie's hospital room without crossing the threshold. He had somehow sidestepped all of the hospital paraphernalia. "You got magic platelets on the way, Maggie, ole girl, just in time for you to make the wedding next weekend."

Maggie's face lit up when she saw him. "Thanks, Nat," Maggie said. "Don't think I'll make that wedding, but I'll be thinking of you."

Liz flushed. "Nat, you can't come in here. How did you get past the nurses' station?"

Nat looked at Liz and did a double-take. She pushed him out the door and into the waiting room where she removed her mask. He looked down at her with alarm. "What happened to your hair, Mom? Are you sick?"

"No, I'm not sick. I told you on the phone I cut my hair."

"You said *cut your hair*, not *shaved your head*."

"Well, I might not have been clear enough."

"Why?" Nat said, and then his eyes darted to Maggie's room, and he knew.

"That's why," Liz said. "It'll grow back before you know it."

Nat raised his eyebrows. "Okay, that's that."

"Think it'll upset Lexa—with the wedding and all?" She didn't want everyone to feel sorry for her thinking she might have cancer, and she certainly didn't want to detract from the bride in any way.

"No, why should it?" Nat looked confused. Liz knew he honestly hadn't considered all of the possibilities she fretted over. "I'll tell her, though, just so she's not surprised."

"You do that, honey. Tell her your mom will be the one in the church wearing the baseball cap."

"You wouldn't . . . ?"

"No, I won't wear the baseball cap. Now, go on. Get back to your friends, and thank you. Thank you all for doing this for Maggie. I love you more than you'll ever know."

*****

Liz was relieved to see Richard when he dropped by later that afternoon. Caregiving was labor intensive; she welcomed another person in the room, if for no other reason than to take a break and go to the bathroom.

Richard sat quietly as Liz went through a routine she'd adopted during her long days. Maggie dozed on and off. The mouth sores were better; and despite Maggie's ongoing struggle with back pain, she found some relief with foot massages and moist heat. Dr. Rao had been pleased with her response to the new round of platelets provided by Grandpa and Chase.

Later if Maggie felt like sitting up in a chair, Liz would give her a pedicure. However Biblical, the act of washing her feet provided unexpected comfort to them both.

"Richard," Maggie said after a period they'd mistaken for slumber, "what happens when you die?"

Richard gave an uncomfortable little laugh. The question had startled him. He hadn't come expecting to discuss theology. To this point his weekly visits had involved local news and gentle encouragement. "I don't know, Maggie."

"You're a minister. It's your job to know."

Richard made a tent with his fingers at the base of his chin. "I played hooky that day in divinity school." He was assessing Maggie's genuineness. Was she seeking answers or simply posing an unanswerable question in an effort to shift her focus from the pain?

"I don't believe you."

Richard became more solemn. His eyes focused on the ceiling as if he expected God to intervene with an appropriate answer. Instead he asked, "What do you think happens, Maggie?"

"No fair," Maggie rebuked. "An answer that's a question is no answer." She seemed weary and not sure whether or not to continue the conversation. Liz watched Richard shift uncomfortably in his chair, as if he'd let an important opportunity slip by.

Then Maggie spoke again. "I once read a quote that stuck with me, can't remember exactly how it went." She thought for a moment. "Something about not being aware of anything before we're born and after we die, and comparing the two."

"'There was a time when we were not; this gives us no concern. Why then should it trouble us that there will come a time when we cease to be?' William Hazlitt," Richard quoted.

"You did too do your homework," Maggie looked up. "That's what I used to believe."

"And you don't anymore?" Richard said.

"It changes somewhat when you're standing at the precipice."

No one said anything for another couple of minutes. Liz stood at the bottom of the bed and started to rub Maggie's feet. She wanted to dismiss Maggie's statement about *standing at the precipice*, but then thought better of it. She knew there were days Maggie felt like giving up. Better to explore those feelings with Richard than her.

"What do you believe, Liz?" Maggie asked.

"Oh, Maggie, I don't know. I guess I believe if we were supposed to know, we'd know."

Liz didn't want to tell Maggie what she believed. She had come to feel that when you were dead, you were dead. Afterlife was merely a panacea created in pagan history and carried over into mainstream religions to encourage believers to live better lives. Not that she had any opposition to the overall objective. It helped civilizations become more humane to one another.

"Quakers don't believe in a heaven or hell, do they?" Maggie asked.

"Some do. Some don't."

"So you think there's just nothing after death?"

"Quakers don't have a doctrine, per se. You know how they are . . . always searching, no absolutes. Everyone takes their own journey." Liz laughed a small laugh to lighten the conversation and then regretted it. She realized Maggie was very serious.

"I've always believed that death is part of an ongoing process," Richard said.

"Ongoing to what?"

"Well, if we are to become one with God, it isn't something that crescendos at death and is done. If there's something afterwards, then we'll become a part of that evolving process."

"So what's the point to life?" Maggie asked.

"Dissertations are written on that subject," Richard said.

"But I'm asking you."

Liz interjected, "To respect the fact that there is that of God in every man."

"What if there is no God?" Maggie asked.

"God is love," Liz said.

There was a moment of silence and then Maggie looked over at Richard. "Your turn, preacher."

Richard took a deep breath and closed his eyes. "I guess I think of death like I think of the birth of a child. When we were in our mother's womb we were completely taken care of. Someone breathed for us and ate for us and kept us warm. All we did was grow. And we didn't even do that on our own . . . it just happened." He paused for a moment and opened his eyes. "Then unexpectedly, without any desire on our part, the birth process commences."

Liz stopped rubbing Maggie's feet and listened.

"I can only imagine what an infant's brain must think during those hours of birth. It can't be easy. Undoubtedly it must be stressful, maybe even painful. Yet we remember none of it."

"Why do you think that is, Richard?" Liz asked.

"I don't know. Perhaps the beauty of life eclipses the trauma of birth. Do you dwell on the pain you experienced when you delivered your babies?"

"Actually, I don't," Liz said.

"I've never had that experience," Maggie said. "I wouldn't know."

"I haven't, either," said Richard, "but the day I stood in the delivery room and saw my babies born . . . that day I believed in miracles."

"Me, too," Liz added. "It's unbelievable."

"Each of those little forms emerged into this world out of darkness into light, completely dependent that someone would be there to protect and nourish them. I guess that's what I believe about death. We don't know what's on the other side, but we go with trust and faith that there will be loving arms, so to speak, to nourish and protect us as we pass from one life into the next."

"And you believe that the miracle after death eclipses the process that takes place when we're dying?" Maggie asked.

"That's what I believe," Richard said.

"*Walking in the light. Standing in the light,*" Liz said. "Very Quakerly."

Silence rested over the room for a period before Maggie said, "My problem is that I need more time. I still have things to do."

"Well, perhaps this is God's way of helping you prioritize your tasks? Maybe something that was at the bottom of your list needs to be shifted to the top," Richard said.

"Could be," Maggie said. "I'm just so very tired. Do you think there is a reprieve?"

"God repeatedly offers us reprieves," Richard said. "The problem is we always expect to be given one more."

CHAPTER THIRTY

Liz knew that the check-in at the hotel in Charleston would send shock waves through Grandma Hoole, but she didn't know how to prevent the inevitable. Chase promised he had prepared his mother for what to expect, but he had been unusually quiet and distant the past week. Liz could feel the strain on their relationship. The stress was beginning to show on everyone.

They drove two cars to Charleston. Grandpa drove with Liz and Evan. Grandma was in the car with Chase and Nicholas. Everyone arrived tired after the eight-hour trip.

"Chase," Grandma protested as a valet swooped in to retrieve the luggage from both cars and disappeared with the keys, "I can carry my own luggage. This is not necessary."

"I'll get it, Mom," Chase said as he fished out a roll of ones and fives to peel off for tips. "Everybody's got to make a living."

A doorman ushered the family into the lobby and Chase, Grandpa, and the boys went up to the front desk. Nicholas and Evan were both wide-eyed as they surveyed the opulence of the surroundings. It was surely a step up from the Hampton Inn, where they stayed on their trips to St. Paul. Meanwhile, Grandma Hoole breathed into Liz's ear non-stop. "This is ridiculous. We can stay someplace much less expensive than this. There is no need to spend all this money for a bed. Grandpa and I will go stay at Sophie's."

"Grandma, please just try to enjoy it. You know Sophie and Jack are in the middle of renovations at their house. Everyone is staying here and this puts you where the buses will pick you up for the rehearsal party at the beach. Besides, the reception after the wedding is here in their ballroom. It's just a block's walk from here to the church."

"I don't know," she protested. "We'll pay our share of this."

"No you won't. It's a gift. Please accept it and just have a good time."

"Will your mother and father be staying here also?" she asked.

Liz knew their presence wouldn't necessarily line up in the plus column.

"My mom and dad will be here, and Adam gets in tonight. It keeps us all together."

Grandma Hoole stared critically at the elaborate crystal chandelier and eyed the lavish floral arrangements on the pedestals in the foyer before she sat down on a leather high-back settee. "Your boys will start to think everyone has weddings like this. You didn't do all of this for Adam's wedding."

"We did what Adam and Heather wanted for their wedding," Liz said patiently. She knew the comparison was inevitable. "They wanted a Quaker wedding in Cedar Branch. Nat and Lexa have chosen something different."

Chase returned with two room keys and pointed everyone in the direction of the elevators. "Adam isn't here yet, but Nat has already checked in and left a note that he is out at the beach house with Frogbelly and the others. They are getting the cooker set up and the pig is on ice."

"On ice where?" Evan asked. His Tar Heel T-shirt had suffered from a stain of ketchup and French fries at lunch. Liz knew she'd need to wash it out to dry overnight.

"In the bath tub out at Folly Beach," Chase said.

"They put a pig on ice in a bathtub?" Evan raised his voice in alarm as he fiddled nervously with the latch on a case of matchbox cars. "Why did they do that?"

Nicholas chided his brother, "He's dead."

"They've got a dead pig in a bathtub?" Evan look horrified. "Who killed him?"

"Let's not get into this right now," Liz said, fearful that Nicholas might be relishing the opportunity to describe the pig's fate to his little brother. It was a topic he would have already analyzed and probably questioned to death on the drive down in the other car. "Let's get into the rooms, and we'll explain later."

At Grandpa and Grandma's room Chase slid the key card into the door and showed Grandpa how it worked.

"Where's our suitcase?" Grandma Hoole said as Chase stepped back so she could enter.

"They're sending it up, Mom," Chase said.

She walked in and surveyed the king-size bed, side bar, desk, and gold satin curtains that stretched across one entire wall at the end of the room. "Good heavens, how many people will share our bed with us tonight?"

Chase smiled. "Just you and Dad."

"I'll never find him."

"Reach out your hand and I'll be there," Grandpa reassured her and then waved a hand to shoo everyone out. "We'll be fine. It's late and it's been a long drive. You go on now, and we'll see you in the morning."

"Remember," Liz said. "I have to go to the airport to pick up my mother and father at ten. Then I'll come right back here to get you, Grandma, for the bridesmaids' luncheon."

"We'll be just fine. You do what you have to do. Don't worry about us." Grandpa closed the door behind them as he spoke.

*****

Nat and Adam entered their parents' room the next morning in a fanfare of shouts, as they jousted with Nicholas and Evan. As the two younger boys climbed over their older brothers, Chase gave Adam a hug and asked about Heather. Liz was at the ironing board removing the remaining dampness from Evan's not completely dry T-shirt.

"She's doing great. Everything's on schedule." He eyed his mother's head. "Nice haircut."

"You like it?" Liz asked hopefully.

"Well, I had been warned," he said with a genuine smile and rubbed the top of her head.

"You boys need something to eat?" Chase asked, to which there was a resounding *yes*.

Liz watched as they headed down the hall in a gaggle. These were the moments she knew Chase loved the most. He pushed the elevator button. The doors opened and they disappeared. She wanted more than ever to be with them. Instead, Liz was headed to the airport.

*****

Liz's father, James Reynolds, had retired as a chemistry professor at Macalester College in St. Paul in 1985, and successfully transferred his skills into consultancy work with a prominent pharmaceutical company. Still in good health with marketable expertise and no children underfoot or student papers to grade, he had never been happier.

Her mother, Barbara, had retired as Director at the University of Minnesota School of Nursing, where she'd run her staff with precision. After twenty-five years in health care, Barbara remained on everyone's A-list as a favored board member. If she accepted, she could raise money like nobody's business.

James kept his busy schedule; Barbara kept hers. If they didn't get around to an evening together for several days, no one complained. Liz felt fortunate to have parents who were healthy, active and happy.

Liz and Chase dutifully made an annual trip each year to visit her folks in St. Paul. Otherwise, Liz's family remained focused on the Hooles.

Parking around the airport was horrendous, but Liz found a place in time to be waiting at the gate for her parents to disembark. Her father came first with a briefcase and a tote bag filled with files and books. He had a tendency to put on weight, but his wife kept him on a tight regimen of fresh vegetables and fish. He preferred a Wendy's burger with a chocolate frosty when on his own.

Barbara followed several steps behind him. She was petite, immaculately dressed in a travel suit that showed no wrinkles. Her dark brown hair was coiffed in a fashionable bob. Liz looked nothing like her. She was her daddy's girl; curly copper hair, round, and juggling life on a daily basis.

"Daddy," Liz walked up to him, gave him a peck on the cheek and took his carry-on from his hand. He stared at her without speaking before her mother joined them.

"Elizabeth Reynolds Hoole, what in God's name have you done to your hair?" she asked.

"I cut it, Mom. How was the flight?"

"Well, obviously you cut it, but why on earth?"

Liz started to walk in the direction of the baggage claim. "I did it to support a friend who has cancer."

"You couldn't wait until after the wedding?"

"I could, but I didn't."

Liz's mother kept step beside her now with no hopes of letting up. Her father dropped back, apparently not yet convinced this other woman could possibly be his daughter.

"I assume you bought a wig," Barbara said.

"No, I haven't done that."

"Well, you must. You won't walk down the aisle tomorrow like that."

"Mom, no one's interested in me. I'm not the bride."

"Oh, they're interested. They'll be checking out the groom's bloodline. What did Chase say?"

"He said I looked like Ben Kingsley."

"Well, he's right."

Her mother talked about nothing else all the way back to the hotel. They pulled into the hotel entrance behind a large Budweiser delivery truck. Liz told the valet that they would only be a few minutes.

"Mom, we're supposed to be at the bridesmaids' luncheon in thirty minutes. Liz hit the elevator button. "Dad, you're on your own."

As Liz scrambled back to her room to refresh her make-up, she noticed the message light on the phone receiver. She dialed Grandpa's room and Grandma Hoole answered the phone.

"I'm back from the airport. We'll leave for the luncheon in about twenty minutes. Meet me downstairs."

"Yes, dear," Grandma said.

Liz could hear Grandpa in the background. Grandma Hoole spoke to him over the phone. "It was the wrong room, Nathan. Why would a beer truck call for you, of all people?"

"Euphrasia, give me the phone," Liz heard Grandpa say.

"Liz, they called me a few minutes ago from the front desk. It seems there's a delivery truck out front with two kegs of beer for Nathan Hoole. Do you know anything about that?"

"Oh, Grandpa, I'm sure that's supposed to be delivered out at the beach. I'll run down and take care of it," Liz said.

A tall slender man with a wisp of hair and a rather caustic voice approached Liz at the front desk when she inquired about the beer truck. "Madame," he said, "I need to speak to you a moment."

Liz glanced between him and the entrance, where she saw the rear view of a burly man in a Budweiser uniform go out the front door.

"That man," she said, a bit frantically, "I need to stop that man."

"Madame," the concierge remained insistent. Liz paused long enough to see that he had *manager* on his name tag. "While we don't object to guests taking a brown bag to their rooms, kegs are quite unacceptable."

Liz could see the Budweiser man climbing into his truck and she called desperately to the door man, "Stop that truck. Don't let that beer truck leave."

Several people in the front lobby stopped what they were doing to look in her direction, and the manager, appearing flustered, followed her patiently, as one might trail a small child misbehaving in public.

"Wait," Liz called out across the lobby and passed the doorman who stood obediently with the door held open. "You're at the wrong location."

The Bud man was partially in his truck when he heard the cries and paused. *My Name is Dick*, was written across his name tag, and up close his uniform showed stains from a breakfast burrito.

"Dick," Liz said, "do you have an order for me?"

Out of the corner of her eye she could see the manager approaching.

"Nathan Hoole?" he said. "I called the room. They refused to accept it."

"You've got the wrong place. It's supposed to be delivered to Folly Beach."

He seemed more annoyed than eager to correct a mistake. "Lady, this is the address I was given."

"Well, this is the address for the contact, not for the delivery. The delivery is supposed to be on Folly Beach." She turned to the manager at her side now and repeated, "The kegs are supposed to be at Folly Beach."

"Oh," the manager said with appreciative relief.

"Lady, I got five more deliveries to do. That's thirty minutes away from here. It'll take me two hours by the time I deliver and return. It wasn't on the delivery order."

"Well, it should have been."

"It's not. It'll be seventy-five extra and I won't guarantee delivery before five thirty in the evening. I've got to do the other deliveries first."

"Five thirty? That's too late. There won't be time to get the kegs iced down." Liz looked helplessly at the manager, who quickly become her ally. He transferred his caustic glare to the driver.

"Good man, you can't help the lady out here?"

"It's like I said, seventy-five, and five thirty. If she wants to haggle, she can call my boss."

"Hell," Liz said, "just stick the kegs in my car over there, one in the trunk and one in the backseat."

With an expression of relief, the driver quickly complied and handed Liz two papers to sign. She considered writing a comment about the mistake but didn't want to take the time. She'd call later next week and they could duke it out on the phone.

When Liz went back in the lobby Grandmother Hoole waited downstairs.

"Liz, will there be alcohol at this event tonight?"

"Grandma, I have to run upstairs. My mother will be down shortly. Will you two stick together and I'll be back as soon as I can?" They were running late. Liz figured there would be plenty of time to discuss alcohol consumption later. Besides, she thought, somewhat annoyed, she had designated that to Chase's list of things to do.

Liz threw on a dress, donned a straw fedora she'd borrowed from Billie, and regretted her friend wasn't by her side to help. Billie would have been able to finesse the situation downstairs with a flutter of her eye lashes and a twitch of her hips. But Billie had wanted to stay with Maggie. Liz knew that left her free not to worry as much about Maggie. As always, Billie had risen to the occasion in the best possible way.

After a quick once-over with face powder and lipstick, Liz headed back to the lobby on a run. She always had such good intentions of taking an hour to get ready for special events, but never seemed to plan adequately.

Her mother and Grandma Hoole exchanged polite conversation. As she approached them from across the lobby, she was reminded of what complete opposites they were: Grandma Hoole in her loose gray dress with her hair pulled back in a bun, Barbara in her suit, stylish haircut, manicured nails, and color-coded make-up. Liz ushered them both out to the car.

"Whoever sits in the back seat, please hold the beer keg upright," she said as casually as she could. Then she opened the front car door for Grandma.

Liz's mother turned and did what she did best, summoned the valet. She gave him specific instructions on what needed to be done to secure the keg in both the back and the trunk so they didn't roll or smudge the seat. This took an additional fifteen minutes, but she tipped him generously. Liz knew her mother would get special attention at the front door for the remainder of her stay.

*****

"After this luncheon, I'm going to find some wig shops that we can visit in the morning," Barbara said, her mind already made up.

Liz gave an audible sigh. "Oh Mom, please don't. Let it be."

"No harm in looking. I just think for this particular occasion you need to look your best."

When they pulled up to the entrance of the restaurant, Liz was again grateful there was someone parking cars. "Park the car where that keg stays in the shade," she said and handed over her keys with a five dollar bill.

"Yes ma'am," said the young man who gave Liz a wink and tipped his hat.

They walked into a long narrow room with a bar that ran three-quarters of one side of the wall and had eight round patio tables with mosaic tops nestled together in close quarters. In front of the tables to the right, the aunts stood in a receiving line. Lexa's mother, Louise Lloyd, stood at the end, graceful and elegant in a loose-fitting ankle-length emerald silk skirt and an open-neck long-sleeve white blouse. She had a wide belt at her waist accompanied by an oversize buckle with an emerald stone the size of Gibraltar. She stepped out in front to greet Liz and gave her a warm hug. Liz felt like Winnie the Pooh.

Sophie emerged from the line to hug Grandmother Hoole, and then they started the round of introductions. The luncheon was lovely. The bridesmaids were beautiful. Lexa was radiant. Around 2:00 things began to break up. Liz expressed her need to get out to Folly Beach and reminded everyone about the bus service from the church and hotel. Everyone lingered over thank yous and goodbyes; Liz hoped that the line would move through the bar swiftly and not dawdle.

Then her mother and Louise stopped to chat at the front door and blocked the exit. Grandma Hoole stood between Liz and Sophie and averted her eyes from the sights on either side of the room. Sandwiched between shelves of alcohol and a large painting of three caricatures of nude women frolicking on the beach, Liz felt certain Grandma felt caught between Sodom and Gomorrah.

Finally Liz could bear Grandma Hoole's discomfort no longer. She spoke up. "Hate to break this up, but I really do need to get out to Folly Beach." Her mother and Louise nodded and started to release the bottleneck they'd created.

Before they could get out the door, Liz's little niece, Estelle, pointed at the painting and shouted, "Mommy, look at that lady, she looks like Auntie Liz." There was a lull in the conversations. Liz turned to look at the painting for the first time, realizing that the sketch of one woman did have an uncanny resemblance to her. She went crimson from her neck to her forehead. Polite laughter rippled through the group.

Sophie laughed uncomfortably and said, "But that lady has hair, and your Auntie Liz doesn't."

CHAPTER THIRTY-ONE

When Liz arrived at the beach house, the party was already well under-way. Cars lined the road in front. Two small boxy buildings decorated in balloons and crepe paper sat at the entrance of the wooden walkway leading up the side of the dunes to the house. Liz wedged the back of the car as close to the planks as she could get and double parked. She climbed out to solicit some muscle power. Two signs stuck out from the huts. One read, "Welcome Nat's family and friends" and the other, "Welcome Lexa's family and friends." With a jolt she realized the huts were porta-potties, and proceeded up the walkway in storm trooper fashion.

"Chase! There are two porta-potties at the entrance."

"I knew you wouldn't like that."

"This is a rehearsal party. We can't have the guests pass through an arch of porta-potties. Did it cross anyone's mind that this would not be acceptable?" She surveyed the numerous males and ring of empty beer bottles stretching from the cooker to the beach and had her answer.

"Well, let's see what we can do." Chase remained steady and even-handed. Liz felt the break-point coming sooner than later.

"Where is Frogbelly?" She scanned the gathering.

"I think he's over by the pig."

"Well, point me in his direction."

A dozen guys in cut-offs and T-shirts surrounded a drum cooker, each with a beer in hand. Frogbelly stood front and center, working the crowd with a description of a skiing trick he swore he could do without skis. As Liz approached, he stopped dead in his tracks and displayed his perfect teeth from ear to ear.

"Fellows, you are about to meet the prettiest mama of them all. For those of you who have not yet had the pleasure, here comes Miz Hoole, the woman who gave Nat his good looks." There was light applause and several raised beer bottles in tribute.

"Miz Hoole, may I introduce you to Porkchop, our guest of honor?" With that he opened the smoker and revealed a 125-pound pig. "Pretty as a picture, ain't he? We're keeping him at 260 degrees over hickory with a touch of Jack Daniels sprayed over the coals from time to time. He's gonna be divine."

The other young men smiled and raised their bottles in a second toast as Frogbelly praised Liz and Porkchop simultaneously. There was no doubt which one had their highest admiration.

"Frogbelly, may I speak with you privately?" Liz said.

"You bet, Miz Hoole. It would be my pleasure." He stepped away from the group as he gave them a wink and followed her over towards the wrap-around deck. Nat had spotted his mother from down on the beach where he played touch football with his brothers and friends and began to make his way to the house.

"Frogbelly, I have a problem with the porta-potties."

"Miz Hoole, I'm sorry about that, but the landlord insisted that we have porta-potties to handle this crowd. The septic systems for these houses aren't made for this many people."

"I understand that, Frogbelly. My problem is with the placement of the porta-potties at the entrance to the party. Not exactly the receiving line I'd imagined."

"Aren't they cute? Your boys helped decorate them."

"Cute for a KA beach party where your main objective is to impress good-looking girls who find porta-potty décor seductive, but not cute for the Lloyds of Charleston nor for Lexa's grandparents, aunts, and uncles."

"You may have a point there, Miz Hoole." Frogbelly lowered his eyes, with a shadow of remorse on his face. "So what do you want us to do?"

"Well, how about if you and I go down and survey our options for placement and then you organize this fine group of muscular young men to move them for me."

At that moment Sophie came round the house with a box-load of paper plates and plastic forks. "Criminy, I had to park about a half mile away," she said. "There are cars all up and down the road. Liz, do you realize you've got two porta-potties on the walkway up here?"

"Right. We're dealing with that at this very moment. Put that box down and come help us decide a better location for them."

Frogbelly, Sophie, and Liz proceeded down the walkway with Nat and Chase following. The house sat on stilts on top of sand; the ground was uneven and sprinkled with palmetto pines and brush. The wooden walkway provided the only access to the property. A small clearing to the right of the walkway had been leveled to accommodate two cars. On the opposite side of the street was marshland with wild grass and pinto palms. Nothing other than the paved road felt very solid underfoot.

"See the problem, Miz Hoole?" Frogbelly said as they surveyed the land. "The delivery guy couldn't see any other place to put them, either. His equipment wouldn't get them up the hill to the house."

"Well, I think our only option, as much as I'd like something better, is to rope off half of this parking space and put them as far away from the walkway as we can. Then we'll have to encourage the younger crowd to use these and not the two bathrooms inside. Can we do that?"

Frogbelly had been unusually subdued for a few moments, but then rose again to the challenge. "Consider it done, Miz Hoole." With the strong arms of several recruits they completed the task.

Gradually small groups including Chase and all four boys began to leave for the rehearsal at the church. Tables and chairs had been set up. All cans thrown in recycle bins . . . the house in reasonable order.

Sophie and Liz did a quick review. They checked the fridge for slaw, potato salad, and baked beans. Chase had done his job and picked up everything Liz had ordered; bottles of Pepsi, RC Cola, and Cheer wine chilled in the coolers. The kegs were iced down. A barrel of individually wrapped moon pies sat on the far side of the deck out of the sun.

Liz walked out to the group that faithfully watched over the pig. "How's Porkchop doing?"

"Just grand, Ms. Hoole. He's gonna be good."

"What time you think he'll be done?"

"Easily by seven—probably earlier. Then we'll spread out the coals and just keep him warm."

"Who are Spanky and Buck?" she asked. Two young men waved their hands. Buck was tall and lanky with a moustache and close-cropped beard he'd undoubtedly grown to hide his baby face. Spanky was shorter and heavier with blond sideburns, a throwback to the Elvis days. "Which one of you made the sauce?"

"I did, Ms. Hoole," Buck said proudly.

"Vinegar based or tomato based?"

"Ah, Ms. Hoole," Buck let out a little puff and kicked some sand with his foot. "Anybody knows that Eastern Carolina only has vinegar-based barbecue sauce. I wouldn't insult Nat by serving tomato-based at his wedding."

"Well, I didn't know, with Frogbelly from Georgia and all," Liz said.

"No, ma'am, I sure wouldn't have let that happen."

"What else you got in it?"

"Not much else, a little red pepper. I used to add some brown sugar every now and then, but don't do that anymore. I decided the sugar sweetened it up too much."

"Don't let it dry out."

"No, ma'am, I got a Cadillac cooker. See here?" He pointed to a thermostat on the side of the cooker. "Keepin' her between two-fifty and two-sixty degrees. We started out lower this morning, but I've moved it up a bit."

"All right, Buck. Sounds like you know more about barbecue than I do so I'm leaving it up to you. I wanna thank you boys for your work here today."

"Our pleasure."

Sophie left to pick up her family and Liz did a quick change into a comfortable slacks outfit. Big Gus, the banjo player, showed up and began to set up his microphone next to the barrel of moon pies on the deck. The sun began to set on the marsh and the evening became cool. The salt air brought back memories of a few summer vacations at the boardwalk when they added a week to their annual St. Paul excursions. Sea gulls glided effortlessly above the waves. The first bus of guests arrived and the second one followed shortly.

Dishes filled with roasted peanuts right out of the fields of Cedar Branch served a crowd that was congenial and talkative. The background banjo added a lot. When it was time to start serving the pig, Chase stepped to the microphone to welcome everyone. He ended by saying, "Nat has asked that his namesake, his grandfather, Nathan Hoole, offer a blessing before we get started."

Liz had been unaware that Nat had asked Grandpa to say anything. Quakers rarely offered up a blessing other than a moment of silence before a meal, so she was quite touched by the gesture and curious as to what, if anything, Grandpa would say.

"Thank you," Grandpa said quietly as he took the microphone and lowered his head in response to polite applause. "It is a pleasure for my wife, Euphrasia, and me to be here this evening and be part of this celebration. We feel fortunate to have lived long enough to witness the marriage of our grandchildren and we hope to be around when it's time to greet some of our great-grandchildren." There followed a few shouts and claps.

"In Quaker tradition, we ask for a few moments of silence before a meal to give quiet appreciation for the food that has been given us, and to those who have prepared it in our honor. Please join me now in silence."

After some nervous whispers and rustling, everyone became still. Silence has a profound effect because it is so rarely used; the transition was noticeable. Liz sensed the rhythms of nature: the sound of the waves, the caress of the wind against her cheek, the intense appreciation for the moment, the family and friends. She couldn't help but think of Maggie and offered an earnest prayer that the treatment was working—that Maggie was feeling more like her old self. Then in an unusually strong voice, Grandpa broke the silence:

> *"It is with humble gratitude, oh God, that we seek blessings*
> *on Lexa and Nat and their families and friends.*
> *Countless ancestors who have bequeathed to us the rich*
> *and undeserved heritage with which we are blessed have*
> *molded our lives. We give thanks for their sacrifices and for*
> *their vision and for their constant acknowledgements of*
> *Your Divine Being and care. As our histories and values*
> *become woven into the life tapestries of the next generation,*
> *keep us ever mindful of our many and bountiful blessings,*
> *and of our love for and responsibilities towards one another.*
> *Amen."*

Oh, Grandpa, Liz thought. *How perfect. How beautiful. Thank you.*

Porkchop was served up with drama and fanfare and unlimited praise for the BS Frogbelly Big-Pig Team. Big Gus and his banjo proved a delightful addition with the likes of "Reuben's Train," "Cripple Creek," and "Dueling Banjos," and Gus also took center stage a couple of times with a few vocals.

Around 8:00 p.m., Adam stepped to the microphone. "I'm Adam," he said, "Nat's brother. I'm younger than he is, shorter than he is, a little heavier than he is and a whole lot better looking than he is." Light laughter.

"Lexa, when you get one Hoole, you get us all. So make sure you've always got the guestroom ready." Adam raised his beer and a cheer went up.

Next Frogbelly stepped up to the microphone. "Now Nat's good brother, Adam here, would have you believe that Nat is about the smartest guy around. But I'm here to tell you that everything Nat has learned about money, liquor, and women, he's learned from me."

A hoot went up from the KA brothers around the deck.

Out of the corner of her eye Liz noticed Euphrasia with her eyes cast down. Grandpa had a hint of a smile on his face. Across from Liz, her father was enjoying the evening immensely, while her mother, sitting with Louise Lloyd, appeared amused. Nicholas and Evan remained center stage among several attractive young ladies.

"I want to give you some examples of a few of the many ways I helped Nat out," Frogbelly continued. "In fact, if the truth be known, if it weren't for me Lexa probably wouldn't have given Nat the time of day. Let me tell you how Nat Hoole operated before I took charge. Do you know what the first gift was that Nat gave to Lexa after he started to date her? You're probably thinking flowers? Candy? Not even close. On the third date, to show her his deep affection, Nat Hoole gave her a mug with her name on it!"

Hoots erupted from the crowd.

"On the next date he gave her a mug with *his* name on it."

Lexa nodded as the laughter reached an elevated pitch.

"At Christmas he gave her a coffee drip machine, and for her birthday he gave her an assortment of gourmet coffees."

Another round of laughter.

"Lexa, Lexa, Lexa, I don't know why you stuck with him. At this point I sat down with him and said, 'Now Nat, if you're really serious about this girl, then you need help. I don't know how they do things back in the sticks of Eastern North Carolina, but your KA brothers are gonna teach you some tricks of the trade.'"

Frogbelly became even more animated. "Number one—never give a girl anything that plugs in. Number two—any kind of glassware you ever wanted, you will get as a wedding gift."

Applause and more cheers from the crowd. "And number three—unless you're picking up the tab in a restaurant, forget food, it's a no-winner. Nat, there are only a few choices you have. Diamonds are always good. Did you get your diamond, Lexa?"

Lexa nodded.

"Thank *me* for that," Frogbelly said with loud exaggeration. "If left to Nat you'd have gotten an engagement watch." Everyone laughed again.

Frogbelly was now completely unstoppable. "In all seriousness, Nat is not just a good guy—he's one of the greats. I have a little story to tell you that shows what a special guy he is and why I'm so proud to be his friend. Last Friday night we had a small bachelor party planned for Nat with some KA brothers. Then we were all going to play golf on Saturday morning. Nat's mom, Miz Hoole . . ." Frogbelly acknowledged Liz with a wave of his hand.

"Miz Hoole over there called on Tuesday to see if there was any way that Nat could drive up to Duke Medical Center on Saturday morning and donate some platelets for a friend in Cedar Branch who is having chemotherapy. Did Nat hesitate? Did he say to his mom, I've got a bunch of friends here for the weekend, can't do it? No, he did not. In fact, IN FACT—he took four of us up with him and made us give blood, too. We were all up there by nine in the morning, postponed our tee time until one and were back in Charlotte to play golf. But the biggest sacrifice of all, was that he wouldn't let any of us drink beer on Friday night."

A roar of disbelief erupted from a table in the corner. Frogbelly nodded appreciatively: "Now, if that isn't enough, Nat and Lexa have actually postponed their honeymoon by one day and changed their tickets to leave from Raleigh-Durham so that Nat can drive up to Duke again on Monday and give one more pint before they leave. What kind of guy gives two pints of blood on the week he's getting married? I gotta give it to you, Lexa, you're getting a heck of a man and you're a hell of a woman to put up with it all. You be good to each other, hear? A toast to Nat and Lexa."

As the crowd applauded, the blood drained from Liz's face. She dared not look at Chase. Instead she glanced at her mother, who shot her a quizzical look. Forty-five minutes later, Chase rose to present the final toast and to thank everyone for coming.

Nothing registered with Liz the remainder of the evening. She shook hands with people as they left, and climbed on the last bus with Nicolas and Evan while Chase stayed behind to help clean up. As Liz walked past the rows of those already seated, Grandpa's eyes met Liz. Without speaking, they both knew that Chase had now connected the dots.

CHAPTER THIRTY-TWO

The next morning Chase and Liz stepped out of the elevator with Nicholas and Evan and headed to the restaurant. Chase had said little more than two words to Liz since the evening before; she felt responsible for the tension between them. In her mind she kept going over what she could possibly do or say to reassure him that she wanted to be truthful, but the answer eluded her. This was the day that had been on their calendars for almost a year now. She wanted it to be perfect in every way. She wanted Chase to recognize her dilemma, and hold her in his arms as he'd always done in the past when they'd had a misunderstanding.

"No time for breakfast, dear," Liz's mother saw her coming and rose from her chair immediately. "Grab a cup of coffee." She turned and looked at Chase. "The boys with you for the day?"

He nodded. "We're going to finish the clean up out at the beach."

"Good," Barbara said, turning back to Liz and pointing to the door. "Let's go."

Liz shot a glance at Chase, but he had already directed the boys to a nearby table where Grandma and Grandpa Hoole sat at breakfast. "Mom, I really don't have time to look for wigs, and everyone saw me bald last night anyway."

"Not everyone, dear," her mother interjected. "Let's just spend a couple of hours. You never know, we might happen upon exactly the right thing. Besides, what else do you have to do?"

She was right. What else does the mother-of-the-groom do on the wedding day? Her moment in the sun had passed with the rehearsal dinner.

Barbara again tipped the valet generously after he pulled the car around. "Lovely party last night," she commented as she fastened her seatbelt and Liz got in behind the steering wheel.

"Aren't Nat's friends great?" Liz said. Her mother's compliment meant a lot and evidently the porta-potties' placement had been discreet enough to be overlooked. "They did a nice job with the barbecue, didn't they?"

"Yes, Nat's friends are great," her mother agreed. "You look tired, honey."

"I'm just too keyed up. Didn't sleep well. Sat up waiting for Chase to get back. He was exhausted by the time he came in."

Barbara surveyed the homes as they turned right around Colonial Lake. "Charleston doesn't look bad, given Hurricane Hugo only a couple of years ago. I expected worse," she said.

"They've done a tremendous amount of rebuilding. Chase and I came down in 1990 for a conference. Things were pretty bad then," Liz said as she turned left on Calhoun.

"So how is the campaign going?"

Liz moaned. "It's not going, not going at all. With Maggie in the hospital and the wedding, I've completely dropped the ball."

"Does it matter that much?" her mother asked.

"What? The election or the campaigning?"

Liz spotted the turn onto Jonathan Lucas Street and thought she saw a car about to relinquish a much-coveted parking space. She stopped dead in the right lane and waited for the car to edge out in front of her.

"The election," her mother said.

"Not that much. Not anymore. My priorities have shifted."

Liz pulled up to parallel park, backed in too wide, and had to pull up and start over again. When she had the car within walking distance of the curb, she took a deep breath and said, "If I had to do again, I wouldn't file. My biggest concern is how much I will disappoint Maggie if I don't put out the effort, and then lose."

"You've got to have the passion," her mother said. "Whatever you do, find the passion. No point in stepping into that circus otherwise. Whatever's left of your family life will be gone."

They got out of the car. Barbara opened the door to the wig shop and did a quick sweep of the merchandise. "Not here. Let's head on out to Mt. Pleasant," and with that she turned and walked back to the car.

At the second shop in Mt. Pleasant they met an engaging saleswoman who read Liz's mother like a book and realized immediately who the buyer was in the twosome. She selected a wig she described as "Aspen Honeynut" and maneuvered the pile of hair onto Liz's head. Momentarily breathless, Liz was riveted by the reflection of her former self. Lord, how she missed those unmanageable curls.

"You like it?" her mother asked. "I think it's quite attractive."

"I love it, Mom. But this wig is much too expensive. I probably wouldn't wear it more than this once."

"We'll take it." Barbara motioned to the sales clerk and followed her to the register. They dodged efforts to be sold adhesive, tape, and an assortment of other accessories. Barbara pulled out her credit card. The saleswoman then offered the name of a hair salon close by that would fit the wig and style it. Over Liz's unheeded objections, she found herself draped in a plastic cape in front of an unflattering full-length mirror while her mother and the hair stylist discussed various options. Afterwards, they had lunch and then set off to get manicures. It was 3:20 p.m. before they headed back to the hotel. For the first time in months Liz felt beautiful. How could hair and nails carry such a wallop?

*****

"Mom," Liz said as they drove back over the Cooper River Bridge, "Are there times that you weren't truthful with Dad?"

Barbara looked at her daughter. "What kind of *times* do you mean?"

"Well, times when you've done something or learned about something you didn't share."

"Shoot, he doesn't know diddle squat about most of the *somethings* I do. If we shared every thought we had during the day, we'd both die of boredom."

When Liz didn't respond after a few moments, her mother broke the silence. "But you're not just talking about everyday *somethings*, are you?"

"No, this is a pretty big deal."

"From the past or present? Generally, my advice is to let the past stay in the past. Can't do anything to change it, so let it be."

Liz thought before she spoke. "It's something from the past that affects the present."

"Are people involved other than you and Chase?"

"Yes, quite a few."

"Will this shared truth result in someone getting hurt?"

"Quite possibly. It might also result in someone being healed."

Barbara looked back over the river. "How did you stumble upon this truth, anyway?"

"At work."

"Are you bound by confidentiality?"

"Yes."

"Then you have no choice. The decision has been made for you."

"I know."

"Life gets complicated, doesn't it?"

CHAPTER THIRTY-THREE

The wedding came straight out of the pages of *Bride* magazine. Whether or not mayhem reigned in the bridesmaids' quarters or the mind of the mother-of-the bride, it appeared to be the wedding of every girl's dreams. Estelle emerged as an adorable flower girl and she shyly dropped lavender rose petals down the white tapestry that covered the main aisle. Her younger brother, Stin, accompanied Evan, who carried the ring as if he held the British Royal Crown. Both dressed in pint-size tuxedos, smiles followed them down the aisle. One top button on Evan's shirt had come undone, revealing a slight burst of a blue Tar Heel T-shirt underneath his tie. Liz imagined she was the only one who noticed.

The nine bridesmaids each floated down the aisle in whimsical lavender dresses that danced around their slim figures like a gentle breath of summer. Their long hair, adorned with strands of violets, fell loosely over their shoulders.

The groomsmen waited at the altar: confident, handsome, each in command of his own corner of the world. It could have been a movie. Nat stood at the center in front of the altar with Chase as his best man. Adam stood next to Chase and Nicholas stood on the end of the line of six fraternity brothers, taking his role in this drama very seriously. He quite liked the tuxedo look.

For the first time all weekend Liz felt equal to any woman there. Her dress fit perfectly and the wig gave her a new level of confidence. She sat next to Louise Lloyd with her mom and dad, Grandma and Grandpa Hoole, and the Lloyd parents in Pew #43. As predicted, Grandpa wore a suit with an open collared white shirt, no tie, and Grandma had on a black skirt and sweater with an off-white blouse. Their attire attracted no attention. Nobody cared.

Pew #43 was rather famous in the history of Charleston. It had been enlarged and squared off with seats stretching three-quarters of the way around. Originally built for George Washington's visit on May 8, 1791, it accommodated Robert E. Lee seventy years later. The pew was directly opposite the enormous pulpit that brought the focus to the front quarter of the church. The obvious disadvantage would be that anyone sitting on the right side of the church behind the pulpit was unable to see the front altar. Thus, all the parents and grandparents of the bride and groom sat together in the one enlarged pew, as was the custom.

The steeple bells struck 7:00. Two trumpet volleys announced the arrival of the bride as Alexandra Louise Lloyd entered on her father's arm to the organist's rendition of "Rondeau" by Mouret. Mrs. Lloyd stood. The congregation followed her lead.

The bride was radiant. Her father seemed a bit pale. Liz fantasized that he had just done the mathematical calculations of what this elaborate affair cost him. More likely, however, age had tapped him on the shoulder and reminded him that this lovely young woman had been but an infant in his arms a short time ago.

The bride looked like an angel. Tiny pearl beads in the veil reflected the light and danced over her head and bare shoulders like fairy dust. A continuation of beaded work across the back of the dress and down the bridal train accentuated the image of a princess. While Liz had never paid much attention to fashion, she fully appreciated the beauty and poise of her soon-to-be daughter-in-law. Lexa held her head high. Her posture was perfect. She smiled with genuine warmth in recognition of friends and family from one side of the church to the other. Her father escorted her to the front of the altar where they stopped, with her on his left, and Nat on his right.

"Dearly beloved, we are gathered here today . . ." began the priest as Daniel Lloyd stood with his powerful shoulders like a stone wall between the couple. After a prayer, the priest began a short homily on the sanctity of marriage.

Daniel was immobile.

"And who giveth this woman for marriage?"

There was a long pause before Daniel Lloyd said, "Her mother and I." The priest nodded for him to take his seat, but Lexa's father remained planted in place. The priest looked momentarily confused. His eyes beckoned for Lexa's father to join the congregation. Daniel did not respond. After a second futile attempt to unhinge him with a slight gesture of the hand, the priest asked that everyone bow their heads in prayer.

Someone began to sniffle near the altar. At first Liz assumed that it might be the maid-of-honor, or even the bride herself, but the sniffling soon turned into sobs. Liz glanced over at Louise. Louise Lloyd scanned the crowd, too, first in the direction of the grandparents, and then around the church.

As eyes combed the pews a small voice began to quiver softly. Then, as if her heart would break: "I don't want anyone to give me away. I want to stay with my mommy and daddy." Estelle, the flower girl, was crumbling. She held her basket of rose petals precariously in one hand as she tried to wipe her nose and eyes with the other. It was then that Daniel Lloyd broke rank and on bended knee crouched next to her.

"It's all right, honey. Nobody really gives you away. You always have your mommy and daddy." He offered the child his hand and walked her back to where Sophie and Jack sat. Then the omnipotent father-of-the-bride slipped into Pew #43, sat, and melted like ice in a warm glass of tea as manly tears began to roll down his thick craggy cheeks. Liz fumbled in her purse and found her handkerchief.

*****

The Mills House, hardly more than a block from the church, provided the perfect venue for the reception. At 10:00 p.m., Grandpa and

Grandma Hoole took the two tired boys by their hands and offered to take them upstairs. "You two take your time," Grandpa said. "Euphrasia can go ahead to our room and if I'm asleep when you come in, just wake me." Chase gave him their extra room key and thanked them.

By midnight, most of the older guests had left, and those who remained on the dance floor were whirling to rhythms that challenged the over-forty crowd. Chase struggled with the change in tempo. Liz was ready to leave. They slipped out of the ballroom and into the hallway leading to the elevators. Liz laced her fingers into Chase's hand.

"You look beautiful," Chase said.

"Thank you," she said, grateful to hear once again the tenderness in his voice.

Chase slipped the key card into their room lock. Grandpa Hoole lay awake on top of the bedspread opposite the two boys. He roused and sat up as they walked into the room.

"Did you get some rest?" Chase asked.

"I'm fine," Grandpa said. "The boys went right to sleep. Just been lying here thinking."

"Well, let's get you back to your room. We hope to get off tomorrow around noon. Plan to eat a big breakfast," Chase said.

"Listen," Grandpa said, his voice a bit strained. "Perhaps you and I could drive back in one of the cars alone?" He glanced over at Liz. "Maybe Liz would take Grandma and the boys with her?"

"We could do that," Chase said.

"I have something I need to tell you," Grandpa said. He lowered his head and moved towards the door. "I think just the two of us in the car together might help."

"Okay, Dad," Chase said, and turned to look at Liz after his father left. Liz held his stare. Without speaking they both knew what Grandpa needed to say in the confines of a car where neither could walk away from the truth.

CHAPTER THIRTY-FOUR

It was a long drive home, much of it in silence. Chase and Grandpa Hoole followed Liz and Grandma on I-95 to Florence. There Liz pulled off to get the boys hamburgers at a drive-thru, but Chase passed the exit and kept going.

"What I wouldn't give for a sweet potato," Grandma mourned. "It's been three days." Grandma Hoole had become an ardent believer in the value of sweet potatoes. Long ago she came to the conclusion that sweet potatoes far surpassed the noble apple as the real source of health and longevity. She and Grandpa ate them religiously at lunch and dinner and there were always cold sweet potatoes in her refrigerator for snacks.

"Do you know what it is?" Grandma Hoole asked.

"What?"

"You know, what Grandpa wants to tell Chase?"

"I'm not sure," Liz said, which was the truth.

"Nathan's been brooding for quite a while. I hope Chase can help him work through whatever is bothering him."

"He's been brooding?"

"He's a very private man and doesn't often voice his personal feelings, but I know. He's become quite involved in this thing with Maggie, going all the way to Durham to give blood. When that boy they called Frog-whatever said at the rehearsal dinner that you asked young Nat to go and give blood, I thought maybe you asked Grandpa, too. Did you?"

"Yes, Grandma, I did."

"Why?"

"Well, I've asked everybody," Liz said, stumbling a bit over her words. She couldn't lie to Grandma. She just couldn't. "You know how worried I am for Maggie."

Grandma Hoole looked out the window. "You didn't ask me."

Liz's mind went blank; she had no response. She could neither lie nor tell the truth. She said nothing, and wondered again when silence justified the absence of truth?

After hamburgers the boys began to doze on and off. "That wedding ended up costing quite a lot, don't you think?" Grandma said.

"Yes, it did."

"I can only imagine what else the same money could have done."

"I'm sure there are lots of things. But in the meantime, the celebration provided salaries for a whole lot of people who made the dresses, cooked and served the food, played the music, and cleaned the hotel rooms. It brought people from far away together for a short period of time to laugh and remember to love one another. Those people are all grateful someone wanted to spend money on a wedding,"

"I guess so," Grandma said, but couldn't keep from adding, "I think it would have been just as nice without the alcohol."

Liz wanted more than ever to change the subject from money and Grandpa's brooding. "Grandma, what was Grandpa like when you met him?"

Grandma's thin lips relaxed in reflection. "A serious young man, very serious."

"Not the party type?" Liz joked, never having seen either Grandpa or Grandma do more than to blow out some candles on a cake, and find enjoyment in the faces of their grandchildren.

"Well, we attended Guilford, after all, and we are considered *slow* Quakers from the old school. But I know Guilford has made some major concessions, and well, I won't even mention what I've heard about parties these days." She raised one eyebrow and looked at Liz out of the corner of her eye.

"How did you two meet?"

"In an accounting class. He was the star student."

"I didn't think Quaker schools recognized star students. Not wanting to encourage gains through competition, as Adam phrased it."

"No, Adam is right. They don't. He was a star to me though."

"Why was that?"

"He was so intense; so serious, studying all the time or working. He had put his tuition together through a bunch of scholarships and part-time jobs. It was hard for me to find any spare time in his schedule to flirt with him."

"Why, Grandma Hoole. You, a flirt? I would have never guessed."

"I had to do something to get his attention."

"What finally won him over?"

"I learned how to make him laugh. You would have thought he'd never had a day of joy in his life. Then one day we started to laugh. It was over something silly. I remember exactly. I had made him some brownies and taken them to the men's hall where he lived. When he came down and ate one, he tried to be very polite, but it was obvious he didn't like them. I took a taste and realized I'd forgotten to put any sugar in them. We started to laugh." Grandma's face brightened and her eyes lit up.

She continued, "Then several of the other men from his hall came out and made a fuss about Nathan getting brownies and not sharing them. So Nathan told them his best girl had made them, and he hoped they'd enjoy them. When he offered them the plate, they grabbed up those brownies like dollar bills. Each of them ate their brownie and told me how wonderful they tasted, though their expressions told me otherwise. When they left, Nathan and I fell to the ground in laughter. I think he even used the example for a paper he wrote in ethics class on the Quaker testimony of truth. He said it got quite a discussion going."

"But then you dropped out of college?"

"He had called me his best girl. Nathan didn't lie. I knew we would get married. Once we'd made the decision, we couldn't wait. It's not like young people today. They go ahead and live together for two or three years and then they get married. We wanted to be together, so we got married."

She leaned her head back on the car seat and continued to reminisce. "Had a small Quaker wedding. My parents came. Nathan's parents came. People brought food. I remember a beautiful June day."

"You could have still kept up with your studies, though."

"One of us had to work. Nathan's education was the most important. We always figured I could go back once he had his degree. I got a job as a secretary for a bookkeeping firm and we made do. When Nathan finished a year later they offered him a job as a bookkeeper. We were careful with our money and I planned to start school in the fall and then I got pregnant with Chase. I stopped working after he was born."

"Why did you move back to Cedar Branch?"

Grandma paused and gave a deep sigh. "I really thought we had no choice. We needed to help out his mother after his father died. Nathan seemed terribly reluctant. There was something in Cedar Branch he didn't want to come home to. I learned not to ask too many questions. It only drove him deep into himself."

"Did he ever tell you what it was?"

"No. He struggled with it . . . really struggled. I finally told him that there was nothing in his past that I needed to know. I thought maybe it had to do with another romance, or maybe something between his mom and dad. But I didn't care. We had made our vows to one another and once we did that, I knew he'd never break them. We belonged to each other. What was past could stay in the past."

Liz kept her eyes on the road and wished with all her heart that's what would happen.

"Nathan's struggle is one between himself and God," Grandma continued, "and I believed that the two of them would reach consensus. For much of his life, I think he has."

She turned and looked at Liz. "Having you and Chase and the boys close by has meant so much to him. But then something stirs him every now and then, and he's lost again to that inner struggle."

Liz didn't say anything for a bit. The boys were starting to fidget with one another in the backseat. "What finally persuaded you two that this was where you belonged?"

"His mother. One day when we called her on the phone, she became very upset, and sounded confused. His Uncle Charles called to say that a neighbor found her walking along the road and she didn't know how to get home. We felt like she couldn't live alone any longer. So here we are today in the very house where Nathan and his father grew up. I don't regret that," Grandma said. "The accounting office turned out well. It's been a good life."

"You know he tells everyone he never could have done that without you," Liz said.

"That's nice to hear." Grandma seemed pleased.

They pulled off I-95 onto the two-lane road that took them to Cedar Branch and the boys began to doze again.

"I'm surprised Grandpa didn't go back into farming, like his dad," Liz said after they'd gone a few more miles.

"We'd have never made any money at farming. His Uncle Charles wanted him to join the two farms and raise more horses, but Nathan dismissed the idea immediately."

"Really?"

"Nope, it was always the numbers. Nathan liked to be able to work alone. He could run the numbers in his head. Didn't even need to put them on paper, although, of course he did anyway. I don't think we could have possibly done as well in farming."

"You've both been very generous. Cedar Branch is lucky to have you there."

"Nathan believes that you have a responsibility to invest back into the community that invests in you. If we make money from the people or the land in Cedar Branch, he insisted that we not take that money and spend it in a city someplace else. Small towns need people to invest in things closest to their homes."

*****

Liz pulled into the drive at Grandpa and Grandma's and put the car in park. When they walked into the back door they saw Grandpa sitting at the kitchen table. He barely acknowledged either of them.

"Nathan, what in the world is wrong?" Grandma Hoole asked. A single plug-in swag light with a simple white shade cast a shadow over his face. It made his lips look blue and his skin gray. Had he been lying on the floor Liz would have immediately thought he'd had a heart attack.

"I'm tired, that's all," he said wearily. "Wanted to wait up for you and know everyone got home safe."

"You and Chase didn't think about waiting up for us back there." Grandma made a gesture to the outside road. "You just disappeared up the highway."

"I'm sorry," Grandpa said without further explanation.

"It wasn't a problem, Grandpa. We did fine," Liz said. "Can I do anything else for you two before I go home?"

"No, dear," Grandma Hoole said. "I'll just have a sweet potato, and then I'm going right to bed. It's been quite a weekend, though. We both thank you for all the driving you did."

"Nathan?" Grandma gestured as she opened the refrigerator door and pulled out a pottery bowl with four large sweet potatoes. "It'd make you feel better."

"I think not, Euphrasia," he said.

Liz leaned down to give him a kiss on the cheek. The boys stood in the doorway as a reminder that they were both tired and ready for bed. Grandpa looked over and beckoned them nearer. "Come here, you two. Give your old grandpa a kiss before you go." They each ran over and let him embrace them in a bear hug. He released them and then looked up at Liz. "Thank you for everything."

They scrambled back into the car and drove back to their house where all of the lights were on. As the car pulled in, Chase immediately came out the door and without a word began to unload the luggage. He did it with such regimentation that Liz found it disconcerting. The boys climbed out and headed into their bedroom. Liz searched Chase's face for anything.

"So," she finally said, "are we going to talk?"

"Not now, Liz. Just go on to bed."

Liz tucked the boys in and took a shower. Then she lay exhausted and wide awake. Sleep would not come. Finally at two in the morning she climbed out of bed and put on her bathrobe. Chase sat on the porch swing. She grabbed an extra blanket and joined him. He took the blanket and wrapped it around himself.

"I'm sorry I couldn't tell you, Chase," she said.

"I understand."

"I can't sleep."

"How did you find out?" Chase asked.

"Went to check Maggie's blood type and realized it wasn't the same as her father's. Then Grandpa came to talk to me. He wanted to be a bone marrow donor."

Chase nodded his head, "Figures."

"Do you think we can keep this within the family?"

"Probably not."

"Who'll get hurt?"

"Well," Chase took a deep breath, looked over at Liz and raised his eyebrows. "Of course Dad's worried about Mom and you and me and the meeting. And then there's Maggie."

"Oh, Lord, Chase, I don't want Maggie to know."

He tilted his head and sighed. ". . . And the reputation of the Judge." Chase stopped, raised the palm of his hands to his forehead as though he couldn't stop the thoughts that now swirled. "That's just for starters. We haven't even considered the Perrys and what might happen in the black community."

"What do you mean?"

"The lynching of Isaac Perry . . . it's a deep wound. There's going to be some reaction, possibly very angry reaction. People will question whether or not the lynching could have been avoided or at the very least, the Perry family saved from their suffering if Grandpa had stepped forward."

Liz stared at Chase in disbelief. "Oh, Chase, surely not, not after all these years, not after all the good Grandpa has done in this community. People can't possibly demonize him."

Chase shook his head and motioned to the blanket. "Come over here," he said. Liz slipped in under the blanket next to him as he wrapped his arms around her.

"The black community may boycott the pharmacy."

"What?" The thought had never crossed her mind.

"Economic reprisal. It's been done in the past. That would be two-thirds of our business. We'd go under in a few months, weeks even."

"I just can't believe that. Is Grandpa concerned about that?"

"He is."

"What did you tell him?"

"I told him we'd cross that bridge when we came to it. For now we'd just take one step at a time. We've agreed to meet with the elders at meeting first."

"Grandpa *is* an elder," Liz said.

"I know," Chase said. "I imagine it's the first time in the history of our meeting that an elder will be eldered."

"What do you think they will say?"

"I don't know. They've all looked to Dad for leadership in the past. This will be hard for them, but they will seek clearness and most important, I think they will look for a way to do what is right for those who have suffered."

"You don't think they would ever disown him from the meeting, do you?"

"No," Chase said. "I haven't heard of that happening in decades."

Liz said nothing, but wrapped her arms tightly around Chase. She worried about Grandpa and Grandma and she worried about Maggie. How on earth would Maggie feel if she learned that the Judge was not her real father? And then, there was LuAnne; Maggie and LuAnne were friends. They could talk this through—couldn't they?

Off in the distance a faint blue light moved through the swamp. Liz followed its slow progression and finally said, "Chase?"

"I see it," he said. "Swamp gas—that's all."

CHAPTER THIRTY-FIVE

Liz pulled into the front of The Quaker Café dog tired from the week-end. But she'd promised Miss Ellie that as soon as she got back from the wedding they'd go to see Maggie together. Miss Ellie wore a jaunty wool scarf and a teal blue hat to match her slacks. Liz had on slacks and a slipover sweater with her UNC baseball cap. Miss Ellie dressed to visit. Liz dressed to work. "Don't you look nice," Liz said as Miss Ellie eased into the car.

"You know," Miss Ellie said, "the Judge would never let Maggie come to the café in shorts or jeans when she was little."

"Really?" Liz said.

"That's the honest truth. He considered it *going to town,* even though it's just a few blocks away, and he always insisted she dress appropriately when she came with him for a meal."

"Times have changed," Liz said, becoming more self-conscious of her own clothes. After all, they were off to Durham, the big city.

"They certainly have. Why these days, you wouldn't know some-times whether people were going to town or headed for a beach party."

"Keeps things from getting boring."

"Well, it's a new day, a new way. People have different expectations," Miss Ellie said. "But, tell me about the wedding."

"It was wonderful, Miss Ellie. It really was. I'm sorry you couldn't be there."

"I want to send something to Nat and Lexa, maybe something for the kitchen. I thought perhaps some biscuit sheets?"

"I'm sure they'd appreciate that," Liz said, as she wondered whether Lexa had ever cooked a biscuit in her life. She knew that Nat hadn't. She didn't even cook them, herself, anymore. The biscuits of choice were always Miss Ellie's.

They discussed the wedding as Liz drove. She told Miss Ellie about her parents and the wig, the rehearsal party at Folly Beach, Estelle's tears at the wedding, and the reception. She didn't mention Frogbelly's toast or the unraveling confessions of Grandpa Hoole. Liz hoped against hope that somehow all of that might remain a private family matter in a small town where personal becomes public overnight.

"How's Maggie? Have you talked to Billie?" Miss Ellie asked.

"Talked to her this morning. Maggie's fair, getting better. LuAnne went with her to Durham over the weekend and they had a good visit."

"I want to tell her some things today, if she's up for it . . . some things about her daddy. I've decided she should know," Miss Ellie said. "But I hope what we share at the hospital can remain just with the three of us."

The burden of secrets weighed heavily on Liz. She didn't wish to be trusted with any other personal history. "Miss Ellie, I would be happy to leave the room while you talk with her. If what you have to say is something that you've thought important enough to keep to yourself, there's no reason I should know."

"Actually, I think I'd like for you to be there, just in case."

"Just in case what, exactly?"

"Just in case she gets upset; you might know better how to handle it."

Becoming even more uncomfortable, Liz said, "Miss Ellie, if you think what you want to tell her might upset her, perhaps you shouldn't tell her now."

"If not now, when?"

"When she's better."

"What if she doesn't get better?"

Liz turned to Miss Ellie with a look of complete surprise. "Don't say that. She's got to get better." Unexpected urgency crept into her voice.

Liz, better than most people, knew what Maggie faced. She knew the odds, but somehow Maggie had always come out on top; she refused to believe she wouldn't do so again.

Miss Ellie looked away from her, aware that she'd hit a nerve. Maggie's health was an ongoing topic in The Quaker Café. Daily Miss Ellie listened to people recount stories of someone they knew who had cancer. Miss Ellie wanted to return from the hospital with a good report, but at the same time she was realistic. Life has a way of forcing you to consider all the alternatives.

*****

They put on the gowns and masks before they went into Maggie's room. Despite Miss Ellie's attention to dress, she was transformed into just another caregiver on the floor. Maggie was sitting up in a chair and looked at her hard before she let out a long sigh and reached out her hand. Miss Ellie took it and immediately hugged her.

For the first hour they talked about the wedding while Liz rearranged the pillows, and then sat on the floor and rubbed Maggie's feet.

"Did you wear my necklace?" Maggie asked.

"I did," Liz replied. "It's beautiful. Lots of people commented on it."

"I want you to keep it," Maggie said. "I want Billie to have something, too. Miss Ellie, you heard me say that. I want Liz to have that necklace."

"I heard you, dear," Miss Ellie said. "She certainly deserves it."

Liz objected, but that discussion seemed finished.

Miss Ellie started to talk . . . brought regards and well-wishes from the denizens of the café. Frank Busby was the same as ever. Doc Withers said there'd been a spike in rabies, mostly among raccoons. Henry hoped the rain would hold off so they could turn the peanuts and let them get good and dry.

Liz sensed when Miss Ellie started to look for an opening to shift the conversation. Finally . . . "Maggie, did you know that your father and I were high school sweethearts?"

"I think I knew that, Miss Ellie. He told me several times that you had always been one of the special people in his life, going way back."

"He asked me to marry him."

"Did he really? I didn't know that. Why didn't you?"

"Well, we were in high school . . . too young. By the time I turned eighteen he had gone to college."

"You could have waited for him," Maggie said.

"Well, yes, I could have, but your grandparents didn't really think I was a good match. I knew that all along."

"Their loss." Maggie squeezed Miss Ellie's hand.

Miss Ellie turned to face Maggie more directly and cupped Maggie's hand with both of hers. "Then Walter Cartwright came along. He lived down in The Neck and went to school in the next county. Captain of their football team . . . fine looking. I always loved the dimple in his chin. Do you remember that?"

"Sure I do. He was a sweetheart."

"His mother always told him that dimple was where God reached down and touched him and said, *This one is special*. She was right. I fell in love with him."

"You found yourself a good husband," Maggie said.

"We got married, had the two girls. I waited tables at the café. Walter, he worked as a mechanic down in The Neck. Corbett was gallivanting around the country, going to law school. I'd hear stories about him and wondered sometimes what my life might have been like if I'd married Corbett Kendall." Miss Ellie paused.

"A lot different," Maggie said.

"Who knows? When he brought home that delicate little thing from New Orleans, she was hardly bigger than a soda cracker. She no more belonged in Cedar Branch than a fleet of limousines, but your father, he couldn't see that. He was busy over in Raleigh trying to be somebody."

Maggie looked slightly offended, but Miss Ellie didn't notice. She kept talking. "I'd look at that pathetic little wife of his and feel sorry for her. There wasn't anything in our town for her." Miss Ellie slowed down and rubbed Maggie's hand. "Can I get you something to drink or a snack, maybe?"

"No, Miss Ellie. You just keep talking. I like your stories."

"Some of them aren't easy to tell. There was that terrible business with Isaac Perry and afterwards your mother dying and all. Our town had some bad times and no one knew exactly how things would end up."

"I don't think it ever ends," Maggie said. "People bury the past inside them and just let it fester. It's like mildew. You think you've gotten rid of it, and then the weather gets hot and sweaty. Overnight the fungus takes over."

Miss Ellie cleared her throat. "I want to tell you something about your father I don't expect you know."

"I have a feeling there's a lot I don't know."

"The money in the will . . ."

Maggie interrupted her, "I know, Miss Ellie, and I hope you don't think I resent that for a minute. You were probably the closest friend my father ever had."

Maggie pressed Miss Ellie's hand to her cheek and then looked her squarely in the eyes. "As soon as the courts release the will from probate, you'll have a check. I hope you retire and buy some nice things for yourself."

"I wanted to explain that to you," Miss Ellie said, stress apparent in her voice.

"You don't owe me any explanations."

Liz rose from her chair. "I'll just slip out to the waiting room for a bit, get a Coke."

"No," Miss Ellie insisted. "Liz, please stay. I want you to stay."

"The money isn't for me," Miss Ellie said. "It's for my children. Your father left me a lump sum, specifically for my boy, Josh, but I plan to divide it between Josh and his two sisters."

Maggie adjusted her pillow and sat up a little straighter in the chair. "Why for Josh?"

Miss Ellie bent her head without speaking for what seemed like a long time. Finally she looked back at Maggie. "Josh is his son."

Maggie stiffened immediately, her eyes wide open. "His son? My daddy's son?"

Miss Ellie nodded her head. Maggie shut her eyes and took a deep breath. The room was silent.

A nurse slipped in to change the IV drip. "Everybody doing okay?" she said in a cheery voice. She looked at Maggie and saw her eyes shut and whispered. "Sorry, didn't realize she was asleep."

When the nurse left the room, Maggie spoke without opening her eyes. "I have a brother? Wow." She blew out a long breath.

"Josh is your half brother." Miss Ellie pulled a tissue from the side table next to Maggie's bed and wiped away a tear.

"Why didn't anyone tell me?"

"We really weren't even sure, Maggie. It was just one night after your mother died. Walter and I were deep in debt, and he had become very depressed. Without telling him, I went to your father after my shift at the café to ask to borrow some money."

Ellie stopped and blushed. "I'm ashamed to even say this; I started to cry. He wrapped his arms around me. Suddenly, we were in high school again . . . just him and me. Life was a lark when we were young. Your father made everything look so easy. We ended up in bed that night. When I left he gave me a check."

"Oh, Miss Ellie," Maggie reached over and put her other hand on top of Ellie's. "He loved you. You do know that, don't you?"

"I do know that, but the next morning I felt so miserable, so cheap. Corbett and I were always better friends than lovers. I tore up the check. I told him that I loved Walter and we would work out our money problems on our own."

"I'm sure he felt badly, too," Maggie said.

"He did. He apologized. Things were very strained between us for a while, but it's a small town. In small towns there are a lot of things that happen behind closed doors. In the morning you still have to walk back onto the street and look your neighbor in the eye. Life goes on."

"Did Walter ever know?"

"No, he didn't," Miss Ellie said. "I'm sure he didn't because a month later Corbett went to Walter and told him he thought Cedar Branch needed its own auto repair shop. He asked Walter if he'd consider leaving the shop in The Neck and managing a new one if the Kendalls provided the capital. Walter considered your dad a saint. He never stopped talking about the big break we got. I guess the rest is history. We did well. Eventually Walter and I bought the shop from your dad."

"And Josh?" Maggie asked.

"Josh," Ellie smiled and shook her head. "Who would have ever believed? One night? When I got pregnant, I was sure the baby was Walter's. He adored that child. You and Josh used to play together at the café. You remember?"

"Sure, I remember. He and your two girls were in and out all the time, between the café and the repair shop. Then he left for boarding school and hardly ever came home."

"Yes, Corbett talked to Josh at the café about going away to school and encouraged him to apply. He'd tell Josh he could get a scholarship. He told him that so much we all believed him." Ellie looked over at me. "Reckon I could get a soda somewhere?"

"Just down the hall, Miss Ellie. I'll go get you one," Liz said.

"A Coke would be good, thanks."

When Liz returned she handed Miss Ellie her Coke and sat down with one of her own.

"Walter didn't want Josh to leave, but he admired your father and thought a prep school might give Josh a leg-up in the world, so he tried not to discourage him. Then lo and behold, when Josh turned fourteen, he applied to boarding school and got a full scholarship."

"Surprise, surprise," Maggie said.

"Of course, I suspected your father paid the tuition, but Walter and Josh didn't know otherwise. Josh loved Woodberry. He stayed there year round, helped at their camp or in the admissions office in the summers. We hardly ever saw him in Cedar Branch again. We'd go up once a year for homecoming. Your dad would drop by when he had a meeting up that way and take him out to dinner. Josh loved that."

"And then he went to St. Mary's College in Maryland?" Maggie said.

"You knew that?" Miss Ellie said.

"I saw the invoices in the files, but I hadn't put it together."

"When we drove him up to Maryland the first year, I watched him hobnob so casual with the other boys and throw his head back and laugh like your father. What Corbett realized when Josh was fourteen, I knew for sure when he was eighteen. Josh was a Kendall."

Maggie closed her eyes again and squeezed Miss Ellie's hand. "I think I need to get back in bed, now," she said. Liz went through the process of helping Maggie move from the chair to the bed and repositioned the pillows.

When she was finally settled, she asked, "Why are you telling me, Miss Ellie?"

"The will, and now with this bone marrow thing . . ."

"Does Josh know?"

"He didn't know up until now, which is why I'm telling you. I called and asked him to give blood to see if he might be a match for you as a donor. He couldn't understand why I became so insistent. Finally I told him."

"How does he feel about it?" Maggie asked.

"He's confused right now . . . needs to work it through."

Maggie seemed uncertain. "Thank him for me, will you?"

"I'll tell him."

"Would he like to talk?"

"Would you?"

"I guess so. Why didn't my father name him in his will?"

"I asked your father not to, Maggie. We planned for me to pass the money on to Josh at my death, but I have decided I can't give something to Josh without giving equally to each of my girls. I didn't want the girls to know that Josh had a different father. That's probably a pipe dream now. No telling how long before the entire town knows."

"And you weren't going to ever tell Josh?"

"No, I wasn't. Corbett left that decision up to me."

"Miss Ellie," Maggie said with a certainty that surprised Liz. "Josh needed to know. I needed to know. Still, I'm glad Walter's no longer living."

"Maggie, if Walter were living I never would have said the first word."

CHAPTER THIRTY-SIX

As long as Liz had been in Cedar Branch, all visitors who came to Grandpa and Grandma's house entered through the back door and sat in the den. The two large recliners signaled a passage of Quaker custom from the simple to the more comfortable. The living room was rarely used except at Thanksgiving and Christmas. A dark room with heavy curtains to hold the heat in winter, it still had most of the original furniture from Grandpa's youth. Liz expected that Grandma might redecorate at some point before she realized that redecorating constituted frivolity. When what one has is adequate, why should anyone want more? The two rooms symbolized the past and the present.

Grandma Hoole met Chase and Liz at the back door. "Thank you for coming," she said. "He's in the living room. Last night we talked for hours. I've asked Anna Reed to join us."

"Anna Reed?" Liz asked.

"I thought it would be good to have an elder here."

"Does he want her here?" Chase asked.

"He does. He thinks the time has come to speak to the elders and we agreed she'd give the best counsel. She'll be honest but have compassion."

"What do you want us to do, Mom?" Chase seemed hesitant.

"Your presence is all I ask. He needs you for support."

It was not without irony that Grandpa had chosen the living room to sequester himself. A glass of untouched orange juice sat on the side table. The curtains were drawn and a small desk lamp filled the room with shadows. Liz immediately wanted to push open the curtains and let in more light, but there was no light outside at this hour. Grandpa stared into a corner, a man consumed by the guilt he'd carried for fifty-six years. Liz's heart broke knowing the pain he undoubtedly felt.

Chase pulled a straight-back chair closer to the sofa. Liz did likewise and Grandma Hoole sat down on the couch next to her husband of fifty years. She had thought she knew everything she needed to know about the man she'd married. Apparently, what she knew wasn't enough. Grandpa looked up but said nothing.

"Nathan," Grandma said gently. "Chase and Liz are here."

"And Anna?" he asked.

"She's on her way."

As Grandma spoke Liz realized how much Grandpa leaned on her. In her mind Liz had chided him for not being a more assertive partner in their marriage. She realized now that Grandma's clearness of purpose had given him the strength he needed.

"Dad," Chase began softly. "We're going to work through this together."

"I have spent my life trying to right the wrong I did so many years ago, but I'm not sure that redemption is even a possibility anymore," Grandpa said. "I stayed silent far too long."

"Nathan," Euphrasia said gently. "Leave it in the hands of God. Even King David was forgiven. You are no less than he."

A slight tapping at the back door told them Anna had arrived. Grandma rose to let her in. One year older than Grandpa, Anna grew up in Cedar Branch as a birthright Quaker; born into a family of Quakers. Their parents had been second cousins. She had outlived her husband and two children, who had both died of cystic fibrosis. Liz had a great deal of admiration for the fact that Anna never complained, but always found God in her life and expressed appreciation for all that she had received.

Anna entered the room, leaning heavily on a cane that made her instantly recognizable throughout the town. Her decisive use of her crutch became legendary. She used it to point at what she wanted, motivate those moving a bit too slowly, and stop traffic when she ventured across the road.

"Nathan," she said as Grandpa rose. They exchanged an embrace. Anna gave each person a hug before settling into a straightback chair that Chase offered her.

Anna slipped into the familiar plain language using *thee* and *thy* she and Grandpa had been raised speaking. The usage had emphasized equality in place of social distinctions but had fallen away among most people with their parents' generation. While it had confused Liz at first, she came to appreciate the usage as a sign of affection and an affirmation among the elders who still spoke it.

"Euphrasia tells me thee is deeply troubled."

"I am," Grandpa said, his eyes lowered.

"Tell me thy story." Anna reached out and placed one of her hands over his. The arthritis was visible in her fingers and nested in her back, yet her eyes and mind remained as clear as a fresh blanket of snow. She listened.

Grandpa told the story he had told Liz and then Chase and finally Euphrasia, each separately. This time there were no tears, only a sense of release as it poured out like water through a canyon.

"And thee never sought counsel from the elders?" Anna asked softly.

"I feared I would be read out of meeting," Grandpa said. Anna nodded in understanding.

"And thy parents?" she asked.

"I spoke with my father, only after I could no longer bear my pain alone."

There was silence. For Liz this was the first time she had heard Grandpa reference his father.

"What did thy father say?" Anna asked.

"He grieved deeply. I shall never forget the pain I inflicted upon him, as I know he suffered throughout the remainder of his life. After seeking clearness from the Lord, he and I went to the Sheriff."

Anna paused.

"Did thee tell the Sheriff of thy affair?" Anna asked.

"I did. I told him I had been with Sarah Kendall when Isaac came in to help her unsaddle her horse. I told him I did not believe that Isaac had done anything wrong. I confessed I ran from the barn when Corbett Kendall arrived."

In Quaker fashion, Anna took time between each question for extended amounts of reflection. Such discussions were not to be rushed.

"What did the Sheriff say?" Anna asked.

"He became very agitated." Grandpa began to rub his forehead. "He asked if we intended to accuse men in the community of killing an innocent man. My father said if that be the truth then we would not argue it."

Grandpa now wrestled with his words knowing that herein lay another junction where he could have cleared the name of Isaac Perry. "Our challenge made the Sheriff extremely angry. He began to yell at me. *How quickly did I leave the barn? Was I in the barn when Corbett Kendall walked in? Did I see Isaac approach Sarah? Was I there when she pushed him? Did I know why she pushed him? Did I actually see the fight between Corbett and Isaac? Could I swear that Isaac did not hit Corbett? Why had I waited to come forward?*"

"After I answered each one of his questions as truthfully as I could, the Sheriff told us our accusations had no foundation. He warned us that if I were to testify that I had an affair with Corbett's wife, he was sure that Sarah would deny it. He claimed that Sarah had signed a written statement that Isaac had threatened her; and there was proof that Isaac had struck Corbett. They had all the evidence they needed. He advised us to cease any further accusations for fear of escalating the tension already dividing the town."

Grandpa stopped and took a deep breath. "I was stunned. *Sarah had said Isaac threatened her?* I couldn't believe that Isaac would raise a hand to hurt Sarah, or that she would accuse him of such an act. And then I had to question myself about whether she would deny the affair. The fact that she left town with Corbett was my answer."

Anna sat in reflection. No one else spoke.

"The elders, Nathan? Thee and thy father never went to the elders?"

"I did not." Grandpa shook his head. "My father told me he would speak with them, but I don't believe he ever did, for I am sure they would have called me to present myself, and I would have been denied my membership. Undoubtedly, my father wrestled with this untold truth the rest of his life. He compromised himself to protect me and to shield my mother from the heartbreak if I were disowned. That, too, haunts me."

Grandpa took a long deep breath. "I can never forgive myself for what I did to the Perry family. If I had been forthcoming, I am sure the Quaker meeting would have responded to the way the Perrys were shunned by the white community."

"We should have responded to their need, regardless," Anna said. "We also stand at fault." More silence. "What did thee do after that?"

"I worked on the farm planting through the spring, and in the summer my father told me he had arranged for me to go to Guilford College in the fall. I was so grateful to him; so relieved to leave. I honestly didn't want to ever return."

"But God wanted thee back here," Anna said.

"I guess He did."

"He gave thee Euphrasia to help thee weather thy storm," Anna added as she acknowledged Grandma with her eyes.

"He did, didn't He?" Grandpa looked across at Euphrasia with warmth. "She has been my blessing."

"Now," Anna said, changing her tone from one of inquiry to one of enactment. "What must thee do now?"

"My time has come to present myself to the elders," Grandpa said.

"Yes," Anna said. "We'll go to the elders, but thee must seek guidance from the Lord for redemption. We will stand in the light together and a way will open."

"I have tried to ease the pain and suffering, Anna," Grandpa said, "but to no avail."

"No, Nathan, thee hast tried to ease *thy* pain and suffering. Thy goal must be to ease the pain of others. That is not to say that thee has not been a generous and giving man, but thus far thy generosity has been an effort to rid thyself of guilt. First thee must own the past and truthfully acknowledge those who have suffered because of your failure to act. Only then shall thee be redeemed."

Euphrasia took his hand in hers. "All of these years we've stood in the light together. The Lord will not fail us now."

CHAPTER THIRTY-SEVEN

Never before in the history of their meeting had an elder been eldered. Never before had the elders had to address the consequences of a member failing to *speak truth to power*.

Grandpa Hoole sat with Euphrasia to his right and Chase and Liz to his left on one of the long pine benches in the meeting house. Four elders sat facing him on what was appropriately called the facing bench. Elevated slightly above the others, the bench was where the elders sat together in front of the body of silent worshipers each First Day as referenced by Quakers. For twenty-five years Grandpa had joined the elders on the facing bench. He had declined the meeting's bidding to become an elder for several years, professing his unworthiness, but after repeated encouragement from the members and his family, he had humbly accepted.

This evening, the elders would understand for the first time the reason for his reluctance.

Anna arrived early and greeted each member of the Hoole family with a hug. She had already met with the three other elders and discussed her conversation with Nathan so that individuals would have time to *hold him in the light* prior to their meeting. This was to be a meeting of counsel, not condemnation. Their task was to seek a peaceful path that would bring resolution and ideally, forgiveness.

Leland Slade sat to the right of Anna. Leland was a bachelor whose greatest love was the soil that permanently discolored his hands and nails. He spoke rarely, but with clearness if he chose to put his thoughts to words. He never sidestepped the hard decisions, or softened the truth.

Kate Pearson, the most recently appointed of the elders, brought with her the rare insight as the grandmother of three biracial children and the mother of an openly gay son. As a birthright Quaker who had lived her life in Cedar Branch, she had been challenged to broaden her acceptance of alternative lifestyles in a way that few of those in Cedar Branch had yet embraced.

Duncan Howell sat as the remaining elder. A slight man in statue with piercing blue eyes and thinning gray hair, he had spent his life as a math professor at Guilford College. He and his wife had retired to his home in Cedar Branch ten years earlier and had become a tremendous asset within the meeting. The meeting could always depend on Duncan for a deliberate, thoughtful approach to whatever task was at hand.

Once assembled, with no small talk as a distraction, the members present folded their hands, closed their eyes and began with silent prayer. There were no spoken words for at least fifteen minutes. Anna broke the silence.

"We are here this evening to seek clearness on how to respond to an injustice that happened in our community fifty-six years ago. Isaac Perry was falsely accused of an injustice and hanged."

Silence.

"The man was hanged. You can't change that," Leland said.

Silence.

"The injustice entails the fact that a member of our meeting may have been able to reverse that injustice had he come forward. A family has suffered irreparable damage," Anna said.

Silence.

"The family must be told the truth," Kate said.

Silence.

"There are ramifications that must be considered," Duncan spoke. "The victims are a black family. There is racial hostility that surrounded the event, and the black community never believed in the guilt of Isaac

Perry. From the beginning the incident increased racial tensions. I agree, the truth must be told, but we also need to do that in a way that creates a path to peace and not to violence of any kind."

Silence.

"Euphrasia and I have talked at length, and I regret that I was not able to trust in her sooner to discuss my transgressions. I am a weak man. As always, she gives me strength," Grandpa said. "We are willing to meet with the Perry family and discuss compensation."

Silence.

"While that is generous of thee, Nathan, I believe we must look beyond financial compensation," Anna said. "Money does not replace all that the family has suffered. Consider the pariahs that the Perry family became during those regretful years."

"Let us consider the need for the entire community to know the truth," Kate added. "Certainly it would be important to the Perrys that Isaac's innocence be proclaimed for all to hear. Let us lay a foundation to insure this will never happen again."

Silence.

"I remain concerned about how this discourse is to begin," Duncan said. "Who will start? To whom will it be told? We must take into consideration the fact that there may be outrage, cries for vindication, threats, and increased fractionalization as the white community retreats to claim ignorance, and the black community advances to assign guilt."

Silence.

"I believe that I should be the one who stands alone and accepts responsibility," Grandpa said. "It is I who am at fault. No other."

"We all stood silent," Kate said. "A lynching gang took justice into their own hands and was condoned by those in power. We, as a meeting, should have stood in the way of this atrocity. We failed to speak truth to power. If we had, perhaps you, Nathan, and your father, would have had the courage to step forward."

Silence.

"May I make a suggestion?" Liz said. She was tentative, as she was there by Grandpa's request and rarely had taken part in the meetings for business, much less any discussions among the elders.

"Of course," Anna encouraged her.

"I want to say how helpful Reverend Broadnax was as he assisted Maggie through the delicate process of planning her father's funeral. He is highly respected within the black community and he has worked with Grandpa Hoole and others within our meeting on the implementation of a number of community projects. Perhaps we should solicit his help in deciding how best to move forward."

Heads nodded. Silence returned.

"Can we reach consensus to discuss this issue with him?" Anna finally asked.

Heads nodded again.

Silence. No one spoke.

"If we have consensus, we shall proceed. Duncan, would you and Nathan arrange to meet with Reverend Broadnax and report back to the elders?"

"Before we break, may I raise one last concern?" Anna turned towards Grandpa. "Nathan, does thee plan to tell Maggie Kendall the truth? Perhaps she deserves to know before the others?"

"I do," said Grandpa. "As soon as she is well enough to hear it, I do."

Chapter Thirty-eight

"There's a problem, Liz." Billie was on the phone a few days later.

"What?"

"Maggie's got a fever. Dr. Rao says it's from an infection. He's started her on an antibiotic."

"How could that be?" Liz asked, as if she'd never been to nursing school. Hospital infections were one of the nightmares of the business. Buildings full of sick people with compromised immune systems and thousands of airborne germs. Gowns, gloves, endless lectures on sanitary precautions and still, 100,000 patients died in hospitals every year from infections they acquired while there. Liz quoted those statistics again and again to her own staff before each and every blood drive.

"Do you think we had anything to do with it?" Billie asked.

"No, I don't," Liz said. "You can't think like that. What else did Dr. Rao say?"

"I don't understand it all. He wanted to know when you would be back."

"I'll be there in the morning. Are you coming home?"

"No, her fever is still up. She's a bit delirious sometimes. Keeps saying she wants to go home. I'm staying."

"I'll be there in the morning. Hang in there," Liz said, and started to mentally figure out what needed to be done for her to take a leave of absence from work and arrange for babysitters. She longed for the old days when her biggest problem was getting the kids out the door and arriving at work on time. What had once felt like morning chaos had come to embody a cherished memory of a predictable routine that promised nothing more unusual than a struggle with Evan over his dirty blue T-shirt.

Chase and his father were to meet with Duncan and Reverend Broadnax that evening. Chase knew that Liz might be at the hospital all night. She gave him a hug and a kiss as he went out the door and whispered, "I'll be thinking of you and Grandpa. I love you."

"I love you, too," he replied.

*****

When Liz arrived in Maggie's room things had taken a dramatic turn for the worse. Oxygen tubes ran around her ears and into her nose. Her eyes remained closed. Billie looked exhausted and frightened.

"Is she asleep?" Liz whispered.

Billie shrugged her shoulders, unsure herself.

"Maggie," Liz said softly. "This is Liz. I'm here next to you. Can you hear me?"

Maggie's eyes flickered. She opened them, looked straight at Liz and appeared to acknowledge her presence and then closed them again. Liz took her hand and squeezed. She felt a weak, uneven response.

"Has Dr. Rao been in today?" Liz asked Billie.

"He was in early this morning, around six thirty and told me he'd be back at his lunch. Liz, I really didn't understand anything he said, something about the ANC count and sepsis. I don't know. It's all Greek to me. Said they were trying some antibiotics to get control of it."

"It's an infection that's resistant to a lot of antibiotics. That's the problem. They have to find one that will attack the bacteria before the bacteria takes over."

"Could it kill her?"

Liz looked down at Maggie, not sure whether she could hear or not. One never knew. She made a hand gesture to Billie to lower her voice and said, "I feel certain they can handle this." In reality, she didn't feel certain at all. She walked Billie to the door, "You all right to drive?"

"Yeah, I'll make it home."

"Be careful. Get some sleep and call Richard and tell him, would you?"

"Of course I will," Billie said, and slipped out the door.

For the next three hours Liz rubbed Maggie's feet and put lotion on her arms and legs. She sang all of their favorite songs, choking up at times and having to stop mid-chorus. She watched the blip on the monitor as it stretched endless waves across the screen measuring a heartbeat and pulse. Occasionally Maggie opened her eyes for a few seconds, seemed to search until she saw Liz, and then closed them again. Just past one o'clock, Dr. Rao came in the room. The first thing Liz noticed was that he wasn't wearing his Tar Heel shirt. The UNC cap stuck out of his lab coat pocket, but he didn't bother to put it on.

"How's my Tar Heel doing?" he asked, but his monotone voice lacked its normal bounce. Liz could see the worry in his eyes. He walked to Maggie's side and took her hand. "Maggie, can you hear me?" Her eyes fluttered. "Maggie, we've got a glitch here. We're working on it. You stay with us. We will fix it."

Liz thought she saw Maggie's head move ever so slightly as if she wanted to nod, but it was barely recognizable. Dr. Rao motioned Liz outside the door.

"This isn't good, is it?" Liz said.

"It's certainly not what we had hoped for, but don't give up. I've seen cases like this turn around before."

"Even with her immune system as compromised as it is?"

"It can happen."

Liz nodded.

"You will stay with her?" he asked.

"Yes, I plan to."

"Good. That will help."

*****

Liz stayed by Maggie's side the rest of the day. Reluctant to leave, she stepped out at 10:00 p.m. to call Chase. He was home.

"How did it go tonight?"

"All painful, but Reverend Broadnax was very concerned that we handle this situation carefully. He's afraid that if the Perrys aren't given the opportunity to vent their anger and frustration privately at first that it could spill over into the entire black community."

"Really?" Liz was stunned at such a possibility. It just hadn't dawned on her that after all the good Grandpa had done, he would not be forgiven. "What does Reverend Broadnax suggest?"

"He suggested that he meet with the Perrys first, to let them voice their feelings and expectations. Ideally, Grandpa and the Perrys could make a statement to the church congregation together. He also agreed that it might help for you to speak to LuAnne."

"When?"

"As soon as you can."

"How's Grandpa?"

"Pretty exhausted, but I think he finds relief in knowing that this is coming to a head. How's Maggie?"

"Not good, Chase. I'm staying overnight."

"All right, call me tomorrow."

"I'll do that. I love you."

"I love you, too, honey. Tell Maggie she's in our hearts and prayers."

When Liz got back to the room, Maggie was weeping uncontrollably. Her eyes were wide and the sobs interfered with the oxygen tube so that she gasped for breath. "Where have you been?" she sputtered out between breaths.

"Maggie, Maggie." Liz stroked her forehead. "I just went to call Chase."

"I thought you'd left me. Don't leave me alone like that again." Her words came in sputtered intervals between the sobs. Don't let me die alone."

"I won't," Liz choked. Tears swelled into her eyes.

"I don't want to stay here, Liz. Get me home to Cottonwoods."

"Oh, Maggie!" Liz tried to hug her but the tubes made an embrace awkward. "As soon as you get a little stronger, we'll take you home. I promise." Liz hit the call button for a nurse and appreciated the immediate response of a tall woman with calm cool eyes and a soothing and reassuring voice.

Maggie began to regain her composure. The nurse stayed with them until her breathing became regular again. "Do you have any pain, Maggie?" the nurse asked.

"Yes," Maggie whispered and ran her hand over the right side of her stomach.

"On a scale of one to ten?"

"Nine," Maggie whispered.

"I'll check with the doctor," the nurse said, and left the room. A few minutes later she was back and connected another sack of fluid to run simultaneously into the IV drip. Liz didn't even ask what it was. Maggie began to doze again and Liz sat in the chair next to her the rest of the night. Whatever turnaround Dr. Rao hoped for needed to happen soon.

*****

Dr. Rao arrived before the sun the next morning. He wore no Tar Heel regalia at all.

"Maggie," he called to her several times and then went so far as to shake her shoulder. Gradually she began to acknowledge him. "I'm going to back off the pain meds some, so you won't be so sleepy, but you tell us if the pain gets worse. Okay?" She gave a partial nod and closed her eyes again. He turned to Liz and motioned her into the hall. It had been a sleepless night, with Liz worrying that Maggie was in pain every time she moaned or twitched. She kept buzzing the night nurse, whose reassurance did little to comfort her.

"Do you still think she might make it?" Liz asked.

His eyes betrayed his worry. "That's a no-win question, but I will tell you that the pain in the upper right abdomen is not good. To be honest, our window of opportunity for reversal is smaller than it once was."

Liz called Billie at 11:00 that morning. "Not good, Billie," she said. "They're running tests, but Dr. Rao appears discouraged, and Maggie is not very responsive."

"Maybe we should get a room at one of the hotels," Billie suggested, "and trade off during the night?"

"Probably," Liz agreed. "Would you call Chase for me? Tell him things aren't getting any better. Tell him to call Grandpa, too."

After lunch Dr. Rao returned and tried again to talk to Maggie. "Tar Heel, you still with me?"

"The pain," she mumbled.

"Is it bad?"

"Yes."

"Can you still fight?"

"I don't know," she breathed out a whisper and grimaced.

"We want you to fight, Maggie. Fight like a Tar Heel."

There was no snicker, no partial smile, and no attempt at a nod from Maggie.

"I'm going to help you with the pain," he said, and a morphine drip was wheeled into the room.

"I'm dying," Maggie whispered to Liz after Dr. Rao left. With her heart exploding in her chest and tears rolling down her cheeks, all Liz could do was bend over and kiss Maggie's forehead. She needed to be a tower of strength, to say something inspirational or empowering. Instead here she sat weeping and slobbering all over her. She knew Maggie was right.

*****

After Billie arrived in the afternoon, they sat together in silence. When Maggie's blood pressure began to drop, Liz called the nurse.

Dr. Rao was in the room within thirty minutes. His eyes said it all; those beautiful dark eyes offered no reassurance.

Maggie's kidneys were failing and there was little hope. He suggested that if there was anyone else who should be with her, now was the time to call.

Richard, Gill, Chase, LuAnne, and Grandpa arrived at ten. They all hugged and shed tears together. Liz asked about Miss Ellie. Gill said she had chosen not to come. Chase went to get some extra chairs.

Gill had brought a tape recorder and tapes of Haydn and Mozart, which he plugged into a corner outlet; the music filled the air as a requiem mass. Around midnight Richard offered a heartfelt prayer. Afterwards Chase suggested to Grandpa that they get a hotel room. "We'll come back first thing in the morning," he assured him.

Grandpa Hoole shook his head and didn't move. Forty-five more minutes passed. At two in the morning, Maggie stirred and began to mumble. Liz got up to lean in closer to her. Gill turned off the tape recorder.

"Daddy? Daddy?" she whispered, "is that you?"

No one said a word.

"Daddy?" she said louder this time. "Daddy, where are you?"

Grandpa Hoole raised his head. "I'm right here beside you, Maggie," he said.

Liz caught her breath and looked at Chase. Then she looked at LuAnne, whose eyes immediately shifted between Maggie and Grandpa Hoole.

"I can't see you," Maggie said.

"Walk in the light," Grandpa said as he rose and brushed her hair back from her forehead. "Wherever you may be, darling, walk in the light."

There was a long pause and then a sigh. "Oh, yes."

CHAPTER THIRTY-NINE

Billie and Liz sat on the ground of the Kendall family cemetery with their backs against the brick wall. November had turned breezy and the winds had blown many of the pecans to the ground. Liz wore a stocking cap pulled down over her honey-nut wig of curls. Billie's pink pullover matched her pink jeans. Webster ran around sniffing between the stones, excited to be off his chain, but a bit confused. After scurrying back to Billie for an occasional pet, he'd rush off again.

"I have a new grandbaby," Liz said.

Billie looked over and a paradoxical look crossed her face. "Girl or boy?"

"A little girl, Mary Elizabeth Hoole."

"Funny, isn't it? Life and death all happening at the same time."

"Yeah," Liz said as a tear began to form. "She's got one blue eye and one brown eye, Adam tells us."

"Ah, honey . . ." Billie slipped her arm about Liz's shoulder and gave her a squeeze.

Liz pulled a Kleenex out of her pocket and wiped her nose. "I love pecans," Liz said as she looked up over her head at the massive limbs above them that continued to drop the nuts into the cemetery. "They're like manna from heaven. God drops these little gifts into our lap and all you have to do is pick them up and crack them open."

"I'm sure you can come and get all that you want," Billie said. "You and LuAnne, she loves them, too."

"So what do you think, Billie?" Liz said as she stared across at the stones. "Where do we put Maggie?"

"I think we should cremate the body and bury her ashes with her father's grave."

"She was never sure whether she wanted to be cremated or not," Liz said.

"Well, she was definitely sure about not wanting to be out there by herself."

Billie motioned to the other side of the wall.

They continued to stare at the cemetery as if somehow their thoughts could shift stones and miraculously cause an available plot to appear in one place or another.

"I feel like we could have done better by Maggie," Liz said, tearing up again.

"In what way?"

"Oh, I don't know . . . gotten her back to Cottonwoods? She didn't want to die at Duke. Allowed more people to come and visit her? Flowers? She would have appreciated lots of flowers while she was alive. What good will they do her now?"

"That wasn't our choice, Liz, plus she was the one who said 'no visitors.'"

"I know. Rationally, I know, but I still want to have another shot to do it all over again and get it right. Maybe we should have played more music for her, read her poetry, helped her put her life in perspective. All of these things might have made everything right."

"Right? How in God's name do you get death right? Or life, for that matter? It never goes the way you planned."

Liz ached. So many things she would have done differently had she known the outcome.

Billie stood up and dusted off the back of her jeans. Liz knew that Billie was grieving, too. They had different ways of showing it.

"We'd have to take down the wall if you want to forget cremation. I don't see any other way," Billie said.

"Another thing Maggie didn't want to happen."

"Well, she didn't want to be buried outside the wall, and she didn't want to be cremated. That gives us very few options unless we stack coffins."

"If they take out a wall, it'll be a mess for the funeral," Liz said.

"We'll have to just live with it. In ten years no one will know the difference."

"I'll call the funeral home and get Jackson down and see what he says," Liz said. "He's good at this sort of thing."

"The additional bricks are going to have to match."

"Absolutely! I want to be here when he comes," Liz said.

Liz stood up alongside Billie and brushed leaves and dirt away copying what Billie had just done. Time to start doing. A strong wind brought cold air through the grove and they heard the sound of more pecans hit the ground like little balls of hail. "I'm just curious. Did she know I lost the election before she died?"

"She knew that Clinton and Hunt had won. She asked me before you got there."

"Did she ask whether or not I had won?"

"She never asked," Billie said. "I think you were always a winner in her mind."

The two headed to the house as Liz picked up a pocket of pecans on the way in and cracked them together in her hands. "Let's make our list for the funeral before Reverend Shannon and Reverend Broadnax get here," Liz said.

"You think we'll just do a repeat?"

"Pretty much," Liz said, "although I think we can forgo the walk from Cottonwoods to the church. It's going to be cold, and besides, I don't think Maggie would want it. That walk was for the Judge, and only the Judge."

*****

This time an integrated church service didn't seem to excite the same amount of controversy. It was cold and cloudy, but the Jerusalem Baptist Choir again lived up to their reputation. Reverend Shannon and Reverend Broadnax took turns at the pulpit. When the drummer started his first drum roll, Reverend Shannon stopped, pointed his finger directly at him and said, "I've been warned about you, young man, and I'm ready. Bring it on."

This got the expected laugh. From then on they worked together like two trapeze artists catching one another in mid-flight. The congregation loved it.

Maggie would have approved of the open house in her honor at Cottonwoods. Billie had mulled wine and Russian tea in two large pots on the stove. On the center table in the den sat a five-tier wedding cake with a picture of Maggie on the top.

A number of the elderly, including LuAnne and Grandpa and Grandma Hoole, stopped by briefly, but didn't stay. Liz caught LuAnne as she started out the door. "Can we talk sometime soon, LuAnne?"

She hesitated and said with more reluctance than Liz expected, "I suppose."

When a series of toasts were initiated in memory of Maggie, it turned into a grand memorial. Applause erupted from the crowd and more rounds of "Here's to Maggie." When all was said and done, the only thing missing was the guest of honor. It was her kind of party.

Chapter Forty

Liz and Chase entered the Quaker meeting for worship emotionally drained. The silence remained unbroken. A deepening sense of communion began to descend on the service and from it emerged a unified presence that blanketed and bound together everyone in the room. Many refer to such an occasion as a gathered meeting. If ever Liz had experienced a gathered meeting, she did on this day. She prayed for guidance for what to say to LuAnne. When it was over she believed with all of her heart that whatever happened next would strengthen the community. She was wrong.

*****

Liz had arranged to see LuAnne after church. As she pulled into her driveway she reminded herself that her connection with LuAnne had been through Maggie and the Judge. Beyond that and an occasional exchange of pleasantries in the grocery store or pharmacy, she had not been involved with LuAnne's family.

The small one-story brick house on the outskirts of town was immaculate, as Liz expected. A sofa and large recliner sat before a television set. With the addition of two small side tables and lamps, the furniture filled the living room. Well-known reproductions of a black Christ and Leonardo da Vinci's *Last Supper* hung prominently on the walls surrounded by several crucifixes of varying sizes. A small kerosene heater set in front of a fireplace on low, making the room warm but not uncomfortable. LuAnne accepted an embrace, but was less responsive than Liz anticipated.

"LuAnne, I'm so sorry about Maggie," Liz said. "Thank you for coming to the hospital with Reverend Shannon in the end. I feel certain Maggie knew you were there."

LuAnne was quiet. She gestured to the chair for Liz and moved to the sofa where she sat with her arms crossed in front of her. She pulled a Kleenex from a box next to her. A coffee table in between them was filled with an assortment of small ceramic angels, apparently a collection item.

"Not much family left," LuAnne said. "The Judge, Maggie . . . both dead. Johnson in jail. I just got Johnson's girl and boy now."

"Oh, I'm sorry," Liz said, waited a moment, and then leaned forward. "LuAnne, I want to talk to you about Nathan Hoole."

LuAnne shifted uncomfortably on the sofa. "Reverend Broadnax came by, told me."

"You were absolutely right. He was the other man in the barn the night that Isaac was murdered. All these years, and you were the one who figured it out."

LuAnne pressed her lips together tightly and nodded.

"We didn't know. Honest to God, we didn't know until just recently." Liz felt a strong need for LuAnne to believe her. "I want you to know he did go to the Sheriff and the Sheriff wouldn't believe him. He tried to tell his story."

"He didn't try very hard."

"The Sheriff didn't accept his word. He didn't want the men who had lynched Isaac to be accused."

"Why didn't he stay behind in the barn?" LuAnne asked. "Why did he run?"

"He was scared. He didn't want to be caught. For the same reason Isaac ran."

"No, ma'am," LuAnne snapped at Liz. "Not for the same reason Isaac ran. Isaac ran because he knowd he might get killed for doing nothing wrong at all. Mr. Nathan ran because he'd been caught with another man's wife."

Liz lowered her head, "That's true," she paused. "My father-in-law has regretted that his entire life. He wants to try to make amends to your family."

LuAnne clucked her tongue and shook her head. "Why are you here, then? Why ain't he here, down on his knees in front of me? He not brave enough to even do that much?"

"LuAnne," Liz pleaded. She wanted so much for LuAnne to offer forgiveness; to say that she understood, but Liz realized now that what she'd hoped for was unrealistic. "It was my idea to speak to you first. I thought it might help. He will be here. He is willing to speak to the Perrys and anyone else you think needs to hear the story."

"He needs to be arranging to stand on a platform in the middle of the county and tell the world that he was a coward and a liar," LuAnne shot back with more venom than Liz expected.

"If that's what the family wants, I think he's prepared to do that," Liz said.

"Leastwise, he's been living. He had a life . . . a good life. A wife, children, grandchildren . . . a lot more than Isaac had."

"You're right," Liz said.

"Somewhere there's got to be justice."

Liz felt lost. She didn't know where to turn or what to say. "Will you tell Johnson that his daddy died an innocent man and the truth will finally be told?"

"Johnson already knowd that. He knowd that all along, just like me. What you think he's been fighting for all these years? Fighting to get the mad out of him. Fighting because he lost a daddy for no good reason at all. You hear that, no good reason at all. Do you and Mr. Hoole have any idea at all what you done to that man?"

"We can only imagine," Liz conceded. Silence pursued and Liz felt the tension escalate. "What do you want us to do now?" she asked helplessly.

LuAnne shifted in her chair. "I don't know."

Liz grimaced. "Will you meet with Reverend Broadnax and discuss what you expect from Nathan Hoole? Grandpa has agreed to do his best to accommodate whatever you think is required, no matter what."

"I don't know." LuAnne shook her head and pursed her lips. "Maybe for Johnson's kids, Isaac's grandkids. Maybe there's a way they can turn the page and move on. But . . ." and LuAnne paused and her eyes began to water, "I want them to know their granddaddy was hung an innocent man and I want them to know that I did everything I could do to help my family."

Liz sat quietly for a few more minutes. She wanted more than ever to hold LuAnne in an embrace that promised forgiveness, but she wasn't sure now whether that time would ever come.

LuAnne rose, having said all that she wished to say. "I'll call Johnson. He deserves to know. Then I'll talk to Reverend Broadnax."

That was that.

CHAPTER FORTY-ONE

Liz dropped Nicholas and Evan off at school and returned to the pharmacy the next morning. She knew Grandpa would be there. She and Chase had talked about her discussion with LuAnne and Liz was disappointed that there had been unexpected hostility.

"Maybe I made a mistake," she said to Chase. "I should have left this in the hands of Reverend Broadnax. I don't know all the history or anything about Johnson and his family."

"There are a lot of moveable parts going in different directions at the same time," Chase said. "No one thought this was going to be easy."

Grandpa sat at one of the corner tables with a bag of roasted peanuts beside him. Chase stood in the back with Timmy Bates. Liz kissed Grandpa on the top of his head and sat down across from him. "Hi, Grandpa," she said.

He patted her hand.

"Reverend Broadnax called last night," she said. "He's arranged to meet with the Perrys."

"Chase told me," Grandpa said.

Timmy saw Liz and turned to carry his bags of peanuts over to her. She fished in her pocket and pulled out two quarters. He smiled, handed her a bag and started for the door.

"Did he say anything else?" Grandpa asked.

"Said there was a lot of anger, a lot of questioning. He's not sure the best idea is for you to meet with them right away. They're going to talk about what to do." Grandpa nodded. "People aren't ready to offer forgiveness. He wants to be sure you understand that."

"I understand," Grandpa said.

The front door to the pharmacy opened and Helen Truitt walked in dressed as if she was on her way to Norfolk instead of the local pharmacy. "Good morning, all." She waved a hand at Liz and Grandpa and turned to where they sat.

Liz got up to intercept her, but Timmy had already stepped in front of Helen holding out his bags of peanuts for sale. Helen hesitated and then tried to get around him.

"What can we do for you?" Liz asked as she blocked Helen's approach to Grandpa.

"I need a refill on this medication." She pulled out a small container for pills, bypassed Timmy and headed for the back counter.

Liz stayed by her side. "I wanted to say how sorry I am about Maggie," Helen said.

"Thank you, Helen." Chase took the plastic bottle from her and started some polite conversation. He wanted to give Grandpa an opportunity to leave if he wanted. It wasn't the best time for a Truitt encounter.

Not to be deterred, Timmy turned and followed Helen to the back.

"I dropped by Cottonwoods Saturday after the funeral but so many people. What a crowd and with no receiving line or anything, I didn't stay long. I didn't see you," Helen said.

"Well, it was hard to know how to set it up, but we appreciate your concern."

"And that's the end of the Kendalls. It's hard to imagine, isn't it?"

"It is," Liz agreed.

Helen looked up at Timmy and began to rummage around in her pocketbook. He waited patiently. "No hard feelings over the election, I hope?"

"Certainly not."

Liz realized for the first time she hadn't even spoken to Helen since before election night. "You won fair and square. I wish you the best with a difficult job."

"Well, you have to admit, I do know more about this county than you do; and with Maggie's will, you'll be busy anyway. You are the executor, aren't you?"

Liz screwed her mouth into one of those I-can't-believe-you're-asking-me-that-right-now expressions, but true to form, Helen ignored the facial cues. Then the front door to the pharmacy opened and LuAnne walked in. She turned directly towards Grandpa at the corner table.

Liz shot a glance at Chase. He stood with his back to the room as he filled Helen's prescription, but Liz saw him look in the mirror and follow LuAnne with his eyes. Helen turned slightly to see who had just come in, and then turned back to face Liz. Timmy waited patiently for two quarters and eyed LuAnne, another potential customer.

"Excuse me a minute, Helen." Liz walked behind the counter over to Chase.

"Let it be," he said. "Let them talk."

"This isn't the best place," Liz said.

"LuAnne obviously has something she wants to say now. See if you can get Helen and Timmy out of here and then lock the front door."

Liz watched Grandpa rise to his feet when he saw LuAnne. He hadn't expected her, either.

"Helen," Liz began in an effort to think of a way to get her out of the pharmacy as quickly as possible. "If you'll go on over to The Quaker Café and order me some toast and coffee, I'll join you there in a minute. I can tell you what I know about the will."

"And my prescription?" she asked.

"I'll bring that along with me."

Helen seemed unsure at first, but the temptation was too great. She handed Timmy four dimes and two nickels. Liz put her arm around Helen's shoulder and guided her to the front door. "Come on, Timmy," Liz said in an effort to get him to leave LuAnne alone. "I'll buy you some breakfast."

Timmy immediately shifted his attention away from LuAnne and followed Liz and Helen.

They walked past Grandpa and LuAnne. Liz heard LuAnne speak. Helen asked Liz if she wanted whole wheat or white toast. LuAnne opened her pocket book. Helen opened the front door. Liz ushered them out, quietly locked the door behind them, and flipped the "Open" sign around to "Closed."

When Liz turned, she caught her breath. Chase had frozen at the pharmacy counter, the color drained from his face. LuAnne stood facing Grandpa, holding a Smith and Wesson.

"It's Mr. Corbett's gun," she said.

Grandpa didn't move.

"The same one he should have shot you with fifty-six years ago." Her hand trembled. "You don't know how many times I thought of doing exactly that. You over there on the other end of town living your life as if nothing happened. Isaac not living at all, and his family falling apart."

She sat down and rested her hand on the table between them, the barrels still aimed at Grandpa.

"What sort of man makes a Christian woman want to do that? Me and my God, we're struggling," LuAnne's voice quivered. "Sit down, Mr. Hoole."

"LuAnne," Liz whispered. "LuAnne, don't."

Chase inched towards the table and LuAnne momentarily scanned the room as if aware of other people for the first time. "Miss Liz, you and Mr. Chase just sit over yonder. I got some talking to do. Mr. Hoole here, he got some listening to attend to."

Neither Chase nor Liz moved as LuAnne raised her voice for the first time. "Sit down. Didn't you hear me say sit down?"

Liz and Chase both pulled out chairs at the small table nearest each of them. They'd been on opposite sides of the room and they sat about twenty feet apart, eyeing one another for any clue as to what to do next.

292

"LuAnne," Grandpa said, "this is just between you and me. Let my son and daughter-in-law leave?"

"Just between you and me?" LuAnne's voice escalated and her hand steadied, her finger on the trigger. "Is that what you said to Miss Sarah when you took her to bed? *This is just between you and me?* Is that what you said to Mr. Corbett when you left him swinging a shovel at Isaac in the barn? *This is just between you and me?* Is that what you said to Old Man Kendall and the Sheriff when they were out raising a lynching party? *This is just between you and me?* There ain't no so such thing *as just between you and me,* Mr. Hoole. There's always other people who get hurt by someone's foolishness."

LuAnne closed her eyes momentarily and shook her head. She put the gun down on the table. "*Just between you and me,*" she sighed.

Chase and Liz both eyed the gun, but neither was close enough to grab it. Grandpa could have. He could have knocked it off the table at the very least, but the gun seemed not to hold any power over him. LuAnne's words had his back to the wall.

With his head bowed he confessed. "I have caused great pain to others, to you and your family. I understand your need to seek revenge."

"Dad," Chase stood, alarmed at his father's submission.

LuAnne immediately picked the gun back up and glared at Chase. "Didn't I tell you to sit down? We're here talking. Ain't no way a black person seems to be able to get you white folks to listen unless they point a gun at you."

"LuAnne," Liz said. "Maggie always listened to you. Don't you think the Judge thought what you had to say was important? I tried to listen to you. I really did."

"All these years, and not one white person ever came to say 'I'm sorry.' Not one . . . but you, Miss Liz," LuAnne nodded at Liz. "You the only white person who ever said you was sorry 'bout what happened to my family. Sorry about the lives that was ruined. You was listening. That's true."

The room became eerily quiet and still. There was a knock on the door and Frank Busby looked through the picture window and waved to be let in. "What do you want me to do, LuAnne?" Liz asked.

"Tell him we're busy just now." LuAnne lifted the gun from the table and slid it back into her pocket book.

Liz looked over at Chase, but she had already made up her mind. She got up and walked to the door. She cracked it open. "Sorry, Frank," she said. "We need a little time before opening this morning, a bit of a family issue has come up."

"Can I help with anything? Work the counter for you?" Frank looked confused. This was highly unusual.

"Thanks, not right now Frank. We'll be open in another hour," Liz said, and closed the door. She sat back down and looked over at Chase who frowned at her. "We're listening, LuAnne," she said.

After another long pause, Grandpa spoke up. "There is not a day that goes by that I have not prayed over what I did and the guilt I have felt. I have tried to stand in the light in hopes that a way will open."

LuAnne looked confused. "What good does it do to stand in the light, Mr. Hoole, if you wouldn't stand by Isaac and me?"

Grandpa closed his eyes and bowed his head. His chin began to quiver.

LuAnne clicked her pocketbook shut and rose. "I'm going now," she said. "There ain't nothing I can do here that will make things any better. I can't kill nobody. I can't forgive nobody. There's too much you stole from me, Mr. Hoole. Too much that ain't coming back. Talk to your God about that."

*****

Rumors swept through Cedar Branch like the November leaves that blew into the gutters and across the harvested fields. Grandpa didn't return to the pharmacy the next morning or any other time that week.

Everyone who came in asked Chase for more details. Chase deflected each question with as much discretion as he could. *He didn't wish to comment.* He couldn't help but notice that no one from the black community had entered his store at all.

Chase and Liz rarely went to the mid-week evening worship service held at the Quaker meeting on Fourth Day, but this week they knew they should. Grandpa and Grandma would be there. They debated whether to take Nicholas and Evan, and decided their children's presence would show support. It was important for children to know that every person, young and old, experienced difficult times in their lives, and the community had an obligation to gather round and help.

The meeting house was filled, which was highly unusual for mid-week meeting. Every one of the fifty-two adult members living in close vicinity had come. It was somber, with none of the greetings that usually occurred when people entered. Instead, there was a weighty silence. Heads remained bowed, hands folded together. Sensing something different, Nicholas and Evan sat still. When Evan reached out for his brother's hand, Nicholas took it.

At the close of meeting Grandpa rose. "I will be speaking at Jerusalem Baptist Church on First Day," he said. "I have told my story to the elders of this meeting. Based on the number present this evening, I realize that at least parts of that story have been retold elsewhere. I feel that the members of Jerusalem Baptist deserve to hear my confession in its entirety before the story becomes more public." He paused, steadied his voice and concluded, "I would be grateful if you would hold our community in the light during the difficult days ahead. My actions from years past threatened to reignite hostilities, which are the least desirable outcome. I ask you to pray with me that we might avoid such an incident."

*****

On the way home, the boys sat unusually quiet until just before Chase pulled into the drive and Evan spoke up. "I just have one question."

Chase and Liz braced themselves. "What's that, honey?"

"Why weren't the Judge and Maggie raptured?"

Chase sighed a sigh of relief, and raised his eyebrows as he deferred to Liz. Liz cleared her throat and took a deep breath. "God doesn't rapture people, honey, at least not so far as Quakers believe."

"But he raptured Jitters."

"No, he didn't really. That was something I made up."

Evan's eyes opened wide and a knowing smirk appeared on Nicholas's face. "Jitters wasn't raptured?" Evan asked.

"No, he wasn't."

"So what happened to him?"

"Jitters was dead. When his box fell off the bench on the float, one of the cats saw him and grabbed him. I got Jitters away from the cat, but he looked so bad I didn't want you to see him or think somehow it was your fault. I wanted you to remember him the way he looked when he was alive. That's why I made up a story."

Evan looked hurt. He thought for a minute and Chase and Liz waited before opening the car door. "You saw Maggie when she looked bad after she died," Evan said.

"You're right. I did," Liz agreed.

"And the Judge?"

"I did."

"Did you cry or feel like it was your fault when they died?"

"Yes, actually, I did, sort of," Liz admitted.

"Are you sorry you saw them that way?"

"No," Liz paused a moment before she spoke, "I'm glad I was there for them when they needed help. I hope I did some good."

"And so will you remember them looking awful?"

"No, I will always remember them as very much alive; as wonderful people who were both good friends."

After a thoughtful pause Evan said, "What did you do with Jitters, Mom?"

"I buried him."

"Where?"

"In our back yard."

"In the silver box?"

"Yes."

"I should have been there," Evan said.

"You should have," Liz agreed. "I made a mistake. If you like, we can go out to where I buried him and I'll show you. We could say a little prayer together in appreciation for all the joy he gave us."

"Okay," he said, accepting his mother's apology. Liz marveled that as quickly as that she had been blessed by the simple, unconditional forgiveness of a child.

CHAPTER FORTY-TWO

Grandpa and Grandma Hoole sat on the front row of Jerusalem Baptist Church with Chase and Liz on one side of them and Sophie and Jack on the other. Nat had driven up from Charlotte. Lexa remained at the house with Nicholas, Evan, Estelle, and Stin.

LuAnne Perry sat on the opposite front bench between Johnson's two children, Felicity and Alex. Felicity resembled her Aunt LuAnne, about the same height and round in all the same places, but without the excess weight or lines that came with age. She was dressed modestly in a white blouse and burgundy pants suit. Several silver necklaces draped around her neck and fell halfway down her blouse accompanied by a dangling pair of silver earrings. She wore a pair of spike heels for fashion and additional height. Carefully coiffed, straight, thick black hair rested on her shoulders.

Alex wore an army uniform, starched and pressed, with spitshined shoes. He towered over his sister. Repeatedly he crossed his long thin legs and then uncrossed them, shifting uncomfortably in his seat. He seemed unable to find a place to accommodate his arms; first by his side, then across the back of the pew, then bent forward with his elbows on his knees.

LuAnne's jaw was set. Her eyes focused straight ahead. She wore a long-sleeve blouse and a corduroy black jumper with no waist. A coat was draped over the back of the pew. Cousins and friends filled the space on either side of them. Liz regretted that she knew the names of so few in the black community. She knew that Maggie would have been able to speak to everyone. Chase recognized most.

A young man played a keyboard to the right of the pulpit and Reverend Broadnax walked to the front rows and leaned down and spoke first to LuAnne and her nephew and niece before walking over and speaking to Grandpa. "May God give you strength," he said, placing his large hands on Grandpa's shoulder. Grandpa nodded.

Reverend Broadnax stepped up to the elevated pulpit at the center of the front of the church. He wore a clergy robe of Ghanaian kente cloth with a gold cross woven into the front. The Jerusalem Baptist Choir entered the sanctuary down the center aisle and up to the choir loft behind the pulpit singing "Walking in the Light of God." A large reproduction of a painting of Jesus praying at Gethsemane hung on the wall above them. The congregation stood and joined in. After the hymn, Reverend Broadnax offered prayer and then welcomed guests.

"We are fortunate to have many joining us from our community today. This is an unusual morning. It will be an unusual service. A service you will remember, because today we will make history in our town of Cedar Branch. We will turn the page on a chapter from our past and we will begin to tell a new story; a story of promise, a story of opportunity, a story of commitment to something better. Before you walk out of this church today, you will be inspired. You will have new hope. You will believe in the power of good over evil. We will be changed. Do you believe that?"

There were a few "Amens," which did not satisfy Reverend Broadnax.

"I SAID . . . DO YOU BELIEVE, because if you don't you might as well go ahead and walk out right now. This is not an easy story to tell. It's gonna make you mad, maybe as mad as you've ever been before, but being mad isn't what's going to turn this story around. Being inspired to do something, something GOOD, IN THE NAME OF THE LORD. I SAID . . . DO YOU BELIEVE?"

A boisterous "YES" resounded from the congregation. "SAY IT AGAIN, one more time so I know that you are sure. DO YOU BELIEVE, MY BROTHERS AND SISTERS, WE CAN LEAVE TODAY WITH A WAY TO TURN A TRAGEDY INTO A NEW BEGINNING? If you believe, then holler out to the Lord, I BELIEVE."

"I BELIEVE" burst forth in unison.

"Brothers and sisters, we come together today to publicly acknowledge for the first time a terrible injustice inflicted upon one of our members over five decades ago. Fifty-six years, my brothers and sisters . . . fifty-six years have passed and finally the truth will be told. As Paul wrote from his prison in Rome to the saints in Ephesus: *laying aside falsehood, speak truth each one of you with his neighbor, for we are members one of another.* Members, one of another," he repeated.

"Nathan Hoole is with us today. Many of you know Nathan. I have worked alongside him as members of numerous committees throughout the past years. I have known him as an honest man. But like many he has lived within his own prison wall concealing a long-hidden truth. Today he has come to speak the truth and in so doing, to redeem the name of Isaac Perry in the eyes of the entire community and history. Nathan . . ."

Reverend Broadnax stepped aside and sat down in the chair behind the pulpit. Grandpa rose. All eyes in the church were upon him. There was no rustling of church bulletins, no shifting in seats, no shuffling feet. No one coughed, opened and closed a pocket book, or quieted a restless child. The word had already started to spread. Today the members of the congregation would hear for themselves. Nathan made the only sounds in the sanctuary as he climbed the six steps to stand in front of a jury of his peers.

As he raised his eyes and looked across the room, Grandpa realized for the first time that members of the Quaker community sat scattered throughout. They had not assembled on the back few benches, nor come to sit directly behind him and his family members. Instead, all fifty-six members including a few from meetings in Virginia Beach and Greenville sat throughout the church, sitting among the black membership.

The first one he saw was Leland, his black round hat visible immediately. There was Anna and Kate, Dana, Duncan with his wife, and other white faces throughout. Timmy Bates sat next to Miss Ellie on the back row, along with Frank Busby. Grandpa's mind paused a second in recognition of a fourth figure beside them, Helen Truitt. To the right, a flash of pink caught his eye, and he recognized Billie and Gill at the end of one aisle. Momentarily overcome, he raised his eyes to the ceiling to regain his composure. Then in a voice loud and clear he began.

"Fifty-six years ago I committed adultery with the wife of Corbett Kendall. When Isaac Perry arrived unexpectedly, I was ashamed. I ran and hid in fear of what might happen to me. In so doing, another man's life was tragically taken and his family ostracized for a crime he never committed. I am told his son has never come to terms with this injustice and struggles to this day with the hatred that keeps him behind bars . . . a consequence I could have possibly reversed if I had spoken sooner. I come before you today to tell you the truth as I know it, not in order to seek forgiveness for myself, but to re-claim the name of Isaac Perry for his family and to attest to his innocence."

Grandpa took a handkerchief out of his pocket and wiped his forehead, then, step by painful step he retold the story in its entirety. At the end, he paused before saying, "I am unable in any way to restore to the Perrys their great suffering and loss. I pray that God will have mercy on my soul."

Grandpa returned to his seat. LuAnne had begun to weep at the first mention of Isaac's name, and her nephew and niece cradled her in their arms, holding each of her hands in one of their own. The Jerusalem Choir rose and sang "The Storm is Over Now."

As the choir concluded, Reverend Broadnax rose to the pulpit as if he were Icarus rising towards the sun. His arms stretched out above him to the heavens. He had a plan, and he wasn't about to let this opportunity pass. His powerful voice thundered through the church.

"WE ARE A COMMUNITY, a community I tell you! Black, white, yellow, or brown, we cannot deny our interdependence. We cannot deny our shared history. We may grieve, and our Lord knows we have plenty to grieve about, but out of this grief must come action."

301

A few "Amens" began to resonate for the first time in the service.

"What good does it do to drift along on human error? None, none whatsoever!"

A *pop* from the drummer alerted everyone that preachin' time was upon them.

The congregation remained attentive. Tears had dried and people readjusted their posture, straightened their backs, and moved to the edge of their seats. They could tell that what came next would require up and down action.

"What is our common goal here? Our common goal is to create from this tragic history some good. Our goal is to redefine the legacy of Isaac Perry so that he will be remembered, NOT as a VICTIM, but as *an instrument of God's work* here on earth. DO I MAKE MYSELF CLEAR?"

As heads began to nod, there was scattered applause.

"We have two grandchildren of Isaac Perry sitting with us today. Felicity, Alex, will you please stand."

Felicity and Alex looked a bit taken back by the Reverend's direct request, but they stood obediently.

"Felicity is seventeen, am I correct?"

Felicity nodded.

"And Alex is twenty-one. These young people are on the brink of heading out on their own. Alex, here, is already serving his country in the military."

There was applause.

"They have been deprived of a father most of their lives. Their mother is ill, staying with friends in New Jersey. I spoke with her on the phone, but she was unable to be with us here today. But she supports whatever we are able to do to help her children. WE ARE A COMMUNITY."

Another *pop* of the drum, and "Amen" was heard through the church.

"We are a community! As I look around our church this morning, I see members of the Quaker community who have joined us. Friends, thank you for coming. I know you have come to support your brother, Nathan, but I also know you have come to support LuAnne because you believe as we do that WE ARE A COMMUNITY."

Several "Amens" resounded.

"I see Ellie Cartwright in the back row, and Frank Busby. Thank you for coming. Timmy Bates is with us. Timmy, you are always welcome in our church."

A big smile stretched across Timmy's face and he rose and did a partial bow to everyone.

"I see the lovely Miss Billie McFarland and her husband. Billie often volunteers her time at our Senior Center. Thank you, Billie, for coming."

"And then, we are honored to have our newly elected commissioner with us today, Commissioner Truitt. Commissioner Truitt, I'm going to offer you the pulpit in just a few minutes. We'd like to hear from you."

Helen flushed. She had come that morning as a personal request from the Reverend. Completely unprepared to speak, she had assumed it would simply be a political gesture on her part.

"Brothers and sisters . . ." the Reverend lowered his tone, and the congregation leaned forward. "Do we as a community have a responsibility to help these grandchildren of Isaac Perry? To give them the educational opportunities that Isaac wanted so much for them to have?"

"Yes," voices shouted.

"Do we, indeed, have a responsibility to ALL of our children to help them attain the educational opportunities that they deserve so that they can be forces in this world, forces to build and strengthen our community and to raise families who contribute back to this community? Do we have that obligation, I ask you? DO WE?"

"YES" came louder this time.

"SAY IT AGAIN, ONE MORE TIME SO I'M SURE I HEARD YOU RIGHT."

A resounding "YES" filled the room.

"Then my friends and neighbors, I propose that today we initiate the Isaac Perry Educational Scholarship with our first priority to assist Isaac Perry's grandchildren to complete their college educations."

There was applause.

"But ALSO to ultimately assist all African American children who live in Cedar Branch to go to college, whichever college they choose; a community college, a state college, Howard, or Harvard University."

"YES, YES" rose in unison.

"Can I get an Amen?"

"AMEN, AMEN!"

The Reverend suddenly turned to the choir. "I think we need to sing to that, don't you? A happy song, a song of celebration."

As the choir obeyed with several zippy choruses of "Oh Happy Day, Oh Happy Day," Helen steadied herself for what was to come. Had she attended more black churches she would have been better prepared. What she didn't yet realize was that she was a fish on the line about to get reeled in.

As the choir ended, Reverend Broadnax leaned onto the podium with the force of his weight and slowly eyeballed the congregation. "How much? How much do you think we should raise so that this young man and woman can finish college?"

"Ten thousand" was thrown out. Reverend Broadnax frowned.

"We're not talking about sending them to beauty school. We're talking about AN EDUCATION. We're talking Norfolk State, Shaw University, the University of Virginia, Georgetown. We want our children to become doctors, physicists, computer scientists, and engineers. We want our children to be senators and governors and President of the United States."

Half of the congregation was on its feet now, applauding and shouting, "AMEN."

Reverend Broadnax stopped and looked at Felicity. "If you could go anywhere, where would you want to go to college, honey?"

Surprised by the question, her mouth twitched: then she whispered, "Chapel Hill."

"And you, son?" The Reverend nodded to Alex.

Alex sat up straight. "Howard, Sir. I'd like to go to Howard University."

The Reverend slammed his hand on the pulpit: "One hundred thousand dollars! We're gonna start with one hundred thousand, but that won't do it, because we're working on building something permanent, not just for these two young people, but for ALL of our young people. We're building a trust and we can only take five percent a year. No, my friends, that won't do. We need to raise more than one hundred thousand dollars."

"Two hundred thousand!" jumped out from someone in the congregation. *"Three hundred thousand!"* another said.

"NOW, we're starting to talk ED-U-CATION," the Reverend said. "We're starting to talk about sending our children to the *best* schools for the *best* educations so that they can get the *best* jobs and raise the *best* families for our community. NOW WE'RE TALKING."

There was applause and general agreement as the drum and keyboard danced off one another in a short duet.

When things quieted, Reverend Broadnax was ready. "I make a motion, I make a motion here today in our church, and I know this isn't often done, but I'm doing it anyway, I make a motion here today that the Jerusalem Baptist Church establish the Isaac Perry Educational Scholarship in memory of Isaac Perry with a goal to raise five hundred thousand dollars within the next two years."

A few eyebrows went up and one or two audible gasps of surprise were heard.

"I propose that we raise a half a million dollars in the next two years. Do I hear a second?"

Numerous seconds were called out, as well as a resounding "YES."

"Now," said Reverend Broadnax, "I'm going to ask Miss LuAnne Perry if she will chair that committee for us. I'll work with you LuAnne and we'll put together a board of directors from our church and an advisory board from the community. Would you do that for us, LuAnne?"

"Yes!" LuAnne said loudly, with unexpected vivacity.

"We're going to need the help of the whole community—the *whole* community. We're going to need fund-raisers and grants and personal contributions from individuals and organizations and our county commissioners. Madame Commissioner, would you please join us up here at the pulpit?"

Helen Truitt froze. She looked from side to side, unsure whether she could rise or not, until one of the deacons stepped forward and offered her his arm. She took it and returned a weak smile. She seemed a bit unstable as she walked to the front. Reverend Broadnax assisted her up the steps and then kissed her on the cheek, another unexpected gesture that caught her off guard.

Realizing how swiftly the Reverend had shifted attention from the Hoole family to the Perry family and Helen Truitt, Liz watched him with admiration. Grandpa and Grandma, Chase, and Sophie carefully followed his message.

"Commissioner, this is turning into a wonderful opportunity for our community, wouldn't you say?"

Helen looked out across the sea of primarily black faces, plastered on her smile, and said, "Goodness, yes, a wonderful opportunity. I've always believed that education is the key."

"Then you won't have any trouble getting a motion from the other county commissioners to support such an endeavor?"

"I can't imagine why not," Helen said in all truthfulness.

"The commissioners would be willing to support us as we seek grant funding through outside organizations, foundations, and governmental agencies. We'd need this type of money to become a priority for the commissioners, a priority over jails, wouldn't you think, Madame Commissioner?"

Helen hesitated, again looked across the room. That took her a bit off guard. She collected her thoughts and said, "Money that goes to children's education, I will always support." There was applause. Helen smiled.

"That's wonderful of you, Commissioner," Reverend Broadnax said. "We look forward to being a line item in the budget. Now, Madame Commissioner," he continued before she could absorb what he'd just slipped by her, "in support of what we are trying to do and as a show of your commitment, could we count on a fifty thousand dollar pledge from the Methodist Church?"

Helen blinked and swallowed. The room went silent. "Well, we're a small church," she stuttered a bit. "I'm not sure I can speak for the church."

"Madame Commissioner, someone must speak for the church. We have to be able to show foundations that we can match any contributions we receive from them. We have to show them that our entire community is behind us. We're counting on you to go to your church and lead the fund-raising there for a fifty thousand dollar contribution."

Helen tried to collect her wits. The clicking of a cane on the back of a pew broke the uncomfortable pause and Anna Reed rose with some effort. "Reverend, while it is not in the Quaker tradition to make any commitment that does not have consensus from our members, I feel led to rise and speak. I believe you can count on a fifty thousand dollar contribution from the Quaker meeting, perhaps more."

"Hallelujah!" Reverend Broadnax sang out. "Let the Lord be praised."

A chorus of "Hallelujahs" echoed throughout the room.

"And the Methodist Church?" He returned his attention to Helen. "Madame Commissioner, if the Methodist Church will match the Quakers, we will immediately jump-start this scholarship here today with one hundred thousand. You will help to attest to the fact that the children in sixty-five percent of the families in your constituency will have more access to higher education."

Helen looked out over the congregation and said hesitantly, "Yes, we will try."

"Hallelujah, again, praise to the Lord. We have just raised one hundred thousand on our first morning and have affirmation that the county commissions will support our requests for funding from outside organizations and consider this scholarship as a priority in their annual budget. Can we do better?"

Helen was stunned, but the Reverend was still rolling. "Madame Commissioner, you are the President of the local Women's Auxiliary, are you not?"

She looked at the minister with a blank expression.

To Liz's surprise, Chase rose. "Reverend Broadnax, I would like to pledge twenty-five thousand from the Men's Club here in town and ask the Women's Auxiliary to match that pledge."

"Glory be to God, the Lord is speaking to us today, my brothers and sisters. The Lord is speaking. When the Lord is speaking, we want to listen. We have one hundred and fifty thousand already in commitments. The men and women's club will each contribute an additional twenty-five thousand."

He gave Helen a hug without waiting for any affirmation from her; she was like a rag doll in his mighty grip.

"I have pledge cards here in my hand. The Lord's been speaking to me all week long, and I knew this day was coming. The Lord told me to be prepared. There are about three hundred people here today. That's a good crowd. We're going to pass these around and as the choir sings I'm going to ask you to look into your hearts and see if each person here can come up with two hundred today for the Isaac Perry Educational Scholarship. Two hundred dollars in cash, a two hundred dollar check, or a two hundred dollar pledge would give us over sixty thousand dollars! We would leave this church today with a total commitment of over two hundred thousand dollars in memory of Isaac Perry. Can we do that? CAN WE DO THAT? YES! WE! CAN!"

The choir jumped into "This Little Light of Mine, I'm Gonna Let it Shine," as the cards and offering plate circulated. Reverend Broadnax generously handed Helen a pen. "A check, if you have it," he smiled. "I'll put mine with yours."

"I left my purse back at the pew," Helen whispered.

"Deacon Roberts," the Reverend motioned for one of the deacons to come over. "Would you collect Commissioner Truitt's pocketbook? She'd like to go ahead and write a personal check."

As the choir sang, Reverend Broadnax pulled out two hundred dollars in cash and then almost as an afterthought, pulled out another fifty. "Let's make it an even five hundred," he said as he waited patiently for Helen to write her check. Together they dropped their offerings into the plate. Then, and only then, did the deacon offer to accompany Helen back to her seat. She seemed to require more help on the way back than the trip up, but she had just had an important education in how to raise money, *the Reverend Broadnax way.*

The service ended with a last hymn and a lengthy prayer of thanksgiving for a community that stands in the light of God. Reverend Broadnax had done his Quaker homework.

As Reverend Broadnax went to the rear of the church to greet parishioners, Grandpa and Grandma stood, unsure how to approach LuAnne, but feeling the need to remain and speak. Grandpa would not turn his back and walk away. After everyone else departed, Reverend Broadnax returned to where the two families stood. The Reverend looked at one family on one side of the aisle and then the other.

"LuAnne," Reverend Broadnax said, "I know this doesn't end the pain, but it's a start."

"Anything that saves our children from jail or an early death is a start."

Grandpa stepped forward. "I may not be worthy to stand by your side, but I want you to know I will make myself available in whatever way you see fit to use me."

"Mr. Hoole," LuAnne stiffened her jaw.

"Nathan, please call me Nathan."

"Nathan," she swallowed and then turned her head up to meet his eyes, "you keep looking for that light of yours. I'll keep praying."

Grandpa nodded. "And by the grace of God, a way will open."

Author's Note & Acknowledgments

This book has been a long time in coming and I thank those listed below for their patience, time, and help. Some people I called numerous times and they have been gracious enough to provide thoughtful answers. I compiled pages of information that do not appear in the novel. Often a paragraph or two may be all that is written after lengthy discussions. In this way, however, I came to know my characters better and their lives and stories evolved.

First and foremost, a special thank you to Kathryn Lovatt, SC Arts Commission 2013 Prose Fellow, who has reviewed my work repeatedly and taught me valuable lessons during the past six years. Her steady guidance and insightful suggestions have been vital. She has her own list of writing publications, including the 2012 and 2013 Press 53 Open Awards for short fiction.

I am sincerely grateful to Barbara and Bob Gosney who have thoughtfully read this book and discussed with me relevant issues concerning the Religious Society of Friends (Conservative) in North Carolina. Any misconceptions of Quakers that might be conveyed merely illustrate my attempt to heighten the tension in a novel. Any other conclusions would be unjustified. I have nothing but the utmost respect for the Quakers I know and with whom I am affiliated.

I am grateful to Dr. Sreenivas Rao, an oncologist of great compassion and ability, who provided care for my youngest sister at the end of a terminal illness. He is portrayed in name only as one of my characters, and is not connected with Duke University. He took hours to explain to me the exact protocol for the treatment of AML in 1992 and offered me the breakthrough I needed by explaining the possible need for platelet compatibility. I used only a small portion of the wealth of information he gave me. Any mistakes are mine. He asked that I inform readers that new techniques in gathering bone marrow makes the process much easier than it was twenty-two years ago.

In addition I'd like to thank Bill Futrell, Gene Bennett, Louie Brown, Dick Dabbs, Michael Hewitt, Charles Slade, Jay Bruner, Carter Jones, Jamie Muldrow, and Gwen Gosney Erickson for their contributions. I wish I could have used every word of insight they gave me—perhaps in a later book. For helpful long talks, critiquing, and continual inspiration, I am indebted to Pamela Sibley Slade, Brenda Hewitt, Anna Burgwyn, Martha Greenway, Mary Brent Cantarutti, Cathleen O'Brien, the South Carolina Writers' Workshop, especially the Camden group, and the Book Pregnant blog authors who have encouraged me throughout.

Several individuals have taken time to edit my manuscript. Thank you to Pat Mulcahy (wow, that one was major), and Marti Healy. To my mother, Louise Bevan, and my husband, Bill, I can never repay you for the proofreading you've done and your infinite encouragement and support. The beautiful prayer that is offered by Grandpa Hoole for his grandson is, in fact, one that my mother wrote and gave at my own son's rehearsal dinner.

This book has made it this far because of the incredible faith, persistence, and confidence of Catherine Drayton. The luckiest thing that happened to me in publishing was when she offered to be my agent. She is a woman of talent, integrity, and graciousness. If anyone ever wants to know why you need an agent, ask me. I extend additional thank-yous to Charlie Olsen and Lisa Vanterpool at InkWell Management. Finally, I'm thrilled to be working with Danielle Marshall of Lake Union Publishing, who has encouraged me with her energy and enthusiasm. I feel very fortunate.

ABOUT THE AUTHOR

Brenda Bevan Remmes lives with her husband near Black River Swamp, South Carolina, in an old family home filled with the history of generations past. Her stories and articles have appeared in *Newsweek* and Southern publications and journals. She spent her career conducting rural health education programs for the Schools of Medicine at both The University of North Carolina and The University of South Carolina. *The Quaker Café* is her first novel; she is working on a sequel.